DEATHWATCH
SHADOWBREAKER

Further tales of the Space Marines

DEATHWATCH
A Talon Squad novel by Steve Parker

DEATHWATCH: THE OMNIBUS
An omnibus by Steve Parker and many more

KNIGHTS OF MACRAGGE
An Ultramarines novel by Nick Kyme

BLOOD RITE
A Blood Angels novella by Rachel Harrison

• DARK IMPERIUM •
by Guy Haley

BOOK 1 – Dark Imperium
BOOK 2 – Plague War

SPEAR OF THE EMPEROR
An Emperor's Spears novel by Aaron Dembski-Bowden

BLOOD OF IAX
A Primaris Space Marines novel by Robbie MacNiven

• MEPHISTON •
by Darius Hinks

BOOK 1 – Blood of Sanguinius
BOOK 2 – The Revenant Crusade

SPACE MARINE
CONQUESTS

THE DEVASTATION OF BAAL
A Blood Angels novel by Guy Haley

ASHES OF PROSPERO
A Space Wolves novel by Gav Thorpe

WAR OF SECRETS
A Dark Angels novel by Phil Kelly

OF HONOUR AND IRON
An Ultramarines novel by Ian St. Martin

APOCALYPSE
A Primaris Marines novel by Josh Reynolds

DEATHWATCH
SHADOWBREAKER

STEVE PARKER

A BLACK LIBRARY PUBLICATION

First published in 2019.
This edition published in Great Britain in 2019 by
Black Library,
Games Workshop Ltd.,
Willow Road,
Nottingham, NG7 2WS, UK.

10 9 8 7 6 5 4 3 2 1

Produced by Games Workshop in Nottingham.
Cover illustration by Marc Lee.

A CIP record for this book is available from the British Library.

ISBN 13: 978 1 78193 963 5

Printed and bound by CPI Group (UK) Ltd, Croydon, CR0 4YY

For Bryce.

It is the 41st millennium. For more than a hundred centuries the Emperor has sat immobile on the Golden Throne of Earth. He is the Master of Mankind by the will of the gods, and master of a million worlds by the might of His inexhaustible armies. He is a rotting carcass writhing invisibly with power from the Dark Age of Technology. He is the Carrion Lord of the Imperium for whom a thousand souls are sacrificed every day, so that He may never truly die.

Yet even in His deathless state, the Emperor continues His eternal vigilance. Mighty battlefleets cross the daemon-infested miasma of the warp, the only route between distant stars, their way lit by the Astronomican, the psychic manifestation of the Emperor's will. Vast armies give battle in His name on uncounted worlds. Greatest amongst His soldiers are the Adeptus Astartes, the Space Marines, bioengineered super-warriors. Their comrades in arms are legion: the Astra Militarum and countless planetary defence forces, the ever-vigilant Inquisition and the tech-priests of the Adeptus Mechanicus to name only a few. But for all their multitudes, they are barely enough to hold off the ever-present threat from aliens, heretics, mutants – and worse.

To be a man in such times is to be one amongst untold billions. It is to live in the cruellest and most bloody regime imaginable. These are the tales of those times. Forget the power of technology and science, for so much has been forgotten, never to be re-learned. Forget the promise of progress and understanding, for in the grim dark future there is only war. There is no peace amongst the stars, only an eternity of carnage and slaughter, and the laughter of thirsting gods.

'This thing I have done for us all, for we cannot fulfil our destiny in a universe of dead worlds.'

– Aun'dzi

Address to the Aun'T'au'resha (pre-recorded)

2526.316.3 T'au

ONE

'Wrong side of the line this time, Lyndon. She made a mistake. Dragged you into it. Don't make it worse. We can help her, but only if you talk to me. The longer you wait, the greater the chance she dies out there.'

The speaker moved in closer. Lyndon could feel hot breath on his face, noted the sharp scent of recaff on it.

'We already know about the shipments, the fringe-world smugglers, the charters into t'au space. I admire your loyalty, but think, man – no transmissions, no word of her for months. If she weren't in trouble, why the silence? The ordo can't just sit on this.'

The pitch-perfect tones of the confidant, all understanding and sympathy and reason. Every sound, every look, every gesture was calculated to convey that this was a fellow on your side, a man with your best interests at heart. All he wanted was a little information. Just a few words, so easy to speak, so unbearably painful to keep to oneself.

Bastogne, he called himself. Not his real name.

He was good, but Lyndon knew the dance. He'd been on the other side of it often enough. Didn't make it easier. Too much was at stake. Her ladyship had asked for trust. She needed time. Lyndon expected to die here in order to buy her that. It was the best he could realistically hope for now.

Had the abduction team consisted only of this interrogator and his muscled goons, Lyndon's confidence in his ability to stay silent would have been supreme. But there was a fly in the balm – a man-shaped fly sitting on a wooden stool in the far corner, robed and hooded, tattooed with the marks of both the ordo and the Adeptus Astra Telepathica.

An ordo psyker.

Sartutius, the others had called him. He sat in silence, pensive after his earlier failed attempt to pry information from Lyndon's mind with his fell sorcery.

The pentagrammic wards tattooed on Lyndon's flesh and laser-etched into his bones were holding off the psyker's invasive mind-assaults, but for how long? Sartutius never seemed to blink those useless all-white eyes. He never looked away, no doubt intent on Lyndon's aura, probing for gaps, eager to exploit any cracks that would let him inside.

Yes, Lyndon's wards were strong, but given enough time and the right kinds of pressure, an ordo psyker almost always got the answers he or she was looking for.

A bead of sweat rolled down Lyndon's neck. No respite from the heat in here.

The interior of the crude structure was baking hot. A single room, twelve metres by seven, the walls thick, the floor rockcrete. Solid. Probably soundproofed and scan-shielded, too. The interrogator and his team weren't sloppy. They'd have prepped the place well.

Oil stains on the rockcrete floor, heavy-duty pulleys attached to the rafters – the place had likely been used for vehicle repair or storage in the past. Metal slats high in the walls were tilted inwards a few degrees. Through them, spears of hot midday sun sliced into the room, muted by the grime on the windows but still bright enough to leave trails when Lyndon closed his eyes.

The windows were high, the glass clouded and milky. No one would be seeing in.

'Trying to help you here,' Bastogne continued. 'The ordo takes care of its own.'

Groxshit, thought Lyndon.

Everyone in the ordo knew the truth – the larger factions within warred constantly for power and control.

He pressed his lips together, felt pain where the lower lip had been split in the scuffle of his kidnap and re-split in the subsequent beatings.

He hurt all over. It got worse every time they dragged him up out of that hole and smacked him awake. And it wasn't going to get better.

Dust motes danced a slow waltz in the air, moving gracefully on the interplay of warm microcurrents. Time seemed to pass at a crawl in here. Before the beginning of this morning's round of questions, he had lain with hands and feet bound, a black sack tied over his head. They gave him food and water, just barely enough to keep him functional. Isolated and blindfolded, most hostages quickly lose track of time, Lyndon knew. It was a common technique, all part of breaking them down.

But mental time-keeping had been an early part of Lyndon's basic training. By his count, they'd been holding him for three days and six hours. And that meant alarm bells were ringing loud and clear elsewhere.

There was a sudden hard yank on his outstretched left arm. A surge of fresh pain followed as rough rope bit into his wrist. The masked thug holding the left rope had adjusted his grip. Now the one on the right, just as powerfully built and identically masked, shifted his grip, and more of Lyndon's nerves sang out. It was only these ropes and the graft-muscled brutes holding them that kept him upright. He no longer had the energy to do so himself. He suspected several bad fractures in his legs.

Simple-minded thugs. Brute force. No finesse. Had he not been bound and injured, he could have killed both in a matter of seconds.

But here he was, strung to pulleys in the ceiling, stripped to the waist, face bruised and swollen, cuts and contusions all over. He was limp, beaten as badly as he'd ever been.

Clever of them to use that paralytic when they did the snatch. It's what he would have done.

They had placed a false tail on him at the port, just clumsy enough to be noticed, not clumsy enough to be a clear dupe. While Lyndon had been busy avoiding the more obvious tail, he hadn't spotted the snatch team. He should have known they'd never trust his capture to just one man.

Sloppy. And now he was paying for it. But he wouldn't let her ladyship suffer for his mistake.

There had been no time to bite down on the cyanide tooth. The paralytic they'd hit him with had been so fast-acting, so potent. Neurox necarthadrine or some new derivative. He was unconscious before his head hit the street. While he'd been out cold, they'd extracted the tooth. The fact that he was still breathing meant they'd also nullified the tiny cortex bomb in his skull.

No clean, quick death for field agent Urgoss Lyndon. Not while he knew what these men did not.

He felt Bastogne's breath on his face again, this time close to his ear.

'We're trying to help her. I wish you could see that.'

The ordo seal was legitimate. Lyndon would have known a fake. Besides, Bastogne had *Inquisition operative* written all over him. Despite the heat, he wore a long, black grox-leather coat and gloves. Somehow, though everyone else in the room was sweating rivers, he was as cool as ice.

'You know,' said Bastogne, stepping back but still facing his captive, 'I admire your loyalty, your integrity. You're good. Well trained. I respect that. We're the same, you and I. Same sense of duty to the ordo, to our handlers. Had mine disappeared, you would be asking the questions right now instead of me, desperate to help an inquisitor who, in all probability, needs urgent aid. I wonder if you'd be quite as patient with me as I am being with you.'

Lyndon had nothing to say to that.

Bastogne turned away for a moment and sighed. He came back in close. Hovering there, he spoke softly in Lyndon's ear.

'I would help you, you know, if things were reversed. I'd know that it was the right thing to do. Damn it, man, think of the Imperium. We want the same thing. The enemy is out there, not in here. If you're helping anyone with your damnable silence, it's the stinking xenos.'

Lyndon almost managed a snort, but his mouth and nasal passages were bone dry. All that came out was a wheeze. He hung there, breathing hard through those dry, split lips, eyelids fluttering as he teetered on the edge of passing out again.

Bastogne shook his head and gave another sigh, heavier this time, then began slowly walking around Lyndon.

'What am I to do, then? If you won't talk to me, how can I help? Doesn't it bother you? She may be dying out there. The t'au may be cutting into her flesh as we speak, eager to gain whatever she knows. Hear the death clock ticking. A retrieval team sent now, today, might be the only chance she has.'

Lyndon let the words roll off him. His ladyship had been clear:

Nothing and no one must interfere with my plans. You will give your life if you have to, but reveal not a word. I tell you now, the stakes have never been so high.

There was a sudden rush of movement from behind him. Pain exploded in his kidneys. Bastogne had struck him a savage body blow.

Agony became all of his reality. The breath burst from his lungs. He sagged almost to his knees, but the twin thugs yanked him up again, sending more fire through his singing nerves.

Throne and saints, thought Lyndon. *Let it end. Let me keep my silence and just die.*

Bastogne snarled and spun away in disgust, the tails of his long black coat flaring, his veneer of kindly patience abandoned at last. Behind him, Lyndon coughed wetly.

'Damn your ancestors,' Bastogne spat over his shoulder. 'If you don't tell me what I want to know, I'm going to start enjoying myself. You don't want that.'

To the others, he barked, 'Keep him upright.'

The heavies pulled in the slack again. Lyndon was raised almost onto his toes. He hissed in agony.

Bastogne walked over to a plasteel table set flush against the west wall and opened a black case. Looking down at the contents with some distaste, he spoke quietly, as if murmuring to himself.

The tiny I-shaped pin on his collar picked up his words.

'My lord, I think I've taken this as far as I can go with conventional methods. This is ordo conditioning at the highest level. He can't be broken without extreme measures.'

Another voice – calm and level, but grainy from so much distance – responded via the micro-vox-bead in Bastogne's left ear.

'It was to be expected. Time to move this forward. I want Sartutius to try again. After that, use one of the worms, but not before.'

Bastogne frowned. There in the case, in a transparent cylinder of toughened permaglass, several slick purple forms writhed and slithered against each other.

He looked over at the cowled figure in the corner, seated on his wooden stool, hands clasped, exuding the fell atmosphere which clung to all so-called *gifted*. The psyker's tall wooden staff rested against the wall beside him.

'You're up again, witchblood.'

There was a frustrated mutter from the cowled man, but he took his staff in hand and raised his frail form gently from the stool. With his other hand, he drew back his hood to reveal a face deathly pale and deeply lined. Networks of pale blue veins laced his papery skin, flowing everywhere. The veins were joined by wires that trailed back to a psychic amplifier bolted to the base of his neck. In the centre of his forehead was the stark red tattoo of the schola that had trained him in the marshalling of his foul power, the same schola that had subsequently sanctioned him for ordo use.

As he brushed past Bastogne, the psyker paused briefly. 'This is pointless, agent. I have told you already. He is too well protected. If it were tattoos alone, we could flay him. But to break the wards on his spine, on his skull… He would die before I could–'

'Do as his lordship commands,' snapped Bastogne. His

dislike for the psyker was never far from the surface. 'And do it fast. Or what good are you?' He gestured down at the worms in the tube. 'If you can't, we go to the last resort. The chrono is ticking. We'll need to move soon.'

Sartutius scowled, but he crossed to stand directly in front of Lyndon and raised his right hand. Spreading his fingers, he pressed the tips to several points on the prisoner's head. He began to chant, his voice a low, monotonous drone.

Lyndon tried to pull his head away, but he was too weak. The psyker's fingers held him.

The sunlight in the room seemed to flicker and dim.

A sudden chill pricked the skin of those present.

The walls seemed to withdraw a little as unnatural power tainted the air.

Bastogne watched, back to the wall, as far from Sartutius as space allowed. The masked heavies turned their eyes away. They hated being near the sanctioned psyker, especially while he exercised his unholy gift.

Beads of sweat began to form on Sartutius' pale, bald head. Bastogne saw the trembling begin, saw the muscles of the psyker's jaw clench as he exerted more and more ethereal force. Something foul began to prickle the skin of everyone in the room. Sartutius' body became tense, trembling with effort. Bastogne thought the man's sparrow-frail ribs might crack any second and his chest collapse. Blood began to seep from the psyker's nose and the corners of his eyes.

The chanting rose in tone and volume.

Then it stopped.

With a sharp cry, Sartutius reeled backwards, almost tripping on his robe. He stumbled, righted himself with his staff and staggered breathlessly back to his stool. He was breathing hard, soaked to the skin. With his long cotton sleeves, he dabbed at the blood trails on his face and neck. When his breath had returned, he hissed at Bastogne, 'Damn your eyes, man. I told you there was nothing more I could do. The wards hold!'

Bastogne growled back, 'If his lordship says you try, you bloody well try.'

But Sartutius *had* tried, and it was clear that Epsilon's bone-engraver had done all too good a job on her agent.

There was only one option left.

Bastogne reached in and lifted the cylinder from the case. Somewhat gingerly, he pressed the release on the hinged titanium cap. With his other hand, he took a pair of slim metal tongs, dipped the ends into the top of the cylinder and withdrew one of the squirming creatures.

The worm's puckered facial orifice immediately rolled back, revealing a cluster of red cilia that began questing in the air, seeking living flesh. At the base of those cilia, Bastogne saw glimpses of the small black bone-cutting beak.

By all the saints, how he hated these things!

He closed the cap and placed the cylinder with its remaining worms back in the case. With the tongs held well away from his body, he crossed back to the centre of the room and the wretched man suspended there.

He stopped a metre in front of Lyndon and raised the worm slowly towards his face. Sensing the proximity of a living host, the worm's cilia began moving frantically, greedily. The creature writhed, struggling to break free from the grip of the plasteel that held it.

'You know what this is,' said Bastogne, voice low, resigned. It was not a question.

The regret was genuine. Truth be told, he didn't want to do this. Lyndon was forcing him, and for what? The ordo always got what it wanted in the end.

The prisoner raised bloodshot eyes under a bruised and swollen brow and saw the squirming organism just inches in front of him.

He twisted away in panic, feebly yanking on his restraints. The two men holding the ropes tensed, fixing him in place, the muscles of their forearms hardening like lengths of plasteel cable.

Lyndon knew this creature. Seven years ago, he'd had to use one, and for seven years, he'd tried and failed to forget that day.

'Don't,' he breathed. 'Epsilon still serves the ordo. I serve the ordo. I cannot tell you what you want to know... But have faith. Please. Just... don't do this.'

The look of reluctance on Bastogne's face as he brought the creature closer to Lyndon's nose was no act. 'I have orders, agent. The ordo needs to know why she went dark. I need her location. Give me reason not to use this before it's too late.'

How Lyndon wished he could talk. His mind was already busy making the sentences he could speak to avoid this worst of fates. The worm meant more than death – it meant an agonising descent into madness, the dissolution of his mind. Once it was inside him, it could not be stopped. And still, no matter how much he yearned to escape that fate, he would not – *could not* – betray her ladyship's trust. Epsilon's discovery was of greater importance than the life of any man. The chance that Al Rashaq was no mere legend, that it could conceivably be found and exploited... It was worth many more lives than his.

It could change everything.

So Lyndon held his tongue and steeled himself for the mind-destroying agony that was about to become his entire existence.

TWO

Haluk scowled, baring white teeth in a darkly tanned face.

All around him, heresy.

Faithless dogs. Traitors. Xenos-loving scum!

He pushed his way between them, jostling, shoulders set hard, knocking one or two off balance. No false apologies. These people had forgotten their debt. The God-Emperor of Mankind had not suffered in singular agony for the last ten thousand years that man and xenos might live as one.

The Tychonite majority – the city people, as Haluk thought of them – had cast the Imperial creed aside, so greedy to share in all that the filthy *pogs*[1] had offered.

For over three decades, this world had been part of the t'au domain. Since day one, the Tychonite majority had embraced

1 *pog* – from *pogyo*: a root vegetable, blue in colour, very cheap, highly nutritious and a staple food of the Tychonite human population. Used among Kashtu people as a derogatory term for the t'au.

the blue-skins as saviour and kin. Not so the old tribes, the loyal, the unblinded.

Someone bumped into him from behind. Another from his left. Brief apologies. So damned busy here in the capital. The crowds so dense. And the noise, the constant buzz of conversation, the braying of beasts laden with goods...

So unlike the haunted, rain-drenched havens of the far north.

The souk through which Haluk moved was a tangle of covered alleys and small market squares filled to bursting with brightly robed figures haggling over price and quantity. There were grains, spices, fruits, salted meats, even officially approved narcotics in unprocessed, leafy form.

No women, of course. They were forbidden from entering the souk. Since the first days of commerce on Tychonis, the markets were places for men alone. Women were thought to bring bad luck here. In their presence, negotiations would fail, partnerships would dissolve, agreements would fracture. Whole businesses would collapse and die. On seeing a single female, even a girl-child, the superstitious traders would throw their hands up to the sky, swear coarsely and pack up shop for the day.

Haluk was glad to see some things, at least, had not changed.

His gladness was short-lived. Though no women were present, the crowds were dotted with others that did not belong. A multitude of aliens mingled and bartered with the merchants and shoppers. Some were of the so-called *integrated races* – a mish-mash of diverse and bizarre beings from far-flung worlds which had submitted to the domination of the arrogant t'au.

Most, however, were t'au themselves. Water caste. Merchants and traders.

Blue-skinned dogs!

Typically shorter than their human counterparts, they were not easily spotted in the densest parts of the throng. But every so often a gap would open in the churning sea of commerce and Haluk would see one of the wiry, bony, blue-skinned curs in spotless robes accented with high-tech accessories and shining status tokens. His upper lip curled in distaste. The hairless, earless heads; the noseless faces; the four-fingered hands... How he despised them.

As Haluk glared unnoticed at a pog merchant with particularly dark blue skin, he found himself wondering how they did it, how they managed to speak, to move, to gesture in such a *human* way. It seemed so effortless to them.

Was it something they did consciously, this mirroring? A clever trick to make themselves seem less alien, to ingratiate themselves?

Conscious or not, Haluk saw through the deception. He saw behind the mask. The Speaker of the Sands had chosen well. His heart was hardened and his mind unclouded. He would not be swayed from his purpose.

The t'au trader made a jest to the three men with whom he was bargaining. All laughed – warm, genuine, friendly. Haluk turned away, unable to stomach more.

These men fraternise with murderers. Do they know nothing of our struggle?

He pressed on. Currency was changing hands all around him, the incessant buzz of conversation and negotiation punctuated with the jangle and clink of coins. Here in the western capital, Chu'sut Ka – simply Chusuk before the invasion – Imperial coinage had been replaced by lozenge-shaped discs of a strange alloy, light but incredibly strong.

T'au money. T'au rules. T'au culture.

They have tainted everything.

Not so in the rebel-held Northern Territories, the so-called Drowned Lands where Haluk had been raised. There, the people still used the Imperial ducat and centim, coins that bore the proud double-headed eagle, the aquila of the Imperium of Man.

Once the reckoning was over, all men would use them again.

So much had to be put right, but it would all come to pass in time.

The Speaker's visions had been powerful. The dream of the loyalist tribes would become a reality.

I will not live to see it, thought Haluk. *But that is the price all martyrs pay. My reward awaits me in the Life Hereafter.*

He moved on, eyes hard. Voices called out to him from the brightly coloured stalls on either side, announcing today's prices, but he was not here to trade. He was *kharkeen*, a holy warrior on a sacred mission. Here among the crowds of the faithless, he hid in plain sight, waiting for his hour to arrive, to the eyes of those around him just another unremarkable local in an unremarkable place on an unremarkable day.

It was critical not to draw attention. To climb the tower too early was to risk being marked by t'au surveillance drones. He raised his eyes to the deep blue sky visible between the gaps in the market awnings. No sign of the murderous machines from down here, but they were there, ever present, humming and drifting over the city, looking for rare signs of unrest.

How Haluk hated the drones. To die at the hands of a mindless machine diminished a man's soul. It was not a fitting end for a kharkeen. He feared it, that unworthy death. No matter what, he would not let a machine claim his life this day.

He stopped at a stall, feigning interest in a pair of boots, hand-made, crafted in the old way. As he pretended to consider buying them, he realised he was thirsty.

So dry here in the summer. So different from the north. It is good. The planet longs to return to the days of the great deserts. She strains under the smothering swathes of green and blue that the pogs have forced on her. We will help her cast them off. Soon, she will shimmer again with the bright gold of endless sands, and our way of life will be restored.

That would take a total reversal of the blue-skins' vast planetary engineering project. Their great machines would need to be researched and reset. Simple destruction would avail the Ishtu and Kashtu people little now. As Haluk understood it, the balance point had been tipped. The new weather systems were more or less self-sustaining at this point.

It had taken centuries for the t'au to turn this former desert world into an agricultural juggernaut supplying foodstuffs to worlds in a dozen other seized systems. It was a change that had all but destroyed the old desert communities and their ancient and noble culture, as it had pushed them to the far north and south where no others chose to live.

They should have finished the job, but they did not. We will make them regret that.

The original Tychonite tribes had been well adapted to desert life, to a life that constantly tested and challenged living things. It made men strong and resilient. An easy life made men fat and wasteful. Self-indulgent. The evidence of that was all around him in the souk today.

Up ahead, he spotted a trio of tall, broad-shouldered men in brown uniforms. They cut through the crowd like ships through water, the merchants parting before them on reflex.

Polished stubber-guns and tokens of rank winked as they caught the sunlight.

ISF. Integrated Security Forces.

Men who had pledged themselves to t'au military service.

Haluk moved to the side, turned his face away from them and began bartering with a food-seller over the price of a chilled uanoor – a sweet purple fruit native to the more temperate mid-northern latitudes.

The ISF officers went by, paying him no mind.

Haluk wished he were armed. He visualised himself stealing up behind them with a poisoned blade and stabbing all three before they could turn. The Speaker and the Kashtu elders had insisted he carry no weapon on him. A wise decision.

The ISF had joined with the t'au fire caste in pushing his people out, driving them from their homelands. The far north had been their only choice. Haluk had seen the vids, seen men cut down by other men on the orders of the pogs. His people had fought fiercely, but they had been less experienced in those days, unaccustomed to combat with a highly technological and well-organised enemy.

'Well?' demanded the chubby merchant from his silk pillows. 'What say you?'

Haluk was already turning to move on as he said, 'I suddenly find myself bereft of appetite.'

The merchant muttered curses at his back as he walked away.

There was no lessening in the density of the crowds as the sun moved across the sky. Haluk pressed on, pushing through a gaggle of noisy men in the bright orange, yellow and red robes of spice traders. He clashed shoulders with one and the man stopped to glare, expecting to force an apology from Haluk's lips. He was a large man, well fed, and well appointed judging by the gold he wore. He was probably used to being respected, but if he thought he would intimidate Haluk with that indignant glare, he was wrong. Haluk stared back, eyes cold and hard, as threatening as storm clouds.

The man found his courage rapidly abandoning him under the tribesman's eyes. He relented without comment, turned and moved off with his fellows. As they walked away, Haluk heard him tell the others, 'There's something ill about that one.'

Pigs! Their lives were so easy here in the capital. *Their* children didn't die of lung-rot. Swamp-haunters never stole *their* young women from the food-gathering parties. Kroot patrols didn't roam here, slaughtering anyone they came across.

Here was safety, health and prosperity for all; just bend the knee before the alien, turn away from the truth, forget that one's very life was a gift from the God-Emperor. Simply turn from His light and embrace the rule of the xenos.

Bow before the wisdom and munificence of the Aun.

Haluk discreetly made the cursing claw with his fingers.

Life was not *meant* to be easy. The Emperor did not endure eternal suffering so that ungrateful men might live easy lives.

The Emperor wanted men to be strong. How else would they survive in a galaxy filled with vile and murderous abominations?

For all their talk of the Greater Good, their beloved alien credo, the t'au were still a race of invaders, as eager as any other to expand and dominate, whatever it took. Where men resisted, the t'au made war.

Haluk had been awakened to hatred of the xenos by his mother, Galta. She had often read transcripts of the Speaker's speeches to Haluk and his siblings before bed.

No father. Pictures only. Galta's husband had been killed on a reconnaissance patrol before Haluk's birth.

Haluk would go to sleep with dreams of becoming a great hero to his people. In his dreams, the man in the pictures spoke to him of honour and glory.

Even at six years old, he would wake demanding to be trained.

Encouraged by his fervour for the transcripts, his mother had asked some of the elders to tutor him in the books of the Imperial creed. By the time he was twelve, Haluk could recite verbatim over seven hundred passages from the writings of various celebrated Imperial saints and Great Ecclesiarchs. How proud she had been! She had hoped he would one day join the Ministorum, but for that to happen, the usurpers would have to be driven out. Even to the most optimistic and dedicated of the faithful, that did not seem a likely prospect in his lifetime. So when Haluk reached the age of nineteen, having grown into a hard, lean, athletic man like his late father, his mother had given her blessing and permitted him to enter the ranks of the holy warriors. The Speaker himself had come to conduct the initiation ceremony with its sharing of the bonding drug, nictou, and the taking of blood oaths.

That was the day Haluk had become kharkeen, and his path to great glory had begun.

Weaving his way east through the souk, Haluk recalled the tears that had run down his mother's cheeks, a mixture of pride and sorrow.

The kharkeen were not fated to die peacefully in their beds. There would be no grandchildren to soothe a mother's heart when news of his success came, only the knowledge that her oldest son would walk forever in the warm light of the Great Saviour and eat from His Bountiful Orchards. She'd had that knowledge, at least – that and the hope that perhaps Haluk's younger brother, Farid, would not follow the same path.

She hadn't lived long enough to find out.

She and the women of her foraging group had been out in the mangroves south-west of their home when a kroot patrol had caught sight of them. The beaked ones slaughtered without compunction. They did not take prisoners. They revelled in butchery.

Farid had collapsed, shaking and weeping, when their mother's remains were brought back to the settlement. A single round to the head had killed her, but much of her flesh had been stripped from her bones. The bite patterns were those of great, sharp beaks.

The kroot were known to eat the flesh of those they killed.

Haluk had not wept. Kharkeen shed tears only for the God-Emperor's pain. Instead, he said a prayer that his mother's spirit-journey to what lay beyond would be swift and straight, then steeled his heart and renewed his commitment to the secret mission the Speaker had given him.

Above the noise of the crowds, the hot air of the souk filled with shrill, musical bird-calls, breaking him free from the painful memories.

The calls of the *kjantil*, a small avian species which the people of Tychonis had, for as long as history could remember, trained to sing precisely on the hour. This call marked the second hour after midday. It was the sign Haluk had been waiting for. Pushing through a gaggle of men bartering over sacks of sajarti rice, he turned into an alley that opened at its far end into bright sunshine and the broad, baking expanse of the main highway that led to the Inner Districts.

Already, beige-armoured figures had started appearing on the corners of the roof gardens and terraces lining the road. T'au security forces.

Surveying the streets below, they fingered the grips of their long-barrelled energy weapons. Haluk had seen how accurate and deadly those weapons could be.

He felt his heart racing, his breath quicken. His moment was almost at hand.

He turned left and headed north along a narrow street that ran parallel to the main road. He moved against increasing foot traffic now as word spread through the crowds that the procession was approaching. The markets were emptying, everyone moving towards the main road, eager to see the return of the planet's most senior military figure.

Shouldering people from his path, Haluk turned down a narrow alley on his right. At the end of it, he found the iron gate he was searching for. There, tied around one of its bars, was the scrap of red cloth he had been told to look for. The gate was unlocked. He pushed it open. The old hinges creaked. He stepped through, closed it behind him and slid beyond it into the cool shadow of a pillared path.

At the end of the path, he entered the base of a minaret and began ascending a spiral staircase of old sandstone. The air inside was still and cool.

He had climbed barely ten metres when, too late, he heard someone descending towards him in a hurry.

He froze. The staircase was narrow. No cover.

Suddenly, a figure in the dark brown fatigues of the ISF appeared around the curve of the central column. There was a blur of movement, a barked order to halt.

Haluk's veins flooded with ice.

He looked down the barrel of a raised stubber.

This was wrong.

No one should have been here. Assurances had been made. The way should have been cleared.

THREE

Thick walls of plasteel-reinforced rockcrete soaked up Lyndon's desperate pleas. He did not fear death itself. Never that. He had served well. He believed in the Imperial creed. But the manner of his imminent death and the implications for Epsilon's work… Those he rightly feared.

Of all the myriad fates an Ordo Xenos field agent might face, he had never once imagined it would end like this.

The *synovermus* would burrow into Lyndon's nasal cavity, releasing a powerful psychotropic mucus as it went – a mucus that would radically alter Lyndon's perception of time and simultaneously obliterate his will. Seconds would stretch out like days, and his mind would lose all hold on itself, become pliable. Inner walls would tumble. And all the while, the creature's tiny beak would be carving a channel through flesh, nerve and bone to its eventual target, the cerebellum, there to lay its eggs before curling up to die.

Despite the physical and mental trauma of the worm's

journey through his head, Lyndon would still be alive when the larvae hatched mere moments after being laid. They would emerge and feed, and that would be his end. By then, however, Bastogne would have the information he needed, and Lyndon would die having given up his handler and every secret in his head.

Through bitter tears of resignation, Lyndon began praying to the Emperor.

Bastogne reached out and gripped a handful of Lyndon's sweat-soaked hair. He yanked his head back and held it tight as he inched the worm closer to the prisoner's nose. Lyndon hadn't the strength to resist. Bastogne moved slowly, eager to give the man as much chance as possible to speak out and forego the need for this. But only blood and prayer issued from Lyndon's lips.

Bastogne already knew in his heart that Lyndon would not break. Had things been reversed, he would have chosen the same path. The ordo asked much of its agents, but not without good reason.

The future of the Imperium depended on men and women ready to die for it.

Heart heavy, Bastogne pressed the worm to Lyndon's nostril.

Immediately, the creature plunged its cilia into the hole and began tugging itself up the dark channel of flesh. Bastogne had not released it quite yet. It strained hard against the tongs.

Lyndon's prayer became a scream through clenched teeth.

'Where is Epsilon?' shouted Bastogne desperately. 'Where is she?'

Lyndon struggled against every instinct for self-preservation he had. *I will not give you up, my lady. For the Imperium. For mankind. Find what you are looking for. Make everything right. Do not let me die in vain.*

With a final curse, Bastogne released the creature and watched in fascinated horror as it hauled its soft, glistening body up into the nose of the doomed agent.

Lyndon roared helplessly through gritted teeth, his nose bulging as the worm fought its way inside.

'You did this to yourself, man!' snapped Bastogne. 'Not me. *You!*'

Turning, he hurled the tongs angrily against the wall and stepped away. He didn't want to be close enough to hear the first crunch of that tiny black beak.

As it was, he was spared the sound, diverted from it by a louder one, a sudden clatter from behind.

He spun to see Sartutius standing bolt upright, stool toppled, his blind eyes wide, face rigid with tension.

'We are discovered, Bastogne,' he gasped. 'They have us!'

Before the psyker had finished speaking, the voice of Bastogne's master sounded over the vox-bead in his ear, tones clipped and harsh. *'Perimeter breached, agent. Auspex monitors show multiple heat signatures converging on your location. Arm yourselves. They're closing fast. None of you is to be taken alive!'*

Bastogne didn't need to be told twice. Time was up. An opposition field team had found them. More bloodshed was inevitable now. He drew a fine master-crafted hell-pistol from the holster beneath his coat and spun to face the others.

'We're about to have company. Arm up. Now!'

The two heavies released their ropes at once and raced over to a crate in the corner.

Always against the clock, thought Bastogne as his men prepared to defend this place.

The interrogation was in its final stage. If it were to bear any fruit at all, the next several minutes would be critical.

Throne and saints, just give me a little more time.

Lyndon collapsed in a heap, breath shallow, mind spinning, time and agony already beginning to stretch out before him like an endless road. He lay shaking and whimpering as the worm worked its beak against the first resistance it had encountered inside his head. The crunching and cracking from within was deafening to him, but in the sudden flurry of activity, the others didn't even register it.

Bastogne's associates swept up a pair of big, drum-fed heavy stubbers from the cache, cocked them and moved, each covering one of the room's two plasteel doors.

Sartutius gripped his staff and cowered in the corner. His skills did not lie in combat witchcraft, but perhaps he might escape notice and slip away if he could manipulate the attackers' senses once they were inside the room – if they got inside. The doors were solid plasteel and the locking bolts went deep... but no – he was lying to himself. They wouldn't hold out against an ordo assault team for long. Entry was inevitable.

How foolish, all of this, thought the psyker bitterly. *We wear the same mark. We should be shedding xenos blood. Not our own.*

The seconds slowed. In the relative calm before the approaching storm, the air was thick and hot. Beams of burning sun seemed to creep across the floor. The four-man interrogation team was so tense that the sounds of suffering from the man on the floor became mere background noise.

'How many?' Bastogne asked his master over the link, but if his lordship answered, Bastogne never heard it, because at that moment the doors exploded inwards, slamming back against the rockcrete walls, thick hinges torn and twisted with the force of the breaching charges.

Bastogne's ears rang with the double crack of man-made thunder.

Smoke and dust billowed into the room.

He and his heavies tensed, muzzles raised, fingers on triggers, but no figures appeared through the doors. Instead, a crisp contralto voice rang out.

'Throw down your weapons immediately and lie face down on the ground, by order of the God-Emperor's most Holy Inquisition. Do not resist. Our authority is absolute. Disobey and die.'

No one moved but Lyndon, curled up on the floor like a child, twitching and whimpering.

Bastogne cursed and called back, 'I am an agent of the Holy Inquisition, here on the direct orders of an inquisitor lord. You are interfering in a level-nine Ordo Xenos operation. Leave the area at once. Do not attempt to enter this building or we will open fire.'

Again, the voice of the other. 'You are performing an unsanctioned interrogation of a friendly asset. This will not be tolerated. I say again, throw down your weapons and lie down on the ground now. If you do not comply by the count of ten, we will enter with lethal force.'

At that, the voice from outside began its countdown.

Inside the building, Bastogne looked at the wretch by his feet. He crouched beside him and placed the muzzle of the hell-pistol to his head. When the opposition assault squad stormed the room, he would have to execute Lyndon immediately. It would leave him open, unable to fire on the attackers, but he could not risk the man falling into their hands.

One last time, he hissed at his prisoner, 'Where is Epsilon? Can you hear me, Lyndon? Where is your damned mistress?'

Lyndon lay shuddering and howling in pain.

'Sartutius,' barked Bastogne. 'Last chance. Do a mind-rip! We've got seconds only before they–'

'Beyond my power!' snapped the psyker. 'It will kill us both!'

'Damn you, witchblood. I'm ordering you to try!' He swung his muzzle up towards the psyker. 'Or I'll paint that wall with your brains!'

Hissing with rage, but knowing the threat for truth, Sartutius scurried forward and crouched by the prisoner's curled form.

A mind-rip, Throne damn it! Didn't this bastard know what he was asking? Even if Sartutius didn't die, the line between his soul and the prisoner's could be blurred forever. He might lose himself, become someone else, an amalgam. In Terra's holy name...

'Psyker!' barked Bastogne as he thrust his pistol's muzzle against Sartutius' left temple.

Sartutius swallowed, thrust a hand out, grabbed the prisoner's head, closed his eyes and began to channel every last bit of power that was available to him.

Bastogne stepped back, giving the psyker room, but he kept his hell-pistol raised. When he was sure Sartutius was doing as commanded, he turned his eyes back to the ruined doorway in front of him.

Over the vox-bead in his ear, Bastogne's handler spoke once again.

'There must be no evidence linking me to this operation. None.'

Bastogne knew exactly what that meant. 'Thy will be done, my lord.'

'Make your last appeal to the God-Emperor for His mercy,' said the voice, *'and know that I honour you for your sacrifice. Your work has been righteous. Your rewards will be eternal.'*

'Ave Imperator,' replied Bastogne. 'It has been an honour and a privilege to serve, my lord.'

Outside, the assault team's countdown reached two, then one, then zero. Four hissing canisters bounced into the room and began belching out clouds of stinging green gas. It quickly filled the air, billowing into every corner, causing the defenders to double over and collapse, their bodies wracked by painful muscle spasms. Bastogne raged, even as his lungs began to burn. He should have expected gas. Sartutius dropped to his knees beside Lyndon and coughed wetly into his sleeve. He kept his right hand pressed hard to the prisoner's skull, pushing forward with the attempted mind-rip. Pale psychic fire licked upwards across his forehead from the sockets of his sightless eyes.

Through stinging, gas-induced tears, Bastogne thought he saw something ephemeral, something ghostly and vague, ebbing upwards from the prisoner's skull.

Sartutius was screaming now, tone and pitch matched perfectly to those of the dying prisoner, and the faint, ghostly stuff poured upwards into his mouth, nose, ears and eyes. Then, suddenly, it stopped, and all sound and motion from the tormented prisoner stopped with it, shut off like a light.

He collapsed, dead, in peace at last.

But no peace for Sartutius. The psyker reeled backwards, his wiry muscles locked, his skin stretched tight, his face a terrible rictus of pain. The witchfire flames from his eyes died out. Blood ran in streams from his ears.

He collapsed in a heap on the floor at Bastogne's feet.

'Tell me you got something, witch!' roared Bastogne.

Sartutius was gasping hard, barely able to breathe. He was a ruin. He felt his life flooding from him. This was death. As expected, the effort of the mind-rip had broken him. It had been too much. Voices in multitude bubbled forth in his mind, rising rapidly, clamouring to dominate, drowning out his own inner voice. Louder and louder. Soon he would be lost completely, his soul buried under the boiling depths of so many monstrous, inhuman others fighting among themselves to possess him, to become manifest in the physical realm.

But before that, a single word.

'Tychonis,' he gasped. Control over his body was almost gone.

'Tychonis,' he managed one more time. 'Now kill me, damn you. Before it's too late!'

Bastogne heard him, saw the white eyes turn black as tar, saw the lips pull back over teeth now sharp and triangular where seconds ago they had been flat and even. He watched raw red seams split open along the psyker's cheeks from lip to ear, and gasped as the mouth hinged open far wider than any human jaw ought to. The tongue, twice the length it should have been, began lashing around like a red whip, cutting itself raw and bloody on the razor-like teeth.

A dozen voices laughed and growled and shouted in strange and ancient languages from that hideous maw.

Horror gripped Bastogne. He could scarcely comprehend what he was seeing, but he managed to press his pistol to the fallen psyker's head.

'In Terra's holy name,' he muttered as he pulled the trigger.

The pistol kicked hard. The psyker's head vanished in a blast of light and heat. The body rolled on top of the dead prisoner's, smoke curling from the cauterised neck.

The long-range vox-link was still open to his lordship. Bastogne had but a second now.

'Tychonis, my lord. Do you hear me? She's on Tychonis!'

If there was any answer, Bastogne never heard it. At that moment, eight respirator-masked figures in body armour stormed the room, four through each doorway, weapons raised. They raced towards each of the incapacitated defenders, savagely kicking the hell-pistol and heavy stubbers out of their hands. One of the intruders hoofed Bastogne hard in the side and he collapsed face down on hot rockcrete. Another immediately knelt on his back, driving down viciously with one knee, pressing him hard into the floor.

Not one shot was fired. These men had orders to take everyone alive. The prisoners would need to be interrogated if their handler was to be unmasked. Bastogne would, in all likelihood, find himself facing a synovermus of his very own. Would he resist? Would he be as strong and resolute as Lyndon had been?

It was not a question Omicron could allow him to answer.

Far away, an order was given.

From a stealth-cloaked ship high above the planet, something metallic dropped. As it streaked towards its target, it left a thin ribbon of white, a bright contrail cutting vertically through the deep azure of the mid-afternoon sky.

Twelve seconds later, an area over one kilometre wide in the western slums of Falcara City, the northern capital of the planet Syrion, was utterly obliterated.

The city lay shrouded in thick ash, smoke and dust for days afterwards. When a wind from the south-east finally picked up, drawing back that smoky veil, the citizens left alive surveyed the damage in grief and confusion. Of the homes, the businesses and the people which had brought life and noise and colour to the area, only burning embers and an eerily perfect crater remained.

Such sudden and mysterious devastation. Over eighty thousand dead. The planetary inquiry would last decades, but the truth would never emerge. Those who came close to it would vanish, and the event would eventually pass into local legend.

All of it for the sake of a single, simple word – the name of an insignificant backwater planet that was no longer part of the Imperium of Man.

'Tychonis,' muttered the old inquisitor lord.

He rose from his command throne, ignoring the stiffness in his joints, ordered a course set through the warp and left the bridge in the hands of the ship's captain.

As he stalked the gloomy stone corridor back to his quarters, he turned it over in his mind. The flames in the wall sconces danced and guttered as he swept past them.

'Why Tychonis? What drew you there?'

And why now?

FOUR

Haluk tried to swallow in a mouth suddenly dry.

His heart raced.

The black port of the gun barrel pointed right at his face seemed to swallow him.

Time slowed to a crawl.

There they stood – two men, one in civilian robes, death-commando from the north, and the other…

What? ISF? A t'au-aligned Tychonite traitor?

The man was hard-faced, flint-eyed, roughly ten years Haluk's senior. He was tall and broad like most of the men that policed the capital alongside the fire caste troopers.

For a long moment, the two simply stared at each other, barely breathing, nerves jangling.

Then words. 'Long we bled upon the open sand.' His tone was low, his voice gruff.

Haluk breathed. The tension in his neck eased. He knew

the response. 'And from that sand,' he said, 'shoots of truth and purpose did grow.'

The man lowered his weapon.

Not ISF. *Haddayin.* An infiltrator. A fellow servant of the cause.

Still, he should have been gone already.

'The drones just finished a pass.' He tapped a metallic t'au glyph on his uniform. 'All they found was a member of the security forces running last-minute diligence. You'll have the window you need.'

Haluk nodded. He wondered if the infiltrator was a city-born sympathiser or had come from the rebel tribes. Kashtu, Ishtu and city-born – all were of tan skin and black hair. There was no way to know; any giveaway in speech or manner would likely have got the infiltrator killed or imprisoned already. Haddayin service to the cause depended on a flawless facade.

Haluk respected such men. He knew the rawness of his hate for the pogs precluded him from the kind of vital work they did.

'You'll find the weapon at the top,' said the infiltrator. 'Don't miss.'

'I won't,' said Haluk, the mere suggestion of it irking him. 'But why are you here? I was not told to expect you.'

The man paused. 'We were not meant to meet, it's true. But I wanted to leave something else for you up there. It took me a moment.'

'I don't understand.'

'A chance at life, kharkeen. I anchored a rope to the tower wall.'

Haluk scowled.

'Do not be offended,' said the haddayin. 'I know you are

ready to give your life. But if you move quickly... Would the cause not be better served by your survival? Martyrs are a one-shot weapon. I've always thought it wasteful. If there's a chance–'

'The Speaker has seen my ascension to glory in the scrying sands.'

'The Speaker,' said the man gravely. He shrugged. 'Then so it will be, I suppose. Fate is fate.'

One did not doubt the Speaker, least of all in the presence of a kharkeen. The infiltrator gave a shallow bow and resumed his descent. Haluk angled his body that the other might pass him on the narrow stair. As the man drew parallel, he offered his final words. 'Saint Sathra watch and keep you, kharkeen. Saint Isara speed your soul on its journey. I'll hold your deed in memory and see the tale passed on.'

He vanished round the curve of the staircase and was gone, but his words stayed with Haluk all the way to the top of the minaret.

So it will be.

It has been foretold. My fate is set.

Today, I die.

He had thought himself ready, his acceptance complete, certain of the promise of elevation in the eternal life after this one.

But now, chill slivers of doubt began to press at the edges of his faith. Fear and the animal need to survive gnawed at him.

What about choice? What about free will? He did not doubt the Speaker or his visions, but... What if he turned around right now? What would happen to the cause? Just how much did the dreams of his people rest on his actions this day?

Surely the future was not so binary a thing. Surely success

in the years that followed did not rest on a single act of sacrifice today.

Emerging from the stairwell at the top, he found himself high above the city, sheltered from the beating sun – and from any eyes overhead – by the eaves of the tower's sharply tilted roof. The sky was so wide and blue it seemed that the whole of existence lay beneath it. On the eastern side of the parapet, by the inner edge of the waist-high sandstone crenellations, he found the man-portable missile launcher he had known would be waiting for him. The weapon looked old, covered in scuffs and scratches.

A one-shot weapon only, as was he.

It was foretold.

Damn the haddayin for igniting these doubts now.

What if surviving to fight might make a bigger difference?

No. The Speaker would have seen that in the scrying sands. He was the God-Emperor's instrument on Tychonis. It was by his visions and his leadership that the yoke of alien occupation would be thrown off. Haluk's death today would be a flagstone on the path to the redemption of his people and his world. His place in history was assured.

One shot.

The weapon's laser-targeting system meant Haluk wouldn't need more than that. His training had been comprehensive. Strict. Gruelling.

He was fully prepared.

The missile was pre-loaded and the targeting systems were on standby, but as Haluk bent to lift the launcher, he felt a powerful urge to check something.

Walking around to the other side of the tower, he spotted the coil of thick rope the sergeant had left for him. He reached down and tugged on it. It was anchored solidly to a plasteel piton.

He growled at himself, again conflicted.

I should be past this. Why am I still torn? If I run, I risk being taken alive.

Capture was not an option. What might the blue-skins draw out from him? What terrible methods did the pogs use?

Committed to death in duty, kharkeen did not train in anti-interrogation methods.

Haluk cursed himself for his momentary weakness and whirled away from the rope. He marched determinedly back to his firing position. Mere moments remained. Peeking over the lip of the wall, he surveyed the scene forty metres below.

The highway was thronged with people now, all jostling for position. Hab windows on every floor in every building were crammed, mostly boys and men who had shoved, elbowed and shouted their way past sisters, wives and mothers to get a better view.

The infiltrator had said the drones had completed their pass on the towers. Sure enough, they hovered over the lower rooftops now, guns and lenses tracking left and right looking for potential threats.

Haluk muttered a hateful curse as he watched.

The air began to fill with the eerie humming of alien engines. T'au gunships swung into view from ramps and intersections along the highway, hovering a metre off the ground, sliding like insects on the surface of a pond into prearranged positions. Their guns swung to cover the dense assembly of a curious and colourful crowd.

You see? thought Haluk. *Safety and prosperity to all those who bow to the T'au'va. But little trust.*

Members of the security forces made a long line on either side of the road, facing the masses, weapons in hand. Haluk was disgusted to see so many humans among them, proudly holding weapons across their chests, so ready to kill any of their own people who threatened their t'au masters.

As he looked down at the spectacle-hungry masses and the might of the security forces restraining them, he felt himself being pulled headlong towards a nexus, a point in time on which great future events rested.

More ground vehicles started to emerge from the heat and dust at the far end of the road now, engines adding their strange voices to the rest, creating a curious low vibration in Haluk's chest.

First came a vanguard of sleek skimmers, their cockpits open to the air. Then came two heavy craft bristling with gun barrels and missile racks. They had about them the visual aspect of an ocean predator, their hulls of metal and advanced ceramics curving and sweeping like organic forms.

Then, at last it appeared before him – the craft he had spent so long studying in vids and picts, visualising in his mind, the overwhelming, overriding focus of the days and weeks leading up to this one.

It was the personal vehicle of the blue-skin wretch responsible for more Kashtu and Ishtu deaths on Tychonis than any other living being.

Commander Coldwave.

Haluk's whole body tensed.

In that single moment, this thing which had dominated his thoughts for so long was made suddenly, imposingly solid and real.

Flanked by the support craft of an honour guard, it prowled along the highway, a heavily armoured troop transport with the honour markings of the warrior-leader to whom it belonged.

As it glided closer to Haluk's position, he hefted the missile launcher and settled it on his right shoulder. The weight of it pressed down on him. He adjusted until he was about as comfortable and steady as he could make himself.

The crowd below grew quiet, hesitant, watching in awe and respect. No cheering and clapping. The t'au found such raucous displays distasteful.

The fire caste supreme commander had been in the south for months. He had always shunned the spotlight and his movements were seldom made public knowledge. But the Speaker had known. Long before this morning's public announcement over the Tychonite infocast system, the Speaker had known that Coldwave would pass this way at this hour on this day.

And a single kharkeen might thus strike a great blow against the enemy.

The moment had come.

Coldwave's Devilfish armoured transport slid into firing range.

FIVE

With his heart pounding and a prayer on his lips, Haluk sighted through the lens of the missile launcher's scope and tracked right. The crosshairs rolled over the polished fuselage of the Devilfish.

He thumbed the safety off and pressed the activation rune for the laser target designator. A bare moment after the invisible laser painted the side of the transport, the t'au military presence and their human cohorts jolted into action like they'd been stung. The energy in the whole area changed completely. Helmed faces whipped around towards Haluk's position. Drones lifted from their holding pattern. Fireblade squad leaders started calling out to their cadres, gesturing sharply. Several squads broke from the road and started charging through the crowd, converging on the minaret from several places at once.

So Coldwave's Devilfish had a lock-on sensor.

No matter. Haluk had his target dead centre.

He kept his right eye pressed to the weapon's scope. In the peripheral vision of his left, he noted three gun drones cutting straight towards him through the air. Blood roared in his ears. His brain was screaming at him to flee. Instead, he gritted his teeth, pushed the weapon's charge lever to *Active*, pressed forward on the firing lever with his thumb and squeezed the trigger.

The weapon roared, deafening him. He was almost blown from his feet. He shut his eyes involuntarily, blinded by the sudden ignition of rocket fuel. When he opened them half a second later, he saw a streak of white smoke arcing down towards the transport.

He had time to marvel at the gentle, graceful curve of the trail before he was blinded again by the flare of the explosion. The noise was like a thunderclap, short and sharp. It reverberated in the stone beneath his feet. The tower shivered.

Righteous zeal filled Haluk's wildly beating heart. He had done it. He had struck a blow against the usurpers in the name of the God-Emperor and all that was right.

The t'au fire caste leader was dead!

Be proud, Mother. Terra's Holy Light surely shines upon me now.

But Haluk was wrong in that. Perhaps the Emperor's attention was elsewhere that day.

Luck, certainly, was not with him. As he let the launcher drop at his feet, he watched the smoke clear, pulled away like a veil caught on a breeze.

The sight it revealed made him cry out in denial.

Down in the streets, people were shoving and scrambling to get away from the main thoroughfare, desperate to get back to the cover of the alleys and away from more explosions. Shutters slammed over the windows that faced onto the highway. The security forces were forming a cordon around what should have been the twisted, burning wreckage of the transport.

Should have been…

The transport was untouched, not even blackened by the blast.

But how? The missile had exploded. Haluk had done everything he had been trained to do. Burning debris should have been raining down from the sky. Those inside should have been so much charred meat.

Haluk felt like his heart had dropped out of his chest, but there was no time to stand and try to process it all. The drones were almost on him. The knowledge that he had failed to kill the t'au military leader changed everything. This was not the glory he had been promised.

He was no longer content to die here. Not now. The promise of eternal reward had been snatched from him, his most fervent hopes undone.

Giving himself over completely to the survival instinct he had been wrestling with, he raced around the walkway to the other side of the tower, grabbed a double armful of the coils of the infiltrator's rope and heaved its length out over the crenellations. The rope plunged downwards, uncoiling as it fell. It stopped just a few metres short of the ground.

The hum of the drones was pressing on his ears. They swung around the sides of the tower – two from the left, one from the right – just as Haluk took firm hold of the rope and pitched himself over the edge.

He swung out in a controlled spin and landed his feet against the wall. From there, he began a frantic descent.

The drones swept in closer, descending in parallel with him, taking up position four metres off to his sides and rear.

A burst of flat t'au speech, mechanical and lifeless, emanated from all three at once.

Haluk ignored it, his mind given over completely to the descent.

The voice switched to Uhrzi, the most common variant of Tychonite Low Gothic, the official human language of occupied Tychonis.

'Cease all movement immediately.'

Desperate now, hardly thinking at all, Haluk switched from arm-over-arm. He hooked the rope into the crook of his elbow and began to drop at speed, the fabric of his robes protecting him from burning abrasion.

He dropped fast, but the drones dropped with him, guns levelled.

'Cease movement. This is your final warning.'

Only ten metres to the ground. Nine. Eight. Seven.

When the guns fired on him, it was the sound more than the explosive pain of the pulse rounds smacking into his flesh that snapped his focus away from the rope. So distinctive, that strange, angry buzz.

His strength left him completely. He lost his grip, plunging the rest of the distance to the ground below, hitting it with a loud, wet crack. The back of his skull shattered. A pool of hot, thick blood began to spread out around his head. Lights swarmed and danced behind his eyelids.

He opened them and looked up at the sky, cloudless and blue. In his peripheral vision, he saw the drones settle around him in a cordoning pattern. They turned their guns outwards.

He was no longer any threat.

Everything was growing dark. He heard the sound of many pairs of booted feet running towards him. There was shouting in both Uhrzi and T'au.

Haluk was fading fast. He couldn't turn his head to see, but he sensed he was being surrounded. Figures moved at the edges of his vision. Suddenly, the flat, noseless face of a t'au fire warrior leaned over him, close and low, scowling, snarling, barking a string of questions in that arrogant, contemptible way common to all pog soldiers.

Haluk tested his right arm gingerly. It moved, albeit painfully slowly. With great effort, he forced his hand into the folds of his robe. The officer leaning over him snapped ferociously, this time in Uhrzi.

'Don't move, gue'la. You are dying.'

Haluk felt his hand close over the tiny device he sought. Through bloodied lips, he grinned. Perhaps a little glory after all.

'Pro Terra Imperator,' he wheezed, blood bubbling from his mouth.

He pressed the small red button on the detonator and ignited the explosives under his robes, ending his part in the liberation of his world.

Eight t'au security personnel died in the capital that day, all kills of the Ishtu death-commando Haluk uz-Kalan. Four human security officers also died immediately in the blast. The three drones that had gunned the rebel down were blown to hot fragments. A further sixteen members of the t'au and human security forces were injured.

The greater effects of the attack were felt only after, and for much longer, just as the Speaker of the Sands had always intended.

Coldwave had never been a viable target – not for so simple a plan as this.

The real target that day was unity – the cross-species trust between the people of Tychonis and their blue-skinned overlords.

In the climate of surging doubt and tension that sprang from the attack, and in the months of increased security measures that followed Haluk uz-Kalan's death, not just in the bustling districts of Chu'sut Ka but in all the integrated towns and cities, thousands of men and women were forcefully detained for questioning. Those with something to hide were subjected to measures few would have expected of the t'au. People vanished. Some were released – not because they were thought innocent, but because observing them might lead t'au intelligence operatives to higher-value suspects.

Among the people of the souks and recaff houses and narco-dens, words of criticism and outrage became more common.

Perhaps the Greater Good was not all it purported to be, men whispered to each other. Perhaps, despite all the promises, some were more equal than others in the glorious t'au regime.

That was what the Speaker of the Sands had sought to gain. *That* was what Haluk uz-Kalan's life bought for the loyalist cause.

SIX

The room never changed. And why would it? Those who met within cared not at all about its decor or lack thereof. After all, it did not actually exist. It was a no-room, a psychic construct only, a simple tool, nothing more. It allowed the two minds now occupying it to discuss matters of great import without the distraction and discomfort of total astral disembodiment. Those minds were projected and maintained in that ethereal space by the life-sapping, flesh-withering efforts of their individual psychic choirs, each a collection of lobotomised psychic minds all slaved to their respective master astropaths.

This was what it took to bridge the vast distance between the *Saint Nevarre* and *The Lance of Sion*, two ships currently almost half a segmentum apart.

The table in the centre of the no-room was of the same unnaturally symmetrical grain as before. The flames in the wall sconces still guttered and danced in strange synchronicity, each a copied instance of a single fixture. The chairs were plain, their surfaces neither warm nor cold, neither hard nor soft. There was only enough detail, enough realism, to appease the human mind so that it might disregard the surroundings as utterly mundane.

No, the room had not changed since the last time these two met in secret conclave.

But much else had.

'The master astropath confirms we are secure on our side,' said one.

'Likewise at this end, my lord. Cleared to proceed,' replied the other.

The simplicity of this astral environment had another benefit – it was easy to spot glitches. Had any asymmetry crept into the psychic fabric of the room, any hint of unexpected detail, the implications would have been significant and the course of action immediate. The meeting would be ended at once. Anything at all – a single flame out of sync with the others, or some tiny variance in the table's grain – would mean outside interference.

A psychic intrusion attempt.

A breach.

It could come from a thousand different sources, for many were the minds that longed to hear the most secretive sessions of the Emperor's Holy Inquisition. Whatever the source of an infiltration, the result would be the same – instant termination of the mindscape and an immediate return to the physical realm.

As ever, there was too much at stake.

No, thought Omicron. *This is different. The stakes are even higher now.*

It was a dark thought. So much work, so much progress

since *Night Harvest*. *Blackseed* was further along than ever. So much had fallen into place.

Now it all hung by a thread.

A full century ago, when he first set foot on this long and arduous road, taking the mantle of Omicron and all its attendant responsibilities from his late mentor, he would never have believed he might actually come this far. The opposition had proven less competent than he had first given them credit for. Far from fools, of course. Deceivers and exploiters all – manipulators and illusionists, puppeteers and gamesmen of the very highest order. But in taking them on, their very capabilities had brought out his own and, thus far at least, his had consistently proved the superior.

Only he hadn't foreseen this. Not *this*. The members of the ordo played the most dangerous of games. Assets disappeared – many were tortured and killed, others simply never heard of again – and as many questions went unanswered as not. But this time, one of his own, one of his best and brightest and most highly placed...

His hooded avatar leaned forward across the table and stared at the identically cowled figure seated there.

Sigma.

Omicron had invested five and a half decades in this one. Time well spent. That investment had been returned many times over.

I knew you'd be worth it. You had the right kind of fire in you. And exactly the kind of Achilles heel I needed to draw out your best.

The boy and his sister – she deathly ill – had been stowaways on an Imperial freighter. Omicron had been tracking the illegal movement of xenos technology between cells of a multi-system extremist pro-alien terrorist group. He had thought to find eldar shuriken rifles in the freighter's hold.

Instead, he found a boy who would, in time, evolve to be a far deadlier weapon.

He chuckled scornfully at himself, still surprised on occasion at the strength of this patriarchal pride. Naively, he had thought himself beyond such feelings. Some within the ordo thought him a paragon of ruthless, cold efficiency. They would have been surprised to know he was still so human. But such feelings were a weakness nonetheless, and that was something he could not abide.

The blade that kills you is the one you least expect.

He hardened himself. There was deadly business to discuss. High-level assets would have to be put on the line. There would be deaths. Very probably Space Marine deaths.

'Epsilon has gone off-grid. Dark. Without authorisation.'

On the other side of the table, Sigma's avatar stiffened visibly. The weight of the words and their implications hung there in the astral space between them.

'Probability she's dead?' asked Sigma. 'What does your coven say?'

'Dead would be simpler, old friend.'

Yes, he thought. *Let him hear me say 'friend'. The bonds must remain strong, more so now than ever before.*

'And we would not be talking now,' continued Omicron. 'But my coven has been scouring the aether since she missed her last transmission deadline, and it appears her soul is still grounded in the physical realm. Were it disembodied, the coven could have forced it into seance. Their divinations are not often wrong, and their conviction is strong on this one. I am inclined to believe them – she is not an easy one to kill. They also believe there is a significant event-nexus in her near future. Highly significant. And that makes the problem of her disappearance all the greater.'

Of course, there were ways of being dead without one's soul transcending. And there were countless reasons why an inquisitor of Epsilon's rank and responsibilities might fail to report as ordered, none of which were reassuring. In every single case, the implications for all that Omicron and his faction had been working towards could not have been more grave.

'How long has she been missing?' asked Sigma. 'How overdue is her last astropathic contact?'

'The tower on Galathis was due to relay a status report forty-three days ago. The Listener there reports no transmissions forthcoming. Nothing got through, not to Galathis nor to any of the other relays. No distress calls. No fragments. Nothing. Epsilon's movements for the last ninety-one days are a blank.'

Sigma's avatar leaned forward, elbows on the table, and clasped bone-white hands. 'The very difficulty of tracing an agent who has deliberately gone dark is testament to the training you gave us. She may have had no choice. There's a chance that seeking her out is the wrong play here.'

Omicron nodded. 'I've accounted for that. But this goes well beyond the usual protocols. There are signals she could have given prior to dropping off the map.'

'What of her retinue? Her assets? Someone must know something. Even dead bodies tell tales.'

'Those we could locate, we picked up. Interrogations proved fruitless for the most part. Members of her network either knew nothing or opted not to cooperate, loyal unto death. Significantly, a number of those interrogations were cut short. Our opponents within the ordo have been particularly proactive and tenacious. Armed elements stormed several of our active sites. A number of operators under my own direct command were lost as a result.'

'You exacted an appropriate price of your own, I'm sure.'

Omicron allowed himself a slight smile. 'Oculum pro oculo. I'm confident the opposition gained nothing tangible. They will still be smarting from their last attempt. But this is the most overt move our political enemies have ever made against us. The implications are twofold, I think.'

'That they were watching for just such an opportunity, and that they believe there is a chance they can get to Epsilon first,' said Sigma.

Omicron nodded. 'They have never had such a fine chance. To acquire one of the core members of our cabal, one I trusted as deeply as I trust you, trained in the same way and to the same ends, someone who knows enough to destroy *Blackseed* and all we have built... Yes, it's worth almost any price to them. They must be frothing at the prospect. Were I in their shoes, I would spare no effort.'

Sigma shifted, leaning back in his chair, arms sliding from the table to settle on its armrests. 'There is, of course, the possibility that they have Epsilon already and the strikes are a ruse to cover it. Could she have defected? I mean no offence, my lord, but, much as it pains me, it would not be the first time an ordo inquisitor has... switched allegiance.'

Omicron felt the same brief wash of denial he'd felt when that very thought had first occurred to him. But feelings changed nothing. Epsilon may indeed have gone over. Still, even as he admitted this to himself once again, his gut rejected it. It just didn't strike him as truth.

'I can't rule it out,' he said. 'But her indoctrination and psycho-conditioning were every bit as comprehensive as your own. You share many qualities, you and she. Her loyalty has never been in doubt, nor her commitment to our ultimate aims. Something else is afoot here. I'll not believe her a defector until I have exhausted all other possibilities.'

'Xenos, then,' offered Sigma. 'Epsilon may have been taken captive before she could signal. I am assuming, of course, that as part of *Blackseed* she was conducting an operation with a high probability of hostile contact.'

'Capture was my first thought. On the surface, an obvious answer. But why, then, the resistance from her assets during interrogation? We are not talking about mere conditioning. There was hope. Faith. They went to their deaths willingly with knowledge they would not share at any price.'

'Nothing was extracted? At all?'

Sigma's surprise was warranted. Ordo methods always ensured something to work with.

'Ultimately, we were able to snag a single thread. It cost us much.' *And now we get to it, to the moment I put you in play.* 'A single word is all we have to go on – Tychonis.'

Sigma's avatar paused as the inquisitor searched his memory.

No. Nothing.

The avatar shook its hooded head.

'Tychonis,' said Omicron, 'was a low-yield Imperial fringe world until it was cut off by the warp storm Occulus Draconis, the Dragon's Eye.'

'That storm abated a century ago,' said Sigma. 'The system was not reintegrated?'

'It was a desert world. Low population. Low- to mid-value natural resources only. The proposal was scrapped over costs. For a while, the human population was victim to the depredations of the dark eldar. The t'au swept in, eliminated that threat and turned the planet into a fertile agri world during their last expansion.'

'The t'au? What was she doing in t'au space? You're sending me in, of course, so I'll need access to her records.'

'What I can share under emergency protocols, I will

transmit to your ship's archives at once. There will be omissions, for your own sake as well as mine. Encryption will make processing slower than I'm sure you would like, but you'll understand the need when you review the material. Once you've processed it, make your initial assessment of the assets you require. I'll see you have everything you need. Because mark me well, locating and recovering Epsilon is the most important thing I have ever asked of you. Failure in this is not an option. Only a handful know the truth about *Blackseed,* and each of those knows only their part. Epsilon, however...'

'She knows enough to end it, then.'

'She has been to Facility fifty-two. She has overseen key aspects of the work and more besides. Enough that, were it to come out, every last one of us would be declared *traitoris* and marked for death. Of the cabal, nothing would remain. Of all we have achieved to date, only ash. Let me reiterate – we face not only the fall of *Blackseed,* but the collapse of everything you and I have ever built in the name of mankind. There will be no mercy for us.'

Sigma leaned forward on the table again, head bowed in thought.

'And if we find her?'

'I need answers. Why did she go dark? If she has talked, to whom, and of what? How much has been compromised? What are the ramifications? I cannot get these things from a corpse, and I cannot plan countermeasures without them.'

'I understand, my lord. Tychonis, then. If she is there, my assets will find her.'

'I have already activated sleepers within the Tychonite populace. The blue-skins are watchful. Like the eldar, they are not easily deceived. But also like the eldar, their weakness lies in their arrogance, their self-assurance. Agents on the ground have been told what to look for. I await word. The time and distance involved…'

'Why was Epsilon in t'au space?'

'She was initially deployed to the Eastern Fringe in order to covertly observe their military operations against tyranid incursions there. She was never tasked with going to Tychonis. Her last reported movement was groundfall on a world called Dalyx. The t'au had fallen to the tyranids there two decades prior. A dead husk of a world is all that remains now, but decrypted t'au records secured in a previous kill-team operation led her to seek out an old research facility. Since their first clashes, the t'au have been looking for an answer to the tyranid problem as desperately as we have. Why she would ultimately end up on Tychonis is a mystery, if indeed that is where you'll find her.'

'She was tasked with observation only?'

'With one proviso – in the event that a nascent genestealer presence was discovered on a t'au-populated world, Epsilon was to secure several t'au specimens, male and female both, infected with the tyranid geneseed.'

Sigma's head lifted at that, the sharp movement betraying his surprise. 'An extension of *Blackseed*.' After a second, he nodded. 'Of course. The blue-skins have no known psykers. The potential benefits to the project… It should have been obvious to me.'

'Peace, my friend,' said Omicron. 'The scope of the project has grown. You were assigned to other critical work. *Blackseed* would not be so far along but for all you achieved with *Night Harvest*. The inclusion of t'au subjects in the programme is potentially promising, yes, but it is merely an offshoot – an avenue of research that has yet to prove its worth.'

'If she is unrecoverable, do you wish me to secure infected t'au specimens?'

'If she cannot be recovered, you will take over her mission and procure them for transport to Facility fifty-two. Detailed orders will follow by astropathic link. Our time here is almost up. To risk maintaining this astral space any longer invites intrusion or a trace. All relevant files will be transferred to the *Saint Nevarre*. Make your resources request once you have reviewed the data. Assign assets as you see fit, but spare nothing in pursuit of your goal. As you will see from the files, Tychonis is firmly in t'au hands. Consult your coven. A kill-team will need to be deployed.'

'Scimitar then, my lord.'

No, thought Omicron. *Not Scimitar. At least, not* just *Scimitar.*

He had been told, warned, by that enigmatic voice in his mind – a voice he thought of as 'the great herald' – that his ambitions would falter were the Exorcist Rauth and the Death Spectre Lyandro Karras not somehow brought into the middle of all of this.

But would the Death Spectre recover in time?

'Talon,' said Omicron. 'If the kill-team Alpha can heal and deploy in time, his skills could be pivotal to recovering Epsilon.'

'Scimitar are more experienced, more obedient, my lord,' countered Sigma. 'Codicier Karras has never fought the t'au outside of simulations and sensorium relays.'

Omicron shook his head. 'Broden is too rigid, too orthodox to lead an operation like this. Scalpel over sledgehammer, at least until we know more. *Night Harvest* could have collapsed into disaster. Karras is the reason it did not. Experience aside, he and his team are the better choice, though you ought to place him under the tactical command of one with more direct experience of the t'au.'

Sigma bowed. 'Your will be done, lord. I have just such a one, but the Death Spectre will not like it. None of them will.'

'They are Deathwatch,' replied Omicron with a wry smile. 'It is not in their mandate to like it. Just make sure they get the job done.'

Omicron rose from his chair, signalling an end to the discussion. But Sigma was not quite finished.

'One last thing, m'lord.'

'Ask it,' said Omicron.

'Epsilon... Did she have a Deathwatch kill-team with her?'

That was astute, thought Omicron. *Good.* 'Eight operatives. Battle-hardened. Excellent service records. No word from any of them.'

'A Librarian?'

Omicron's avatar shook its head. 'None with psychic aptitude.'

Sigma nodded.

'If that is all,' said Omicron, 'go, and know that I trust you to resolve this. *In nomine Imperator.*'

Sigma also rose from his chair. He bowed. '*In nomine Imperator.*'

With that, the room around them began to dissolve, to peel and flake, rising up like ash on a warm current as if the whole illusion were a painting on fire or paper being burned from a wall. So, too, did the cloaked avatars disintegrate until nothing of them remained.

The minds of the two Ordo Xenos inquisitors snapped back into their respective bodies and the voices of the astropathic choirs which had been raised in hymn gradually lowered.

The song ended on a last long and mournful note.

Minutes later, the master astropath aboard the *Saint Nevarre* started to receive highly encrypted data. He gave himself over to the deepest of trances. His eyes rolled back into his head.

His hands began scribbling madly, frantically, on the reams of parchment placed in front of him.

When the writing stopped, his servants rolled his work into tight scrolls and delivered them into the hands of the acolytes on the Mechanicus decks for crypto-cogitator processing.

Three hours later, seated in an antique ironwood and grox-leather chair in his private quarters, Sigma finished absorbing the last of the details. The hyper-focus drugs he had taken were starting to wear off, right on time. Over ship comms, he ordered Cashka Redthorne, ship's captain, to make for the waystation at Mandrake Point. It was a trading and refuelling hub roughly midway between Damaroth and the edge of the T'au Empire. Already, plans were forming in his mind.

The *Saint Nevarre* swung around to face galactic east. Her warp engines powered up, prickling the skin of all aboard. Moments later, she punched a boiling white hole in the immaterium, then plunged into it like a spear cast into churning waters.

The turbulent rift in reality closed behind her.

Operation Shadowbreaker had begun.

SEVEN

Time, like the torrents of the Black River, flows only in one direction. But like those ethereal currents that carry one's soul to the afterlife, it does not flow uniformly. There are rapids and crashing falls and gentle, slow-moving shallows.

Moments of joy and victory seem to flash by.

Moments of pain and torment seem to last an age.

Karras could no longer sense these currents. The flow had become immeasurable to him. There was nothing to gauge it by. He existed. This much, he knew. He could think. He could wonder. His conscious mind was intact. But he had struggled up from the inky black of oblivion into a world entirely of the mind. He could no longer sense any physical form. Nothing to tell him he still had fingers, or eyes, or either of his two hearts.

All he had was thought, and at first his awareness hung in a void of utter nothingness, waiting.

Lost.

Eventually, the colour and landscape of memory slowly drifted into focus around him. He saw the skull-and-scythes iconography of his Chapter engraved on a thousand mausoleum doors. He saw votive candles winking in the orange gloom of a corner of the Reclusiam. He saw broad-backed figures bowed in prayer before an altar on which lay weapons of war once wielded by legends.

There were other memories, too, things he struggled to recognise or reconcile with, fragments of another life. These were memories of a past his Space Marine conditioning had long suppressed but had never truly erased.

A forest filled with the sounds of battle.

So real.

Gunshots echoed off the black trunks. A woman screamed his name, begged him to run.

His mother.

He ran, but his legs were short, his lungs small, those of the child he had been. Thorny branches and the frigid air stabbed at him as he sped between the trees.

A great roar sounded from ahead and to the left. Something vast and black ripped through the sky so close that dead branches rained down around him.

There was a boom that shook the earth. A wall of flame reared up right before him. He swung right and ran harder, putting everything he had into pumping his arms and legs. He didn't turn to look behind. He could feel the heat on his calves and the back of his neck. Fire wanted to engulf him, to wrap itself around him and greedily consume his flesh.

Behind him, burning trees cracked and collapsed. Their fall made the flames surge, rearing up like bright dragons tossing their mighty heads, all violence and rage. But they wouldn't catch Lyandro Karras.

He was the son of the hunt leader, fleetest of foot and strongest of sinew among the children of the Okosha. No mere fire would take him. Not if he just kept running.

Up ahead, there was a break in the trees. He sprinted for it.

In his focus on the chaos behind him, however, he had neglected to keep note of precisely where he was. On any other day, he would have known that the eastern edge of the forest marked the lip of the great chasm. They called it Talan's Fate, though many more than the mythological Talan had found their end at the bottom. In all the fear, panic and confusion, Karras didn't have time to think of where he was running to, only of getting away.

He burst from the trees at full tilt. There was no way he could have stopped himself. His eyes went wide the moment he knew what he'd done. Time slowed to a crawl. He watched his right foot thrust out ahead of him to step down on nothing but empty air.

Momentum carried him straight over the edge. Dark death yawned up at him. His eyes stared down into the black abyss that was about to claim his life. No death by fire, then. Nor by the growling blades of the grotesque red giants which had just stormed his village.

Gravity.

Gravity would kill him.

At least it would be quick.

Just as his heart leapt into his throat and his body began its descent, something swept out across the edge of his peripheral vision – something a deep, dark blue, cold and hard as stone.

It hit him across the midsection and encircled his waist.

Karras' fall was suddenly and violently arrested. Breath exploded from him. He hung in mid-air, looking down at the deep black bottom of the chasm's vast, hungry throat. His heart was pounding like a hammer beneath his ribs.

The thing that held him drew him back over the lip of the abyss. He saw the deadly void slide away to be replaced by beloved brown earth, pine needles and patches of unmelted snow.

He was breathing hard, his nine-year-old lungs still aflame with the effort of the escape and the adrenal blitz of imminent death. He felt something grip his upper arm. With absolute ease, as if he weighed nothing, he was turned around in mid-air and found himself staring straight into the terrible visage of his saviour.

How well he remembered that moment. The bravest, most reckless boy of the tribe had frozen in abject fear. Never had he seen such a face – skin the white of sun-bleached bone with beard and eyebrows to match. Eyes like pools of fresh-spilled blood. No whites. It was a face straight from the haunting tales old Sheddac would tell by the light of the cooking fires.

Khadit.

The word rang loud in his mind – an old word from a language he'd never heard, and yet, looking into that wise and terrible face, its meaning had been as clear as a mountain stream.

Visions came attached to it, visions of gloomy places where bodies were shaped by pain and ancient knowledge, of dark chambers where impossible things were taught and mastered.

'We must get you away from here,' said the giant, and his voice was so deep that Karras could feel the words shaking his ribs. 'We must get you out while they are still distracted.'

As Karras recalled this, relived it, he realised he had never learned who *they* were. Space Marines, of course, as he knew now. Heretics from one of the accursed Traitor Legions. But in all the years since – over a hundred of them – his giant saviour had never spoken of that day. All too soon, psycho-conditioning and the demands of Space Marine selection had programmed Karras to neither ask nor care.

Why, as he hung in an unknowable void, was it all bubbling up within him now?

Memories of childhood run deep. Suppressed, yes, but never truly erased. What has happened to me? Why is this coming back to me now? Where am I?

He let the memory continue to play out. Still holding the child he had just snatched from the air, the albino giant had angled his head and spoken into a transmitter on his gorget, a string of sharp words Karras hadn't understood. There was no mistaking the tone of command, though.

Moments later, thunder filled the sky, echoing along the canyon walls. A great ship the colour of charcoal swung into view, its rear ramp already lowered. It hung there in the air above Talan's Fate, jets growling, spewing fire.

The giant had slung Karras over one massive armoured shoulder and leapt.

Karras saw the ground fall away and the abyss yawn beneath him once again. His stomach flipped with resurging fear. His saviour's boots clanged loudly as he landed on the outstretched ramp. The aircraft dipped an inch with the impact, then nosed left and thrust upward. With his left hand, the giant grabbed the edge of the craft's fuselage and pulled himself and Karras further inside. Still carrying the child over one shoulder, he strode further into the compartment. Behind them, the ramp began to rise towards the shut position. Karras looked out on a sight he had only ever seen from the nearby mountainsides.

There below him was the forest, vast and ancient, the home of the tribe, provider of all they had ever needed, all he had ever known. The ship swung south. The ground wheeled below him, and Karras saw great clouds of black smoke and the glow of vast fires raging out of control in the place where his people had lived since the tribe's first tale began.

The ramp was half closed now. It was the last he ever saw of his birth world. In the seconds before it closed completely, in the last slice of sky visible, Karras saw movement to the south-west – three slender, elegant ships shaped like arrowheads. They streaked off into the distance.

The ramp slid home. Locking bolts rammed into place.

The white-faced giant placed him gently down on a seat far too large and, without either of them speaking a single word, they began to talk.

It was the first time anyone had addressed Karras mind to mind.

In that moment, he learned of the Imperium and of the Emperor on Terra.

On that day, he discovered purpose.

Vivid as it had been – the reliving of that day, the details, the sensations – it dissipated like smoke from a bolter barrel now. Karras found himself back in the unknowable void, just a disembodied spark of identity and experience.

This is not death. It cannot be. I remember Chiaro. I remember all of it. Voss and the others... They dug me out.

A feeling of great dread swept over him. Memory muttered a fell name, and his emotions surged. He shrank back from it, but it insisted on his memory, and soon he was remembering in detail, whether he wanted to or not, the encounter with the daemon on the ethereal waters of the Black River.

Hepaxammon. Prince of Sorrows.

The entity's presence had sullied the river, made the raging waters stink with foul decay. It had broken through the boundaries of its own realm to issue Karras a dark ultimatum – pass a message to the Exorcist Darrion Rauth or face dire consequences.

Karras had almost died that day, his armour shattered, his body speared and pulverised by rocks both sharp and heavy. But he had not. The *Saint Nevarre* had returned for him. Hepaxammon claimed agency in bringing it back.

But the lips of all daemons are black with lies, thought Karras.

A psychic construct placed at that point on the primary timeline by Athio Cordatus had bought Karras his escape, pulling him out of the Black River and the daemon's torment.

You knew, my khadit. And yet... Could you not have prepared me?

There was shame and a certain bitterness at the thought. Had Athio Cordatus known ahead of time, he would surely have prepared his protégé. The Death Spectres Librarius must have divined the daemon's intrusion only *after* Karras had left Occludus, his Chapter's crypt-world home.

Had they seen this, too? This... this what?

Where was he? Why was he here, trapped in this bodiless state?

Answers would not come. The absence of any sense of time and space threatened to madden him. Nothing to grasp. Nothing to ground him. All he had here were memories of the past, and those that came to him were not of his choosing. He was being forced to relive things he did not invoke.

He saw again the three deaths he had endured as rites of passage.

He remembered the slaughter he and his brothers had

unleashed on a dozen alien-held worlds in the Ghoul Stars, saw good friends die and others raised to great glory by their deeds. He recalled ceremonies celebrating great victories and remembered others less joyous, honouring the heroic sacrifice of brothers lost in desperate battle.

And then, after all this, there came again his flight through the winter woods of his birth world.

Only this time, it did not play out quite the same.

The memory started as before – the screams from behind him, the sounds of gunfire, the roar of hungry flames and the stabbing winter air in his young lungs. This time, however, at the moment his body angled right towards the eastern edge of the trees, everything around him abruptly froze. It was as if he were in a sensorium feed suddenly paused.

He ran on for a few steps, but the stark absence of noise and blazing heat struck him so hard that he stopped, turned and looked back. The only sound now was his ragged breathing. It slowed as he stood there in total confusion.

The trees glowed with fire, but the flames didn't move. Nothing did. They had no hunger, no heat, nothing but shape.

And then a voice, soft and strangely accented. Feminine.

'We knew they were coming for you.'

Karras spun, turning towards the source of the sound.

There was no one there.

'It was we who stalled them while your warrior brethren got you out. Ignorant as ever, you mon-keigh did not even detect us.'

The voice sounded so close now that Karras felt hairs prickle on the back of his neck and arms.

'I gave the orders myself,' it continued. 'We could not allow you to fall into the hands of the Great Enemy. What terrors you would have wrought had your fate been to ravage the stars as one of the Foul. Such an abomination you would have become.'

Karras spun again, angry now, scowling fiercely.

Finally, he found himself facing the source. There before him stood another child, apparently of an age close to his own. She was a pale, slender thing with long blonde hair, fine-boned and elegant, dressed in richly jewelled robes of shimmering white silk.

This is no memory, he thought. *This is an intrusion!*

The girl regarded him without smiling, her face unreadable.

Karras spoke, and found to his surprise that it was his adult voice, his Space Marine voice, that issued forth from his child lips.

'Who are you?' he demanded.

'Aranye,' answered the girl. 'It is a contraction, but it will suffice.'

Taking her eyes from him, she crossed to a tree and stared at the detail of the bark, stroking it with one delicate hand. 'Your memories are richly detailed. You had a fine mind, even before the implants and the training. I was not mistaken about your potential, nor about the threat you represented.' She glanced over at him. 'May still represent.'

She turned back to the tree. 'We shall soon know if I am to regret my part in your journey.'

'And what journey is that?' Karras growled.

A flicker of a smile crossed her small, perfect mouth. She looked him up and down. 'I see a nine-year-old boy running for his life while his people die behind him. Die *because* of him. Let no guilt assail you, however. Their lives meant little. In truth, you were something of a bargain, as you mon-keigh might say.'

She continued to study the bark of the tree, apparently fascinated by the folds and tiny cracks and bumps, by how some parts were smooth and others were rough.

Karras was about to explode at her, to deny her words, but he could not. She had not spoken falsely. Part of him had always known. His people had been killed – all of them – and he was the reason. The murderous red giants had come solely for him.

'How did–'

She cut him off mid-question. 'Countless tribes on countless worlds are watched. You know this. The most promising have always been marked and tested. The darkest, foulest foes of your bloated, cancer-riddled Imperium are ever in a race to deny your ranks and swell their own.'

'You talk of the Traitor Legions.'

She turned, eyes suddenly intense. 'How narrow the path you walk, Death Spectre. Such storms surround you. An abyss on either side, and such a narrow path between. Be thankful you were never trained to read the future. Were you able, you might not dare another step towards it.'

Karras closed on her, fists clenched at his sides. 'What nature of thing are you? You didn't invade my mind just to taunt me.'

'I am here to help prepare you,' she said. She raised a hand and brushed her hair over one ear. 'And you already know what I am.'

Karras' reaction was immediate and powerful. He saw the ear, how pointed it was. It was the final marker that gave her nature away.

'Xenos,' he growled. 'Damnable eldar!'

He tried to rush her, but his body would no longer obey him. Young muscles strained against invisible bonds.

He snarled and raged, fighting desperately to push forward.

She remained icy calm as she stepped straight towards him. When they were standing eye to eye, barely half a metre apart, she placed a cool hand to the side of his head and said, 'It is time to see for yourself, Space Marine. It costs me much to be here inside your mind. Heed these warnings or risk bringing destruction down on all you love.'

At that, the forest vanished, and she with it.

All was utter darkness, and Karras was falling.

Aranye's voice sounded in his head, this time different, mature, aged by centuries, or perhaps even millennia. 'I will be watching,' she said. 'Act with care in the times ahead. Do what is right, or I will do what I must to stop you.'

The darkness receded. Red light trickled into his vision. He was still falling, but the sensation changed. He felt his adult body encasing his consciousness again, felt gravity pulling on his muscles and joints. He was heavy, grown far beyond the genetic limits of normal men. He felt the comforting weight and warmth of power armour around thick, gene-enhanced muscles. He tried to move and found himself restrained. Lights winked before his eyes.

Alert runes on a tactical display.

He was in a drop pod. It was thundering through planetary atmosphere, the heat inside rising. This was an assault drop. Everything about it was familiar and clear. He could hear the roar and feel the deep shudder as the armoured pod smashed through the sound barrier.

Seconds later, his stomach heaved violently and the pull of gravity shifted. His organs lurched inside him. The braking jets had fired. The pod landed with a great, juddering crunch. The hatches, like five titanium petals, blew their locking bolts and burst open.

Karras looked out upon a mountain range of black crags covered in crisp white snow. Overhead hung a heavy, graphite-coloured sky.

The impact clamp which had been holding him in place clicked free. He stepped out of the pod.

He knew the place all too well, but no assault drop had ever happened here.

He could name all of the high peaks before him. There, the tallest and sharpest – that was Yurien's Claw. He had been tested there as a neophyte, forced to navigate the pass in deep winter, hunted by rock leopards, armed only with a knife. Six aspirants had ventured out. Four had died.

Why Occludus? What game is this?

It all seemed so real, so tangible. Even the bitter chill of the air nipped at the tip of his nose and stung his eyes. He looked down at his feet and took another step. The snow crunched under ceramite and plasteel.

Home.

He turned, knowing what he would find, and was not surprised. There, high on the mountainside behind him, was the towering Western Gate of Logopol, fortress-monastery of the Chapter.

It was as glorious as ever – exquisitely carved, shining white and gold against the dark grey sky. At first, his hearts soared to see it, but the joy swiftly fell away. Not a soul moved on the mighty watchtowers. No Thunderhawk gunships or Stormtalon fighters cut across the skies. He looked around. No more drop pods, either. Only his.

'This is all a lie,' he muttered.

But it feels so damned real.

Whatever power the eldar witch had used to conjure this, it was as flawless and convincing in its detail as any psychic construct or sensorium feed he had ever experienced, almost as convincing as reality itself.

But it was *not* real.

Angered, he turned his red eyes to the sky and shouted, 'What do you want with me, xenos witch? What is the point of all this?'

Nothing. Just his own words echoing back at him from the black crags.

Capricious as they were, the eldar had contrived to bring him here for a reason. But there were no answers to be had out on the icy white slopes. That much was clear.

With no other choice, Karras put one booted foot in front of the other and began his climb towards the Western Gate.

EIGHT

Arnaz forced himself not to hurry, but his self-control was being tested tonight. Something itched at the corners of his awareness. As he threaded his way through the alleys, he fought the impulse to look back every few seconds. Pointless anyway. All who fought the War of Patience – what the tribes called the Kavash Garai – knew the t'au could make themselves all but invisible when they wanted to.

Arnaz's tradecraft was as clean as ever. No slips. No threads for them to follow. He just had a bad feeling tonight, a feeling that he stood out somehow.

He was wrong. In dark blue robes bearing the appropriate glyphs, he looked just like any other member of the city administration, a mid-ranking functionary heading home after a day of work in the name of the Greater Good.

His cover had been built over a decade. It was solid.

If his steps betrayed a little haste, a little anxiety, well… Who wasn't anxious in the capital these days? Things were changing rapidly on Tychonis now. After the attempt on Coldwave, the t'au were cracking down on every manner of criminal and known sympathiser from here to the smallest of the agri towns on the borders of the Drowned Lands.

The fire caste were relentless, and the ISF were even worse, as if their loyalty to the Aun were in question on account of the attacker being human.

Hardly times that encouraged a calm demeanour, especially since Arnaz and the men he was meeting were precisely who the blue-skins sought.

Only, Arnaz was no simple rebel. He had been placed here by a far greater power than the Speaker of the Sands. He served a mover of pieces in a much greater and deadlier game than mere planetary rebellion.

For years, he'd had no word from his off-world master. His remit was to entrench himself, foster solid contacts and information streams, and wait. He had actually thought himself forgotten, left here to live out a lie that was gradually becoming his truth. He'd wondered at what point he'd stop being a sleeper agent of the Inquisition and start just being a member of Tychonite society. Where did the act stop and real life begin?

Then, just months ago, word had come via psychic relay. He had been activated. The Imperium had turned its eye to this backwater world at last.

He had upped his security measures. Fresh tension coloured his days.

He rounded the last corner and saw, just up ahead, the sandstone hab he was looking for. There in the small side window stood the green bottle with the lit candle in it, exactly as Gunjir had told him to expect.

He stopped at a short wall and pretended to adjust the

straps on his right boot, a last little act allowing him to check over his shoulder before he committed himself.

Nothing. Nothing that could be seen. Nothing that could be sensed.

He straightened, cinched his waistband a little tighter, smoothed his robe and went around the back to a small stairway cut into the ground. This he descended, stopping by the door at the bottom. There, on a heavy portal of lacquered Cycadian oak, he tapped the prearranged sequence.

There was the slightest of grating sounds, barely audible, from above. Looking up, he saw a tiny pict-lens set in the sandstone door frame. It swivelled to focus on his face and stopped. For a second, nothing happened. The lens just stared at him.

Arnaz heard locking bolts being slid aside. The door opened a crack. A weathered face with the nut-brown skin so typical of the capital's human population squinted at him with eyes of pale violet.

'Evening's greetings, my cousin,' said Arnaz.

'Blessings on the dawn,' said the other.

'The day was dry. I saw a canyon hawk fly south over the market.'

'The hawk sees much. Perhaps he saw you.'

'He did not see me, cousin. His eyes were on the horizon.'

'As are the eyes of all the Iczer-Makan.'

Iczer-Makan. The Far-Sighted Men.

The use of that name, never uttered casually, told Arnaz he had answered satisfactorily. The man behind the door moved aside, opening the portal further and allowing Arnaz to enter. Beyond was a short hallway ending in an arch over which hung a richly embroidered curtain of deep red fabric and golden thread.

The older man pulled the curtain aside and gestured him through, revealing a small, low-ceilinged room filled with men seated on cushions. A sharp mix of smells – fresh recaff, spiced bread and body odour – hit Arnaz in the face like hot breath.

He saw Gunjir sitting on the far side, facing him as he entered.

When he saw Arnaz, Gunjir rose, smiling, flashing those eight gold teeth of which he was so proud, and gestured for Arnaz to come sit in the empty space on his left. The others, all of whom Arnaz had long known from his files but whom he had never met in person, eyed him with sullen reserve.

Good, he thought. *They are not too quick to trust.*

Arnaz bowed to them, then sat cross-legged on the empty cushion. At that point, the man who had led him inside also sat, directly opposite Arnaz, and began a round of introductions. He used first names only, each so common that were one to be called out in a crowded souk, a hundred men would turn to respond.

Arnaz made the appropriate respectful responses. These men were no fools. Each was a leader in charge of several significant cells. That they had gathered here together was a sign of the times. The War of Patience was a delicate thing, expected to take decades, even centuries. With the Kashtu and Ishtu utterly outnumbered and outgunned, it required the long view. Most men were incapable of giving their lives to a war that would not be won in their lifetime. These men were different. They did not care that most of them would not live to see the fruits of their labours and sacrifices. It was their faith that mattered, their belief in the right of the Imperium to hold dominion over all worlds in the known universe.

The God-Emperor of Man was the one true god.

The teachings of Saint Sathra and his protégé, Saint Isara, could not have been interpreted otherwise.

The man to whom the house belonged, he who had opened the door for Arnaz, was called Diunar. He mumbled something to a man on his right, youngest of the group by the look of him, and Arnaz found himself quickly furnished with a cup of recaff and a small, hard biscuit of baked rice and urix-weed. The biscuit was sweetly spiced, complementing the hot recaff well. He had long ago learned to embrace the strong flavours so loved by these people, though the first few days after he had been smuggled onto the planet had largely been spent with one end or the other suspended over a bio-waste atomiser.

Hard days. First footing on a new world was always so. He'd lost weight rapidly, but that was no bad thing for his cover here. Only the men and women of the Integrated Security Forces – what the blue-skins called the Gue'a'Sha – were expected to hold more muscle than ordinary citizens. The t'au had strong thoughts on such things. One's physiology was expected to fit one's role in society.

Those beliefs had gradually permeated into the human cultures they embraced. Thus, soldiers were by default larger and stronger than merchants and men of other callings.

With Arnaz having now sipped from the cup placed in his hands, Diunar got things underway.

'As we meet in my home,' he began, 'Melshala[2] bless it, Sathra keep it safe, I will speak first. Some of you know me. Others do not. All present are of the blood of the true people. We are of one purpose. Let any who betray that purpose

---

2 Melshala: Uhrzi term for the God-Emperor of Mankind, literally 'father of all men'.

have their souls cast into the black and endless void for all eternity. As you will have heard through the network today, the Aun has ordered the ending of the current curfew from the tenth day of Salbado. An official announcement is to be made tomorrow. The city guard will continue patrolling in force and will retain the power to perform random searches, but the streets may once more be walked at any time of the day or night.'

A short man with a crooked nose – he had introduced himself as Sadiv – spoke up. 'It is good,' he said. 'High time the people were free to move about the city as they please.'

'Is it?' asked another. This one was called Rava. As Arnaz looked at him, he noted a deep and abiding sadness in the man's eyes. He had known great loss. Arnaz recalled his file. A son, his only child, gunned down by fire warriors during an arms depot raid. To maintain cover, Rava had been unable to attend his son's funeral or visit the boy's grave. 'I am not so sure, cousin. Fuller streets mean more eyes to see us as we go about our business. The traitors among our own race are a greater threat to our cause than the warp-cursed pogs. We cannot know on sight who might side with us and who might not. At least the pogs wear their sympathies in the colour of their skin. These curfews have at least kept the streets clear for us.'

'Laha,' said Sadiv, an old Kashtu word indicating conditional agreement. 'But every time we break them, we risk too much. For any of us to be taken alive–'

Gunjir interrupted, his hand raised. As the oldest, his gesture immediately commanded silence from the others.

'What righteous liberation, cousins, ever succeeded without such risks? The Dictator knows we operate here in the city and in every town and city across his stolen world. If he is ending the curfews, it is to maintain the support and favour of the blue-tongues[3], not because he believes the threat to his rule is eliminated. The commerce guilds have been petitioning for an end to the curfews for weeks. The citizenry complain and grow restless. Certainly Aun'dzi would prefer not see our cause gain further support. The curfews have embittered so many.'

'Laha, laha,' said Arnaz, interjecting for the first time, 'but we must not overlook the fact that it may be a strategy to draw us out, to make us careless.'

Gunjir nodded. 'Whatever the Dictator's motivation for lifting the curfew now, I shall not relax my guard, and nor shall any other who values his life. The Aun knows we will have to act again to maintain and build on the support we've gained in the towns and cities in these recent weeks. He will expect us to add to our momentum. We can't let the people settle back into comfortable complacency. The pogs know this. They will be watching for our next move.'

A stout man with a white streak in his dark red beard cleared his throat and placed his right hand over his heart, indicating he wished to speak next. This was Urqis.

'Coldwave has returned to the city yet again, gathering more prisoners to take south. What does the Speaker say of this? Do we strike again while he is here? And what of his constant need to move inmates from the city's internment blocks? Haddayin brothers there report no overcrowding.'

Gunjir shook his head. 'No word of a further attack on Coldwave has come to me, cousin, but Arnaz received word from the north more recently than I. The Speaker believes

---

3 Blue-tongues: slang term, highly offensive, for those humans who embrace the t'au philosophy, integrate into their society or otherwise seek favour with them.

the path to our rightful future is entwined with the arrival of the newcomer, this woman of the black feathers. Arnaz?'

'I will tell you what I know,' said Arnaz. This was why he had come. It was true that he had received encrypted comms from the Speaker. Of all the men here, only he knew the rebel leader's true identity. And in turn, only the Speaker knew Arnaz for what he was – no tribesman, but an agent sent from afar.

'But I have never beheld the woman,' he told them, 'save in these picts.'

He pulled several small squares of glossy paper from his robe and passed half to his left, half to his right. Each man gasped in turn as he laid eyes on them.

'Your shock mirrors my own, my cousins. When I saw the two that escort her, I doubted my own eyes.'

'Resh'vah[4]!' whispered Rava in awe.

'Space Marines!' said Sadiv. 'Space Marines have come!'

---

4 Resh'vah: literally 'holiest of sons'.

NINE

Logopol.

From its crypts and catacombs to the immense and heavily armed fortress built atop them, it was a vast and complex place. Images of death and transcendence were everywhere, engraved onto walls and doors, glorified in fine statuary, stained glass and mosaics, dazzling in their craftsmanship yet darkly morose. One thousand active Space Marines called the crypt-city home, though never had that number gathered here at once, not even on Founding Day. Some went out never to return. Others never left. Many of these were the Chapter's serfs, numbering in the tens of thousands, their entire lives dedicated to duty in the service of their warrior lords.

By their blood and toil did the city endure, allowing their masters to focus on their role in the endless, galaxy-wide war.

As Karras strode through the mighty gates of laser-etched titanium, he saw not a soul. No serfs. No brothers. No one.

None watched him from the bastion walls or from the

black balconies of the Great Keep. He would have sensed them even had he not seen them. And yet, there *was* energy here. Presence. Something was pulling at him. As he stalked through gardens filled with black and leafless trees, through training grounds, halls and sconce-lit corridors, the feeling became a certainty.

He was being pulled below, down into the great catacombs where the honoured dead lay silent, their noble duty fulfilled. There at the bottom he would find the ancient dome, the Temple of Voices, and in its cold central chamber, the terrible Throne of Glass so prominent in the Chapter's lore.

The Shariax.

The moment he thought of it, he knew it was to that ancient throne he was being drawn. The certainty sped his steps.

Automated vator-cages descended only part of the way. The catacombs were far older than Logopol itself. No one knew just how old, but they had been in place long millennia before the First of the First, Merrin Corcaedus himself, had ever set foot on this world. From the final corridor into which the vator doors opened, it was a long walk down a dark spiralling stair lit only by the soft orange light of undying candles. A man might drop a stone over the edge of the stairwell and say his own name a dozen times before hearing it strike the bottom, if indeed he heard it at all. Few came this way save to inter the dead deep in hallowed earth. A chosen few, Karras' khadit foremost among them, might be called down here at the behest of the Chapter Master, who, once seated on the Throne of Glass, would never again see the light of the Occludian day.

From the bottom of the stairs, it took Karras another half hour to reach his destination, and the stride of a Space

Marine is far longer and faster than that of an ordinary man. He passed through the Halls of Honour, past the calcified and enthroned bodies of every Chapter Master the Death Spectres had ever known.

Though all this was illusion, some trick of the eldar witch, Karras still could not allow himself to pass by those who had sacrificed themselves on the Throne of Glass without saluting each, fist to chest, and offering up a whispered prayer of gratitude and profound respect.

All had been slowly petrified as the Shariax leeched their life force away. Why each had knowingly embraced such a fate was knowledge beyond Karras' rank, but the need must have been great indeed.

He tried not to think about the fact that Athio Cordatus would, most likely, be the next Death Spectre to embrace that dark fate.

It was the way of the Chapter that each Chief of the Librarius be made Chapter Master when time demanded. The Shariax accepted only the most powerful psykers.

It was even conceivable, though humility made him scorn the notion, that Karras himself might one day be forced to sit upon it.

No, he thought. *Most Deathwatch never even make it home. Likely my fate lies elsewhere.*

After briefly praying at the feet of the petrified Corcaedus, last and largest of the enthroned masters, Karras entered the great cavern in which the Temple of Voices awaited, silent and brooding and monolithic, its pillars rising to points near the cavern roof, its great dome rimed with dirt and age but eternally strong.

He crossed the broad stone bridge that led to the entrance. Beneath him, far down in the dark, the icy waters of an underground river murmured like an army of ghosts, watching him, muttering about his trespass here. This was not a place Karras would ever have ventured without being called directly by the psychic impulse of the Megir.

Freed by the knowledge that all this was a lie ripped from his memory, he strode forward with purpose, eager to have it done with. At the arched stone doors, he stopped, wrestling the urge to show reverence, then placed a gauntleted hand on each and pushed. It took a great deal of strength. The doors were heavy, but he was powerful and they swung aside, grinding as they scraped across the stone floor. Dust and a light shower of debris fell from the ceiling as if no one had been here for many, many years.

He tried to ignore the forebodings that arose in him, but they grew more insistent as he neared his goal. Passing through two more sets of smaller, lighter doors, he found himself inside the final antechamber beyond which lay the main chamber.

He crossed to the final set of doors and breathed deep. The air was cold and dry and smelled of dust.

That was wrong. It should have smelled of incense.

He realised his primary heart was pounding.

Do not trust what you find beyond these doors, he told himself. *The alien attempts to manipulate you. Nothing more. She serves only the needs of her insidious people. Do not be deluded. Not by any of it.*

With that, he placed a hand on each of the stone inner doors, took a deep breath and pushed his way into the sacred chamber.

This was a place that shunned light, where the Chapter's greatest and most noble came to make a long, slow, fatal act of self-sacrifice. It was a sacrifice made mostly in the dark.

Those whose gifts allowed them to be in far-off places and see far-off things needed no light. Powerful psykers often went physically blind over time, their optic nerves no longer necessary given the greater potency of their witchsight.

The Shariax itself gave off a ghostly bluish glow that pulsed like a heartbeat. Very faint, but illumination enough that Karras' enhanced eyes allowed him to see his surroundings by it.

He moved towards the throne apprehensively and noted the large figure seated there. The silhouette was unmistakable. There, the curve of each broad pauldron. There, the sculpted helm, decorated with honours in the form of laurels crafted from silver and gold and inlaid with precious gems.

He knew the helm. It belonged to his khadit, his mentor.

So here, in Aranye's version of Logopol, Athio Cordatus was Chapter Master.

But this is no future that will come to ever pass, thought Karras, *if she thinks Logopol will ever stand abandoned.*

There was another thing she had got wrong – none who took the throne did so in armour and helm. On ascending to the position of First Spectre, the new Chapter Master presented his armour and weapons to the one who would follow his sacrifice next, and that was always the Chief Librarian. So why was this figure before Karras dressed in full Adeptus Astartes plate? It made no sense.

If she pulled all this from my mind, she knew this already, and her choices are deliberate. What does she mean by this?

Yet another inconsistency came to him now, for though the throne was clearly occupied, the one atop it radiated no psychic presence. His soul should have been so bright, so potent, that it could be felt from orbit. But even so close to the locus of that power, there was nothing. Not even a trace of an immortal soul.

Karras girded himself and strode forward determinedly. He flexed his will, causing faint wisps of psychic light to coruscate around him. The added illumination showed him the seated figure in much greater detail.

The armour was indeed that of the Chief Librarian, but it looked ancient, caked in dust. There was nothing of Cordatus' life force and spirit in that chamber.

As Karras came to a stop at the bottom of the dais, the figure moved. It lowered its head to look at him. Dust fell from the helm. Its visor lenses flared red. They locked themselves to Karras' eyes.

Wordlessly, the armoured figure shifted again, tossing something heavy.

Karras caught it.

When he looked down at the object in his hands, what he saw made him cry out in denial. He dropped it and staggered back a step.

The severed head of his mentor hit the floor and rolled.

When Karras found his voice, it was not to the seated figure on the Shariax that he roared. It was to the air around him, to all of this, to the one who had created it and placed him here.

'Eldar witch!' he raged. 'Blood-cursed xenos! Show yourself so I can cut you down!'

The figure on the Shariax laughed at him, a harsh sound that boomed and rasped from the helm's vocaliser grilles. With gauntleted hands, the figure reached up and undid the seals below the jawline of the helm. Then, slowly, deliberately, it raised the helm from its head.

Karras glared at it, and the white balefire of his psychic power flared. But what he saw made him reel backwards once again.

There upon the Shariax, grinning down at him, he saw himself.

The features were precise, down to each individual scar, and yet it was Karras as he had never been, his mouth twisted with malign glee, a bloodthirsty madness in his eyes.

'What is the meaning of this?' Karras demanded, rage rushing back over him to replace shock. 'Answer me, damn you!'

The false Karras laughed again and rose to full height. Karras dropped into a combat stance on reflex. He felt his power responding to the threat, welling up within him as it always did when he was threatened. He began to coalesce that ethereal strength inside him. He would obliterate this thing, this insult. He would rip this whole damned nightmare apart.

Even as he thought this, the false Karras flexed its armour-plated muscles… and stretched all four of its arms.

Karras hadn't seen the extra appendages until they unfolded – long, bony, covered in glistening chitin, and ending in three blade-like talons.

He had seen such arms before. All too many of them, and all too close.

Genestealer!

Behind the monstrosity that dared to wear his face, he saw the pulsing of the Shariax quicken. It began to glow brighter, as if sensing the surge of violence that was about to erupt. Karras felt the light from it burning his soul, scorching him. He kept his range, stepping back as the four-armed abomination began to descend the steps of the dais towards him.

At the bottom, it stopped, its shoulders squared, all four arms splayed wide for slashing attacks. Karras saw now that it was taller than he. Its skin had a waxy quality and, as it grinned again, he could see that the teeth were pointed and sharp like tiny white daggers.

When it spoke, its voice had become that of the eldar witch, incongruously musical and feminine.

'You think I toy with you, Death Spectre? I would waste neither the time nor the power. I do this out of need. The paths before you are many. To your kin, you are the Cadash. Or let us say that you may be. They place too much hope in you, and it may undo them. Others still have seen flashes of you in futures they are working to create. They will use you to bring about their ambitions.'

The false Karras, the tainted Karras, gestured down at its own body, then turned its gaze pointedly to the left and right at those terrible outstretched arms.

'To yet others, you represent the gravest of threats, the undoing of all they have achieved. You can scarcely imagine. Time and Fate boil and churn around you. It is a maelstrom of possibility. Unreadable. So many paths branch off into horror and suffering. So few lead to the light. Will you be a saviour? A destroyer? Or something greater or worse than either?'

Karras felt sick with revulsion. Words! Just words!

He did not believe any of this.

Damn her arrogance. I'll have her life!

'I am a soldier,' he snarled. 'No more, no less. My fate is to fight and die.'

The abomination laughed, not with Aranye's voice, but with one low and bestial. It gestured with all four arms to Karras' right and left. He sensed movement all around him. Armoured feet sounded on stone. He turned, right hand raised and ready, condensed psychic fire flaring from a ball of power that was growing in his palm. He would burn all around him to ashes.

Before he could launch it, however, the sight of those that surrounded him froze both his hearts.

In their hundreds, on every side, were his brother Death Spectres. They crowded around him, hissing like beasts from beneath cracked and rusted battle-helms.

Each bore the same terrible twin pairs of limbs as the false Karras, mark of the tyranid geneseed.

Karras heard Aranye's voice again, though it issued from the air this time and not from the abomination's mouth.

'Be wise in your choices, Lyandro Karras. Look beneath the surface. The chain of events has already begun. Tychonis will decide much.'

As the last of those words echoed in the domed ceiling, the twisted false Death Spectres began pressing in towards him, reaching out with their lethal claws.

Karras gritted his teeth and opened his inner gates to more of the power he commanded.

'Xenos tricks and lies,' he growled. Then, much louder, 'I deny you!'

Empyrean power reached a crescendo, coursing through him, barely restrainable now. He readied himself to unleash it with a battle roar. Just before he loosed it, he felt cold hands press firmly against each side of his head, and with that touch, all his power left him, bled away in an instant.

All went dark. All went silent.

No dome. No Shariax. No unholy abominations.

For several seconds, he was just that mote of awareness again – a soul lost in a formless void. Then light and sound exploded all around him. Gravity yanked on him. He staggered, steadied himself, opened his eyes and saw muddy ground. Blood-red clouds tumbled through a purple sky.

Rockets and artillery shells screamed overhead.

So close.

So low.

Deafening.

He saw the fighter jets and Marauder bombers of the Imperial Navy tearing through the air. All around him, the ground was carpeted deep with the dead. Men, women, children – all torn to pieces, their blood turning the earth into a crimson mire.

To his right, he heard the sharp report of gunfire followed by desperate cries. He saw figures clash in great tides, shining chitin striking polished armour plate.

Lasbeams scored lines across his vision. Metres away, an artillery shell bit into the ground and exploded, throwing him from his feet straight onto his back. Dirt geysered up into the air and rained down on him, drumming on his armour like hailstones. He looked up at the clouds and saw something vast and dark breaking through them.

At first he took it for a ship, long and sleek of prow. But as more of the object eased itself from the cloud cover, he saw that it was organic, a creature almost city-sized, with great tendrils stretching from its vast torso. There were apertures all along its body. From these, swarms of flying monstrosities emerged. They turned their heads towards the conflict on the ground and dived.

Karras rolled and pushed himself up.

'None of this is real!' he bellowed at the sky. 'Do you hear me, eldar? None of this is real. It means nothing!'

There was no answer.

Karras roared in frustration. He looked down at his hands, at his legs. Full battleplate, with all the weight and reassuring power it conferred. It *felt* real. He heard the blood rushing in his ears, felt his primary heart beating. Runes projected on his retinas by his helmet systems told him his heartbeat was elevated. Adrenaline, too. He flexed his fists.

What was happening to him? What was this?

Had he been broken on Chiaro after all? Was he now trapped in his own insane mind?

Or was this some trick of the daemon? Did the eldar witch exist at all?

He could smell the stink of blood and burning bodies. He could feel the wind through his armour's advanced sense-feeds, the pressure of the air, the tug of the gore-sodden ground on his boots.

What if this is real? he asked himself. *What if I suffered some kind of psychic seizure or collapse? What if I'm really here?*

He could be sure of nothing. No, not quite nothing. He was certain his recall of that day in the burning forest was just a memory. He was sure the trek through abandoned Logopol and the twisted horrors in the chamber were false.

Those things did not happen. They did not!

But this?

He looked again at his armoured fists – one silver, one black.

I am Deathwatch.

Battle raged around him. Another shell landed close, shaking the ground, throwing up gouts of fire and great clods of earth.

He felt so present, so grounded.

He checked his mag-locks and webbing for weapons.

None. No bolter, no pistol, no grenades, nothing.

He slid one hand back to see if his knife was sheathed at his lower back where he usually wore it. It was not. *Arquemann*, too, was gone. The precious force sword his mentor had entrusted to him should have been slung between his shoulder and his armour's power pack. It was not.

He was unarmed in the middle of a warzone, alone in a

muddy clearing among rocks and bodies and shell-blasted trees, mayhem and death on all sides, great tyranid organisms breaching the skies, Imperial forces fighting desperately to push them back.

He searched for a landmark, for something that would tell him where he was, anything at all that might give him an idea. His search was cut short. Figures loomed up out of the mire, surrounding him, hissing and chittering, their eyes hard and cold like black stones.

He'd faced such things, seen good brothers die, swarmed by them and hacked apart.

They advanced on him as one, long, scythe-like talons raised for a lethal downward stroke.

Termagants!

He longed for *Arquemann*. Four tyranid warrior forms were more than a match for most Space Marines at close quarters, but with force sword in hand, his eldritch power coursing through it, the odds would have been altered dramatically.

As they closed, the beasts breathed loudly. Drool dripped from their razor-lined jaws. Here was prey!

But if the creatures thought Karras unarmed in the absence of any visible means of defence, they were very much mistaken.

Real or not, Karras wasn't about to take any chances. He brought forth his power, joining it to his violent intent. He spread his arms, hands open, and dropped into a combat stance. Flickering arcs of blue-white power writhed up and down his vambraces like electrical serpents. He felt the pressure building in his mind, a great welling of force. He wrestled it under control, shaped it to suit his needs. In his mind's eye, he marked his targets, marked the path he wanted the deadly energy to take.

The termagants closed on him. They tensed their haunches,

ready to leap, ready to carve him apart. The moment they sprang, Karras unleashed blinding spears of psychic lightning upon them.

There was a great cracking sound, like the splintering of bones.

His vision went black. He felt himself falling forward, his skin suddenly wet and icy cold.

He struck solid ground, knees and forehead smacking hard on smooth marble. He pushed himself up on his palms just in time to vomit. Thick mouthfuls of a strange, sweet-smelling gel gushed out. He tried to open his eyes, but they were gummed shut.

His body hurt. It ached all over. He felt pathetically weak.

He convulsed again, bringing up more of the strange, sticky substance. There was a bitterness to it, despite the sweet smell. Not something he recognised.

Raising his right hand from the floor, he wiped forcefully at his eyes. A rough voice sounded from a few metres in front of him.

'No, brother. Step back. Let him gather himself. Give him time. But keep your guard up.'

He knew that voice. Only Space Marines spoke Gothic so low it shook the air like that.

Marnus Lochaine.

It was the voice of the Storm Warden, the First Librarian of the Watch at Damaroth.

Karras forced his eyelids open at last. He found himself looking at a floor of black marble flagstones coated in thick, transparent slime. His vision was flawless, as sharp as it had ever been.

I know I lost an eye killing the broodlord. How is it I can see perfectly?

He looked down at his hands braced on the black marble. He saw his fingers splayed there.

Something else is wrong, he thought. *Something is different.*

He brought his right forearm in front of his face and turned it this way and that.

A chill ran down his spine.

Where was the scar he had earned on Calvariash? Where were the burn marks that had dappled his flesh, the acid burns he had suffered at the Siege of New Golodin? And where were his wards, the pentagrammic and hexagrammic tattoos he had worn since his acceptance as a full battle-brother? Where were his protections? What had happened to him?

Confusion etched itself in deep lines on his face. He pushed himself from the floor and shakily stood up…

… to find himself facing five Space Marines in full armour, three of which were pointing bolters straight at him. A fourth was pointing the nozzle of a flamer in his direction too.

The last figure, and the only one without a visible weapon, was Lochaine.

Karras met the Storm Warden's gaze and was surprised to find the eyes so cold and hard, devoid of the rapport the two had built up during Karras' time in Deathwatch training. No smile of greeting graced those stern, craggy features.

'Is this real, Lochaine?' Karras croaked. His voice was rough. Speaking hurt his throat. 'Throne and Terra,' he rasped, 'tell me this is real!'

Lochaine stared at him a moment, then spoke. The words stunned Karras, chilling him to the bone.

'Who are you?' the Storm Warden demanded. 'Who are you, and whom do you serve? Speak now or die!'

TEN

'Throne and Terra!' exclaimed Rava.

There was no mistaking the figures in the pict – figures of legend, icons of Imperial Glory.

They were the will of the God-Emperor made flesh.

For a moment, the men gathered in the basement sat in mutual silence, stunned, unable to process the implications of what they were seeing.

Urqis spoke first. 'I do not understand this, cousins. These resh'vah… they walk with the pogyos. They are armed, yet they do not kill. In all the tales–'

Gunjir cut in. 'Tales are tales. We cannot know what this means until we know more about the woman. She is clearly a person of power and influence. Why she is here, it is far too early to say. The Space Marines appear to be bodyguards. See how they flank her?'

'A prominent Rogue Trader?' offered Diunar. 'Matriarch of a Noble House? A political envoy from the Imperium itself, perhaps. No visible bondage. The fire caste troopers beside her – are they there to protect her or to contain her?'

'Would that we knew,' replied Arnaz.

'How came you by these?' asked Sadiv.

Arnaz met his gaze. 'I have a contact.'

'It is enough that you brought them to us,' said Gunjir. 'No more need be said of how. For security's sake. Many brave haddayin risk more than we rightly ask every single day of their lives just to keep us informed. Some things need not be shared. Protect your source, Arnaz.'

'Melshala bless them and keep them,' said Rava, his head bowed. 'Saint Sartha cloak them from loathsome eyes.'

Sadiv let it go, but he was not wholly dissuaded from his course.

'These picts are from one of the spaceports, and that is not a pog ship. It is of Imperial manufacture.'

'She landed at Kurdiza flanked by two Sky Sharks,' said Arnaz.

'Sky Sharks don't operate outside the atmosphere,' said Urqis. 'Either she was escorted here by t'au spacecraft or she came of her own accord. But which is it?'

'I was told fire warriors were already aboard her ship when it touched down,' said Arnaz. 'I cannot confirm it, but I was also told of damage on the starboard side of the hull. An engagement or a forced boarding, perhaps. The angle of the picts is unfortunate.'

'So she is a prisoner,' said Sadiv.

'Flanked by armed Space Marines and with wrists unbound?' countered Rava. 'Marks on the hull may have had nothing to do with a forced boarding. Micrometeorites. Old battle damage.'

'Too much speculation is as dangerous as too little information,' said Gunjir. 'Until we have facts, the status of the woman and the presence of the resh'vah raise too many questions. I can see no course of action that doesn't require more information.'

'You will have answers when I do, cousin,' said Arnaz.

'Where did she go from Kurdiza? Do we know that much?' asked Sadiv. 'Might she be in this very city even as we speak?'

Rava became excited, agitated. 'We must try to contact her. Surely, guarded by the Adeptus Astartes, she is a formal representative of the Imperium. A negotiator or envoy, perhaps no more, but she must learn of our struggle to overthrow the invaders. If we could secure off-world support–'

'She may already know,' said Diunar. 'It may be why she has come.'

'She was taken from the spaceport in a Devilfish with significant close support,' said Arnaz. 'The convoy headed east from Kurdiza, but she could be anywhere by now.'

'Has the Speaker been sent copies of these?' asked Diunar, holding up the picts.

'An encrypted data crystal was sent north with a courier the moment I had them.'

'We must try to get the woman's attention somehow,' insisted Rava. 'If we cannot contact her directly, we must demonstrate our commitment to the war. An attack on a high-profile target. Even were she not in the city, if she has any information flow at all, she will hear of it. She could get word out.'

'Reckless,' barked Urqis, fists clenched on his thighs. 'This woman appears with two of the resh'vah just as the curfews are being lifted. I don't believe in coincidences. What is the Aun doing? He will work the woman's presence to his own ends somehow. Action without proper thought would undo us all.'

It was all Rava could do not to stand up and spit on the floor. 'Acha!' he growled. 'Toothless Urqis! Always counselling caution! Will you bear arms at all when the day comes, I wonder? Or will your caution keep you from the fight?'

Old Diunar moved swiftly for his age. In the blink of an eye, he was in a half-crouch, his knife gripped, the base of his blade peeking from its sheath.

'Walah!' he cried out. 'Enough! You are a guest in my home, cousin, and so is Urqis. In offending him within my walls you sully my honour. I make a blood claim, and I offer it to Urqis.'

Rava paled visibly. His head sank between his shoulders. He could not meet Diunar's blazing eyes. Arnaz was impressed. Diunar's presence was formidable. It was no wonder he was a leader of men. He was the old ways maintained and personified, a man of the real Tychonis, a desert man, pledged to the war.

Or rather, he was, thought Arnaz. *Such a pity he has already been turned.*

Not that anyone else in the room knew it.

'Cousin, forgive me,' pleaded Rava, turning to Urqis. 'If you would have my blood as price, I present my arm to you. Let your blade bite as deep as anger demands.'

Urqis sighed and shook his head. 'My blade thirsts for blue blood, not red. It will bite no man here. You spoke in anger because the fires of hate burn in you as brightly as they do in me. If I am cautious, cousin, it is because I know the fragility of hope. Haste will kill us as surely as a t'au rifle. The xenos will fall when the time is right, and we will do this thing together, you and I. And our blades will be stained blue, not red.'

Rava bowed and turned next to Diunar.

'What of you, my cousin? Will your blade take its due?'

Their host shook his head and settled back on his cushion. 'I cannot allow any to speak so to another of the faithful in my home, but I disregard the claim. Urqis speaks my heart as well as his own. Blue blood, not red. The water in our cups is cool and clear, cousin.'

An old phrase. A desert phrase. It meant all was well.

Rava bowed. 'By your example...'

Gunjir spoke up, having observed that all tensions were now duly dissipated. 'The matter is done, and we have others to discuss before daybreak. Come. Who will speak next?'

The six men spoke for three further hours of secret weapons shipments, of disappearances, of t'au supply routes, of the rumours in the markets and reports from the haddayin who had infiltrated the Gue'a'Sha. The hour grew late and the sky began to lighten as Diunar at last rose to see each of his guests out of his basement. They left one by one, separated by several minutes, each cleaving to shadows still dense and black before the sunrise. Finally, with Gunjir gone, only Diunar and Arnaz remained. It seemed to Arnaz that his host had deliberately contrived for things to be this way.

At the door, Arnaz bowed to the older man and said, 'Sathra bless you for your hospitality and the risk you take in giving it.'

Diunar nodded and accepted the blessing, but he raised a hand and placed it on Arnaz's shoulder before opening the door to let him out.

'Blessings back, cousin. May the saint cloak you from alien eyes. But before you go, I would ask you to take a risk of your own in return.'

'Go on,' said Arnaz. He had expected something like this, but that didn't lessen his disappointment.

'Your source at Kurdiza,' said Diunar. 'Such an asset is too important to the cause to be known to only one man. If anything should happen to you–'

'When Gunjir spoke of protecting our sources, cousin, I saw you nod agreement. Now you ask outright.'

Diunar inclined his head apologetically, but his stance was otherwise firm. 'Shared between six, the risk of capture and interrogation is high. Too high. Shared between two, between you and I and no other, it serves the cause better. Too much cannot be allowed to rest on the shoulders of any single man.'

'Laha! I see the logic in your request,' said Arnaz, 'but still.'

Diunar looked pained. He shook his head. 'Ah! Under the eyes of Melshala, what a fool I am. I see I have yet to earn your trust. That is as it should be, cousin. You are wise. I will endeavour to earn it hereafter. I should not have asked. Age makes me impatient at times. As a young man, I believed I would see the t'au cast out in my lifetime. Knowing better came hard to me. Your forgiveness, then.'

'No, cousin,' said Arnaz. 'It is I who ask forgiveness. You speak only for the good of the cause, I know. And you are right. If you will swear to me a solemn oath before the great saints and on your loyalty to the Golden Throne, I will share my burden of knowledge with you. In truth, I will feel the lighter for it. I, too, worry that too much depends on individual men.'

They were words he had rehearsed, and the solemnity he managed to put behind them was beautifully acted.

Diunar hardly hesitated. He made his oath – on the surface of it, as sincere and zealous as any Arnaz had ever seen. But he knew better.

Ah, if your life had been different, old man, you would have made a fine deep-cover agent.

'Amadi,' said Arnaz. 'Ugnil Amadi, a sergeant in the spaceport security forces. He gets information to me through his sister Larshi, a worker in the powercell factory just south of the Ru'Xie access gate. Both were raised in the Dumru enclave to the far south before it was cleansed by kroot patrols. They are intensely loyal to the Speaker. They can be trusted.'

Diunar closed his eyes and gave a slight bow. 'As can I with their secret. And with yours. Should anything happen to you, I swear to offer them any help I can in fleeing to the Speaker's side.'

Arnaz grinned. 'They are fighters and their hearts are aflame. They will not flee, but they would join you here for whatever fight may follow.'

'Then I would welcome them as family,' said Diunar. 'And now, with the burden shared, it is best you go before the burning eye crawls skyward. Melshala protect you.'

'And you,' Arnaz responded. 'A blessing upon you and your home.'

Diunar closed and locked the door behind Arnaz. Outside, Arnaz listened as the bolts slid home. As he climbed the narrow stair to ground level, he grinned and shook his head.

If it was that easy to trick me, you old lizard, I would have been dead a long time ago. As dead as you will be when the t'au have no more need of you.

After Arnaz had left and the door was locked behind him, Diunar went to a small sub-chamber just off the main basement room and busied himself at a cogitator console. He selected frames from a vid-file, then zoomed in and cleaned up several sections. He hit a rune. The cogitator printed out three stills, each an enlargement of Arnaz's picts from Kurdiza – the woman in black and her Space Marine bodyguards.

Then he printed out several picts of the men he had met that night.

His heart felt like lead, so heavy it was almost pulling him to the floor.

Get it done, he told himself, *then drink yourself into oblivion, you weak, selfish old bastard.*

As he gathered up the picts, he paused to look at the woman in black.

Who was she? Did she bring hope? Not for him. For him, it was probably already too late.

Wearily, picts in hand, he doused the lights and ascended to the ground floor of his hab. He was bone-tired, weary and sickened by what he had become. Tonight had been extra hard. He'd been so careful not to show outward signs of his distress, but that Arnaz had a wily look. He was different somehow.

The t'au had left him no avenue of escape. Blue-skin scum! He was trapped utterly, powerless to throw off their control. Love was his weakness. If only he had been a colder, harder man.

From the top of the stair, he shuffled into the main room. With a deep sigh, he sank into a seat at the old table of moulded plastek on which he took his meals. He leaned back and rubbed his hands over his face.

What had he done to bring this curse down on himself and his household? He had always honoured the Golden Throne of Terra and the Imperial creed. He had lived his whole life fighting for a future free of the usurpers. Now he was subverting that future. His dreams woke him nightly, crying out in guilt and denial. Death was better than this, but he had not the courage for it. To take one's own life was to be damned forever in the warp. And there was still that tiniest flicker of hope. If the t'au were as good as their word, then maybe...

He wasn't surprised when he saw the air in the far corner shimmer, displaced by something that quickly resolved itself into a humanoid figure dressed in distinctive curving armour.

In clipped alien tones, it barked at him. 'Report, gue'la.'

Diunar thrust his chin at the stills on the table.

The xenos stalked across to his side.

As they both looked down at them, Diunar said, 'Amadi. A security forces sergeant at Kurdiza. He has a sister, Larshi, working in the Ru'Xie industrial zone – the powercell factory. Together, they supply intel to the Speaker's people here in the capital. From here it goes north by courier.'

The alien stood staring down at the picts. 'Gur'dya'al,' it said, then added in Low Gothic, 'It means mask-wearers. Spies. We suspected so.'

'I know what mask-wearer means, damn you,' hissed Diunar. He tapped his finger on the image of the woman. 'I want to know what *this* means.'

The t'au operative gave that low gurgle which passed for a laugh among his kind. Then he, too, tapped the finger of a gloved hand on the photo and said, 'Gue'la, *no one* yet knows what this means. We call her the Qua'shai'dha. It is difficult to translate. It is close to say *the feathered serpent who makes great promises*. She is of no concern to you.'

'As you say,' said Diunar. 'What *is* of concern to me is my wife and daughter. When do I see them? I have done as asked. It is enough.'

The alien swept the picts from the table and was already crossing to the front door as it replied, 'We decide when it is enough, five-toes.'

Diunar rose, shoulders set, fists clenched, anger coursing through him. 'I want more assurances that they are unharmed.'

'You will be with your family soon. The commander will be informed of your compliance. Await further word from us.'

There was a brief crackle and hum, a sound just on the verge of human hearing. With it, the alien melted back into shimmering air. Diunar watched the door open. The alien's voice, now disembodied as if it were the voice of some taunting spirit, addressed him one last time.

'Remember, gue'la. We see you. We are everywhere. We see everything.'

The door closed.

To be certain the damnable creature was gone, Diunar went to the door, waving his arms around in the air to make sure it really was empty.

His fingers found nothing. With a snarl, he double-bolted the door and returned to his seat.

He put his elbows on the table and placed his head in his hands.

'Pog filth,' he muttered. 'You see everything? You didn't see Amadi take those picts.'

The thought hardly made him feel better – he had just given Amadi and his sister up. Hours only, maybe even minutes, remained before they would be dragged off for torture.

Two brave haddayin... and he had just doomed both of them. And for what? So he might see his wife and daughter again?

You are the lowest of cowards, he told himself, lip curling up over his teeth. *Ancestors forgive me. I am a cur. Remah, Shirva, if only they had killed you outright. If only I could be sure I was free to take revenge.*

But because they might yet live, he was not free at all.

No one on Tychonis was free.

* * *

From a second-storey rooftop overlooking Diunar's hab, Arnaz watched and waited, knowing that movement would come. The streets and alleys were devoid of all traffic. The curfew would hold for another hour. He knew the patrol routes, knew the schedule. He would not be caught out. And he had to be sure.

He held a small, multi-spectrum auspex scope to his right eye, cycling back and forth through vision modes as he swept it around the circumference of the hab. When Diunar's front door opened and closed again, Arnaz felt a twitch of satisfaction edged with sorrow.

How and when did they turn you, tribesman? What was your price?

To the naked eye, nothing emerged from that door. But through his scope, Arnaz watched the multi-coloured shifting of displaced air as it outlined a shape at its centre, roughly humanoid. Familiar.

Still with his eye pressed to the scope, he reached down and slid a power knife from his boot.

'Got you,' he muttered.

ELEVEN

The air in the Reclusiam at Watch Fortress Damaroth was cool on Karras' skin. Strangely, he found more comfort here, now, than he ever remembered feeling in the Reclusiam on Occludus. But then, he'd never been this troubled back on his beloved Chapter world.

After all he'd seen, the visions and torments and falsehoods, it meant much to be somewhere real, somewhere he could trust. Through the fabric of his black fatigues, his legs felt the chill of the stone pew on which he sat. His fingers brushed the book of litanies he held. He felt the texture, the solidity of the grox-leather cover.

The psychic intrusion he'd experienced in that infernal eldar healing machine had been so vivid, so detailed and convincing, but this was different on a fundamental level. His mind and body knew instinctively to trust it.

This is *real,* he told himself. *Know it. Don't doubt it.*

The soft glow of a thousand votive candles threw shadows

out onto the great stone pillars on either side of the nave. Above the double rows of pews, glorious and ancient banners hung, resplendent in their colours and rich embroidery, detailing great battles and disastrous crises averted by the selfless heroes whose stories filled the deep and secret archives of the Watch.

One of the banners depicted a Deathwatch-serving Ultramarine crushing an ork skull under his ceramite boot.

I wonder what Prophet and the others are doing now. They must think I'm out of commission… Maybe I am.

At the far end of the Reclusiam, beneath the fine, self-illuminating stained-glass works of art, were seven statues, figures of legend, the heroes of the First Watch. So stern and proud, and so finely sculpted they almost looked ready to spring to life. It was impossible to look at those bold, noble faces and think of them as harbouring any notion of self-doubt.

Simpler times, perhaps.

The Reclusiam was such a quintessentially Adeptus Astartes place. It was so much easier to feel centred here. He was thankful for that. Apart from the barely human servitors that carefully cleaned and maintained it, only the Adeptus Astartes were permitted to set foot within these dark granite walls. It did not matter to which Chapter they belonged. To most, the Emperor was father and idol, a figure from the ancient past one strove to emulate in His indomitable strength and prowess. To some the Emperor was godlike, a creator deity as celebrated by the Ministorum and the Imperial creed whose unblinking eye was ever upon them. To the Death Spectres, to Karras, the Emperor was a little of both, for it was He who had granted Corcaedus his great vision at the foot of the Golden Throne. It was He who had blessed

Arquemann with a soul, He who had sent the Founder out among the stars to find the Shariax and establish the new Chapter on Occludus. Not a god, as such, but a being of an order above all others.

Why the Emperor had done these things was beyond Karras' comprehension. Perhaps the reasons became known to those who sat upon the Shariax. Perhaps not.

The Shariax. The Throne of Glass.

The memory of what he'd seen seated upon it during the eldar's psychic trespass of his mind sent a fresh chill up his spine. Such grotesquery. To see himself mutated, perverted into that which he despised… to see his khadit's dead eyes staring up at him from the severed head on the floor…

A scowl twisted his face.

It did not matter that the visions had been a warning. What mattered was the insult to his Chapter and the feeling that… that he was now tainted somehow. It sat in his stomach like a nest of coiling black asps.

The alien machine had made him whole again. It had saved his life. He lived and breathed and would fight on in the name of Emperor and Chapter because of it. But what were the hidden costs?

Given the choice, would I have allowed them to save me in that way? Knowing what I now know?

He cursed himself for the futility of such thoughts.

The choice had never been his. What was done was done. He lived. He would serve, and with more resolve than ever before, fuelled by his outrage, his renewed hatred of all that was alien.

As he looked at the statues of the Seven Sentinels, the First Watch, all exquisitely carved in black marble and detailed in silver, he thought of the Watch Council. It was they who had stored the eldar machine here. Had the Ordo Xenos commanded that? Had Sigma's coven known it would be needed? Or had Marnus Lochaine's Librarius seen the day of its need in the Imperial Tarot or the reading of ancient and holy rune-carved bones?

Had this been pre-ordained somehow?

So much talk of destiny and great purpose surrounded him. All he sought was to serve like any other, to die in battle with honour.

To the blasted warp with all their talk of the future. Let me be as any other Space Marine. Set me against the foe. Let me live a life of war that is simple and bloody and brutal and pure.

He wanted to growl his frustration, but the Reclusiam was a place of silent reflection, and it held him silent now.

The Seven Sentinels of the First Watch stared back at him impassively, their stone-cut features without judgement, set only in grim determination, certain of their purpose, committed to their alien-slaughtering mandate with boundless zeal.

Leaning forward, he rested his forearms on the back of the pew in front of him, clasped his hands and lowered his eyes from those marble faces. He gazed at nothing and focused on his breath, working to clear his mind, to find peace in thoughtlessness, just for a while.

After several minutes, the hinges of the Reclusiam's great bronze doors creaked behind him, and a draft blew into the room, causing the candle flames to dance.

Karras did not turn.

He heard heavy footsteps approach him, then the rustling of fabric as someone sat heavily on the pew behind his. Normally, without conscious command or exertion, Karras' psychic senses would have reached out and tested the aura of the newcomer, identifying him. But that was another change the eldar machine seemed to have wrought in him.

His eldritch power, if any remained at all, seemed so diminished he could hardly feel it, like a river reduced to a trickle. This time, unlike during his training at Damaroth before Second Oath, it was not because of a warp field damping implant.

After a moment, the newcomer spoke, his voice hushed but still deep and clear. 'There are entire chambers of the Librarius archives dedicated to the stories and records of the Seven,' it said, and Karras knew from the first word that it was Lochaine. 'Some are even declassified now. If you have yet to read them, try to find the time before you redeploy. They have much to teach. The Watch would not be what it is today but for their boundless resolve and selflessness.'

Karras half-turned in his seat. 'And just what *is* the Watch today,' he said, 'that it employs eldar machines to heal its members?'

Lochaine paused a moment. 'Given your position, brother, the comment is not unfair. Your outrage is understandable. But remember this – Sigma could have let you die. Truly, had it been any of your team but you, I fear he may have done just that. Healing your body in such a manner, I know, is hard to accept. But it was not a decision made lightly. Not by the ordo, nor by the Watch Council. The Inquisition's influence here is hard to overstate. We do not operate in a vacuum.'

'As I've learned well,' said Karras.

Lochaine let that hang in the air.

Looking at his hands again, Karras said at last, 'It is hard to accept that my life has been… spared this way. Every last scar is gone. Each was a part of me.'

'And each well earned in blood and pain, I know. But scars only *tell* of experience. They are not experience itself. The xenos machine did not erase the skill, the knowledge. And new scars will replace the old soon enough.'

'If you think such will satisfy me–'

'What satisfies you is not my concern, Space Marine,' said Lochaine, his tone suddenly hard. 'It is duty that must be satisfied. Oaths that were taken. You are bound by them. Think on that.'

True enough, Karras conceded, but it was clear Lochaine was somewhat unsettled himself. It was in his voice. It seemed hardly a coincidence that the damnable xenos machine had begun to collapse and dissolve, atom by atom, mere moments after it had spilled the rebuilt body of the Death Spectre onto the floor.

The eldar were known to have powerful seers. Something about the way the machine had destroyed itself spoke of a purpose met. They had somehow contrived this or, at the very least, had had a willing hand in it. And that made the Storm Warden uneasy. What did the eldar care if one lone Space Marine – *this* Space Marine – survived?

Lochaine shook it off. Too much conjecture. Not enough to work with.

'Debate has always raged in the Watch Council,' he said. 'We suffer from factionalism as much as any Imperial body. Given the nature of what we do, perhaps we are even more inclined to it. Many among us, the purists, would have it that all trace of xenos existence must be cleansed from the galaxy. They will touch nothing of xenos make. They will not learn the language of the foe, even where such knowledge might offer important tactical insight. Then there are the rest. I count myself among them. Our mission is too great to be blinded by zealotry and miss critical opportunities. Knowledge properly applied is power. Sometimes the purists find themselves with a Watch Council majority. Other times not. But the debates rage, nonetheless. So it is in every Watch fortress and station across the Imperium.'

Lochaine paused.

'We do not often speak of it openly, but you need to hear it, Karras. There was much argument about whether to concede to Sigma's wishes and place you in the machine. In the end, it was the Librarius that argued most strongly for it. The futures surrounding you are... complicated.'

Karras' eyes narrowed. Again, the talk of fate and futures.

'Ours is not a short and simple fight,' the Master of the Librarius went on. 'Not since the time of the Warmaster's betrayal, ten thousand years past, has mankind faced darker days. Beset on all sides, it is our survival, not our dominion, that hangs in the balance. The Watch Council believes we must embrace every weapon, every opportunity. Good intelligence is key to our survival.'

'Clearly, the Inquisition concurs,' said Karras. 'Sigma apparently operates with a free hand. You mention factionalism in the Watch – what of the ordo?'

'As with any Imperial body, we can assume there are struggles within for power and control. But none are better at keeping their business behind closed doors. Let Sigma's business within the Ordo Xenos remain his own concern. What should we care? We fight. One day, we die. We endeavour to die with honour, selling our lives dearly. You would have died already, brother, and your Chapter and the Watch both would have lost a valuable asset. This feeling that you have been tainted somehow will pass. Duty will soon erase your doubts, as will the imminent tests. We swear our lives to the service of the Golden Throne. You look at your hands, Karras, and lament the loss of your scars, but that thought diminishes you. They will bleed again. The Watch Council has been told little of what befell you. It is unlikely the ordo will ever share the details, and your oaths preclude you from saying much. But I saw you when they brought you in. It was clear that you fought to the very last. Trust me. It is a fine thing that you were saved, no matter the method.'

'Trust you?' said Karras. 'I barely trust my own senses anymore. Things happened inside the machine. Xenos trickery. Visions. A psychic intrusion.'

'The purity tests will prove that there has been no taint. You will see soon enough, though they will not be easy to bear.'

The purity tests – the reason he had been brought to the Reclusiam in the first place. The High Chaplain Qesos and Lochaine both would need to approve his return to service. No sign of taint would be tolerated. His service and his life were not yet guaranteed by any means.

But it was not some taint from the mind-invasion of the eldar that concerned Karras most. It was thoughts of Hepaxammon.

The eldar may have had a hand in healing his body, but it was the daemon that claimed responsibility for his recovery.

He recalled the abomination's ultimatum – the threats against his Chapter, the message for Darrion Rauth.

Again, that feeling, like snakes in his stomach.

'The tests. What happens when I pass?'

'Sigma has ordered your immediate return to Talon Squad. Alpha status intact.'

Karras processed this in silence. Part of him wished to be released from the inquisitor's service. Let him be part of a standard kill-team, unattached to the blasted Ordo Xenos.

But another part wondered at it – why the insistence? What had Sigma's coven seen? Did it align with the hopes of his Chapter? Of his khadit?

'I never served under an ordo handler, Karras,' said Lochaine. 'I can well imagine how it must rankle. Speak to Kulle. He is due to return to the Silver Skulls soon. He has served long and with distinction, and he will be granted his Honours of Fulfilment. But he served under a handler for years before he made Watch sergeant. Perhaps he can offer a perspective I cannot.'

Karras recalled the face of the Silver Skull, his instructor during assault training in the kill-blocks. Kulle had shown an openness and respect for Librarians where others were wary, even disdainful. Perhaps it would be wise to seek him out.

Lochaine went on. 'Those that survive to return home are the ones who adapt the fastest and do not let pride or rigidity kill them. I urge you to silence the questioning voice inside you. Hold to your faith in your wargear and the honour of your Chapter. Hold to your oaths. Meet your objectives. Compete your missions. The years will pass more quickly that way. Soon enough, you will find yourself on a ship bound for Occludus. You will return changed, a more powerful force for your Chapter. An inspiration to your brothers. A source of strength when they need it most. That is the prize, Karras. Keep your eyes upon it.'

Karras made a decision then. It seemed to come of its own accord, the words leaving his mouth before he realised he was speaking them.

'I want deeper access to the archives. I need to know more about Sigma. Everything the Watch has on him.'

He heard Lochaine shift uncomfortably behind him.

After a moment, the Chief Librarian said, 'You have little idea of what you ask, I think. What would you be willing to sacrifice to gain that access?'

'Sacrifice?'

'Of all the archives at Damaroth, those concerning the Inquisition require some of the highest clearance levels we have. You would have to petition both your Chapter and the Watch Council for permanent secondment here. Do you understand? Deathwatch till death, never to return home, as it is with me. Truly, brother, the knowledge you would gain would be worthless to you by then. The Watch fortress would be proud to have you, but such is not your fate. Scant as they are, the records would not satisfy you in any case.'

'Then I'm to endure in silence. Even when I doubt everything this damned inquisitor says, even when every instinct within me is telling me it's wrong. There were things we saw on deployment–'

'Assumptions are dangerous. You know this. You were not placed under Sigma's command to judge him or to second-guess him. The Holy Inquisition stands apart for a reason. Respect it. It is the Eye That Sees, the Ear That Listens. To separate the Watch from the ordo is to blind us, to rob us of vital intelligence. Where then would we send our kill-teams? How would we know where we were needed most if not for the cooperation of the ordo? Come to terms with it, brother. All of it. The Inquisition acts in the interest of the human race. May the Seven Sentinels forgive me, but the truth remains – we need them just as much as they need us. Would that it were not so, but it is. So look instead to the honour of your Chapter and the oaths you have made to the Watch, and serve them both as you are sworn to. Let there be no more anguish over what has passed. You live. Your service continues. War beckons. What more can a Space Marine rightly ask?'

'Aye,' said Karras. 'To serve with honour.'

It was all he could say. No other words had a chance to

form. At that moment, from an antechamber on the right of the nave, High Chaplain Qesos entered, striking in his black armour and golden skull-faced helm. With a wordless nod, he told them it was time.

Lochaine stood and placed a hand on Karras' shoulder.

'The purity tests will be gruelling. Think no more of past and future. Save all your energy for the here and now. You will need it.'

Karras rose.

'Come,' said Lochaine. 'Let us get this over with.'

TWELVE

The sun was strong and high over Chu'sut Ka.

Shas'O T'kan Jai'kal, known more simply as Coldwave, felt the midday heat pressing against him, an almost physical force, its brightness bouncing off the stuccoed walls and arches and pricking at his eyes. And yet it was nothing to the heat and dryness of the canyons and plateaus around the Na'a'Vashak.

That place which the gue'la called the Tower of the Forgotten – how he wished he'd never had to set foot there. All his recent surging self-hate and doubt were linked to the accursed place, to what was being done there under his supervision.

So too, however, were all his hopes.

Despite the sun's sting on his head and hands, the rest of his body felt cool and comfortable. His clothing – a simple, formal uniform in tan with the battle honours and trappings of his rank – included a microconductive weave which shifted excess heat to the power-storing unit in his left thigh-pouch, where it charged the spare magazine for his sidearm.

He leaned on the railing of the third-storey gallery, looking down on the gardens below. They were thick with shadowy greens and brightly coloured fruits. Finely laid paths of polished stone, made broad enough so two could walk abreast and talk, snaked lazily through them. Artisans of the earth caste would find much to inspire them here. Coldwave was far from blind to its aesthetic qualities but, like the Aun, he would have preferred something more austere.

Water caste advisers had been adamant, however, that seating the new t'au government here was paramount to the success of human integration. The gue'la were apparently incapable of respecting any authority that didn't proclaim itself with brazen shows of status and wasteful luxury.

Soon, thought the commander, *the percentages will shift. Within five years, our race will be the majority here.*

Things would start to change at a faster pace. Less compromise. It would still all be carefully managed over time – as fast as the prevention of unrest would allow. But it was coming. The water caste would succeed as they always did, as they had on every integrated world in the expansion.

They were masters of gradual cultural subversion by now. Enough worlds had been turned. Their programmes were well tested and refined.

But watching over it all is no place for a warrior, thought Coldwave. *Not for me. Were it not for the rebels, the traitors and the coming of the black-feathered woman and her death-dealers, I would wither of disgrace and disuse.*

He belonged on a battlefront. He belonged on the frontier. Warriors were born to fight, not oversee foul experiments.

In the years since his posting to T'kan, despite his abiding love of the Aun and his dedication to serving him, Coldwave's growing bitterness at being robbed of further honour by his political rivals had been eating away at his core.

He had been a threat to the ambitions of others, and those others had had powerful friends on the Aun'T'au'resha, the Ethereal Council.

He had been sidelined before his star could properly rise.

But it wasn't over. A chance had come in the form of the woman. As much as he hated her, her arrival had changed everything. The way back to prominence had opened before both he and the Aun.

Prominence, or everlasting infamy and shame.

He turned his eyes to the right, to an open, flag-stoned area of the gardens where a small gathering of humans and t'au were seated around a table of white marble. At the head of the table, so regal in bearing despite his simple robes, sat Aun'dzi, beloved of all on T'kan, the Light in the Darkness, the Bringer of Hope and Unity.

Clay goblets of fruit-flavoured water sat before each individual. Even among the myriad strong floral scents of the gardens, Coldwave could zero in on the delicate smell of the refreshments, such was the sensitivity of the t'au olfactory nerves.

He felt a gentle thirst rise in him.

They would finish soon, provided the humans didn't needlessly prolong things as they tended to do. Even this small assembly, unified in purpose, seemed to feel a constant need to compete with each other, currying favour and jostling for status.

Coldwave clicked his tongue several times, a t'au expression conveying both exasperation and disdain.

It's a wonder they ever cooperated long enough to build their Imperium.

He heard movement behind him. Rahin. He knew it was the ISF's commanding officer by scent. The man joined him at the railing, standing a good head taller than his t'au superior.

'News?' asked Coldwave.

'Nothing of the rebels. A couple of disturbances in the markets.'

'The usual trouble, I assume.'

Rahin nodded. 'Pricing disputes that turned violent. Nothing of any real note.'

Such things never happened among the t'au. 'Mutual benefit and the benefit of all' was the coda by which they lived. Negotiations never degenerated into physical attack. The humans were like unruly children in so many ways, and yet their race was far older than his own. How had they learned so little in all that time?

He glanced at Rahin and noted the fondness he felt. The gue'la soldier had always been good company, a trusted lieutenant.

I'm too harsh on them, he thought. *I cannot judge all by the example of some. There are good men, good soldiers among them who truly seek to understand the T'au'va and what it means to serve it. They have embraced it as best they can. Our empire is their empire, and they will learn to serve it better in time.*

It could not be easy for them. The gue'la seemed constantly to struggle with their ancient ape nature.

As we struggled with our own before the Auns appeared.

Perhaps the humans should be pitied. Their race had existed for so long without any real icons of enlightenment to save them and lead them. What choice but to cling to their strange corpse-god of ten thousand years ago and the dark, brutal creed that had grown from his legend?

What might the humans have become if only they had been blessed as we were?

It was a sorrowful thought. Things might have been so different.

One of the trade representatives below gestured to emphasise a point, catching Coldwave's eye and returning his attention to the moment.

There was always so much unnecessary movement when humans talked, as if they had to act out every sentence for it to be heard. At least the meeting was breaking up now.

The commander watched Aun'dzi rise from the table, as tall as the tallest of the humans, and offer the group his best approximation of a human smile. He tilted his head and thanked them for their attendance. He would summon Coldwave and Rahin the moment the delegation and water caste members were gone.

Coldwave was abruptly conscious of the scent traces he was exuding. It would be unseemly for the Ethereal's most trusted military adviser and force commander to present himself while his pores still communicated anything but calm confidence and self-control.

'We will be called momentarily, major,' he said, using Rahin's ISF rank. 'A few seconds alone, if you please, to gather my thoughts.'

'I will await you at the bottom of the stair, commander,' said Rahin.

He bowed briefly and moved off. Coldwave listened to him descend, then slowed his breathing and shifted his hands through a series of slow, precise gestures.

The Vas'ra'gan – the seventeen stations of inner calm. He had been turning to it a lot recently, yet another indicator of just how uncomfortable he was with the joint project at Na'a'Vashak.

A soldier ought to have nothing to do with such horrors.

If there had been any other choice…

He shook it off and refocused on the seventeen stations.

The Vas'ra'gan began to take effect, stilling the waters of his mind, chasing his troubles to the edge like ripples on a pond.

Once the last of the movements was complete, he dropped his hands to his side and breathed normally again. For confirmation, he stroked his jawline with a fingertip and lifted it to the olfactory slit in his forehead.

Good. His scent no longer betrayed any angst. It was less sharp, more earthy, speaking of calm readiness, of presence in the moment.

Below, the water caste representatives and the gaudily dressed figures of the human delegation drifted through the arches in the garden's south wall and disappeared from view. Aun'dzi, regal and serene, watched them leave, then turned his gaze up at the gallery where Coldwave stood.

The Ethereal raised his hands in front of his chest, fingers upwards, palms facing each other a few inches apart. An invitation to join him, as gentle and exquisitely polite as always. He could have commanded Coldwave's obedience in the roughest manner possible and still caused no offence. The Aun was the Aun. He would have been obeyed without hesitation or rancour or resentment no matter his tone or gesture, no matter the register of his voice.

All the Ethereals Coldwave had ever met shared the same gift. They were born to lead. They inspired. They uplifted. Their essence was of the mirror-smooth lake at sunrise, or of the cool evening breeze that soothes the hunter's weariness and lifts his heart on a long march home.

They have given us everything, he thought, *asked nothing for themselves, and have brought us through three expansions, each greater than the last. There is no limit to what we might achieve under their guidance. They are everything to the future of our people.*

And yet some could not see it. Would not. How was it that Farsight, for one, could have been so blind? A tragedy that still had never been satisfactorily explained. And here on Tychonis, the number of dissidents among his own people grew with every passing year. The prison cells at Na'a'Vashak were filled, no shortage of subjects for the damned woman's *procedures*, because more and more t'au were turning from the light, and he was at a loss to explain it.

From the gallery, he bowed to the Aun, right hand over his heart and the fingers of his left hand pressed to his forehead.

Profound respect. Obedience. Love.

Then he turned from the rail and descended the cool, shadowed steps to the garden below. Rahin fell into step silently behind him.

It was time to bask in the presence and attention of the Aun.

If only the things of which they must speak were not so horrific...

Greetings. Formal and sincere. It always began with greetings.

Form and propriety were important to the t'au. Powerfully so.

'Uniter,' said Coldwave. 'Beacon of Truth. Lighter of the Way, look down upon me, forgive my unworthiness, grant me the wisdom to put aside the self for the betterment of the whole.'

The words were almost as old as the stories of the Ethereals' first emergence, and within them they contained the essence of the T'au'va and the guidance that had brought unity where bloodshed had reigned.

The willowy, beatific figure standing before Coldwave inclined its head and smiled in open affection. 'Skilled Hunter, Beloved Protector, True Adherent of the Way, let us stand as equals. We are fingers on the same hand. Let us speak as such, without reserve, for the benefit of all.'

Coldwave, as always on hearing these words, suppressed a rush of shame. They were uttered with such feeling, every single time. The Aun seemed incapable of token pleasantry. He meant exactly what he said, and he said exactly what he meant. And yet, Coldwave could never conceive of himself as equal to one such as this. Only another Ethereal could even come close.

He knew the scent from his pores gave such thoughts away. Aun'dzi would smell it. He always did, and always he had the grace not to mention it, as if the scent were so weak as to pass beneath his notice. Coldwave almost wished the ancient leader would dispense with the traditional response and assert his status more fully, as a member of the fire caste would, as he himself would with any soldier of lesser rank, but the Auns had their own forms, their own ways, and that would not change.

Aun'dzi, again showing grace, moved swiftly past his subordinate's discomfort and acknowledged Rahin with equal warmth. 'How fares the captain today?' he said in perfect, unaccented Uhrzi. 'He looks well as always.'

Rahin bowed low. 'The better for seeing you in fine health, Uniter.'

Aun-dzi tilted his head in thanks and returned his attention to Coldwave. 'You have come to take more of the *rauk'na* south. I know how deeply it troubles you. Does the project really require so many?'

The rauk'na. The ungiving. The self-serving. The t'au who were not t'au.

Coldwave broke the Aun's gaze. 'Much as it sickens me, more are needed. Speed in doing this thing could save many loyal lives. Error margins are large, but there has been progress. I would see this nightmare ended quickly and our business with the woman over.'

'She continues to disturb you,' observed the Aun.

'She is not like others of her kind,' said Coldwave. 'She is a far more dangerous animal, and she withholds much. Clever names aside, Uniter, truly we treat with a two-tongued serpent. Would that we had never found her. In truth, I wonder if we found her at all. I suspect she contrived all of it.'

'And you, captain?' asked the Aun of Rahin. 'What are your thoughts?'

'I believe as the commander does, Uniter. This woman has an agenda I can't rightly guess. And I fear that the presence of Space Marines on Tychonis, should word get out, would tip a heavy percentage of marginals over to the rebel cause. Their image cannot be separated from that of the God-Emperor. They must be kept at the Tower, away from the eyes of the people.'

Coldwave clacked his teeth in agreement with his subordinate.

'Wise counsel, major,' said the Aun. 'For now, then, I release you to return to your duties. You have much to do before returning south.'

'My gratitude, Uniter. There is never enough time. I go to serve.' Rahin bowed, once to each of the t'au, and left to attend to other duties.

The two aliens watched him go.

'He has witnessed the procedures first-hand?' asked the Aun.

'He has.'

'How did he react?'

'As I did, but he sees the need. He knows the shadow of the

Y'he will fall over this world eventually. Probably within his own lifetime.'

'Such a burden I have placed upon you. In due course, it will be shifted to the Aun'T'au'resha, but we cannot present to the High Council too early. If the woman is right, if her project bears the fruit she promises, there will be much darker business to follow. Rauk'na will be needed from all across the empire. At that point, and that point only, we can make our work here known. Until then, we must trust that we do what is in the best interests of all.'

'I believe, Uniter. I see no other choice. If the woman is right, we will be called saviours. If she is wrong, then we are wrong. And history will call us monsters.'

The Aun nodded solemnly, then gestured for Coldwave to sit. As always, Coldwave would not do so until the Ethereal seated himself. Aun'dzi lowered himself gracefully into the chair at the head of the table.

A young water caste acolyte appeared from the left almost at once, bringing fresh goblets, a tall jug and a plate of berries carefully aged and garnished with a selection of cultivated moulds. The smells made Coldwave's mouth water. He waited for Aun'dzi to ask him to pour, as was proper.

After each had sipped from their goblets, Aun'dzi said, 'The price of the woman's aid still puzzles me greatly. She must have a very powerful reason to request complete freedom of movement within t'au space.'

'She has asked for access to data regarding territory our people lost to the Y'he. I have not granted it, but we might learn more by giving her access and observing her searches. Whatever she is looking for must be incredibly important to the Imperium. She would never have brought the project to us, otherwise.'

'Give her access and watch her,' said Aun'dzi.

Coldwave bowed. The woman could be stopped later if need be.

'We must conclude matters at the Tower soon,' said the Aun. 'The emptying of the city prisons has been well noted now. Questions are being asked. And the rauk'na are not a limitless resource. However selfish and misaligned they may be, they are still kin by blood.'

'As you say, Uniter, but if any must pay the price, let it be those who have rejected the Greater Good, who would kill or steal from their own brothers and sisters for gain, not loyal fire warriors ready to lay down their lives by noble choice. Enough of us have died fighting the Y'he while the rauk'na served their own interests.'

Aun'dzi made a gesture, palms together, long fingers intertwined – an old salute to the fire caste who had died for their people and those that were yet to die in the times ahead.

'As you say. Let the rauk'na serve the T'au'va with their deaths, since they will not serve it with their lives. Our loyal fire warriors must be saved. We lose too many and the number grows each year. But we may still pity the rauk'na. I believe their all-consuming self-interest is a kind of illness, not a choice.'

Coldwave processed that, searching his feelings for a moment. 'Pity is not hard to come by as I watch them processed in the laboratory. The infection procedure... Uniter, I am thankful you need not see it yourself. That we drug them first is little consolation. Even in an altered state, they know true horror when they look into its savage, hungry eyes.'

The Aun raised his face to the sky and said, 'We did not, either of us, ask for this. Fate brought us to this day. Fate decreed that this onerous task should fall to us, and us alone.

But we are equal to it. We will do what must be done. Give the woman all she asks for, but continue to monitor her every breath. The earth caste must glean all they can from her while she still believes she can manipulate us. When the moment comes that we no longer need her, we will decide then whether she is to live or die. Until then, make no move against her.'

Coldwave dipped his chin. 'My life for the T'au'va. I will not falter.'

'When will you return south?'

'I meet with Shas'el Kayan before dusk to discuss new security operations. Once I am satisfied with her proposals, I will set out again for the south.'

'She does a fine job in your absence. You trained her well. I will repeal the emergency powers of the security forces in three days. We cannot allow the widening of the divide that has opened between our people and the gue'la. Only in unity does true strength flourish. The gue'la have such great potential as a people, but there is so much they must unlearn first. Truly, of all the integrated peoples, they are the most difficult and yet could offer so much to the T'au'va. The universe does seem to revel in such dichotomies.'

The Aun made a low trilling sound in the back of his throat – mild laughter. It was a warm, rich sound, and the scent molecules he exuded were just as pleasant. Coldwave found himself soothed. It was true. The humans were a tangled mess of contradictions and complexes. And yet, there was something compelling about them. The two races had so much to offer each other. If only the human race as a whole would put aside their ignorant, reactionary ways and their terrible, suicidal lust for conflict. If they could only see with fresh eyes, the fruits of cooperation could be ripe and sweet.

Aun'dzi continued. 'I have ordered an end to the curfews. A sense of normalcy must return to the capital. We must show faith in the majority. Measured against our temperance, the acts of the rebels will appear all the more extreme, and more repulsive for that.'

'There are still several significant insurgent cells active in the city,' Coldwave cautioned, 'not counting those we have so far been able to monitor. The arms shipments we uncovered recently hint at the likelihood of many more. It is this very district I fear for most. If they do strike again, it will likely be at our structures of governance, and at you above all. Their failure in hitting military targets' – and here, Coldwave was speaking of the rocket attack on his own transport – 'will have convinced them to shift their focus. Were I in their place, it is what I would do. And they may yet have weapons of more potency which they have been saving for just such an assault.'

Aun'dzi steepled his long blue-grey fingers and gazed at the bright, polished surface of the stone table. 'The insurgents in the cities are of lesser concern to me right now than the enclaves in the Drowned Lands. The Speaker of the Sands is no fool. The presence of the woman and her bodyguard on this world will not slip his notice for long. He may even know already. The timing of the attack on your transport was not a coincidence, I wager. Discontent is like a cancer. Untreated, it will grow. Whatever it takes to remove it, that is what we must do. A sign of trust, a show of temperance. It is the only way.'

The sun was on its way west now. The shadows in the garden had begun to lengthen as the day shifted into mid-afternoon.

'I have monopolised your time overlong.' The Aun gestured at the berries before them. 'But enjoy these with me and let us speak of less burdensome things for a while before you go.'

So they did. As always, Coldwave felt tremendous peace and honour in those moments. Dark thoughts of his current duties fell away for a time.

All too soon, however, his visit with the Aun was up. The hour of his briefings with his sub-commanders in the city drew near.

At Aun'dzi's request, Coldwave escorted the Ethereal through the gardens to the Chambers of Contemplation. At the arched entrance they stopped.

'You bear such a terrible weight on all our behalf, old friend. Would that I could take more of it upon myself. The fire caste, as ever, is the rock of our people, and the best hope for our future. Go with my gratitude now.'

Coldwave made a gesture of regretful farewell. 'For the Greater Good, Uniter.'

'The Greater Good, hunter. May your contributions be many and great, and remembered with honour forever after.'

THIRTEEN

Karras was tense on the shuttle over from *The Aleste*. As gruelling as they had been, the purity tests were behind him. The Watch had cleared him for a return to duty, though how hotly contested that decision had been he would never know.

He stood in full armour, helm set atop a nearby ammunition crate, and silently went through several of the stabilising mantras he knew. None seemed to work as well as they ought to.

He could have spent the journey in a passenger compartment, but he preferred the shuttle's main hold. For one thing, the emptiness of the hold suited his mood. For another, he was in appropriate company here.

Across from him, held firmly in place by thick titanium chains, sat the Dreadnought Chyron Amadeus Chyropheles.

Immense.

Wordless.

Still radiating all that sorrow and rage.

Karras knew the Lamenter's story. He felt for him. Perhaps more so now than ever before, having seen his own Chapter undone in the eldar witch's damnable mind-manipulations.

But visions were just visions.

Lies were just lies.

Chyron's Chapter had suffered genuine obliteration. The Great Devourer had crashed down on the Lamenters like a tsunami. No Chapter could have stood against such a storm.

Tragic.

Legend said the Chapter had been cursed from the start, part of the infamous 21st Founding. Now there *was* no Chapter. Chyron believed himself the last of his kind.

Karras scowled. He wished there was something he could do for this battle-brother. The Dreadnought's sorrow and survivor guilt only ever dimmed when he was lost in combat, giving himself over utterly to battle flow, his pain submerging till the peace of victory called it forth again. In time, he might face a worthy foe and sell his life dear. It was his greatest hope, but so far, none had equalled him.

Was the mighty warrior staring back at Karras as the Death Spectre thought these thoughts? The Dreadnought had no face to read. No expressions. All he had was angled armour, tank-like, broken by a single diamonite vision block. But for the flickerings of his troubled aura, he was inscrutable when quiet.

If he was watching Karras, he could surely read the apprehension, the tension, on the Death Spectre's face. Karras didn't bother to hide his mood. The last time he had seen his squad brothers, he had been peering up at them from rubble with one intact eye, the other pierced with rock, his body crushed under black stone, bones broken, blood flowing. They had, more likely than not, thought him beyond saving.

But Sigma had known. He had known of the eldar machine.

Were it not for that damnable device, brother, thought Karras, *I might have ended up encased in a chassis like yours.*

There was great honour in being so interred. More, certainly, than owing one's life to a daemon and a xenos machine!

How do you do it, brother? How do you keep fighting when all you held dear was erased from the universe? When there is no brotherhood to return to, how do you stay the course? There is so much I could learn from you. Truly, I honour your strength. Your soul may be the strongest of all of us.

Karras could hardly conceive of an Imperium without the Death Spectres there to fight for its protection. And yet, that was precisely what Hepaxammon had threatened. Not just the destruction of the Chapter, but its fall from glory, the stripping of its names from the halls and rolls of honour throughout the Imperium. To be disgraced. To be excommunicated. To have all they had accomplished over thousands of years purged from record and memory.

Lies. All lies.

Torment was the daemon's purpose. Torment and manipulation. It had overstated its power, its influence. Karras had to believe that. He had to.

He grappled with his thoughts, forcing them to his brothers on Talon Squad, to the four other Space Marines that awaited him aboard the *Saint Nevarre*, four exceptional warriors with egos to match. To be worthy of leading them again, he needed to stand before them unclouded by doubts. They were apex predators, all. They would smell weakness like blood on the air. They needed to see in him a force of certainty and wrath that they could follow once more, not some haunted wretch preoccupied with the lies and illusions of the Imperium's enemies.

I am not that. I am Talon Alpha. And I have work to do.

He was about to resume his mantras when the rumbling growl that constituted Chyron's machine-modulated voice interrupted him.

'You are different, and yet the same, Librarian. There are new shadows in your eyes.'

'The more we learn,' replied Karras, 'the more shadows we come to see. I'd not choose ignorance to spare myself difficult knowledge, brother.'

'Others might. The truth is seldom comforting. But the Raven Guard named you Scholar, and he named you well. Whatever you have learned in your time away has not been to your liking. That much is clear. Remarkable that you live at all. I saw them preserve the mess that was left of you. I did not expect to see you draw breath again. It would have been an honourable death, I say. The foe was worthy. I would have envied you.'

'There will be other chances for such envy, I'm sure,' said Karras, and he found himself grinning. 'I doubt our next deployment will be any easier than the last.'

'In Terra's name, I hope not. Let the foe be obscenely strong and the odds be preposterous. I want to die laughing, drenched in xenos blood.'

A deep, rumbling sound filled the air – laughter as approximated by Chyron's powerful vocaliser grilles.

As Karras enjoyed the sound, a voice interrupted on the shuttle's comm system. *'Docking in three minutes.'*

He lifted his helm from the crate on his right and placed it in the crook of his left arm.

Chyron's laughter ceased. With abrupt gravity, he said, 'You are Talon Alpha. You lead, we follow. Make sure the others know it, Scholar. Whatever Sigma's demands, lead as you did before. You were strong. You got us through. These fresh troubles you carry – bury them. Show the squad your strength. We are Space Marines. We respect little else.'

Karras threw the massive walking tank a grin. 'Good counsel, Old One. As to your glorious death, I'm sorry – fate has a twisted sense of humour. Like as not, you'll outlive us all.'

The sound of docking clamps closing on the shuttle's hull echoed through the hold.

'Aye,' agreed Chyron. 'That is my curse.'

Gravity shifted slightly, a gentle change felt in the pit of the stomach. The shuttle had fully docked now in one of the hangars aboard the *Saint Nevarre*, and the larger ship's grav-plates took over.

Karras strode over to the Dreadnought and unfastened the titanium crash restraints. With a hiss of powerful pistons and a rumble of promethium engines, the massive warrior rose to full height, towering over Karras, dwarfing him in every dimension.

'I hate being trussed up like a grox over a feast fire,' rumbled the Dreadnought.

Two serfs in black jumpsuits appeared at the inner portal, bowed low and crossed to the rear of the compartment, there to initiate the process of lowering the shuttle's ramp.

Chyron swivelled to watch them, then turned his visor back towards Karras. 'I will follow you, Alpha. Into battle. Into glorious death. Let our enemies dread our wrath. That is the way. These new shadows… The fires of battle will burn them away, even if only for a while. I know. Had I eyes of my own still, you would see those same shadows in them. You have my strength beside you. Lead us well. Make me proud that I still serve. Do that for me.'

Karras rapped a fist off Chyron's front armour. 'I'll give

you xenos blood by the ocean if I can, brother. Now let us go meet those other troublesome bastards. They've surely missed us.'

The ramp descended with the smooth, well-oiled silence one might expect of an Ordo Xenos craft. When it hit the hangar decking, however, there was a resounding clang that echoed off the vast hangar walls. In the relative quiet, it sounded like the ringing of a temple bell.

Four black-clad Space Marines stood a few metres apart, all facing the shuttle's aft hatchway. None quite knew what to expect. They knew Karras and Chyron were returning to them, but in what state? Chyron was already so mechanised that his restoration was a given, but Scholar? Last they'd seen, several large pieces of him had been strung together by little more than shreds of nerve and tendon.

When he marched, proud and whole, down the shuttle's ramp, they watched in stunned silence. Here was the Death Spectre at full height, moving as assuredly and confidently as ever, his stride long, his head high, as noble and austere an image of the Adeptus Astartes as any of them might aspire to.

Behind him came the great metal behemoth, thundering down the ramp on piston legs as thick as the shuttle's own landing stanchions.

Karras and Chyron reached the bottom of the ramp and strode forward, all eyes on them.

Four metres from the line, they stopped.

Silence and stillness pervaded as the Space Marines regarded each other.

Karras' awareness was heightened. His vision shifted, augmented by his gift, to show him the auras of three. One, as ever, had no aura to show.

There was turmoil there in the pulsing colours. Doubt. Apprehension. Things Karras could well understand. But there were flashes of positive colour too, even from the Ultramarine.

That is unexpected, thought Karras.

'Talon Squad,' he barked sharply. 'Deathwatch brothers...' A grin spread across his porcelain-white features. 'It is good to see you.'

He clashed his right fist against his breastplate. The response was automatic. Even Solarion saluted back.

It was Zeed, always one to disregard protocol at the earliest opportunity, who broke from the line and strode straight up to Karras. He stopped right in front of him, their faces only a metre apart, his all-black eyes peering into Karras' all-red ones with curious intensity, as if he were examining a strange new species.

Then a broad smile cracked his face and he slapped Karras' left pauldron with a gauntleted hand. 'You mad dog, Scholar,' he said with genuine joy. 'Next time you decide to kill something, don't pull half a planet down on top of yourself. I didn't join the Deathwatch to dig out your suicidal backside.'

He thrust out his hand and they gripped each other's wrists. Then Zeed moved to Karras' side, throwing a short nod at Maximmion Voss. The burly Imperial Fist hardly needed any encouragement. He, too, stepped up to Karras and warmly gripped wrists with him.

Karras smiled down at the short, over-muscled Adeptus Astartes.

Voss' broad features were as open and honest as ever, skin creasing around the deep scars he bore as he smiled. His brown eyes glinted under a thick, jutting brow. 'Do you remember my last words to you, Scholar?' he asked.

'I do,' said Karras.

'I was right. And I'm glad to see you back.' Voss hesitated a moment, then added with a curious glance, 'Your recovery is... remarkable.'

Karras was ready for this. He managed to mask the awkwardness he felt. He fed his battle-brother the only answer he could, the one he had settled on during transit. 'The Apothecaries at Damaroth are unrivalled. I was as surprised as you are.' He raised his left hand and flexed it in front of his face. 'The price of such recovery was the scars I'd earned. But I'll earn many more before this secondment is over. Sigma will see to that.'

'And now you owe him a debt,' said a low, gravelly voice from behind Voss. 'For he did not abandon you, despite his warnings.'

The Imperial Fist moved aside, stepping off to join the Raven Guard in greeting Chyron.

It was Darrion Rauth of the Exorcists who had spoken. It was he who stepped forward next.

Karras nodded to him and extended his hand. 'Brother.'

They stood regarding each other for a long moment. Rauth's eyes were as hard as ever, like black diamonds, studying Karras without reserve.

'Those warding tattoos are fresh, Death Spectre.'

'They are.'

The Exorcist examined them with interest. Finally, he said, 'They did good work on you. The grimoires look strong.'

Karras nodded, then pointedly looked down at his own hand, still extended.

Rauth didn't smile, but that was Rauth. A smile might have cracked that crag of a face. Nevertheless, he reached out and gripped wrists with Karras, and there was force in the grip.

For a moment, the two stood joined in mutual greeting, and there was respect there, though there was also a certain unmistakable frostiness to it.

'He didst return changed,' quoted Rauth, 'and the changes wrought upon him were both hope and sorrow to the people of the steppes, for his strength was multiplied, fed and forged by the losses he had known, but his soul now bore a weight that much greater, and the fire within him burned less bright. And in time, those changes worked a fell magic on him and did seal the fate of his people.'

'*The Chronicles of Uranos*,' replied Karras, 'by Auldre Derlon. Hardly apt, brother. Uranos was a brutal warlord who butchered millions in the name of a false idol.'

In truth, the choice of quote disturbed Karras, though he grinned as he spoke. Did the Exorcist mean to suggest Karras would doom his kill-team? Was it meant as some kind of warning?

Rauth gave the smallest of shrugs and released Karras' wrist. 'It is a quote about a leader's return after sustaining near-fatal wounds. Apt enough in that. I am sure you are as eager to redeploy as the rest of us.'

'No,' said Karras. 'More so. You, at least, have been active. Sigma provided summaries. I read them in transit. Heavily expurgated, of course, but it's good to know that you have been kept sharp.'

Rauth took that without further response. He went to greet Chyron, leaving only one yet to step forward.

'I will not grip wrists with you, Scholar,' said this last, his voice as haughty and sharp-edged as ever. 'We almost failed at Chiaro under your so-called leadership.'

Karras gazed back into grey eyes filled with ice. Before he could answer, Siefer Zeed called out from behind him.

'We'd have fared far worse under you, Prophet! You couldn't lead a slow march across flat ground. Don't listen to him, Scholar. He's the one that missed you most!'

He and Voss laughed together at that. But the Ultramarine blazed as he replied, 'You had your words, Ghost. Keep your damned peace while I have mine.'

Zeed snorted and said to Voss, 'I could hit him seven times before he'd know which side I was on, and he'd still guess wrong.'

Voss chuckled.

Karras ignored the jibe at Solarion and stepped forward to stand between him and the others. 'Whatever your thoughts on how I handled *Night Harvest,* brother, I am glad to see you well. I am disappointed that you hold to your resentment of me, but it matters not. Just do your job. Or I'll give you cause to resent me a lot more.'

There was a flicker in Solarion's aura then – something transient, ephemeral, so fleeting that Karras almost didn't catch it, but he did, and its colour was dull orange edged with blue.

So there is a part of him that is glad to see me returned. Would that it were not quite so small.

'We do not always get what we want, Scholar,' said Solarion. 'I did not wish you dead, but Sigma is a fool if he fails to hold you accountable for almost costing us the Chiaro mission.'

'I am many things, Ultramarine,' said a dry, grating voice from over Solarion's shoulder, 'but a fool is not one of them.'

The members of Talon Squad turned as one. Before them, they saw a spider-like mechanical construct – a pillar of sensors, scanners and vocaliser grilles atop eight spindly metal legs.

As if the puppetmaster would ever reveal himself to his puppets, thought Karras. *He greets me via mechanical proxy. I should have expected as much.*

The inquisitor's proxy scuttled forward, clicking and whirring. When it settled a few metres in front of Karras, the voice continued. 'Welcome back aboard the *Saint Nevarre*, Talon Alpha. You look suitably restored. That is well, because time is against us. I require your presence in the main briefing chamber. Now.'

The spidery construct turned somewhat awkwardly and began to scuttle away, but as it went, it called back to them, 'And you others, be ready for a group briefing as soon as your Alpha and I are done. Do not tarry. It is time once again for the Deathwatch to earn its reputation.'

FOURTEEN

'Why?' asked Karras. 'If you tell me nothing else, tell me that.'

The figure on the tall black throne turned its hololithic head to regard him coolly. Since the figure was projection only, Karras' senses could tell him nothing. There was no soul there to read, no aura, no energy, just photons. This was precisely why Sigma remained above on the three Geller-shielded upper decks, off limits to most onboard. It was easy enough to guess that those decks housed the inquisitor lord's astropathic choir, maybe his psychic coven, and no doubt a veritable army of servitors to take care of more mundane needs. But Karras' mind was blocked from knowing. His astral self could no more penetrate those protective fields than he could sense emotion from this shimmering lie seated above him.

'Why?' echoed the inquisitor through the vox-grilles built into his throne. 'Because it serves me. I chose you to lead Talon. It serves my needs, and my needs serve those of the ordo and the Imperium itself. I may come to regret my choice in time, but your success on Chiaro has borne my decision out so far. You extracted White Phoenix from the mines. Others would have failed. It was unfortunate that eliminating the broodlord almost cost you your life, but, as I said, the odds were against *Night Harvest* from the start. Projections for the survival of the entire team were incredibly low, and yet–'

'And yet you still opted to gamble with Space Marine lives.'

The hololithic figure remained unmoved. 'The objective warranted the risk. Such gambles are what Adeptus Astartes lives are for. Or should I deploy you only where victory is assured? You are ordo assets now. I will wager your lives as I see fit.'

'You speak so of Space Marines. It's well that you appear only as a hololith. I might teach you the price of your hubris.'

The projection shook its head.

'We both know better. You are no oath-breaker. You would not be a black stain on the shining history of your Chapter.'

'What do you know of our history?' said Karras dismissively.

'More than you might suppose,' said Sigma. 'No archives are as extensive as those of the Inquisition. And while the Noble Order of Occludus may seek to cloak itself in myth and secrecy, the eyes of the Inquisition can pierce any veil to which they turn, given time and cause. Something to remember, Death Spectre.'

Karras forced his temper to cool. He did not like the turn the conversation had taken. 'Is that a threat?'

'A reminder of your duty. You and I must operate in extremes. Together. I need to know you will continue to execute my orders.'

'You ask for blind faith. Among the Death Spectres, leadership is conferred for deeds witnessed. I have no such grounds to trust yours.'

'A circular argument. I am an inquisitor lord. That rank alone, independent of all I have done to attain it, is enough.'

Karras answered with silence, teeth clenched.

'Lyandro Karras, if I held you in low regard, we would not be talking now. You would be dead. Recall that I selected the entire team personally. Nothing I do is on a whim. The war we wage must be fought on my terms. It is of a scale that would shock you, and the alternative to our success is too grave to countenance. Be glad your responsibilities and decisions are limited to the immediate and tactical. Leave the greater burden to me. Simply, be my implement, my knife in the dark, my mailed fist. Do what you are best at, what you were shaped for. And honour your oaths.'

'Why the eldar machine?' Karras demanded. 'Was there no other way?'

The face of the figure on the high throne remained impassive, unreadable. 'It was not a decision I took lightly. I know all too well the baggage of zealous hate that all Space Marines carry. There is a place for it, but one must know that place. Ultimately, I authorised your interment in the machine because I needed you back at full capability. My coven has unusual difficulties in foreseeing your future. I had to take appropriate measures or risk losing a much-needed asset. The crucible into which I am sending you next will be infinitely more dangerous than the last. We have less intelligence on the ground this time. Fewer assets in place. And you will be fighting an enemy with technology that even our greatest tech-magi still struggle to counter.'

'You speak of the t'au as if you respect them. In some quarters, you would be hanged for heresy.'

The hololith grinned. 'The Inquisition decides what is and is not heresy. The t'au have their weaknesses, and we will exploit them, but only a fool would refuse to recognise their strengths. I know from your records that you have never faced them. That is unfortunate, for they are unlike other foes, but it is an issue I have arranged to mitigate. You need only know this about them for now – they are an entirely different prospect to the genestealers you slew during *Night Harvest*. This is no ravening horde you face. Raw courage and bloody determination won't win the day this time. Before we go further, I will summon your squad brothers. We will begin the briefing proper once everyone is assembled.'

Karras took a step towards the throne and held up one hand.

'Wait,' he said. 'I would ask one more thing before you do.'

'Then ask, for all the good it will do you.'

'What happened to the woman we extracted? What happened to White Phoenix?'

The hololith gave a dismissive shake of its head. For a second, it flickered out of existence, then blinked back into view upon the tall throne and said simply, 'The rest of the kill-team has been summoned. They will arrive in a few minutes. I give you those minutes to reflect on the futility of asking such questions.'

Assembled again in full armour, the kill-team was a sight that lifted Karras' spirits after the talk with the inquisitor. They were as he was – bred for battle, disdainful of politics and gamesmanship. The straight fight was what Space Marines lived for. Talon Squad may not all see eye to eye, but they had a lot more in common with each other than they did with those around them.

And they were good.

Karras had watched them file in. Pride in his Chapter aside, these were some of the best Space Marines he had ever served with. He had seen them pull *Night Harvest* from the ashes of disaster. Each was supremely skilled, a specialist complementing the talents of his battle-brothers. Together, they were far more than the sum of their parts. Solarion still radiated bitterness and hate. Rauth was still cold, unreadable and aloof. And Zeed was still an irreverent troublemaker. But what had needed to be said had been said. Downtime was always less welcome than war.

The hololith had shifted form again on Sigma's whim. Karras no longer cared. Let the inquisitor labour his point about need to know as he liked. It was the mission ahead that mattered. He would focus on that. Let all else fall away.

As it should be.

It was the figure of a wizened old man in a ragged monk's habit that now sat atop the tall black throne, looking down at them.

'The *Saint Nevarre*,' began the hololith, 'is currently heading towards galactic east on its way to rendezvous with the vessel that will take you to your destination. Between now and your deployment to the planetary surface, you will interface with the ship's archives and update your knowledge of t'au language, specifically the dialect most used by enemy forces there.'

'Spoken T'au cannot be accurately recreated by unmodified human vocal chords,' said Karras. 'In the event that we need to interrogate one of them in their own language–'

'Accounted for,' replied Sigma. He did not elaborate. Instead, he said, 'Your insertion will be covert. Once you have adequate intelligence and it becomes necessary to make a move, you will strike hard and fast. You are deploying to a hostile world. While it is not heavily garrisoned, once your presence is known, the chances of success become borderline non-existent. The window will close fast. Get in quietly, establish contact with loyalist forces on the ground, ascertain the location of the target, secure and employ any necessary local support, acquire the target and get out.'

'And what of me?' Chyron rumbled. 'Am I again to wait like a guard dog at some damned exfil point like a witless gun-servitor? Is my strength to be squandered yet again? I was born to wreak havoc. Throw me into the storm or let me sleep. My patience with these *special* operations of yours, inquisitor, wears perilously thin.'

The inquisitor's holo turned its head towards the mighty Dreadnought. 'When and where heavy force is needed, Lamenter, your qualities will be called up. Ours is not a compact in which I'm required to satisfy your sense of pride or hunger for bloodshed. In this case, there are too many variables to say how you will best be utilised. Decisions will be taken on the ground. It is highly likely that the asset you are to extract will be heavily guarded. Intense combat is likely, losses almost a certainty. My coven has seen as much. Still, if the mission goes to plan, you'll not alert entrenched security forces to your presence until absolutely necessary.'

'What of these security forces?' asked Voss. 'What are we looking at?'

'I'll come to that, Talon Four. The planet to which you will be deploying was once an Imperial world. We call it Tychonis. The t'au call it by another name. It was separated from the Imperium when a warp storm called the Dragon's Eye flared up, blanketing the region in an impenetrable cloud called the Green Veil. Shipping and psychic communications were completely blocked. When the storm spent itself and the Green Veil retreated, the planetary populace found itself under yearly attacks from the dark eldar. These lasted until t'au forces touched down on the planet and eliminated the dark eldar presence, freeing the people from their suffering, at which point most of the human population turned its back on the Imperium and embraced the philosophy and culture of the t'au. So it is today. Ordo assets on the ground report that the t'au have managed to turn vast swathes of what was once desert into highly productive and rich agricultural land. Long-range scans and astropathic reconnaissance bear this out. Atmospheric processing has turned the northern and southern polar regions into areas of extreme precipitation. Extensive canals channel this water to the rest of the planet, allowing for widespread agriculture and habitation, improving the lives of all but the rebel tribes who refuse to integrate. The security forces present are a mix of t'au and human military. There are a few elements from other species the t'au have co-opted. Mostly kroot, but no auxiliary force of significant note.'

'The people of this world,' growled Solarion. 'They abandoned the Emperor's light. It is unforgivable.'

'But not in the least surprising,' said Sigma. 'Your own Ultramarine brothers and the t'au fire caste have fought side by side in the past. You know they are unlike other races. Their regime is not a difficult buy-in for a world on the fringes, unaided in a time of great need.'

'We cooperated out of dire necessity,' snapped Solarion. 'The Ultramarines are as contemptuous of xenos as any Chapter, and any Chapter with an ounce of strategic sense would have committed to that accord in the moment.'

'No one suggests otherwise. Malbede was as you say. Dire necessity. And it is dire necessity that moves the ordo's hand now. A highly trusted inquisitor lord, designated Epsilon, is on Tychonis. All contact has been lost. Imprisoned, most likely, but we cannot be sure at this stage. We need her extracted alive. We can risk no direct frontal assault until we are absolutely sure of her location. Even then, it must be a lightning strike, like a bolt from a clear sky. Do you understand? This is a precision operation, not a hammer blow. Any open act of war may not only cost us the life of the asset, but will almost certainly eliminate your own chances of survival.'

'Asset recovery,' snorted Zeed. 'Another *Night Harvest*.'

'This is nothing like *Night Harvest*,' replied the inquisitor drily. 'The best chance you have of locating and extracting Epsilon is to make contact with the rebel tribes. The Kashtu of the north are best placed to aid you. They have been resisting since the t'au first set foot on their world. They have a network of spies and cells that may be your best hope in gaining vital intelligence, not to mention operational support. They know the situation on Tychonis better than we do. Use them.'

'What do we have on Epsilon's position right now?' demanded Rauth.

'The situation is highly fluid,' replied Sigma. The hololith turned its head towards the Exorcist as it spoke. 'The ordo has assets in place among the rebels and in the cities. Not many, but each is working on locating the target.'

'The rebels,' said Karras. 'They will mistake our coming for some long-awaited sign, correct? They will believe we are their liberation. I would wager you are even counting on it.'

The hololith grinned, and not pleasantly. 'Such assumptions will serve our purpose well. Encourage them. We may need the rebels to launch diversionary assaults. A great many will likely die. Do not let your consciences confuse you. Their rebellion is none of our concern. It is doomed in any case. The world in question is currently of too little real worth to the Imperium to warrant a Militarum recovery expedition. Focus only on Epsilon. Time is of the essence. We don't know how long we have before the t'au find a way to pry highly classified information from her. It may already be too late. In any case, she must be recovered alive so she can be fully debriefed. She is an asset of the very highest level. The implications of a successful interrogation at the hands of enemy forces–'

'And yet your precious ordo lost her to the blue-skins,' said Zeed with a shake of his head. 'Should have had her on a tighter leash.'

'Resources,' said Voss, quickly defusing his squad brother's remark. 'What are we going in with?'

Sigma ignored Zeed's remark and focused on answering Voss. 'Pre-deployment loadouts will be decided and on-site resources will be overseen by your operational commander. I can tell you that you will have Reaper Wing for transport and air support, Chyron for heavy ground. You will also be deploying with a special operations task force – Inquisition Storm Troopers – all of whom read and understand the T'au language fluently.'

'Wait,' said Karras, holding up a hand. 'Operational commander? You mean to say that you will not be overseeing this one yourself?'

'The *Saint Nevarre* shall remain fully stealthed on the periphery of the t'au defence grid. She will not risk entry until the critical moment. Mission command has been assigned to another. One especially suited to the task. You will follow her orders to the letter as your oaths to the Watch and the ordo decree. I emphasise, Talon Squad, that her authority over *Operation Shadowbreaker* is absolute.'

'*Her* authority?' said Solarion.

Sigma's hololith winked out of existence for a brief instant. When it returned, it was followed by a hiss of hydraulics and plasteel on plasteel as the heavy door on the room's starboard side slid up into the ceiling.

A slender female entered the briefing room through wisps of oily steam. She was lithe, almost panther-like in her movements. The Space Marines watched her with mixed expressions as she marched crisply to a position a few metres in front of the base of Sigma's throne. There, she turned and cast an assessing eye over them. Dark hair cut high at the back, longer at the front, framed a caramel-skinned face in which sat two almond-shaped eyes. A dark, ragged scar ran from forehead to right cheek.

She did not smile. Nor did she bow.

She gave no sign of awe or reverence whatsoever.

Instead, she half-turned and spoke over her shoulder to Sigma. 'They are glorious, my lord. Let's hope they are as lethal as they look, because they'll need to be.'

Solarion looked ready to leap forward and strike her. Karras put out a hand and forestalled him.

'Mind yourself, woman,' he said. 'You address Space Marines!'

She turned back to them, her eyes settling on Karras. In answer, she flashed him a bright and supremely confident smile. It transformed her face, one that made her beautiful where before she had seemed as rough and rugged as unprocessed ore.

'Talon Squad,' said Sigma, 'meet Archangel, your operational commander for the duration of *Shadowbreaker*. Until this operation concludes, whether in victory or death, her word is law.'

FIFTEEN

Solarion surged forward.

Karras threw a restraining hand against his breastplate, but the Ultramarine knocked it away. 'First you assign me to the tactical command of a damned Thirteenth Founding psyker,' he raged, 'and now–'

'Control yourself,' growled Karras.

'Prophet has a point, Scholar,' said Zeed. He addressed Archangel. 'How many decades have you seen, woman? Three?'

'Hold yourselves, both of you,' Karras snapped. He faced Sigma's throne and the shimmering figure atop it. 'The inquisitor is about to explain.'

'My decree is reason enough,' said Sigma flatly. He turned his head towards Zeed. 'But in this case, Raven Guard, I will indulge you. So listen well. There is no individual better qualified to lead this operation than Archangel, even among all the Deathwatch assets at my disposal. No other. As to why, she shall speak for herself.'

The woman's eyes fixed boldly onto each of them in turn until she was sure she had all their attention. She showed no fear whatsoever, as if daring them to challenge her. Adeptus Astartes were used to humans being overwhelmed or paralysed with fear in their presence. Not so this woman. Karras observed her aura. It danced and coruscated like that of Cashka Redthorne, the bold captain of the *Saint Nevarre*. Both women radiated that air of supreme confidence and competence that inspired others to follow, even hardened fighting men.

Among the people of the Imperium, there were the lions and the sheep. Most people needed strong leaders. They craved them. They craved the freedom from personal responsibility that comes with putting faith in something or someone bigger and bolder than oneself.

The vast majority were sheep. So it had always been.

Captain Redthorne, at least, showed genuine deference in the presence of the Adeptus Astartes. But this woman, this soldier, lithe and taut, tattooed on neck, forearms and shoulders with the iconography of Militarum special forces, showed no deference. In fact, she expected it. She radiated killer instinct.

This, Karras could see, was not just some ordo agent. This was a veteran of wars fought and won, a genuine killer, a specialist every bit as dedicated to her purpose as each of the assembled Deathwatch operators.

She did not cower before them because she was a lion in a room full of lions. And if she was to be worthy of leading them, she had no choice but to show it here and now. If even a small crack appeared in her resolve, Talon Squad would not take her seriously.

Karras felt a sudden empathy for her. A kinship, even.

Leadership is an honour and a burden both. Show us then, woman, that you are the lion we will need you to be.

'In the field, you will address me as Archangel,' she said, 'but my birth name is Varanezza Althus Copley. Var for short. Copley to those that prefer it. I don't much care what you call me during downtime, so long as you get the damned job done. Operational success is everything. If necessary, I will give my life and the lives of all those under my command to achieve it. I may not be a Space Marine, but I've dedicated my life to waging war for mankind. You will find me uncompromising, but you will also find me open to good counsel. Even grateful for it.'

She continued to eye them. None of the kill-team interrupted as she continued. 'I have fought beside Space Marines before. I know the truth behind the legends. I have read your files. I respect what you are and what you can do. I may not have your physical strength, your inhuman resilience, your centuries of war, but I have proven myself worthy to lead this operation. To lead you until its end. Read my records for yourselves if you doubt it.'

She cast a half-glance at the hololith presiding over all of this. 'Those parts of the records for which you have clearance, that is.'

The briefing chamber was silent. Still, she held their gaze, never looking away.

'The name,' said Voss, breaking that silence. 'Copley. Is that Elysian?'

Always the peacemaker, thought Karras. Voss often found a way to cut through the tension and move things forward. His uses went far beyond raw strength and technical expertise.

'She doesn't have the look of one,' muttered Zeed.

Elysians were typically lighter skinned and slightly heavier in build than the woman that stood before them.

'The name is Elysian, but only half of my genes are. My father was a sergeant in the Forty-first Elysian Drop Troops regiment, the Thunder Falcons. My mother was a refugee from Armageddon. I spent six years in the Guard. For the last two of those, I was head of a special interdiction force that ran assaults on t'au supply lines. After that, I was selected for the Departmento Munitorum's Special Operations Detachment-F. We ran long-range reconnaissance patrols deep into t'au-held territory. I can read, write and understand sixteen T'au dialects and, with a modulator, can speak them too. After that–'

'Enough,' said Sigma. 'The rest they can read in the files.' He addressed Talon Squad. 'Archangel has been heading an Ordo Xenos task force specialising in operations in t'au space for the last eleven years. For the duration of *Shadowbreaker*, Talon will be attached to that task force, designation Arcturus.'

Solarion scowled and turned his head.

Sigma's hololith looked straight at him, its face utterly expressionless. 'Let me reiterate. Talon will form part of Arcturus until mission end. Captain Copley's orders will be followed as if they were my own.'

Silence hung heavy in the air. The tension could have been cut with a chainsword.

Then Archangel took a single step forward and stopped, feet apart, hands behind her back, every inch the officer in command.

'Is that clear, Deathwatch?' she barked.

Battle-hardened men might have fallen in line immediately, such was the strength of her aura of command. But these were not mere men.

Solarion twitched, barely able to hold himself from destroying the woman. Karras felt it, the rage, the lack of restraint from his subordinate. Pre-empting any action, and thus sparing anyone from dishonour, he stepped straight in front of Copley and looked down at her with sharp, clear, blood-red eyes.

He towered over her, but as she looked up at him, again he saw no fear. Her irises were black as coal and just as hard, just as stony.

'Armour lock,' Karras said simply. He was looking at Copley, but he was talking to Sigma. 'On Chiaro, you insulted us with it. You should have trusted in our oath to duty and honour. Tell me you do not intend to repeat that mistake.'

'She will have the override codes for your amour,' replied Sigma's shimmering form. 'You are still too... untested. I will not have you going off mission. Extreme personalities require extreme measures.'

'Extreme personalities?' said Voss.

Sigma's hololith looked at him and nodded. 'The exceptional are always the most troublesome.'

'It is an outrage!' rumbled Chyron.

Karras held Copley's gaze. 'I am willing to trust in your knowledge and experience of anti-t'au operations, woman. I am willing to work with you. But do not ever employ armour lock against one of my team. Be wise enough to know that we are bound by honour and oath. We are Space Marines. It is more than enough.'

Copley held his gaze and nodded sincerely. 'I believe in your honour. I believe in your oaths. All of you. If you swear to respect my authority for the duration of this mission, I will pledge not to use the lock.'

Sigma watched, choosing to let it play out as the woman deemed fit. He had selected her to lead. He would let her do that now.

Karras searched the woman's eyes. Though her face was hard to read, her aura blazed with sincerity, with deep integrity and respect. Armour lock was not something she wanted. He could see in the flashes of colour that surrounded her soul that she disdained it. Sigma commanded, and his authority here was absolute, so she would accept the codes. But on the ground, Karras doubted she would ever use them.

He found himself satisfied and turned his gaze to Sigma's avatar. 'Talon Squad will deploy as part of Arcturus and we will operate under the tactical command of Captain Copley.'

He sensed Solarion readying to protest again and cut him off. 'For the sake of our oaths to Chapter and Watch, we do this. Honour will be served. Do not insult it, and you *will* have our best.'

Sigma's avatar stared back a moment in thoughtful silence. 'Talon Alpha,' he said at last, 'we will take you at your word. You were all selected for this highly sensitive operation precisely because of the esteem in which your talents are held. Find honour in that. Again, I tell you, the odds are slim that any of you will survive this operation. And yet, my coven assures me that our greatest hope – quite possibly our only hope of success – lies with you and Arcturus operating as one.'

He turned his eyes on all of them in turn. 'Go to Tychonis. Embed yourselves with the rebel forces in the north. Gather the necessary intelligence. Then strike hard, and get Epsilon out of there alive.'

He dismissed them, telling them to prepare for transfer to the ship that would take them through the t'au defence network and down onto the planet's surface.

With the audience over, Archangel saluted the inquisitor's hololith crisply, spun on a heel and marched out past the towering Space Marines with a single silent nod to Karras.

The kill-team followed Karras out a moment later via the

door through which they had entered, with no salute for the hololith on the throne.

As they left the chamber, Sigma spoke one last time, his final words echoing behind them. 'Do not disappoint me, Talon Squad. The price of failure this time may be greater than any of us can yet imagine.'

SIXTEEN

Arnaz was certain he'd left no threads that led back to him. After killing the cloaked t'au agent, he had removed the picts the traitor had handed over then dragged the body to a nearby refuse point. The t'au's stealth field was still operational, despite the work he'd done with his knife. He re-engaged it. The corpse would remain invisible until either the power source died or some denizen of the city stumbled on it by chance. Diunar, too, had been eliminated, made to look like a suicide. As Arnaz's knife undid him, the look in the man's eyes was one of acceptance, almost gratitude. He had been coerced. A quick search of the hab had turned up evidence of a wife and child, but there were no signs they'd been present recently. The search also revealed the equipment Diunar had used to record the secret conclave of cell leaders.

Arnaz made sure to wipe the cogitator's data crystal memory after taking copies of all files for study back at one of his safe houses. He'd then left the hab, just before dawn, satisfied that those loose ends were tied up.

That was a week ago – a week of heightened caution, of looking over his shoulder a little more than usual, just to be sure. But he knew his craft. He was better than good. The enemy hadn't caught wind of him.

To the t'au, he was just another part of the system, living as others did, a role to fulfil in society, a contribution to make, family to support.

That last had been hard to accept, but it was a critical part of having solid cover here. Loners drew more attention, more suspicion, especially Tychonites – a people for whom marriage and the raising of children were seen as a duty equal to that of any professional calling.

So he'd taken a wife of average looks and intelligence, someone who wouldn't draw too much attention, and together they'd raised two unremarkable children, a boy and a girl.

And somewhere in the process of faking emotion towards them, he found he had crossed over into actually caring about them. Not quite love, perhaps, but he found great comfort in the time he spent with them, and they were happy with the life he provided.

They knew nothing of his true nature.

Like most in the capital, they adored the Aun and served the Greater Good in every way they could. If the t'au caught on to him, they'd likely be tortured or used as leverage. He tried not to think about that and just made sure he never got complacent.

In the end, though, he could only do so much. He had no idea that on the night of the rebel meeting, he had been marked.

To Arnaz, as he left his family home to begin his working

day, all looked normal. The streets were filled as always by men going to their t'au-designated occupations in t'au-designated robes and uniforms. He detected no shimmers in the air that might have given away a stealth field. Satisfied, he moved off in the rising heat of the morning. To everyone else, he was just Arnaz, a mid-level contract negotiator tasked with securing off-world resources for the ISF. In most cases, that meant making contracts with human smugglers who were willing to bring shipments into t'au territory from the Imperium. It was a position he had carefully manoeuvred himself into over long years, and it allowed him to keep one eye on the movement of weapons and another on the t'au and human military elements in the upper echelons of the city's security force administration.

Fostering trust was fundamental to any agent in deep cover. Arnaz was privy to highly sensitive information with increasing frequency. More and more, he found the line he walked thinning. There were things that, had he shared them with the Speaker of the Sands, would have given him away almost certainly. Despite the worth of such intel to the rebel cause, despite the rebel lives that would surely be lost, there were times he'd had to stay silent, accepting the burden of large numbers of deaths as a result. That had been hard on him, but he'd soon adapted. He'd learned to plasteel himself against such remorse.

Eyes on the war, not the battle.

He adjusted his belt and moved off down the street.

The stealthed t'au drone that was tracking him kept pace, far enough away that its shimmer in the air was indiscernible, close enough to follow his movements with ease, all the while relaying its images back to its controller in the ranks of a fire caste counter-insurgency unit here in the capital. The disc-shaped device had enough autonomous intelligence to gauge exactly how and when to move so that it would never be seen. Arnaz didn't stand a chance.

An hour later, he stepped out of a grav-rail carriage onto a busy platform and made the rest of the journey to his workplace on foot. The drone locked onto him again.

It lost him when he entered a twelve-storey t'au structure surrounded by watchtowers and electronic defences. This was where Arnaz worked. Today, several discussions were scheduled with mid- and high-level ISF officers. Major Rahin Rasaan would be present, commanding officer of the ISF and close adviser to Coldwave himself.

Coldwave, of course, would not be in attendance. Reports had him back in the south at the Tower of the Forgotten and whatever work was keeping him there so much recently.

Arnaz had met Coldwave twice in his time on Tychonis. The t'au supreme military commander was every bit as stern and expressionless as all fire caste tended to be, but there was definitely something different about him. He had a particular quality that was hard to define. Not charisma as men understood it, but there was definitely something. And he was weathered, scarred. This was a t'au that had fought in planetary wars. He had seen more death in his life than any other fire warrior on this planet. It lent him a quiet, powerful air. Arnaz, despite himself, had found the blue-skin formidable, even daunting. And yet he still hoped to spend more time around the warrior, for, apart from Aun'dzi himself, it was Coldwave who was the primary opponent of Imperial interests. It was Coldwave that would stop the rebels ever getting close enough to kill the Ethereal and begin the collapse of t'au rule.

Instead, Arnaz found himself around an oval table with

several fire and water caste members, the latter there to smooth communications between human and t'au members, for the fire caste tended to be so blunt that humans regularly took offence and things could so easily dissolve into argument and misunderstanding.

As it was, the meeting proved significant. Arnaz learned that additional resources were to be shipped to the security forces at the Tower of the Forgotten. There was little explanation for it, but, through the careful wording used by the water caste and the specific avoidance of certain terms, Arnaz began to suspect that the woman in the picts and her Space Marine bodyguards had been moved to the facility.

As prisoners? As something else? He had to find out. At the very least, he felt he had to communicate this update to the Speaker of the Sands. With this information, perhaps the Speaker would be able to scry more of the truth behind all this.

The discussions were long and gruelling. Major Rasaan was as difficult to please as ever, questioning every aspect of the proposals put before him. Whatever was going on at the Tower had the ISF and fire caste more on edge than Arnaz had ever seen them.

As the day came to an end, Arnaz resolved to return to the nearest of his safe houses and send a message north to the Drowned Lands before heading home.

At the close of business, he made the standard formal farewells to both human and t'au and began to thread his way through the streets, careful to double back on himself a couple of times, keeping his eyes open for sign of any tails. He checked the skies several times, using narrow streets to funnel any airborne followers into view.

Nothing.

When he was sure he was in the clear, he headed for the safe house – a small basement in one of the city's busiest habitation districts.

Over the years, he had slowly and carefully managed to insulate the walls, floor and ceiling with shielding that would defy any kind of electronic surveillance. When the door clicked shut behind him and the locking bolts slid home, he breathed deep, allowing himself to relax. The air was stale. He reached out and hit the lights. Two lume-strips in the bare ceiling flickered to life. An air-cycler began to hum gently. In the middle of the room was a simple table and one chair. To the left, a basic bed. Some food and drink in a small fridgerator. That was it. To the untrained eye, the room was entirely void of anything else.

Arnaz crossed to the north wall and stood facing it. Placing his right hand on the wall, he measured out three hand spans and pressed inwards. He felt the wall give just a millimetre. With his left hand about twenty centimetres lower, he measured out a single span and pressed there too. Again, he felt the wall give just a little. To his right, there was a click followed by the slow grind of stone on stone. A compartment, absolutely seamless until that moment, slid out from the wall. Within it was a black unit about the size of an assault weapon case.

No icons, no runes, no logos. Not even a handle.

Arnaz lifted the unit from the compartment and carried it to the table. He set it down and sat in the chair, then reached out his right hand and pressed it, palm flat, to the unit's upper surface. Then he leaned forward and spoke.

'Indigo seven-six-five-zero-nine. Authorisation ultima: designation Sand Spider.'

A needle stabbed upwards into his palm. He knew it was coming, but he still winced at the sharp and sudden pain.

For a moment, he felt rather than heard the ceramite case humming as it confirmed his genetic identity. He knew it was monitoring his heartbeat at the same time. The Inquisition did not take chances. The blood of a dead operative and the codewords alone would not be enough to open the case. The agent had to be alive.

After a second, the humming stopped and vacuum seals hissed. The case juddered as powerful mag-locks powered down. Arnaz withdrew his hand.

The case opened smoothly.

Inside was a fairly standard Imperial rune board, but there was nothing standard about that which facilitated the machine's ability to transmit messages.

There, in a glass dome embedded in the lower half of the case, was the living brain of a psychic human. This one had been put to fine use, extracted, wiped and conditioned to perform a single function only – to transmit encrypted astropathic messages to another distant psychic mind.

Arnaz began typing on the rune board, glyphs appearing in green on the black screen set in the upper half of the case. Fluids began flowing through tubes into the psychic brain. The lights in the ceiling flickered. One went out. Arnaz prepared himself for that terrible sensation, that feeling of hair rising, of skin prickling, of chills in the spine.

A vague, shadowy form materialised in the north-east corner of the room, hunched and human but too indistinct beyond that to tell more.

'Speak quickly,' said the shadow, with a voice that always made Arnaz think of words spoken underwater.

More fluids flowed into the transmitting brain.

Arnaz spoke of the day's discussions and of all they indicated about events at the Tower of the Forgotten.

The shadow drifted closer to him and he found himself growing more uneasy. His skin crawled.

'This is good,' said the shadow. 'We have eyes and ears at the Tower. They will be contacted. Confirmation should come soon. We must be extra careful. The woman is… unreadable. Something, some field, prevents it. The same thing prevents me from seeing her bodyguards. You have done well. Is there anything else to report?'

Arnaz was about to answer in the negative when the shadow hissed, 'We are compromised!'

His first reaction was immediate and automatic. He slammed the case shut. The shadow vanished in an instant.

There was a deafening boom. Parts of the ceiling to his left and right exploded inwards. Had he been sitting just three metres in either direction, he would have been killed instantly. As it was, the explosions stunned and dizzied him, making him reel in his chair.

That tiny moment, that instant of concussion was his undoing.

Shaking it off, he reached desperately for the button underneath the table that would bring the whole building down around him. Too late. Something flashed down in an arc.

He felt like he was watching in slow motion as the t'au combat blade sliced clean through his right arm. His finger had almost been on the button.

His arm fell to the floor.

He sat gaping at it, stunned.

The blade belonged to a t'au fire caste soldier on his right. There were four of them, all in assault armour – a blue-skin special operations squad. They had dropped into the room from the floor above.

As Arnaz looked in disbelief and horror at the blood fountaining from his cleaved elbow, one of the blue-skins on his left grabbed his throat with a gloved, four-fingered hand and threw him to the ground. He hit hard, his head smacking on the rockcrete floor. But he was well beyond that level of pain. His body was already fighting to stem the agony of his severed arm, releasing endorphins into his system so that he could endure.

Through watering eyes, he looked up into four snarling alien faces.

One of them – the unit leader, judging by his markings – lowered his weapon, pressed a button on his left vambrace and jabbered into a pickup embedded at the wrist. He spoke in the T'au dialect common to Tychonis, and Arnaz understood every word, even as his consciousness was slipping from him.

'We took the gue'la spy alive,' said the t'au soldier. 'No casualties. He was not able to activate the demolition charges.'

The t'au paused as it listened to a response through a device over its left ear.

'No, commander. He was able to seal the device.'

Again the assault team leader paused and listened.

'Understood, Shas'el. It will be as you say.' He clicked his comms unit off and turned to the other three members of the team. 'You two, get him to the transport. You, take that black case. An earth caste search team is coming to examine the rest of the safe house, but our work here is done.'

'Central Detention, Shas'vre?' asked one of the soldiers.

Arnaz was slipping fast, tumbling into the darkness of unconsciousness, but the last words he heard still managed to chill him.

'Stem the flow from that wound. This one goes south to Na'a'Vashak. He will be interrogated there. And if he refuses to talk, he will watch his kin suffer right before his eyes.'

* * *

Arnaz's Ordo conditioning was deep. His kin did indeed suffer, and it tore his soul apart to see it and to hear the screams, but he did not give the t'au a single word of answer. He had always known it might come to this. Still, it was the hardest thing he'd ever done, to stay silent as those that loved him screamed his name, pleading for him to speak and end the nightmare. When their screams ended, and their dead bodies offered no more leverage to the t'au, his frustrated blue-skin interrogators turned to inflicting pain more directly on him. This was a relief by comparison. He knew they could not break him. His own suffering was infinitely easier to take than that of his family.

The t'au had no choice but to escalate the pain.

Eventually, it became too much.

As Arnaz began to slip away, blood bubbling from his lips, he grinned at them and finally broke his silence.

'Enjoy your last days of dominion here, you xenos filth. Judgement is coming.'

His eyes rolled back as he took a last gurgling breath.

'Judgement,' he muttered, and then was gone.

SEVENTEEN

Day dawned bright over the vast irrigated fields of the mid-northern latitudes. These were some of the most fertile agri zones on the planet. Drones were already at work, drifting between the towering rows of stalks, spraying for pests and clipping away dead growth. Soon, flesh-and-blood workers – t'au and human both – would come to harvest the crops. Drones could have been coded and fitted to do it all, but people need a purpose in life. The Greater Good protected people from themselves, from indolence, from idleness, as much as it did from any external threat. Busy hands and minds were less prone to be turned from the T'au'va. So human and t'au alike still laboured in fields as men had done for many millennia, and both went home at the end of the day knowing the satisfaction of a job well done, ready for rest and comforts well earned.

The Tychonite sun was a warm golden orb, gently bringing its heat as it crested the flatlands far to the east. By midday, however, once it was high overhead, it would beat down with little mercy. Workers would break for the hottest midday hours. Tychonis had cast off the mantle of desert planet, but that mantle only stayed cast off by virtue of a constant struggle. The t'au's advanced environmental control systems waged a slow war against the original nature of the world and its proximity to its star.

It was a daily battle the t'au were long used to winning. Tychonis was not the first world rendered more liveable by the machines of the earth caste. Terraforming on this scale was a process they had refined over centuries.

To the far north, the fields ended and the marshes and swamps began. On the fringes were the rice fields, worked much in the same way as the rest of the agri zones. But beyond them, the terrain was unworkable, unliveable, the southern borders of the Drowned Lands. The sky that hung there was markedly different, thick with black clouds, their loads heavy, liable to break over the treetops and unleash their torrents at any time. The abundant waters were channelled south along a precise system of t'au-crafted canals and aqueducts, bringing life to the rest of the hemisphere. A similar system existed in the south. The gargantuan t'au installations at the polar caps were constantly freeing up moisture and releasing it into the atmosphere. Other monolithic machines in rings all around the upper latitudes would then generate appropriate wind currents that would carry the moisture where it was needed. To the t'au, weather was a system just like any other. What could be measured could be controlled. And what could be controlled could be utilised. So it was with all things in the eyes of the t'au.

The drones worked on, mindlessly running subroutines that assessed the growth and ripeness of the crops. The first hovering labour transports from the nearby towns and cities would be arriving within the hour.

From the west, the peaceful morning was broken by a roar. Momentarily, the drones turned optical lenses and audio pickups in that direction. What they registered was a ship entering the atmosphere, its super-heated hull cutting a bright and fiery trail across the sky. This was no t'au ship. It had none of the sleek, graceful, almost shark-like lines. Instead, this was a brutish thing, blocky, angular, the work of human hands.

When the ship hit an altitude of ten thousand metres, it deployed air brakes and reverse thrusters to help it bleed off excess speed. It dropped to five thousand metres. Then it dropped to two thousand.

As the drones in the fields below returned to their work, they sent data packets through the airwaves registering what they had witnessed. It all went back to the central nodes of the vast planetary data processing networks, one of which existed in each capital, the Western and the Eastern. Air caste members working in Aerospace Control would pick up the data, process it and make sure it matched approved flight plans and identification codes. Cargo manifests would appear on a screen somewhere. As the craft neared its designated spaceport, it would be tracked by fire caste defence installations.

On the manifest for this particular craft, there would be nothing unusual. Twelve thousand metric tons of seed for crops edible to humans but not to t'au. Eight thousand metric tons of cheap, synthetic, food-safe proteins to be used as nutritional additives. Five thousand tons of rare metals for use in adapted t'au technologies that would be issued to human security personnel. Another five thousand tons of miscellaneous materials for use in construction. There were even human cultural items on board, things the t'au themselves could not replicate or supply, such as works of literature, art, luxury items, all brought here from the Imperium.

The people must be kept content, after all. True integration was delicate – it did not mean total conversion. Human culture was respected here. Even the Imperial creed – those parts of it that were not zealously anti-alien – was tolerated for the Greater Good. No Ministorum church had been desecrated or destroyed. Of course, that decision also served as part of a control strategy. Those who gave worship in the house of the God-Emperor could easily be marked and watched. Convenient for t'au intelligence services, though the smartest and most dangerous of the faithful never fell into that trap.

This particular lander, however, was carrying none of these things, despite what the official manifest said. Its cargo holds held no grain, no artefacts, no raw materials.

Instead, it held three Stormraven assault craft fitted with stealth plating and jamming pods, and as many hardened fighters and as much equipment as those craft could carry.

The sharp black blade of the Holy Inquisition had come to Tychonis.

Fear has a smell. Most men can't smell it – their olfactory nerves are too few, too numb – but Space Marines can. With gene-boosted senses, they could hardly miss it. Karras smelled it now, slight but definitely present. A little acrid. A little sour, but not offensive. Archangel looked as steady as a rock. Just another drop. But she couldn't mask it completely. It was there, just the barest hint of it. It emanated from her people, too, though they, likewise, looked utterly untroubled. They knew what they were going into. A small force inserting straight into enemy-held territory like this – they had done it many times.

But they had lost people, brothers and sisters they had known well, tough soldiers all. And there would be deaths again. Losses. It was inevitable. Trite as it was, the old adage held – no plan survives contact with the enemy.

Special operations doctrine was built on the ability to adapt, to reformulate tactics on the fly. Much would depend on how well Archangel did that.

So a little fear was understandable… in humans. The closest the Space Marines could come was apprehension. More often, they felt only eagerness and impatience. They hungered for conflict. Too long without it, and many of them became dangerous to be around.

Karras didn't judge the men and women of Arcturus for a little fear. He knew it gave most operators an edge. Not an edge that he and his post-human battle-brothers needed, but an edge nonetheless. Better for mundanes to experience fear and master it than to experience none at all.

It was Archangel who held his attention the most. In front of her people, she was a rock, her poise perfect, as if she had all the answers. A born leader.

Her scars, her honour markings, her physique, he thought. *Inquisition or not, she probably understands us better than Sigma does.*

Everything about her aura supported the image of strength she presented. She was a trained and tested killer – tenacious, self-controlled, highly motivated. Honour and a deeper respect from the other kill-team members were things she would have to work hard to earn, but he believed she would. He had already decided he liked her. She was direct. A straight-talker. Unclouded.

And there was nothing to be gained by clashing heads with her. She was operational commander. If she was as good as her records attested, he wouldn't need to step in.

The ship jerked hard, dropping speed.

Air brakes, thought Karras. *Not long now. We need to be ready.*

The drop would be dangerous. All drops were dangerous, but this one had challenges all of its own. *Shadowbreaker* might end right here if the deployment were to be interrupted or otherwise botched. It had to be fast and it had to be smooth. So far, it wasn't either – there had been long periods when the approach codes they were using to enter t'au space were being double-checked, periods when orbital defence guns might have blown them to space debris. But they had got through. Now, another key moment was upon them.

Metal groaned and clanged as the ship shouldered its way bullishly through the protesting air. The hull was still hot. On the outer surface, it was a dull, angry red.

'Clearing ionosphere in three, two, one…' announced the captain over the ship's comms. The straining and shuddering of the outer hull eased. The tortured whines turned to the low growl of buffeting winds. *'Firing forward nozzles. All personnel, brace for further deceleration.'*

Karras felt his stomach lurch as the ship dropped another chunk of speed.

'Welcome to Tychonis,' said Captain Burgess. *'Banking north-east. Switching to an unauthorised course now. We won't have long before they send out interceptors. Let's get this done quick and clean. This is where the games really start.'*

'Keep the channel open,' Archangel voxed back to him. 'I want to hear any comms chatter when they challenge you over the new flight path.'

'Yes, ma'am.'

It wouldn't be long. The t'au had been monitoring them throughout their approach. With *The Pride of Kalvicca* veering suddenly away from the approved vector, alarms would already be going off. Razorshark fighter aircraft would be taxiing down runways or breaking off from their original patrol routes on their way to intercept. Perhaps some were already in the airspace nearby. If so, the time available for deployment would be cut uncomfortably short.

And so it was.

The captain soon reported three fast-moving contacts on his auspex screens. A blue-skin fighter wing was barely eight minutes out.

'We have to ditch now,' Karras told Archangel. 'Tell him to drop us. It doesn't matter about the exact coordinates. We drop now or we're dead. We have to get the camo-sheets and jamming pods up before those ships make a pass.'

'Did you hear that, captain?' Archangel asked over the vox. 'We need to do this now.'

'That's rough country down there, ma'am. Dense. I'm scanning for good ground, but we're out over the swamp and rainforest now. I can't guarantee a safe drop.'

'A safe drop was never on the cards. We know the risks. But we can't be onboard when those interceptors catch up with you. They need to escort you to the spaceport, not run passes out here looking for us. Start the procedure, captain. That's an order.'

'I hear you, ma'am. Initiating drop. We'll need to bleed off a little more speed before I can open the rear cargo door. Hold tight.'

The ship lurched again, violently. Titanium I-beams whined in protest. There was a loud bang, and something buckled, most likely an outer plate. Karras checked his impact restraint, pulling hard. The locks were solid. He looked across the hold at his kill-team brothers. All stood silent, faces masked by their expressionless helms. With witchsight, he could see their moods coruscate around them. They were ready. They just wanted to get on the damned ground, to get moving again. They hated transit, hated the waiting. Zeed's aura, more than that of Voss or Solarion, danced and flickered in his eagerness to engage enemies. Karras knew he'd have to watch the Raven Guard. He'd barely followed orders during *Night Harvest*. The chances that he'd follow the commands of Archangel throughout this op were even slimmer. This operation was about a patient, timely strike and a fast exit. He couldn't have Zeed jumping into any and every fight that presented itself.

Do as you're told this time, Ghost, he urged silently. *We mess this up, we're not getting off this rock.*

Talon and Archangel's people were loaded into the Stormravens and ready in under three minutes. From outside the hull of the Reaper One there came further noise as Burgess' freighter continued to slow. As soon as *The Pride of Kalvicca* hit a suitable airspeed, her massive rear cargo door began its painfully slow descent. Muted daylight, turned dull by thick cloud, seeped into the cargo hold. The wind was less subtle, screaming in, racing round the hold like a mad animal.

Karras didn't see any of this with his physical eyes. The hatch of the Stormraven in which he sat was sealed tight. But he projected his astral awareness out into the hold to watch the other assault craft exit. With his mind's eye, he watched the freighter's massive ramp finally lock into place in the open position.

The ship began to shake harder, never designed to fly with its main cargo door open like this.

Burgess couldn't fly the ship any slower without actually

descending to land. This was it, as slow as she could go. It would have to be enough.

'Reaper flight, prepare to drop,' voxed Ventius, pilot of Reaper One and mission flight leader as appointed by Sigma. Like all three Stormraven pilots, the captain was as much man as machine, permanently built into the cockpit of the Stormraven by the enginseers of the Inquisition. He had become the living brain of the machine, and the Stormraven had become his body. It was not a standard arrangement. Typically, Stormravens were piloted by Space Marines, but this was the Ordo Xenos. They had their own rules. Fusing pilot and aircraft created a synergistic increase in performance that even Space Marine veteran pilots would be hard-pressed to equal. That Ventius and the others had willingly given up their humanity said as much about their love of flight as it did about their loyalty and drive to serve the Imperium. Perhaps more.

'Reaper Three,' continued Ventius, *'deploy on my mark! Three... Two... One... Go!'*

A disembodied Karras watched as Reaper Three rose into the air of the hold on flaring nozzles and fired its drag-chute out the back of the freighter's hatch.

The chute caught the wind with a snap. The lines went taught. With a burst of gentle vertical thrust from its turbines, the Stormraven lifted into the air and was snatched out of the rear hatch. Its vector jets flared hard to stabilise it, then it dropped from view.

Over the vox, a voice reported, *'Reaper Three airborne. Chute detached. Moving north to search for a clearing.'*

'Acknowledged, Reaper Three,' replied Captain Ventius. *'Reaper Two, deploy on my mark.'*

Karras watched again as the second Stormraven fired its

drag-chute out the back of the lander and whipped out just like the craft before it. With a burst of jet-flame, it swung north and followed.

We're up, thought Karras.

His mind snapped back into his body, feeling the weight and strength of it all at once. He flexed his armoured fingers and rolled his neck.

'When does this ride get to the good part?' asked Zeed.

'Reaper One deploying now,' said the flight leader over the vox.

There was the thunk of bolts firing and a cough like that of a mortar launcher as the last Stormraven's drag-chute was fired out of the back of the lander and into the strong winds. It caught and flared hard. Just as it did, Ventius fired the vertical thrusters, pulled the assault craft's nose up just a touch, lifting the Stormraven from the deck of the freighter, and fought to hold the sticks steady as the assault craft was ripped backwards out of the larger ship and into open air.

With Chyron suspended from the rear of the Stormraven by magna-grapple, Reaper One was by far the heaviest of the birds. She cleared the rear hatch by less than a metre. Chyron's massive feet scraped the ramp on the way out, sending up a wave of bright orange sparks.

'Good luck, Reaper flight,' voxed Burgess. *'Emperor watch over you all. Whatever you have to do here, I pray for your success.'*

'Thank you, captain,' replied Ventius. *'May the Emperor protect you. I pray you make it out of t'au space alive.'*

In the hold of his Stormraven, Karras could feel the craft wrestling with wind currents, enforcing its will with the roar of its turbine engines. It was a battle the powerful turbofans won. He felt the craft stabilise, dip its nose, then swing north. The drag-chute was released. It whipped away on the wind.

Within the quarter-hour, its advanced fibres would degrade, leaving no evidence.

Another voice sounded on the vox. *'I have a clearing, Reaper One.'* It was Flight Lieutenant Dargen, pilot of Reaper Three. *'Big enough for all three Stormravens, but only just. Landing now.'*

'Good work, Reaper Three,' Ventius replied. *'Heading to your position now. Don't wait for us. Get the camo-sheets up and the jamming modules online. If those t'au fighters are still heading in on this vector, we've got a few minutes at most. We do not want to get caught in the open.'*

'Copy that, sir,' Dargen voxed back. *'It will be done.'*

Reaper Three was already under its camo-sheet by the time Karras strode out the rear hatch of Reaper One and onto Tychonite soil, or rather grass, for the first time. He threw a glance at it as the men of Archangel's unit rushed past him, hurrying to get a similar sheet up over Reaper Two. From Reaper Three's camo-sheet, Karras saw cables snaking to a small black terminal on the ground by the treeline. One of Archangel's people squatted in front of it, hitting a sequence of controls on the device's runeboard.

Photo-reactive cells kicked in, working to replicate the colours and textures of the terrain beneath the craft. Pictographic camouflage ripped over the sheet, a jumble of shapes and shades that eventually settled to perfectly mimic the surrounding vegetation. Then the soldier hit another sequence of runes and the sheet adjusted, crumpling here, smoothing there, compensating for the shape of the craft and the shadows it was casting.

From the air, it must've looked almost as if the craft had simply vanished. Here again was a display of the power and resources of the Holy Inquisition. This level of camouflage technology was unknown to most other arms of the Imperium. The cost and resources involved, the rarity of such advanced technology…

Truly, the Inquisition was an organisation apart. Even from the ground, it was difficult now to discern anything existed where Reaper Three had landed – just foliage sprouting from a small natural mound. Had Karras not seen the process take place right in front of him, only his enhanced senses or psychic gifts would have told him any better. A normal man might walk right past the covered assault craft and never know it even existed.

The soldier at the console hit the standby rune. Another disconnected the cabling from beneath Reaper Three's sheet and raced to Reaper Two. Once the terminal was connected again, the trooper went through the same steps.

Reaper Two all but vanished a moment later.

Karras turned to see his kill-team emerging from Reaper One, weapons in hand. Archangel's people were already clambering up on the wings and dragging the last camo-sheet over the craft's exterior. Magna-grapples still held Chyron beneath the rear of the craft. For the sake of time, he would be camouflaged under the sheet along with the Stormraven that carried him.

'I hate drops like this,' growled the massive Lamenter over the kill-team vox-channel.

'Just be glad the grapples held,' laughed Zeed as Chyron disappeared from sight, 'or we'd have to leave you hanging in the forest canopy somewhere.'

'Once those fighters pass, shall we see how far I can throw you, little raven?'

'Space Marines. Into the trees,' said Karras, pointing to the southern edge of the clearing, the nearest. 'Now!'

Talon Squad entered the thick shadows of the forest and turned to look out over the clearing. Karras joined them, standing between Rauth and Voss.

'All photo-reactive camouflage activated,' reported Archangel's man. 'Holding steady. Engaging jamming pods.'

'Power down,' Karras told his team. 'Switch systems to full stealth. Minimal output. I don't want our armour giving us away if they do some kind of deep auspex sweep.'

Solarion thrust his chin at the Arcturus soldiers dragging material – weapons and ammo crates, other supplies – to the treeline. 'If those grunts don't get to cover, it won't bloody matter.'

Archangel's people were working hard and fast, but Solarion was right. Seconds counted. They didn't have long. Karras strained his ears. Reading the thought impulse via neural link, his helm reacted at once, boosting his hearing beyond its already superhuman ability. The sounds all around him immediately became sharper, more distinct, more individually defined. His brain filtered out the noises of the forest, the hum of his armour, his heartbeat, his breathing.

Against the sharp calls of a hundred species of local fauna, he picked out the strange thrumming of alien engines, a powerful and agile combination of anti-gravity motors and plasma-based thrusters. From sensorium recordings he had experienced back at Damaroth, he recognised the sound signature of several Razorshark interceptors.

He tensed.

'Archangel,' he voxed to the woman. 'Your people have about eight seconds.'

The sound of the alien jets was clear enough now to be heard by the unenhanced ears of the Arcturus soldiers.

It grew louder.

Archangel voxed a last curt command, and her people engaged the jammers, each set to interfere with t'au scanning methods but not with their communications. A sudden loss of comms would have tipped off the blue-skin pilots.

Everyone had melted into the jungle now. The clearing was empty to the untrained eye. The task force troopers had worked fast and efficiently, but it was a close thing.

Dark shadows suddenly screamed across the glade, filling the air with that mix of whining and humming. The craft were only visible for a single second, but it was enough for Karras to see that he had been right.

Razorsharks.

Deadly effective in the hands of a competent air caste pilot, supremely so in the hands of their most talented. Had these well-armed interceptors arrived any earlier, the glade would have been host to a bloodbath.

After their first pass, Archangel spoke, barely a whisper over the main task force channel. *'Don't move,'* she told the members of Arcturus. *'Not a damned muscle. They'll make three passes. The blue-skins always make three passes.'*

She wasn't wrong. The t'au jets made exactly three passes over the clearing before the sound of their engines finally began to fade, heading eastward in the wake of *The Pride of Kalvicca*.

She knew, thought Karras.

The sensorium feeds back at Damaroth had shown him how t'au operated in the chaos of battle. He'd seen nothing like this. But Copley had known.

This woman knows the t'au far better than we do, he admitted to himself. *She has lived and breathed the Imperium's war against them for most of her life. She has been on the front line her whole military career. No. She has served* behind *the lines.*

He wanted to know more, to experience her past in detail like the sensorium feeds at Damaroth had shown him those of battle-brothers long dead. A sharing of her memories might be immensely beneficial in the assault phase of this op. But she was Ordo Xenos. If there existed any feeds from her actions in the field, they would be classified. Sigma had certainly not mentioned them.

Karras discounted the notion of an unsanctioned mind-dive as soon as it came into his head. Always dangerous, such a dive might undo her ability to lead. Worse still, dive just a little too deep and it might even kill her, not to mention the risks to his own mind were it to go wrong.

Her leadership would do... so long as she lived.

The Razorsharks were still just within audible range when an unexpected noise intruded, followed quickly by another – the scream of a rocket and the sudden explosive crump as it struck its target.

Gunfire rang out in the east, muffled by the density of the jungle but still clear to the boosted hearing and helm audio-senses of the Space Marines.

Having lost one of their number, the remaining two fighters had swung around and were strafing something or someone down below the forest canopy.

'Karras.'

It was Rauth. He didn't need to say anything else.

Karras centred his mind and tapped the flow of ethereal power that was always around him. Closing his eyes, he began murmuring, reciting the Litany of Sight Beyond Sight. He felt his consciousness separate from its living shell and rise up above the treetops. He turned his awareness east and willed his astral self in that direction.

With his mind's eye, he watched two rockets streak up out

of the forest on white trails. One missed its mark and spiralled off to fall into the jungle without detonating. It had forced one of the alien craft to bank hard, however, putting it directly in the path of the other rocket. The Razorshark's sleek hull blew out in a gush of flame and black smoke, debris spinning off it as it cartwheeled down into the trees, gouging a great gap in the canopy.

The last of the t'au interceptors vectored high into the air at a sharp angle, cut back on the throttle, banked hard and began another strafing run. There was a bright stream of fire from its nose-mounted burst cannon. Rounds stitched the trees, hacking them to pieces, but before it completed its attack run, it peeled off and raced south. Either the air caste pilot had recognised that firing blind into the jungle was futile and was keeping him or her in missile range, or an order had come through to return and report.

Karras willed his awareness back into his body and closed himself off from the flow of power from the warp.

'Two of the Razorsharks were shot down with surface-to-air missiles. Man-portables. The last of them pulled away, heading south.'

'The rebels,' said Voss.

Karras nodded. 'The t'au probably don't do flyovers here unless they have good reason. Too easy to be shot down from below, and too hard to see whoever does the shooting. The rebels have probably punished them for coming this far north before, but *The Pride of Kalvicca* breaking from her approved approach vector was too much for them to ignore.'

'Better for us if the rebels hadn't interfered,' said Rauth.

Karras silently agreed.

'The xenos could clear this whole jungle,' Zeed interjected. 'So why don't they?'

Solarion snorted. 'Don't you ever connect to the archives like you're told?'

'That would ruin all the suprises,' said Zeed with a grin.

Voss laughed.

'Resources,' said Solarion. 'This is a fringe world to the t'au. It's not worth it to them. It's also why their planetary defence grid was so permeable.'

'More than that,' said Karras, 'the jungle is a buffer. The worst of the storms, the density of airborne and waterborne fungal spores, the planet's larger predatory bioforms... Anything that helps stop these things reaching the agri zones and population centres stays where it is.'

'All of which you would know, Raven Guard,' said Solarion with a sneer, 'if you just–'

Karras cut him off, sharply raising a closed fist, signalling his team to be silent.

'What is it, Scholar?' said Voss.

With the Razorsharks gone, Archangel was issuing orders to her people, getting them out of cover, directing them to remove the camo-sheets and get everything ready for the journey north into the Drowned Lands and the domain of the rebels.

Karras sent his psychic presence questing through the trees, moving fast, the thick, vine-strangled trunks flashing by. When he found what he was looking for, he returned to his body and, without further word, strode out to stand in front of Copley.

She turned from overseeing her people and looked up at him, squinting against the bright sun so high behind his head.

'It looks like we're in the clear for now, Scholar,' she said. Absently, part of him noted that it was the first time she had used that name. 'Get Talon loaded up. We're moving out.'

'Not yet,' said Karras. 'We have visitors. Multiple contacts converging on this clearing.'

Archangel's hands went to the Ryza-pattern hot-shot lasgun slung over her shoulder. She shrugged out of its carry strap and then knocked the safety off.

'Hostiles?' she asked.

Karras closed his eyes behind his visor. The auras he sensed had a familiar signature, an energy that surrounded them like clouds of steam. He knew it well. Throughout the Imperium, it was pervasive.

Faith in the Imperial creed.

It had to be the loyalist rebels. The Kashtu.

'Armed,' he said, 'but not hostile. Not to us. Just over a hundred souls. They have been waiting a very long time for us to arrive, major.'

'That can't be,' said Copley. 'Even the ordo assets here haven't been informed about our op for security reasons.'

Karras shook his head. He could read the expectation and the excitement in the approaching people almost as strongly as he could sense their fanaticism. 'Our coming was foretold. The one that leads them, this Speaker of the Sands mentioned in the mission files, saw it in the prime futures. These people have been awaiting us.'

Figures began to emerge from the trees now. Strange figures. At first, they looked almost alien, even bestial, creatures of the jungle, born and formed to merge with it, to move through it without being seen. Their clothing was ragged, patterned to match the foliage, cut to mimic its natural shapes. No photo-reactive camouflage for these people. Theirs was simple, but effective enough. Each head was covered, each face masked to look like some beaked creature, long black bristles sprouting from the back. There was something of the kroot about them, Karras realised. Then he saw that the masks and cloaks were fashioned from the skulls and skins of members of that very race.

They were armed with a wide variety of weapons, from long-barrelled lasrifles to weapons pilfered from dead xenos foes. But none of those weapons were raised.

One moved forward from the ranks. He sat mounted on a tall bipedal creature, a half-bird, half-reptile thing with six black eyes and a horned beak. He dismounted, dropping gracefully to the ground. Stepping a few more metres forward of the others, he lifted a hand and removed his mask, revealing a scarred face with a thick black beard.

True to their training, Archangel's people had immediately trained their guns on the newcomers, but the major trusted Karras' words. She barked out the command to lower weapons. Karras noted that the rebels had moved through the jungle so surely and quietly that even the superbly trained men and women of Arcturus had not sensed them until they broke cover. Had his senses not been that of the psyker, even he might not have known of their approach, taking the sounds they made as those of the forest. These were a people well adapted to their environment.

'You should have had eyes on all sides,' Karras told Copley.

'I did,' she bit back.

At that moment, more of the masked figures emerged from the trees, carrying the inert forms of six of Archangel's people.

She growled and brought her weapon back up.

Karras placed a heavy gauntlet on her shoulder.

'They're unconscious, not dead. They still breathe.'

He removed his helm and stared straight into her eyes. 'Listen well, major. In front of these people, you must be seen to defer to me. These people have been told that the Adeptus

Astartes would come to them one day. They must believe I am in command if we are to leverage that properly. For now, I ask that you let me handle this.'

Copley stared back hard into his blood-red eyes.

'Trust me,' he told her.

After a moment, she nodded. 'For now, Scholar.'

Karras stepped past her and made his way towards the apparent leader.

He was ten metres away from the man when, simultaneously, every last rebel in sight dropped to his knees and pressed his head to the ground.

'Resh'vah!' they intoned as one. 'Resh'vah mukta akir!'

Karras addressed Copley and the rest of Talon, speaking low over the vox. 'They were told by their prophet that Space Marines would come. They believe we are here as a reward from the Emperor for their faith. Do nothing to refute that.'

'You read their minds?' asked Rauth.

Karras spread his arms wide, encompassing all the rebels, and gestured for them to rise.

They obeyed at once, eyes bright, so alive, their patience and suffering finally vindicated in the armoured vision of Imperial might that stood before them.

'I didn't have to,' Karras answered.

He crossed to the rebel leader, stopping four metres in front of him, and stared down at the man, eye to eye.

The burly rebel immediately dropped his gaze. Tears, Karras saw, were running down the man's cheeks.

He truly believes the salvation of his people has come at last, thought Karras. *They all believe it. And I must exploit their faith. I must feed the lie. Damn you, Sigma... You knew.*

Karras already saw where this was going. There was a tragic inevitability one needed no scrying powers to see.

Operation Shadowbreaker would bring destruction and death to these people, not the salvation they had long awaited.

Because we are not here for them. We are not here to save these people or this world. Only one is to be saved. Only Epsilon.

EIGHTEEN

The rebel leader, at Karras' urging, managed to put his awed reverence aside and introduced himself to the Space Marines and Archangel. Maktar Kainis was his name. His men called him *sahik* in Uhrzi, which approximated to *edge of the blade* in standard Low Gothic. He was a veteran – two decades of fighting t'au and kroot. The Speaker of the Sands had personally chosen his unit to meet the new arrivals here in the glade, having seen it all in a prescient trance, even down to the presence of the t'au strike fighters.

Karras had questions aplenty about this Speaker, but it was more important at that moment to be underway. The t'au might send another air patrol out before long.

On Kainis' orders, the rebel band turned east, moving from the clearing, most on foot, some on the backs of the loping beasts – called *jharaks* – that the Kashtu had tamed. They melted back into the forest, swallowed by deep shadow, heading to the crash sites of the downed t'au fighters. They would try to salvage what might be put to use. Only Kainis and one other – his aide, Touric – would fly north, guiding Task Force Arcturus to the Drowned Lands.

The two tribesmen joined Karras and Copley in Reaper One.

The camo-sheets and jamming modules were repacked, and everyone got back onboard. The three Reaper flight pilots powered up their turbines. With a long, throaty growl, the Stormravens lifted off from the clearing, leaving scorched grass behind.

They headed directly north, staying low, flying Nap-of-the-earth to avoid detection, following one of the great rivers that cut a broad highway through the dense trees.

As they skimmed over the river, whipping the branches of the trees on either side and kicking up a spray below, Archangel began to question the tribesmen. Neither was used to being addressed as an equal by a woman. They refused to look at her directly, scowled furiously when she spoke and gave long, pointed pauses before they answered her. When they looked up at Karras, it was in confusion, unable to imagine why he didn't strike her for such open insolence in the presence of men. As this continued, Karras sensed Copley tensing, edging towards the limits of her tolerance, readying to unleash her wrath on the tribesmen.

Pre-empting Copley's wrath becoming physical, the Death Spectre fixed his eyes hard on the rebels and said, 'This woman is a decorated warrior of the Imperium, leader of fighting men and a valued ranking member of this task force. Mark me well – if either of you shows her discourtesy just one more time in my presence, I permit her to cut your head from your body and throw it out of this aircraft.'

Both men paled and froze, gaping like fish. They had just

been threatened by a figure from legend, the Emperor's divine will made flesh. Together, they dropped to their knees before him and pressed their heads to the metal decking.

'Forgive us, resh'vah,' stammered Kainis. 'We did not... It is not our way for women to speak unbidden in the presence of men. Among the Kashtu, even wives must await permission before addressing their husbands. But our ways are not your ways. Leniency, lord. We meant no offence.'

'Nevertheless,' said Karras. 'Offence has been taken.' He turned to Copley. 'How many t'au have you killed, commander?'

Copley glared down at the rebels. Her voice was hard when she said, 'Confirmed personal kills – over thirteen hundred.'

'How many t'au have you killed, sahik?' Karras asked Kainis. 'How many of the blue-skins? Not kroot. Blue-skins.'

Kainis looked at the deck, abashed. He could not bring himself to answer.

The number was not even a tenth of Copley's count.

'It matters not,' said Copley at last, letting Kainis off the hook. 'What matters, tribesman, is that our enemy is the same.'

'But thirteen hundred,' muttered Touric. 'What manner of woman–'

'My people and I,' continued Copley, 'are specialists in counter-t'au operations. We have operated behind t'au lines for most of our military careers. There are none better. None. We were selected by the Holy Inquisition itself, highest agency of the God-Emperor beyond Terra's light. So listen to me very carefully. If you want to win this war, the biggest step you will ever take is to learn everything you can from us. Because you are losing it right now. And we are your best and only hope to shift the balance. Be clear on that.'

Karras watched the words take root in the rebels' minds.

'True that we do not know your ways, sahik,' he boomed. 'But while Space Marines are among you, it is *our* ways that matter. Be clear on that.'

'We... we have been a long time without the light of the Imperium, my lord,' offered Touric. 'You have only to teach us, and we will obey.'

Karras nodded. 'Even so, if you disrespect Major Copley again, you will have to fight her to the death in front of your men. And she will kill you and make it look easy, I assure you.'

Kainis swallowed and looked up at Copley from under thick black eyebrows. With effort, he said, 'Major, if by word or deed I cause offence, I ask clemency and that you tell me of my error. Let us spill blue blood together, and hope that no red mixes with it save that of the traitorous ISF.'

'ISF?' asked Copley.

'The Integrated Security Forces,' said Touric.

Copley stared back at Kainis a while, then extended a hand.

It must have hurt Kainis' pride, but he gripped it all the same.

Copley pulled him to his feet. 'The slate is clear between us,' she said. 'We start afresh.'

'Make sure the rest of your people understand,' said Karras. 'This woman and her storm troopers are agents of the Golden Throne. If any of your people treat them as less, Kashtu blood will be shed, serving the enemy's cause, not yours, not ours. Let all understand this.'

Karras had known such men before – other worlds, other cultures within the Imperium. For a Kashtu fighter to die in combat at the hands of a woman was very likely one of the greatest forms of shame imaginable.

The warning had been given, and clearly. Still, it seemed

inevitable that an example would have to be made at some point.

Kainis had risen to his full height, the compact Copley standing only as tall as his chest, but his aura had shifted into dull purples and greens. He was a man diminished in his own eyes.

That may yet be a problem, thought Karras. *Bitterness and resentment may fester in him. He'll bear watching. With luck, we won't be around long enough for him to make a fatal mistake.*

'I will instruct the others,' said the tribesman, 'but it will be better coming from the Speaker. It is the Speaker alone among us whose words carry the power of change.'

As the Stormravens flew further north, Karras and Copley pressed for details of Kashtu strength. How many fighters were there? How were they organised? What level of cooperation was there with the Ishtu in the south? What of material? Distribution? What of these haddayin, the infiltrators, maintaining and spreading their intelligence network from within the t'au-controlled cities and towns?

Kainis did his best to answer. Speaking in the presence of not one, but five of the Space Marines of legend was something he had difficulty processing. Since the Speaker had foretold of their coming, his hopes and expectations had run wild. In his mind, they were the fulcrum on which everything here was about to turn. And yet, facing them now, their massive black forms decorated with skulls and the iconography of death and war, he found himself unnerved. They did not radiate hope and light and promise as he had imagined. They were like cold black totems of death. Thick shadow seemed to cling to them.

He had always imagined them as perfect men, embodying all the qualities he himself prized and more. But here they were, and he found that they were far from human.

Whenever their leader, who had introduced himself as Karras but whom the woman repeatedly addressed as Scholar, looked at Kainis, the rebel felt his blood freeze and his soul wither.

The massive skull. The blood-red eyes. That corpse-pallid face…

Of the five Space Marines present in the hold of Reaper One, only Karras had removed his helm.

The other four… What terrible faces did they hide?

Their sheer size made them seem almost as alien as the t'au. No. These were not figures from the gilded pages of the old books, bathed in light, swords raised, radiant halos aglow. These were beings of terror and slaughter. Nothing he'd ever encountered caused him fear like this.

But perhaps, Kainis told himself, *that is exactly what we need.*

The woman was about to ask yet another question when another voice sounded over vox-speakers in the hold's ceiling.

'Got a landing beacon on the auspex,' reported Ventius from the cockpit. *'Short range. Imperial encryption. Old code, but verified.'*

'To guide us in,' said Kainis.

'Lock on and follow it in,' Copley voxed the pilot.

'Copy that, Archangel. There's a city just coming into view. You ought to see this, ma'am.'

Copley gestured for Kainis to join her. The rebel waited for some sign from Karras.

The Death Spectre nodded his approval.

At the front of the craft, there was little room, but Copley and the rebel were able to peer out from behind the pilot's seat and see the city slowly emerge like great black bones jutting up through dense banks of low cloud and curtains of torrential rain. It was a ruin, crumbling and rotten, every street and thoroughfare flooded.

Back in the hold, Karras donned his helm and interfaced with the aircraft's forward gun-picter. Through the link, he saw the home of the Kashtu in exile – Chatha na Hadik.

It was a dark, moody place. Above hung a sky so heavy it looked ready to fall and crush everything. All around, battered by the tremendous and unrelenting downpour, was a jumble of slender towers and vast, boxy mega-structures – high-density hab-blocks and manufactories, all built in the typical, functional style of the Imperium.

What had once been a thriving planetary capital was now, thanks to the aggressive planetary climate engineering of the t'au, a drowned and lifeless husk. Only, not quite lifeless, thought Karras. Though no living man or woman could yet be seen, he could already sense the psychic resonance of the million souls who called this place home.

A million, where once it held twenty times that.

As the city grew in the lens of the gun-picter, Karras saw that many towers had fallen, their bases ruined by a mixture of age, flooding, old battle damage and the aggressive invasion of the jungle itself, bullishly pushing in from the edges, claiming the space back now that only a fraction of its original populace remained.

Everywhere were the signs of destruction and decay. Towers hundreds of metres tall had teetered and tumbled drunkenly to lean against their neighbours, their windows shattered. From those broken windows, torrents of water plunged to the flooded streets, calling forth in Karras' mind the memory of the waterfalls at the great scarp on Irexus II.

But Irexus II was beautiful, he thought. *Natural. The sun was bright there, and the sky was wide.*

The scenes could not have contrasted more.

As the Stormravens passed through the outer districts,

Karras' enhanced eyes glimpsed movement from the shadowed upper floors of several of the tallest structures.

'We're being tracked by defence batteries,' he voxed to Ventius. 'All sides.'

'Confirmed, Alpha,' returned the pilot. *'Auspex scanners show passive tracking only. The ammo feeds are powered down. Do you wish me to jam them anyway?'*

'No,' said Karras. 'They won't fire.'

Copley and Kainis returned to the rear compartment. 'We'll be landing soon,' said Copley. She gestured to two vacant stations on the wall. 'Sahik, get yourself and your aide into those impact frames.'

Karras kept his attention on the gun-picter feed as the pilot swung left down a broad highway and angled towards a cluster of the tallest buildings in the city, most of which still stood upright as if in proud defiance of the weather and all the devastation that had been visited on their neighbours.

There was vox chatter back and forth between the pilots of Reaper flight and the heavily accented Low Gothic of someone on the ground. Despite the accent, this individual managed to guide the three craft in to land atop a broad, mid-sized block at the south edge of the cluster.

As Reaper One descended, Karras kept watch through the gun-picter in the assault craft's nose. He noted the dim red glow of landing lights. From a distance, in all this gloom and heavy rain, only those lights gave any indication of a landing pad. The building was otherwise unremarkable but for its relative lack of vines and other foliage.

'Brace for landing,' voxed Ventius.

A few seconds later, Reaper One shuddered as its landing gear touched the roof and took the craft's full weight. The sound of the engines receded to a whine then to nothing as Ventius shut them off. Reapers Two and Three touched down a dozen metres to the left and right. Several seconds after all three engines had powered down, the roof shook. Magnetic locks were released. Hydraulics hissed. A circular section encompassing all three Imperial aircraft began to descend into the structure below. Still watching through the Stormraven's gun-picter, Karras saw the platform lower itself into a gaping, lume-lit hangar. Several other aircraft – large cargo lifters, mostly – were present. They looked old and not in regular use. Above the Stormravens, two doors like massive plasteel jaws began closing overhead, blocking out the rain and wind.

After two minutes of slow, controlled descent, the platform reached the hangar floor, stopping with a short but violent judder.

Ventius voxed from up front. *'Clear to disengage impact frames. Opening hatches now.'*

Karras slapped the release trigger and pushed his impact frame up into the lock on the ceiling. The rest of Talon Squad did likewise, along with Copley and her people. The two rebels, having watched the others, followed suit.

The hatch pneumatics hissed. Light from the hanger spilled into the hold.

Karras was first to march down the ramp. At the bottom, he stopped and raised a clenched fist to halt the others.

All around him, thousands of people were on their knees, heads pressed to the ground, chanting with one voice.

'Ja hadiri! Ja hadiri!'

Talon and the rest of Arcturus had studied Uhrzi during warp transit. Karras knew what the words meant. They twisted and coiled in the pit of his stomach.

Hope has come! Hope has come!

NINETEEN

Copley would not back down. She was adamant.

'We've gone over this,' she told Karras. 'The inquisitor's wishes were clear. They represent a potentially critical resource for this mission, and they're desperate, ready to die for their beliefs. You *will* feed the fire, Scholar. I'm sorry, but that's the way it has to be.'

Karras' face was thunder. As he listened, Voss' expression wasn't much better. Neither liked the idea of exploiting a people who had fought loyally against the xenos for decades with no support. Chyron, too, was rumbling and venting black fumes.

Zeed, Rauth and Solarion seemed utterly unaffected by the notion.

For her part, Copley found it fascinating that among the six Space Marines, there could be such disparity. Her own people had been through this kind of thing before. They'd trained guerrilla forces on t'au-held worlds knowing full well that none of them would return alive, a diversionary force only to be spent gaining the main objective.

Whatever got the job done.

'I need you to do this, Scholar,' she reiterated.

Karras growled, his lip curling back over his teeth, but he readied himself to lead the others out onto the platform beyond the door and do as the mission demanded.

In the vast, echoing hall onto which it faced, tens of thousands of rapturous faces were already locked to the presence of a tall, willowy man of about forty years dressed in flowing robes of red and gold. He had been addressing them for several minutes while they listened with hushed reverence. Only the sound of his voice, sonorous and clear, rang on the cool, damp air.

This was the Speaker of the Sands.

In other great halls throughout the old city, the rest of the population watched via live pict feeds, patiently and eagerly waiting for the appearance of those long promised. Most had never thought to see this day in their lifetimes.

In each hall, the sound of the Speaker's projected voice echoed from stone walls draped with ancient Imperial banners. The image of the aquila was everywhere.

It might have been a scene from any of a hundred thousand worlds in the Imperial fold.

The Speaker addressed his people in Uhrzi, talking of their long struggle, their patience and faith.

As he listened, Karras noted how many of the words reminded him of the Occludian dialect of his Chapterworld. Thoughts of home began to threaten his presence in the moment. He forced them aside.

'We,' boomed the Speaker. 'We, the unbowed. We, the unbroken. We, the faithful. Long have we waited for this day. Raise your heads, brothers and sisters. See before you now the proof, at last. The God-Emperor has heard our prayers. His Space Marines have come!'

That was Karras' cue. With a last silent curse, he led the others out onto the platform and into sight of the assembly.

The reaction was immediate. As one, fifty thousand people fell to their knees.

At first, raw, stunned silence reigned. Then murmurings began. And spread. And soon, the air was filled with noise.

'Resh'vah!'

'The prophecy fulfilled!'

'They have come!'

'We have not been forsaken!'

And more – every variant of that emotion that made Karras feel anger and disgust, both at the Kashtu and at Sigma.

Damn you, inquisitor. Damn you for this.

The Speaker removed himself to the side of the platform and dropped to his left knee in obeisance before the Space Marines.

On the vox, Copley spoke. 'Now, Scholar. A sign they will never forget.'

Karras alone commanded the centre of the dais. The other members of Talon Squad fanned out in a line behind him with Chyron rearmost of all.

He removed his helm and gazed out over the kneeling crowd with his blood-red eyes. *So pitiable. So ready to pin all their hopes on someone else.*

He spoke with power and clarity, sure to keep his disdain from his tone. Amplified by the vox pickup in his gorget, his words rolled off the walls like thunder, shaking the air and the flagstones on which the people knelt. 'Brave Kashtu,' he began in perfect Uhrzi, 'loyal servants of the Emperor, enemies of the t'au, your prayers have been heard.'

Silence.

Then the sound of weeping followed by cries that echoed his words.

'The wait is over! Our prayers have been heard!'

This ran round the hall like brushfire. Some fainted. Others wept shamelessly, tears rolling off their cheeks, soaking into their robes.

Karras gazed out at them. Their outpouring of emotion seemed so extreme, so unnecessary. He didn't doubt it was genuine, but it was unsettling.

He understood that the Speaker had needed to keep the rebels together, keep the war alive. That meant binding the narrative of their war into their cultural identity, making it the whole context in which they lived their lives. Otherwise they would simply acclimate to the way things were. The fight would go out of them. They would settle for life under the t'au.

And once-powerful icons would lose their power. Is that not so?

He looked over at the Speaker as he thought this. The man was a fake. Not a whit of psychic ability in him.

Karras decided to move things forward. He gestured for the Speaker to stand and approach him. As tall as the man was, Karras dwarfed him, a vision of armoured death in black and silver. He looked down at the Speaker's face, lined and sparsely bearded, and spoke directly to him.

'You have led these people well, prophet. And you will continue to do so in the Emperor's Holy Name. Stand now on my left and face them.'

The Speaker bowed and, though he looked a little unsure, did as Karras commanded.

'Bear witness, all of you, the loyal, the faithful,' boomed Karras over the crowd. 'See your prophet at my side. His vision has come to pass. Now the real work begins. A great price must be paid. Rivers of blood must flow before the alien is purged from this world. Many will die on both sides before Tychonis is free. But the alien will not endure.'

He let the words sink in.

'The Emperor must be served,' he continued. 'Are you ready to do what must be done, even if it means your lives? Answer! And let your answer now stand as your unbreakable oath before His Adeptus Astartes!'

It started with a single man, a cry of 'My life for the Emperor!'

Another cried out, 'For freedom!'

And yet another, 'Death to the alien!'

Then a thousand cries. Then more.

Almost every voice in that hall was raised in promise. Those that stayed silent were the cowards and the meek, those less sure of their readiness to die for something greater than themselves. But they were so few as to be irrelevant. The Kashtu people had heard the call and answered.

Karras had his oath.

'Now,' voxed Copley. 'A sign to seal it. Something worthy of legend, Scholar!'

Karras flexed his power, opening himself up to the eldritch energies of the immaterium. In his mind, he formed the shape the power was to take. He projected it outwards, channelling it to manifest in the air.

New light, much brighter than that of the scores of sconces and lumes, began to shine down on the enraptured crowd. Awareness of what was happening above them spread like a ripple on a pond, only reversed – outward edges first, ripples moving inwards. Faces turned to the air above the centre of the great hall.

There above them, it took shape, an unmistakable icon

made real – a great two-headed eagle feathered in bright golden flames. It was vast, wings spread, their span almost half the width of the chamber. Karras held it there for seconds only, but before he let the manifestation pass, he caused it to loose a deafening screech from both beaks. The people below cowered in terror, innate fear warring with religious rapture.

Then the monstrous eagle vanished in a sudden burst of brighter light, leaving the people below momentarily blinded, grasping at each other for balance, blinking hard, rubbing their eyes.

The air above them was empty now, as if nothing had existed there at all. And of course, it hadn't. It was a lie. But he had done as ordered.

The people were silent, stunned. What little doubt any had harboured in secret had now been burned away.

Karras addressed Copley on the command channel, speaking through gritted teeth. 'I hope you're satisfied, major. They'd follow us into the Eye of Terror if we asked it.'

'Not subtle, Scholar,' she said, 'but it certainly did the job. Let's put a lid on this now and get organised. I want us to talk to this Speaker in a secure chamber at once. We don't want to be here any longer than necessary. Every hour we take may be an hour closer to Epsilon breaking under interrogation.'

Aye, thought Karras, *if she hasn't broken already. If she's even still alive.*

TWENTY

It was a simple room, the ceiling just tall enough for Karras to stand upright with a few inches' clearance. Warm colours dominated, the tones and hues of the desert sands at sunset, with a smattering of elements in midnight blue. The floors and walls were draped with traditional hand-woven rugs and wall hangings dating back to the tribe's desert days. Imperial iconography in red and gold was evident in most of them.

Copley and the Speaker faced each other in the room's centre, each seated on large cushions in the Kashtu style. Karras stood to Copley's right, level with her, like a fortified tower of black-and-silver stone. Nothing in the room would have supported his armoured bulk. He surveyed the space, absorbing every detail, and considered what the Speaker's choice to convene here might communicate, if anything. The designs and images woven into the fabrics were a link to the age of the great oceans of sand, an age which t'au terraforming had ended. It had been a hard age, one of terrible scarcity, and most Tychonites had been only too happy to see the end of it. But the Kashtu and Ishtu had seen in it the end of their culture, not to mention the insult of man ruled by alien.

Karras wondered if they ever stopped to think what it might mean to return to such times. Few alive now had even an inkling of what such hardship was truly like. Hard conditions made for hard people, but once a people had lived with ease and abundance, to regress by choice was as foolish as it would be difficult.

They might hate the blue-skin oppressors, but throwing off t'au rule should have been the limit of their ambition here. Not a return to a life of thirst and hunger.

How would that serve the Imperium?

Some are doomed to find their worth only in their suffering.

It was a quote from Yubelard's *Hand in the Flames* – a thirty-third-millennium work on mankind's quest for spiritual evolution. Idly, Karras wondered if Rauth would have recognised it.

As he thought this, an old woman – the oldest person he had yet seen among the Kashtu – entered the room with a small tray. She stopped just inside the doorway and cleared her throat to announce herself.

'Granted,' said the Speaker without looking at her.

With permission given, she bowed low, slowly and stiffly, and said in a reedy voice that matched her appearance, 'If it pleases my lords, an offer of small refreshment.'

Copley glanced at her and nodded, not paying the woman much attention, but Karras watched her with interest. He noticed something that Copley did not – though she had bowed in a manner commensurate with her advanced age, the tray she held did not shake. Not even a little.

His power flared gently as he assessed her aura.

He grinned, finding amusement in his discovery. He doubted Copley would take it as well as he, however.

The old woman quietly placed small beige cups in front of Copley and the Speaker, making herself as minimal an inconvenience as possible. She looked incredibly frail, her skin like liver-spotted tissue paper, barely covering the tracery of fine veins in her hands and face. She was hooded in the style of all Kashtu women when in the company of men to whom they were not married, so he could not see her eyes at first, but again he noted that her movements were precise and steady despite her great age.

His eyes were fixed on her while she arranged small dishes of several traditional foods – spiced nuts, dates and the like – before those seated. Again, not even a tremble.

Karras reached up and removed his helm. 'Old woman,' he rumbled. 'Here. Look at me.'

Copley turned and stared up at him from her cushion in confusion. Why was he addressing this servant? There was much to talk about with the Speaker and she was impatient to get to the matter of good, actionable intelligence.

Karras was so tall that it was difficult for the crone to meet his gaze directly, but she straightened as much as her bent back would allow and turned her head a little. So doing, she just managed it.

Under the dark shadow of her hood, Karras' superior vision could see a wry glint in her eye.

'My lord is troublesomely tall,' she said.

He leaned down towards her, stopping his face just a metre from hers.

Copley was struck with thoughts of how large a Space Marine's head is compared to that of a normal human – like the difference between a lion's and a baby's.

'Deception has a place and time, Speaker,' said Karras. 'This is not it.'

The old woman nodded, then turned from Karras and wordlessly placed the last of the dishes on the low table. She reached out a straw-thin arm and touched the knee of the Speaker, who, like Copley, had been watching the interaction in silence.

'Sleep now,' the old woman said softly and with obvious affection.

Abruptly, the Speaker's eyes rolled up into his head and he slumped backwards, his formal headwear falling to roll on the floor behind him.

The old woman patted his knee. 'My beloved boy,' she muttered. 'If only he had inherited my gift… But that is a selfish thought. Better for him that he did not.'

Copley was on her feet, pistol in hand, fast as a striking snake. 'Who the hell are you?'

Calmly, Karras reached out his left hand and forced Copley's pistol down. She glared at him, but she could not resist his strength.

'What is going on here, Scholar?' she demanded.

The old woman turned slowly and straightened, letting her act of exaggerated frailty fall away. Even so, at full height, she was barely level with Copley's chest.

She pulled back her hood. Her smile was deep and warm and real. The skin creased around her dark, bird-bright eyes.

Karras' grin widened. There was an appealing energy about this old woman. She was immediately likeable, radiating a special kind of good humour that only came with advanced age and depth of experience. It was a quality found in such few souls.

'Major,' he said, turning his face towards Copley, 'meet the Speaker of the Sands.'

Copley looked from the shabby old woman to the slumped body of the man to whom she had been talking since they arrived.

The true Speaker pressed her palms together in front of her forehead and bowed. 'Forgive me, honoured lady. But if not for the use of such subterfuge, I would have been dead long ago. And with me, perhaps, the hopes of my people.'

Copley's face twisted. She spoke to Karras, but kept her glare solidly on the crone. 'You knew?'

Karras shook his head. 'I knew something, but the woman's gift is powerful. She cloaked herself supremely well.' He addressed the old woman. 'For future reference, you ought to shake a little when carrying trays.'

In fact, Karras suspected the old woman had been deliberate in giving herself away.

She pulled a cushion towards the low table, this one for herself, and said, 'Will m'lady be seated?'

After a long moment, Copley conceded, but her expression did not change. She sat back down. The old woman now lowered herself onto her cushion so that she was facing Copley with the table equidistant between them.

Copley's voice was like cold, hard flint. 'I could execute you right now for wilful deception of an Inquisition officer.'

The old woman smiled. 'You could. But you won't. And the deception is a necessity, though I've long wished I could do without it.'

Copley bristled. 'What makes you so sure I won't?'

'If your information is as good as it ought to be, my lady, you already know my value. It is I who leads the two tribes. I am the spider at the centre of the web. I am the conduit for the information you will need to find your missing inquisitor. Lyandro Karras knows. Or suspects.'

'My gifts are not as yours, Speaker,' said Karras. 'I am no seer.'

'Then you will need me all the more,' said the old woman, 'if you are not to fail here. I have been preparing for this for a very long time.'

She gestured at the plates of dates and nuts. 'Will you eat with me while we talk? It is our custom.'

Copley's pointed hesitation indicated her reluctance to forgive the woman's boldness so easily, but she leaned forward and took a date anyway, and the old woman followed suit.

'My name is Agga,' she said. 'At least, that is how I am known to most. It means *old mother*. To them, I am simply the withered old woman who serves the Speaker.' She patted the knee of the sleeping man. 'I bring his meals, clean his robes, do all that a faithful servant would. In truth, he is my son, born brain-addled forty-one years ago. Kashtu culture is strict about such things – it demanded that I leave him out in the elements to die as a baby. But what woman can put tradition over her instincts as a mother?'

Here, she looked Copley in the eye. Perhaps she thought to find understanding there. If so, she was disappointed. Copley was all soldier. There wasn't a mothering bone in her body.

Agga shrugged. 'I hid his condition by using my gifts, by taking over his body and acting out his life whenever it called for him to be around others. Hard at first, but I quickly found my power growing the more I used it. Soon, others noticed that his words – the words I spoke through him – were sometimes prophetic. He began to gather a reputation. I suppose I got carried away. Before I knew what I was doing, he had become an icon of hope for the tribe – a role my gender would never have allowed me.'

She turned her gaze up at Karras, then back to Copley. 'I

was right not to let him die. A mother's love at first, but the wisest decision I ever made. I have been able to sustain our people this way. To give them guidance that has saved lives. I have kept us in the fight. I knew you would eventually come. I knew I had to hold out for that.'

'You deceive your people,' said Copley, 'and expect them to fight, even die for you. And they think they are dying for someone else.'

'Not for me,' said the old woman, face thrust forward, suddenly fierce. 'And not for him. For the end of t'au occupation. For a return to the Imperium. It is the *cause* for which they fight. My place in that, my son's place in that... They are matters of need, not of pride.'

She faced Karras, eyes shining, and said, 'I am the last psyker my tribe ever produced. It was my duty. I don't care if or how I will be remembered.'

'Have the t'au not sent assassins?' asked Karras.

The old woman settled back into her cushion, her ferocity extinguished as suddenly as it had flared. 'They tried several times when word of a prophet-leader first reached them. Had they sent psykers of some kind, they might have succeeded, but the t'au have none – at least, not here. Their intent to kill me made their assassins easy to locate along the threads of time.'

Copley scowled. 'If your sight is so powerful, Agga, it should be easy for your rebels to cripple the t'au. Why have you not done so?'

The old woman shook her head. 'Prescience is like a living thing, my lady. There are times it will show you precisely what you want. Most often, one must let it flow as it will. And we have always been hopelessly outnumbered and outgunned. No vision changes that.'

'They could have crushed you at any time,' said Karras.

Agga nodded. 'You've already guessed why they did not. Aun'dzi and Commander Coldwave are no fools.'

'Steel sharpens steel,' said Copley.

Agga shrugged. 'We are not much, but better than nothing in the eyes of the fire caste. How bored and indolent they would become without us. How listless and weak.'

'Here in the north,' said Karras, 'you command the Kashtu. What of the Ishtu in the far south?'

'I am Speaker to them also.' She glanced sideways at her sleeping son. 'Another proxy, though that one is unrelated by blood and has a mind of his own when I am not speaking through him.'

'With that radius of control, could you not have signalled the Imperium for help?' asked Karras. 'Astropathic relays at the edge of Imperial space could have brought your call for aid to other planets.'

'With amplification, I could have. An astropathic tower. There were once two on Tychonis – one in this very city. Both fell to ruin during the assaults of the Tall Ones in the pre-t'au years, deliberately targeted to ensure our world was isolated from support. The knowledge of their repair and operation was lost with those that died in them.'

Copley leaned forward, elbows on her knees. 'You know that we did not come to help your people, Agga.'

Any trace of good humour fell from Agga's face. Karras felt her warmth and light melt away. Her aura shifted, brighter colours giving way to muted ones.

'Tychonis is a fringe world,' she told Copley. 'Even in the days before the Dragon's Eye erupted and cut us off, it was barely worth notice to the rest of the Imperium. You came for the woman, Epsilon, whose prime futures are shrouded in fate as black as the feathers she wears. You came for her, for her knowledge, and a great many of my beloved people will die before you get it. *If* you get it.'

Her words hung in the air, heavy and dark.

'The business of the Ordo Xenos is the business of mankind's survival as a species,' said Copley. 'Our success or failure here has implications for all worlds. We do not ask anything lightly.'

Agga held Copley's gaze a long moment, then shrugged her narrow, bony shoulders. 'We are loyal to the God-Emperor, to the Imperium and the creed. And we are proud. We believe in strength and honour. We believe in the teachings of the saints. We live by these. And we honour, of course, the Adeptus Astartes. They are the God-Emperor's divine will made flesh. And yet, none of this – not one of these things – is the reason I will send my people to face death in service to your mission.'

'But you *will* allow it,' said Copley.

Agga nodded. Karras saw the warmer colours reemerge in her aura.

'Then why, Agga?' he asked.

The old woman smiled up at him, eyes shining like black gems, then leaned forward and picked up a date from the plate before her.

TWENTY-ONE

Copley was done.

Two days it had taken her to go through every bit of rebel intel. The Speaker had helped her make sense of it all, filling in any blanks where she could. For a withered old woman, Agga was mono-blade sharp. Her good humour made heavy work seem light. The time flew. Despite herself, Copley had started to like her.

It was easy to respect Agga for what she'd managed here, keeping these people together, committed to what was, more or less, a truly hopeless fight.

Not that liking her helped anyone.

As Copley took pains to remind herself, *Shadowbreaker* was all that mattered here.

During the two days she'd been immersed in data, the operators of Task Force Arcturus had been assessing the rebel fighters, their materiel, their organisation.

Then they had set about training them.

The rebels had been eager and quick to learn. They were already solid at close range. A few intense sessions with the Elysians quickly improved their mid- and long-range abilities too, to the extent that time and resources allowed.

Arcturus was well practised at bringing up the skills of locals in short order.

Talon Squad, though, had kept their distance. The Space Marines were rarely seen among the rebels. Whenever they did make an appearance, the Kashtu fell to one knee, heads bowed, or simply froze up and stared. Better that the armoured giants remained aloof.

Now, though, with all the knowledge she needed, the moment had come for Copley to assemble her key people.

Karras arrived in the makeshift Strategium to find the other members of the kill-team, with the exception of Chyron, already assembled around a bright, pulsing hololithic table. It was military grade, a well-preserved remnant from the days when this world still had a standing Planetary Defence Force. The massive Lamenter, too large to enter, was attending remotely via pict feed from Voss' helm.

Copley's sergeants were in attendance – her second-in-command, Vyggs, plus Morant and Grigolicz. So, too, were ranking war-band leaders, including Kainis and Touric.

The major looked up as Karras strode in and nodded a greeting. The Speaker, too – or rather, the false Speaker – bowed his head in welcome. Karras looked for the man's mother, his puppeteer, but she was present only through her proxy. Of all those in the room, only Copley and Karras knew that the man in the headdress and robes at the table's controls was not the real leader of the tribes.

With deft fingers, that man now punched a series of runes in the holo-table's control surface. Intersecting prisms of light cast glowing shapes in the air that quickly rezzed themselves into a highly detailed model of Tychonis and its moons.

Fingers flickered over yet more runes, and the projection zoomed in on a broad swathe of the planet's surface – a rectangular section of the equatorial region a thousand kilometres across. This projection rotated until it lay horizontal like a traditional map. The peaks, ridges and valleys were still rendered in exquisite three-dimensional detail.

'There are Militarum commanders who would kill to acquire one as fine as this,' said Sergeant Vyggs.

'How recent are the scans?' asked Rauth. 'Is this old geographical data?'

'Among the haddayin are a scant few who specialise in the stealing of t'au data,' said Kainis. 'Before he ceased to function, Enginseer Zagorian, the last of the tech-adepts on Tychonis, wrote a machine prayer capable of converting stolen data for our use with this table. This scan is a year old, but the haddayin tell us little, if anything, has changed.'

Zeed gestured at the currently magnified section. 'What exactly are we looking at?'

'Speaker?' said Copley.

Agga's son bowed politely and gestured at the hololith. 'This is a geoscan of the Hakkar. It's a region to the south of the Western Capital. As you can see, the area is riddled with deep canyons. We call this canyon complex Urq Gar – the Scarring of Urq – and it was once a site of holy pilgrimage. Here it was that Saint Isara found the lost temple. The t'au have another name for it.'

'What's our interest in the region?' asked Voss.

The hololith spun and expanded, zooming in, distant features becoming clear. It was a dry, desolate place, formed by ancient tectonic trauma, the scars of which were the gorges and deep crevasses that marred the land. The hololithic view continued to magnify, then to descend, a dive that took it to the floor of the widest of the canyons. Those around the tables watched as countless cave mouths and strange sandstorm-carved rock formations whipped past. The view opened out on a large oval valley, and Karras saw at once why this area was of note.

In the centre of the valley sat a high-walled complex, fortified to withstand assault.

'Looks like a containment facility,' said Sergeant Morant.

'A prison,' said Rauth from Karras' left. 'But not alien. That's Imperial architecture.'

'Right,' agreed Voss. 'The basic structure is Imperial. It looks like the t'au made a few additions.' He pointed to several installations atop the towers and walls – t'au defensive emplacements, characteristically rounded and smooth. The rock walls on which they sat were angular and rough, made of tan-coloured stone.

'It was once the planet's largest and most secure penitentiary,' said the false Speaker, 'built far from the cities so that the families of the guilty would not be able to visit them. It was called Alel a Tarag – the Tower of the Forgotten. Or simply Alel. The Tower. The Civitas Enforcers and Judges of the Adeptus Arbites sent many people there over the centuries. It was not a place from which one returned.'

'And now?' asked Karras.

'Now,' said the tribal figurehead, gaze hardening, 'it is loyal Kashtu and Ishtu who are imprisoned within. There are others, too, what the t'au call the rauk'na – those of their kind that resist the Greater Good. The blue-skins have been using it since their usurpation. For long years, we tried to get our haddayin inside. Eventually, we managed.'

'You have an asset placed within the facility?' asked Karras.

'A doctor of medicine,' said Copley.

'The t'au overseer at the Tower was concerned about the spread of disease among human inmates,' Agga said through her son. 'Since his appointment to the Tower medicae staff seven years ago, our man has managed to provide a good amount of intel.'

'Such as?' said Rauth.

The false Speaker glanced across at him, then back to the structure rendered in hololithic light. 'We have part of the layout, mostly the central block and north containment wing. We know that over three hundred human prisoners are currently kept there. Some are Kashtu like us, but just as many are Ishtu from the south. All show signs of torture. No matter how civilised and reasonable the words of the t'au ethereal appear, the reality of his regime lies just below the surface. The truth of the Greater Good is like a thin layer of paint over rusting metal. It takes but a fingernail to scratch it and reveal the foul nature of the xenos.'

'What else do we know?' asked Solarion.

It was Copley who answered. 'The latest update from the doctor arrived six days ago. In it, he relates that Commander Coldwave returned from the capital with several fully loaded transports. Within the transports were dozens of t'au criminals and dissidents, all chained at neck and wrists. No humans. A dozen of them were not taken directly to the south block as they would normally be.'

'Then where?' asked Rauth.

'It seems they were taken below ground. Somewhere under the central operations block.'

'Before the coming of your Epsilon, the rauk'na were only ever brought here in twos or threes,' said the false Speaker. 'Most were kept in city prisons.'

A ripple of intensity ran through the Space Marines around the table.

'She's there,' said Solarion. 'Could you have seen that, Scholar?'

'I told you already, the woman is protected from psychic tracking. Do you really think one of Sigma's peers would be so easy to find?'

The Ultramarine snorted.

'The Tower has always been hard to penetrate with astral sight,' said Agga's proxy. 'It once counted psykers among its inmates. There were wards in place. But, since shortly after Epsilon was sighted at Kurdiza, it has been even more difficult to survey.'

Over the vox, Chyron rumbled, *'Is there anything else to support this?'*

'The doctor believes he heard t'au guards discussing her bodyguards,' said Copley. 'Specifically, their smell.'

'Their *smell*?' echoed Zeed.

Copley grinned. 'With respect, the scent of an Adeptus Astartes is very… distinctive.'

'She's telling you to take a bath, paper-face,' laughed Voss.

Zeed almost got a retort off, but Karras cut in. 'The t'au have a highly sensitive olfactory sense, like a guard dog's.' He looked at Copley. 'That could be a problem for us going in.'

Copley shook her head. 'Not if you wear your helms. Ordo stealth enhancements to your armour suppress scent traces. Epsilon's bodyguards will have had their helms off as they moved among the t'au.'

'In any case,' said Rauth, 'it's clear that we have to hit Alel a Tarag. And fast, before things change.'

'I've been here far too long already without a foe to kill,' said Zeed.

'Do we know what she's doing there exactly?' asked Karras.

'She's clearly no prisoner,' said Copley. 'At least, not in the sense of others there.'

'We know she is involved in some kind of activity in the subterranean levels of the central block,' said the Speaker. 'The doctor has seen her twice only. Both times, she was entering restricted vators that lead to lower levels. Both times, she was in the company of armed fire warriors and her two Space Marines.'

'She had a full kill-team,' said Solarion. 'Where are the others?'

Copley shook her head. 'We have to consider that she may not want to be extracted. She may resist.'

They all processed that silently for a moment.

'What she wants is irrelevant,' said Karras at last. 'We have orders. The Ordo Xenos is calling her back in.'

'Getting in and out of there doesn't look like a very easy proposition,' said Voss. 'Look here. And here. This whole facility is as much a military base now as it ever was a prison. These towers on the encircling blast walls all have anti-air defences. These structures here are almost definitely fire caste barracks. That's an armoury, there. Given the size, I'd expect problematic hardware inside.'

Zeed leaned forward and gestured to another area. 'These are training grounds. See? This is a firing range. These are combat training areas. It looks like this rooftop here is built to handle small-to-medium-sized aircraft. Nothing bigger than a light transport, but it will be an issue if they have reinforcements within fast-response range.'

'Significant entrenched assets,' said Solarion, 'a difficult and very limited approach by air, potential enemy reinforcement during the op and far too many unknowns... This is damned little to work with. Gaining and maintaining situational control will be a tall order from the start.'

'MSRs?' asked Rauth.

The Speaker looked at him quizzically.

'Main supply routes,' explained Copley. Turning back to Rauth, she said, 'A single road running north-west and another running south-east. Both depend on several bridges to cross the canyon network on the way in to the Tower.'

'Some good news, at least,' grunted Solarion. 'Blow the bridges and we can at least isolate the facility from ground-based support.'

Copley nodded to Kainis and said, 'A chance for the Kashtu fighters to aid in the attack.'

Kainis and the other war-band leaders, each sporting a thick black beard and facial tattoos, all looked at their prophet-leader simultaneously.

The false Speaker smiled at them. 'A chance for our warriors to earn great honour and strike against the blue-skins openly. How could we refuse?'

White smiles cracked those typically dour faces, teeth shining against the black of their beards.

'We will hit them hard,' insisted one called Garum, 'and soak the sands blue.'

Karras shook his head. 'Under cover of stealth, you will rig their bridges and blow them. After that, if you must engage their infantry for your own satisfaction, you may do as you wish. Not before. Is that clear?'

The rebel leaders were not used to being addressed so, but this was a Space Marine. They bowed and, in obedient tones, replied, 'As you will it, resh'vah.'

The false Speaker spoke next. 'Alel a Tarag has never been attacked. The t'au charged with defending the bridges and patrolling the local area will have become complacent. I *know* my people can cut off those routes. Reinforcements by air, however, I cannot comment on.'

'We'll handle that if it comes up,' said Karras.

'If Epsilon were on the move,' said Solarion, 'it would be a damned sight easier to hit a convoy.'

'I concur,' said Voss.

Copley shook her head. 'We can't sit and wait for that. Our orders were clear. Locate and extract her as soon as possible. As far as we know, they still have no idea we're here. We need to go hard while that's still true. Situation superiority.'

'Getting in there unseen will be the first test,' said Karras. 'Just how do you plan to achieve it, major? Darkness means little to t'au battlesuits. Camouflaged or not, there's only one viable approach to the valley – right along the canyon. The turret defences studding the walls will be AI controlled. They don't feel fatigue. They never sleep. Even stealthed, our Stormravens will be detected with plenty of time for them to fire on us. If there's no backdoor, no way to strip those defences before an air approach...'

No one disagreed. Special forces doctrine depended on maintaining situational advantage for as long as possible. The smaller force had to keep things stacked in their favour, by any means available. There had to be something... something that would assure them at least a chance.

Having heard Karras out, the false Speaker nodded to one of the bodyguards at his side. The man moved off at once, leaving the Strategium via a door in the rear wall.

Zeed threw a quizzical look at Karras, but before Karras could offer any response, the door slid open again and the bodyguard returned, followed by a shrunken, half-lame old man with a carved wooden crutch.

Those assembled watched with varying levels of patience as the old man shuffled towards the hololithic table. When he stopped, leaning on his crutch to support himself, he was breathing hard. Still, he managed to bow his head and, with all the reverence he could muster, say, 'My lords. It is truly the greatest honour…'

The Speaker moved to the old man's side, placed a gentle hand on his frail shoulder and smiled down at him. 'This,' he told Karras and the others proudly, 'is Murhad Ganeen. This is the man who will guide you. It is Ganeen, beloved of the tribe, who will get you inside the Tower.'

'He can hardly stand under his own power,' Solarion said with a sneer. 'What qualifies him for the task?'

The false Speaker looked across at Solarion, meeting those cold grey eyes, unflinching. A smile creased his face. It was Agga's smile. All her motherly warmth and patience glowed there. Karras alone could see it. The false Speaker's aura radiated with Agga's own energy.

'He is the only man who can,' she told them through her son. 'Because he is the only living man ever to escape from the Tower alive. If the famed Lizard-in-Shadow cannot get you inside Alel a Tarag, no one can.'

TWENTY-TWO

So much cooler down here in the lower levels. Such a relief from the heat above. Gloomier, too, with no apertures to spill blazing daylight into the room and less artificial lighting than the upper levels. The relative gloom reminded her of the sconce-lit corridors of Imperial ships, of the dark sanctity of Ministorum chapels and Inquisition libraria. It made her feel more comfortable than she ought to among the hated aliens.

She glanced sidelong at the figure on her left.

Shas'O T'kan Jai'kal.

Shas'O, his rank. Commander.

T'kan, his planet. Tychonis to the Imperium. His for now only.

And Jai'kal, his name, the name by which she called him in her mind.

Coldwave.

He stood unblinking, unmoving, waiting for the procedure to begin. They'd both watched it before, of course, and more than enough times. But Epsilon never tired of it, never tired of the thrill that this might lead, as so desperately hoped, to something unprecedented and powerful, something that could change everything in the war with the Y'he.

Coldwave, for his part, seemed to watch out of some dark duty, a penance, a need to give witness to the horrors in which he was colluding for the sake of his race.

He had returned earlier that day with the latest shipment of prisoners from Chu'sut Ka. Before them now, on the other side of the impenetrable plaz, was the first of those prisoners to be processed.

If the fire warrior felt her looking at him, he gave no sign. He kept his eyes straight ahead, but she could see how tense he was. His fists were clenched. His jaw was tight. Silently, privately, she enjoyed his suffering. She might have to work with him now, but no amount of cooperation would ever override the deep training and conditioning the ordo had given her. The t'au were the lesser of two evils, but their turn would come, and the Imperium would erase their species.

But not while they are useful.

She turned back to the room beyond, where earth caste techs were strapping the lightly drugged t'au dissident down onto an operating table. This one was male, slight of build, with the fine-boned features of the water caste.

She wondered at the percentages. How many of the rauk'na belonged to each caste? Were there more fire caste rebels than earth or air or water? The t'au would never let her see that data. What they allowed her was so carefully managed. She, of course, never told them any more than she wanted or needed them to know. She and the xenos were locked in a strange dance of lies, half-truths and uncomfortable cooperation.

And all because of Al Rashaq.

She would never have come this far if not for the discovery in the ruins of that tyranid-ravaged world. Not what she had been looking for, but so important that it immediately superseded everything else. Even *Blackseed*. And though the strange, flinty smell of the t'au and their clicking, jabbering ways of speech grated on her badly, she would endure anything for the possibility to serve the Imperium as few on record ever had. She alone, after all, had finally found proof of that legendary, half-mythical installation. In all these thousands of years, only she...

Coldwave muttered something in T'au, not caring to slow or enunciate his speech for her benefit. It didn't matter. Epsilon's skills were sharp. She caught it.

'They are ready to begin,' he'd said.

She saw the earth caste techs hastily retreating from the room beyond the plaz, saw the prisoner struggling uselessly against his bonds. The drugs were wearing off now. The prisoner began shouting, railing in the T'au tongue against the techs as they left.

'What are you doing? What is this? Release me! I have done no wrong!'

The techs vanished through a portal to the right. Heavy doors hissed shut behind them, followed by the click-clunk of near-unbreakable locks.

Seconds later, a large rectangular panel in the ceiling began to lower itself on thick hydraulic pistons. Through the audio relay in the room, Epsilon could hear wet, hissing breaths.

The prisoner turned his eyes up towards the end of the panel that was descending towards him.

Slowly it came into view, a figure in clamps, restrained just as he was and yet not like him at all.

The dissident cried out in desperate fear and anguish.

We are enemies by birth, thought Epsilon, *but we share the same nightmare, and we face the same terrible darkness.*

The panel continued to descend. The monstrosity clamped securely to its upper side was limbless, arms and legs amputated, utterly unable to move anything but its grotesque head and neck. It was no less terrifying for all that, however. The t'au prisoner was wailing hysterically now, begging for aid, for forgiveness and release. Ancient tales of terror, fell visions of monsters glimpsed in sleep – none compared to the horrible reality of the visage that fixed its pale violet eyes on him.

Hungry, eager, unfeeling eyes.

Its jaw opened. Long, sharp teeth glistened with saliva.

'I am t'au,' screamed the rauk'na, eyes finding Coldwave's beyond the glass. 'Do not do this to me. I am your own!'

Epsilon cast another sideways glance at the shas'o. The muscles along his jawline rippled, but his breathing was slow and steady.

'You are not t'au,' he growled in low tones. 't'au serve the T'au'va.'

The panel ceased its descent now, juddering to a halt, bringing Epsilon's attention back to the procedure.

Only a metre remained between the faces of predator and prey. The genestealer's barbed tongue lashed out like a whip. Once. Twice. Still not close enough, but it sent the t'au prisoner into paroxysms of raw panic. Spit rimed his mouth. More flew with every scream. Epsilon recalled her surprise the first time she had watched a t'au infection, noting that the t'au had evolved tear ducts just as humans had and, just as surprisingly, wept from them for many of the same reasons.

That fact hadn't aroused any pity in her then. As tears rolled in rivers down the doomed prisoner's blue-grey cheeks, it aroused no pity in her now.

At the push of a button by one of the earth caste techs, the apparatus holding the limbless genestealer shunted forward about sixty centimetres. The prisoner's eyes went wide. All his panic and thrashing stopped dead. His mind had snapped, broken by the terror of the moment. The creature didn't hesitate. It plunged the sharp, hard point of its tongue deep into the flesh of the blue-skin's neck.

The rauk'na howled one last time, long and heart-wrenching.

For a moment, predator and prey were frozen there in a grim and horrific tableau. Then the beast retracted its tongue. The glistening prehensile flesh disappeared behind those terrible teeth once again.

And the creature became calm, its strongest urge satisfied. It had infected its prey as it had been born to do. It settled back into its restraints. The clamp retracted, pulling it away, and the panel began to rise back up into the ceiling, taking the monster from view.

The prisoner, too, was becalmed, dull eyes gazing into space. The moment the tyranid's tongue pierced his neck, it released not just its potent genetic material but a cocktail of sedatives, relaxants and mind-altering enzymes to ensure the prey did not fight back after infection, did not attempt to self-terminate before the package of tyranid DNA began to work its mutative effects. By the time the prisoner awoke, he would truly be one of *them*.

The sian'ha, the t'au called them. The word had so many nuances. Rendered in Imperial speech, it meant simply *the infected*.

To Epsilon and to *Blackseed*, however, they were so much more than that.

They were hope.

* * *

Coldwave refused to match the woman's pace. Her long legs ate up the corridor at a far faster clip than his, but he would not hurry himself on her account. So he forced her to slow down as they walked to the area she always referred to as *the creche*. On the way, they passed the doorways to the birthing chambers.

He scowled. He hated the noises from behind those doors. The sounds of t'au females giving birth should be a joyous thing, a music celebrating more members of the extended family that was their glorious race. But these births were dark, bloody, fatal affairs.

This thing we do dishonours us all, he thought. *And it is my hands that are the filthiest.*

The Aun had given ultimate permission, of course, but the project proceeded under Coldwave's direct authority. The terrible impregnations were each authorised by him alone. All the blood spilled here at the prison, at Na'a'Vashak, stained his name. And every time he passed these doors, the unnatural screeching of abominable newborns ripping their way out of their mothers' bellies reminded him all too sharply of it.

Of all the worlds in all the spheres, why did the damned woman have to be picked up closest to his?

They could have killed her outright. Should have, perhaps. But she brought with her the promise of an answer to the biggest threat his people faced. Aun'dzi could turn her away. All too well did the t'au know the devastation wrought by the tyranid race. The Y'he could be held at bay for a time, even redirected given adequate sacrifice, strategy and good fortune. But they could not be stopped. Time was on their side. Eventually, they would flood across the septs, consuming everything, and the glory and light of the t'au race would be snuffed out like a flame.

He gritted his tooth-plates. There was no way they could have refused the woman. She was not to be trusted, but without her research, without the data and the proposals and everything else she had brought to bargain with, there would be no hope for an end to the swathe of destruction the tyranids perpetrated with relative impunity.

He glared at her out of the corner of his eye. *This had better bear fruit, you pale-skinned serpent. Because if you have made us do this for no gain, I will sink my blade into you a hundred times.*

The sounds from the birthing chambers receded behind him. Coldwave realised he had sped his steps to expedite that, and became angry at himself, because he knew it would give away the depth of his discomfort to the woman. Did she enjoy his anguish at all this? Surely she knew by now how much it cost him every time. Easy for her. These were not her people they were inflicting horrors on. She claimed to have done much of that already, of course. Somehow, he suspected she felt just as little watching gue'la infection procedures as she surely felt watching the rauk'na.

The human Imperium's greatest monsters were not the war-mad giants in black armour – the hated Deathwatch. The worst of them were smaller, apparently weaker ones that pulled all the strings. He resolved to remember that. It was easy to forget when faced with the might and ferocity of Space Marines, but this woman was more terrible than either of her slaughter-loving bodyguards.

'I bring you the gift above all gifts,' said the woman suddenly as they walked abreast, 'and yet, somehow I fear you dislike me, shas'o.'

Had she read his mind? Did she have *that* power, too? Some of the gue'la, he knew, had impossible gifts. If she were such a one…

'You smell so badly of deceit,' he said, 'it hurts my face. How can any profess to like such a one?'

She laughed. 'Deceit? I give you the chance to save your people. Perhaps your only chance. I could ask for entire worlds, and such would be small payment.'

He was disinclined to respond. She often tried to provoke him like this. He refused to let it work.

Continuing in silence, they soon arrived at the doors of the creche. Heavily armed guards bowed in deference to the shas'o. He nodded back, enjoying their open disdain and lack of acknowledgement towards the foul woman, not that she seemed to care.

The guard on the left turned to a panel and pressed his hand to it, and the doors hissed open. Coldwave and Epsilon passed through into the space beyond. Automatic security systems tracked them as they walked the short inner corridor that led to the main chamber.

'Have the earth caste techs issued updated estimates on the birth of the first purestrains?' Epsilon asked.

'I would have told you,' he growled. 'This is new ground for us too.'

'That's why I said *estimates*, shas'o. The earth caste ought to have some idea by now.'

'The accelerated birth-growth-reproduction cycle is proving difficult to predict. A fourth-generation birth must be close. Perhaps today they will have news.'

More guards, more heavy security doors, and beyond these, Coldwave and Epsilon stepped out into a cavern-like space above a transparent floor of toughened acid-proof plaz. They stopped at the edge of a railing-rimmed walkway and cast their eyes down into the chamber below.

It was impossible to stem the sudden surge of loathing and innate fear at what he saw.

There were dozens of them. So miserably twisted. So sickening, like figures from the darkest imaginings of the pre-enlightenment age. Noting the movement above them, the abominations raised their heads, gazing back at him, eyes shining with unnatural light. Some hissed or screeched, and in their mouths he saw smaller versions of the razor-like teeth of the tyranid gene-stealers they used for first-stage infection. Many had additional limbs, the hands twisted into claws. On some, the hands had not developed at all – the bones of the forearms had grown into scythe-like blades.

Coldwave had seen such things on the battlefield. He had faced purestrain tyranid forms. While he had lived, many he had thought stronger and better than he had not. The memories still caused him pain. He recognised the hallmarks of the tyranid genetic material expressing itself in the horrors below, but these were stage threes. There was still much about them that was recognisably t'au.

And that made it even harder to look upon them.

'Several of these are far along,' said Epsilon. 'Ready for mating. Have any third-stage males been bred to third-stage females yet?'

'While I was at the capital, yes,' replied Coldwave.

There was an edge to the woman's tone now. He had ordered her and her bodyguards to be confined to the upper levels during his short absence from the facility. Much of the project was performed under her guidance, but he would not allow her access to the creche or the birthing rooms while he was not here to keep watch on her. There was still far too much she was withholding from them.

'If the accelerated gestations we saw in stages one to three are any indication,' she said, 'we could see our first pure-strain within a matter of days.'

'What then?' he asked. 'You assured us of isolation from the hive-mind, but how will we know it is permanent? How will we know it is not just the effect of your strange machine?'

'Your people are not as we are. There are ways to test for what we seek that I cannot explain in a way your science would understand.'

'Human witchcraft, then. I have seen it. It is not a subject on which we t'au are entirely ignorant.'

She grinned at that. 'There will be risks. I have told you already of the things I need brought from the Imperium. A rogue psyker for one. Alpha class. If you were not so adamant about vetting all my communications–'

'If our roles were reversed, you would do the same.'

'You want results,' she said with a shrug. 'You will have to make the requisite allowances. There is no reward without risk, shas'o.'

He bristled at the way she spoke to him. 'If you attempt to burn us,' he hissed, 'to betray the trust we've placed in you, I swear you shall be the next one strapped to a table to await the 'stealers' kiss.'

Epsilon's face was a mask of absolute passivity. Not a single flicker of emotion crossed it. 'I don't doubt that, commander,' she replied. 'Just remember that the Aun was free to reject my offer when I came to you. Suggesting an alliance took great faith and sacrifice on my part. It was no small thing to come here without the authorisation of my superiors, but I stand by my decision. Aun'dzi understands the need, as do you. Neither your race nor mine can hold back the dark-that-swallows-all forever. And what I ask in return is so little – data that cannot hurt you, safe passage through your space. There is no knife hidden in my sleeve, no poison waiting to be slipped into your cup, shas'o. We see this through, and you may or may not get the weapon your people need.

In any case, I get my promised safe passage, and you will not see me again.'

Coldwave did not look at her as she spoke. As he listened, he found himself locking eyes with one of the mutations below. The creature glared at him, its face a sick and twisted mockery of his own, still t'au enough to be recognised as such, but too tyranid to be allowed to live. It twitched and trembled with the compulsion to kill him, working its jaws as if it was already tasting his flesh.

Curse them, he thought. *Curse them all, gue'la and Y'he both. And curse us for entering this damnable bargain. It may save our race, but it will rob us of all honour first, and the blood may never wash off.*

TWENTY-THREE

Even with night-vision goggles set to full illumination, the going was tough. The walls of the tunnel were craggy and sharp – natural formations unsmoothed by the hands of men. Perhaps that was why the old tunnel still existed at all. It was unworked because it was unknown, not present on any map. Old Ganeen was the only one ever to get out this way, and that was the year before the coming of the blue-skins.

Ganeen's memory of all the forks they had to take and tiny spaces they had to scramble through had not dulled even a little in all the years since he'd gained his liberty. Again and again, the old man surprised Copley and her team. Every time she was sure she was looking at a dead end, he would push past her with a cackle and shuffle straight over to some utterly invisible gap in the rock. And they'd all be moving again.

Without him, depending on his map and his notes alone, Copley and her infiltration team would have lost hours scouring the walls of each of these false dead ends for the way forward.

Back at the Kashtu base, she had almost insisted that he stay. Ganeen was physically frail, and would almost certainly be a burden to her team. A younger, colder Copley would have denied him his request for a last trip on the spot. His intel, she had thought at the time, would be enough. So why did she concede? On the flight south, staring at his lined and weathered face in the back of the Stormraven, she had searched herself for an answer and found none that satisfied her. Was she growing sentimental?

Now, with the need for his guidance so apparent, she put it down to some intuition, something her subconscious mind had caught but that her conscious mind was too arrogant and judgemental to see. She was damned glad he'd come along.

Up ahead, Triskel, currently on point, pulled to a halt and threw up his right hand.

She moved up to stand beside him and found herself on the very edge of a gaping black chasm.

She shone her flashlight down towards the bottom of it. Nothing. The light hit nothing.

She heard Ganeen chuckle behind her. 'This was the hard part,' he said. 'This was the part where I was surest I was doomed to die.'

Triskel was shining his light to either side. The chasm filled the tunnel completely. No ledges. He turned it to the walls, looking for handholds. They were smooth.

'Lower, boy,' said Ganeen. 'We have to go down a bit to go across.'

'You crossed this?' asked the trooper with some doubt.

'I didn't have a choice.'

'We don't either,' said Copley. She smiled at him. 'But we have the Lizard-in-Shadow, and he's done it before.'

The old man grinned up at her, a gummy smile with just

a handful of remaining teeth. 'I have to go first. I can't tell it to you, not so as you'd make it alone. I have to show you.'

'Do you still have what it takes?' she asked him dubiously.

He thrust his chin at the far side, shrouded in blackness even the squad's night-vision goggles couldn't penetrate from this distance.

'For all our sakes, let's hope so,' he replied.

Ganeen led. Copley followed. Then Ryce, Grigolicz, Morant and Triskel. Grig was the strongest so, with everyone roped together, he was in the middle, the better to help out if anyone on either side of him fell. And if he fell, he'd have both Ryce and Morant to pull him back up.

It was beyond difficult. Without Ganeen, it would have been truly hopeless. How many times in his mind, in his dreams, had he relived this deadly crossing? His old, big-knuckled hands unerringly found each invisible handhold, exactly as he remembered them. Twice he almost fell, but due to frailty, not to any mistake in his memory.

Both times, Copley moved forward beside him, drove a piton into the rock wall to secure both of them, and made sure he was good to go on. The pitons and lines would give them a chance to recover if one or two members slipped at once, but if more than that went down, she knew they'd all die. The rock was just too brittle to support the pitons if three fell.

And so it went, metre by metre, with the old man methodically leading them from hand- and foothold to hand- and foothold, his eyes closed, feeling his way, remembering, until at last they rounded a final bend in the wall and began the climb up the chasm's far edge.

Sweating, breathing through clenched teeth, Grigolicz and

Morant pulled Triskel over. For a moment, they all sat or lay sprawled on the rock.

'I never want to do that again,' murmured Ryce.

Copley looked at the old man. In the torchlight, his eyes were bright, like shining black gems. He looked vibrant, like the years had suddenly, miraculously dropped away from him.

'Feel more alive than I have in decades,' he chuckled.

'Thank you, Ganeen,' said Copley.

'That was really something, old man,' said Grigolicz, grinning broadly.

'Still a little ways left,' Ganeen told them, 'but it gets a lot easier from here.'

It did.

He had them scramble up a few walls to ledges that were invisible from the tunnel floor. He showed them around rocks to apertures that were just big enough to squeeze through. But then something about his energy, his demeanour changed, and Copley felt that this was a moment the old man had been waiting for.

'This is the last one I need to show you,' he said as he pointed along a narrow fissure in the rock she hadn't even seen until he had drawn attention to it. 'After this, you just follow the map I drew. There's nothing hidden from here. It's just about choosing the right tunnels now.'

She glanced at her men then back at Ganeen. 'You can come with us into the base,' she said. 'You'd have to stay in the tunnel underneath it, but when we extract, if you're quick enough to get out and get on one of the Stormravens...'

The look in his eye stopped her. 'That's not how this is meant to go,' he said. 'This place has been waiting for me, just like I've been waiting for you. Speaker said so. I'd have died years ago 'cept he told me I had to live on till you people showed up.' He tapped his chest. 'Got the rot in here. Six years now. But the Speaker told me. He said, *The Lizard-in-Shadow must wait for the coming of the resh'vah. The Imperium has a need for you, Ganeen. You cannot die until you fulfil it.* So I lived. But now I get to rest.'

'Here?' said Copley.

'I'll go back a ways. Sit by the chasm's edge a while. See if the God-Emperor will spare me a word or two now that I've done my duty.'

He chuckled, turned and pushed past the troopers, all of which towered over him.

As he passed them, each put a hand on his shoulder and said, 'Ganeen.'

When he was a dozen metres away, he half-turned and spoke one more time. 'Never met a woman who was more warrior than a man before, major. Reckon those blue-skins have no idea of the storm that's about to hit them.' He laughed and turned back in the direction of the chasm. 'Give them hell, girl!'

Then he was gone, swallowed by shadow, off to make his final peace with himself and see out the last moments of a long life.

For a few long seconds, Copley stared at the curve of rock around which he'd disappeared. He'd looked peaceful. Ready. She wondered if she would feel like that when her time was up. She and her men were about to enter a base crawling with t'au forces. Nothing they hadn't done before, of course, but any time could be the last. No one on her task force expected to retire.

'Ma'am?' said Ryce.

She looked up and found him staring at her. 'Lead on, Ryce.'

He nodded and set off along the narrow path Ganeen had shown them they must take. The rest of the squad followed in silence.

They edged along in the close confines of the tunnel like worms, the rocks scraping at them and their loadouts, forcing them to adjust their kit frequently, to exhale and push hard to get through the narrower spaces. Packs and weapons often had to be dragged along behind them, with one of the operators at the back to help push them through whenever they got caught or stuck, which was more frequently than Copley would have liked. And all the time, the mission chrono kept ticking off crucial seconds.

Talon Squad and the rest of the assault force was counting on her. She couldn't afford to fail. Karras and the others couldn't rush the facility while the defensive batteries were still in play. They'd be shot down without any chance to fight.

In truth, Copley was anxious – not about gaining access to the facility, not so much about any resistance she and her team would face, but more about getting into the t'au electronics systems and shutting them down. Reading and operating t'au holo-menus systems was one thing. She'd done that before in the field. But an ultra-secure facility like the Tower? Surely there would be encryption, and not light encryption either. With the possible exceptions of spaceports, fire caste headquarters and t'au intelligence hubs, the systems at the Tower were probably the most secure on this planet. She had brought her best people for this, but there was no guarantee it wouldn't be beyond them. So much could go wrong.

So what's new? she thought.

Sigma had made sure Copley and her people were superbly equipped for *Shadowbreaker*. The inquisitor lord knew these were long odds. Some of the new toys her people had been assigned were impressive. That thing Morant was carrying. That hacking module. Her task force had not been given access to something like that before. It was something new, at least to her. Great if it worked. But she knew better than to trust mission success to tech. It was people who carried the day. All the advanced gear in the galaxy wouldn't mean a damn without the right people for the job. She looked ahead at the back of Sergeant Morant and was reassured. The short, surly former drop-trooper had been extensively trained by the tech-priests of the Mechanicus in the use of the module. In fact, just in case Morant went down, several team members had been educated in its use, but Morant had a natural talent for the thing. She was counting on him to secure the t'au security and control networks at the Tower when the time came.

Such rare technology. If only she'd had it in her Militarum days. So many lives…

It paid to be part of the Ordo Xenos.

Even so, she thought. *Even so…*

This whole op still hung by such a fragile thread. Common sense told her it was madness for Talon Squad and the others to try to force their way in if she and her squad failed in their infiltration, but the importance of acquiring Epsilon, knowing she was here, was so paramount that, even if Copley and her four-man unit died before taking out the anti-air batteries, the Deathwatch Stormravens would still launch their assault.

They'll be swatted out of the damned sky, but they'll fly in and try for it anyway. We can't risk giving the t'au a chance to move Epsilon. We take her here and now.

The point man, Sergeant Grigolicz, voxed her from up ahead.

'The tunnel opens out here, ma'am. Room to stand. A little cavern about two metres high, three metres across. Just like the old man said.'

'Understood,' Copley replied as she pushed forward through yet another tight bottleneck in the rock walls. 'Start checking the cavern roof. Ultraviolet. Infrared. From what he said, the seam can't be discerned with the naked eye.'

Grigolicz was still searching for it when Copley, Ryce and Morant joined him. Morant hung back at the entrance to the little chamber, helping Triskel get the kit through the last gap. When it was done, Morant turned his goggled eyes to the ceiling with the others and helped search. Triskel unhooked the squad's portable auspex scanner from his webbing and adjusted the dials, eyes glued to the tiny lambent screen.

'The old guy must've been good in his day,' said Morant. 'He did this in complete darkness, right? I can't find a damned thing, even with the goggles at max, ma'am.'

'Nothing on the auspex either,' added Triskel.

Copley stopped what she was doing. 'Turn them off.'

Morant turned to her. 'Ma'am?'

'Your goggles. All of you. Turn them off. He didn't depend on his eyes. Neither will we. Use your hands. Just feel for it – a tiny seam with the slightest give. It's here somewhere.'

Unless it was discovered and sealed.

No. She wasn't about to accept that. It had to be here.

She pulled off her combat gloves, reached up to the ceiling and let her fingertips probe the rock inch by inch.

Eight minutes later, Morant muttered, 'Wait. Ma'am, I think I've got something.'

He didn't move until she was right by him. Even then, he kept his fingers exactly where they were lest he lose the seam.

Copley reached up, her fingers tracing the rock in a small

circle around his own. And there it was. There was the slightest give in a part of the rock when she applied upward pressure. This was what the old man had talked about. This was the aperture through which, malnourished and blind in the dark, he had dropped, not knowing what was below. Luckily for him, and now for Copley and her people, he had not plunged to his death but instead had found a narrow, twisting path to freedom.

He had found his way out and back into the hands of the tribe that had counted him among the Vanished.

And there he waited... for us to come. Thank you, old man.

Too early for thanks, perhaps. The aperture could still have been sealed from above in the intervening years.

Thinking this, Copley freed her knife from its shoulder sheath and worked the point into the seam, then dragged it along, clearing it.

'It'll be heavy,' she told her squad. 'I want the four of you right underneath it, pushing directly up. When it comes free, shift it gently to the right. Take your time. If any of the blue-skins are in earshot...'

Carefully, the squad pressed the slab-like rock free and, with great care and patience, moved it out of the way. At first, it was silent, but as the space opened further, Morant and Triskel had to let the stone go. It was up to Ryce and Grigolicz to push it aside, and that meant the unavoidable sound of heavy stone scraping on stone. They took it as slow and steady as they could. When they were done, all five members of the unit waited, breath shallow, ears attuned to the slightest noise.

Triskel took the auspex from his webbing again and slowly swung it full circle.

'Nothing showing, ma'am.'

'OK,' said Copley with a nod. 'Looks like we're still good to go. Grig, back on point. Get up there.'

'Aye, ma'am,' said the soldier, and he hauled himself up into the darkness of the space above the chamber. Seconds later, his gloved hand appeared, thrusting downwards to grab his weapon and pack. Triskel handed them up.

'How is it looking?' asked Copley.

'Cramped,' said Grigolicz. 'Water and power lines everywhere. Looks like the t'au didn't change any of this. No sign anyone has been down here in a long time.' He was silent a moment, then added, 'Nope. Nothing running through them now. Obsolete. The blue-skins must've installed their own systems on the upper levels. Looks clear, ma'am. Not seeing any laser trip-lines or monitor lenses. No electronic signatures.'

The blue-skins are confident, thought Copley. And why wouldn't they be? Since they'd arrived, this planet has been theirs. With the exception of a token rebel force they could obliterate at any time, there was nothing on this world to make them think an assault on the Tower would ever come.

Not that she was about to get complacent.

'I'm up next,' she said. She moved underneath the opening. Again, Grigolicz thrust his hand down. She grabbed it and jumped, and was swiftly pulled up. A moment later, she reached down and Triskel passed up her kit.

In the unnatural green hues of her goggles' vision enhancement, Copley made out a low-ceilinged tunnel filled with a jumble of old pipes and cables. It reminded her of dense jungle strewn with creepers. She wondered if cutting through any of the tangled cables would give her and her people away, because it looked like they may well have to do so in order to press further. The floor of the tunnel was natural rock, but unlike the little cavern below, this had been cut by las and plasma tools. It was easy to see that by the melt marks. The ceiling was smooth and angular – thick blocks of grey rockcrete reinforced with girders of riveted iron. There was just enough room to walk hunched over, but the profusion of pipes meant dragging their packs behind them in some places.

'Tris?' she murmured.

The trooper checked his auspex. 'Lot of interference here, ma'am. But again, nothing showing. No movement.'

She activated the holo-compass on her left wrist then tapped it off again. 'The old man said to go north from here, about two hundred yards. There should be an access hatch, but it's not the one we want. Another hundred yards after that, the tunnel swings east. We're looking for the first access hatch in the ceiling after we turn that corner. You got that, Grig?'

'Moving off now, ma'am.'

By the time they found the hatch they were looking for, Copley had noted the sweat running from her hairline and down the back of her neck. It was getting warmer the further they went.

Good. It meant they were closing on an energy source somewhere above them. They were pushing deeper into the complex.

Carefully, her men opened the hatch, senses hyper-alert. There were no xenos awaiting them above. This part of the complex seemed to be more or less abandoned, or at least infrequently patrolled. One after another, Copley and her team hauled themselves up.

After handing his pack and weapon up to Triskel, Ryce was the last to ascend. He, Triskel, Morant and Grigolicz replaced the stone hatch as carefully and quietly as possible while Copley surveyed their surroundings and checked her holo-compass again. With the hatch back in place, the squad stood in a rough circle, backs to the centre, weapons raised, awaiting Copley's command. To the north and south, the corridor ran off into pitch darkness. There were work-lumes set in the walls, glowing a dull red, enough light that the squad no longer needed their goggles.

The air was alive with the deep humming of some kind of power generator. Copley moved to the wall on her left – the west wall – and pressed her cheek to it. The rockcrete was warmer than the air temperature suggested it ought to be. Listening hard, she thought she recognised the sound. That particular tone and frequency was familiar.

'A large-scale plasma generator,' she said. 'Two or three levels above us. Probably the main power source for the whole base.'

She'd blown up more than a few of them in her time.

'Explains the interference on the auspex,' said Triskel. 'Damn thing is all but useless in here.'

'Ma'am,' said Ryce, 'shouldn't we rig it to blow? We could take down every system they've got. Plus it would be a hell of a diversion if we find ourselves pinned down.'

Grigolicz snorted. 'Taking down their systems like that could cut off access to our primary objective. Besides, they'll have a backup for critical systems. Maybe even a backup for the backup. We'd just be kicking the nest.'

Ryce was the youngest – fastest with a blade, deadly accurate with a lasgun, able to move as quietly as a leaf on a breeze when he had to – but he lacked the long experience of the others.

'We'll ignore the generator,' said Copley, 'and stick to the original plan. We get inside their security systems and take things from there. This is no demo job.' She gestured up the tunnel with the muzzle of her lasgun. 'Up ahead should be the old stairwell Ganeen used. From there, we make our way to the sub-tunnels that run under the storage block. Just pray to Terra and the Golden Throne that the blue-skins haven't dumped a bunch of heavy crates over our only access point.'

Copley's luck or the Emperor's blessing – whichever it was, it held. The t'au hadn't covered the final hatch. There were no crates atop it. She and her men slipped into the vast, gloomy space of a storage depot on the east side of the facility, not far from the north wing where Alel a Tarag's human inmates were kept.

They heard movement as soon as they emerged. Copley signalled for everyone to stay low and hang back, then slid from cover to cover until she had a better vantage point.

T'au voices, jabbering and clicking as they always did.

She knew the dialect well. Two low-ranking earth caste members on a rest period making small talk about their most recent arranged matings.

This depot was being used mostly for the storing of foodstuffs, judging by glyphs on the containers. A southern section was given over to banks of equipment for the recharging of power modules. Two modified TX4 Piranha skimmers were parked just inside the rolling plasteel shutter of the west wall. They were without armament, probably just used to taxi supplies over to whichever prison block needed them.

Aside from the two earth caste workers closest to Copley, a mix of t'au workers and human auxiliaries moved to and fro, ticking things off on checklists or hefting crates.

None had noticed the arrival of the five Imperial soldiers.

Copley returned to her team and pointed up towards the ceiling. 'That's where we need to be. That upper walkway.

There's an observation room top and centre. It'll be manned, and there will be some kind of control and communications systems there. Let's not give them anything to report. Once we pass the observation room, we continue on the gangway going north. There's an exit in the north wall, upper level. You see it? From that, we can access the enclosed bridge that will get us into the mid-levels of the central block. It doesn't look like they modified the general structure of the place all that much. That's good for us. The old stairwells should still be in place. We don't want to use t'au vator shafts. Careful and quiet. Any one of you gives us away, I'll shoot you myself.'

They grinned at that. They'd heard it before.

She motioned for them to follow and, one by one, with adaptive camouflage systems blending them into the background, they moved from cover, quietly making their way to the plasteel frame that supported the overhead walkways.

Copley went up first, climbing swiftly and silently, her slender muscles bunching and rippling as she pulled herself from strut to strut. Within moments, she was at the top, crouching on the gangway.

She wasn't even breathing hard. It was good to be out in the field again, to feel alive like this, to put her skills to use. At times like these she knew she wouldn't have traded this life for anything.

Crouching low, trusting the others to keep pace, she moved along the walkway towards the door of the depot observation room. When she reached it, she crouched at the edge of the doorframe and slung her lasgun over her shoulder. She drew a wickedly curved, black-bladed knife, flipped it into a reverse grip and waited.

Ryce joined her first, settling against the opposite side of the doorframe and throwing her a nod. Within seconds, the others had stacked up beside them.

Copley used battle-sign, her fingers forming words and sentences in place of her mouth. In this silent language, she ordered Ryce up and over the roof of the control room and down onto the walkway on the other side.

It was risky, sending one of her team up and over like that. A single noise at the wrong moment might give them all away. If even one of them were spotted at this early stage...

But she trusted Ryce. Since his selection for Arcturus four years ago, she had shaped him, moulded him, to the point where he, like every other operator on her team, felt almost like an extension of herself, like a particular sword in the hands of a master swordsman, like a part of her own body.

As Ryce pulled himself up and crept across the roof of the room, he moved with the cautious stealth of a panther approaching skittish prey. His every movement was careful and coordinated. In due course, he dropped silently down to the walkway on the other side and hunched himself against the doorframe. And there he waited.

Copley nodded to the others. She reached up a hand and tested the door. As expected, it was unlocked. Slowly, carefully, she pulled it open and moved silently inside.

A stocky t'au in a dark blue jumpsuit sat at a bank of monitors and controls, munching on the pungent black seeds that the earth caste seemed to love so much. Copley knew the smell. The seeds were toxic to the human liver, but the earth caste t'au couldn't get enough of them, snacking on them almost constantly.

That crunching and munching was her ally right now. As she crept quietly and carefully towards the t'au's back, all he heard was the sound of his own grinding tooth-plates.

Earth caste.

Unmistakable, and not just for the smell their favourite food gave them. Their bodies were shorter compared to those of the other castes, but far denser, far thicker in bone and muscle. Approximately five feet in height, some weighed in at a hundred kilograms, and they were never fat. They were the lifters, the labourers, the inventors, the creators, the engineers.

Copley raised her knife and readied herself for a clean, swift killing blow.

Exhaling between her teeth, she put considerable strength behind her strike. The point of the knife bit her victim exactly where she wanted it to – between the third and fourth vertebrae, utterly separating the key nerves located there and immediately paralysing the target.

The body shuddered. There was a soft sucking sound as the t'au desperately fought to breathe with lungs that were no longer responding. The blue heart slowed and died, and the inert form of Copley's victim began to slide from its stool.

Copley caught it, grunting at its weight, and lowered it quietly to the floor. She quickly checked the control console for any glyphs that would indicate security systems or door locking mechanisms.

There was nothing to suggest emergency security systems, but she found a small bank of glyphs relating to door locks on the closed bridge between the storage depot and the central block – that part of the Tower from which its name had originally come.

Briefly forcing her thoughts into the T'au language, Copley manipulated the controls, punching alien glyphs, unlocking every portal between here and the main block, before turning to her operators and signalling them to move through the room.

Stealth systems still fully engaged, they passed her, joined up with Ryce on the other side and proceeded along the walkway.

Copley came up last. Glancing down, she saw that their presence had not been noted. The t'au and their adopted human workers went about their business oblivious to the killing that had just taken place.

She hoped that would last long enough for them to gain the main control centre. Compared to that, getting in this far had been a breeze.

She knew it wouldn't last.

The first kill had been made. Many more lives would end this day.

TWENTY-FOUR

Karras stood in the shadowed mouth of a cave high in the cliff face, his helmet optics gently whirring, zooming in and out at his mental command as he scanned the outer perimeter of the t'au facility. It wouldn't be long till sunset. He hoped Copley and her team were as far along in their task as they were supposed to be.

The t'au were a diurnal race. Just like humans, they had fought back the night, first with fire, then with electricity. With the need for the fire caste to operate effectively in the dark, night-vision capabilities had followed, built into their helms and battle suits.

And then they'd gone beyond that, fitting their drones with advanced multi-spectrum optics and energy sensors.

Even now, as Karras studied the walls of the Tower at range, that advanced t'au scanning technology would be sweeping the surrounding area, most likely in the form of surveillance and security drone patrols.

At least they didn't have psykers. Not among their own kind. Sigma's data indicated no Nicassar or other t'au-aligned psychic races were present on Tychonis.

One less thing to concern him.

He had sent his spirit out, murmuring the mantra of Sight Beyond Sight, searching, questing for signs of life, the glow of sentient souls.

T'au didn't register strongly in the immaterium. Comparing their aura to that of a human was like comparing a candle to a city on fire.

Or a burning forest.

Memories of his visions in the eldar machine threatened to rise up and distract him. He snarled and slammed shut the doorway to that room in his mind.

Down on the canyon floor and up on the far side, on the plateau above, he sensed the simple spirit energy of desert creatures. He sensed other things, too – humans held within the Tower's north block and beings of other races as well, though these were very few. What bothered him was that the psychic signatures of those souls were much dimmer than they should have been. There was a strange fogginess to his astral sight. It couldn't be a t'au thing. They knew so little of the warp and the realm of the immaterial. As the Speaker had mentioned, the prison blocks had old pentagrammic warding, but this seemed to be something different. For a start, there was a different resonance to it, and it seemed particularly powerful at its centre, a single location somewhere beneath the main tower, the place where Epsilon was rumoured to be.

Whatever it was, it kept his astral presence at bay, unable to proceed where he willed it to go. It was like trying to push two magnets together. He kept sliding off to the side.

He soon stopped trying and withdrew his astral self into his physical body.

The sun was beginning to set in the west, flooding the valley floor with warm liquid light just before it dipped below the horizon.

He turned his gaze to the walkways high atop the perimeter walls of the Tower, visor optics zoomed at maximum magnification. In the day's last light, he saw t'au sharpshooters in their distinctive carapace armour walking back and forth in groups of three. Occasionally, they would stop on one of the towers to gaze out into the canyon before turning and walking back the way they had come.

No appreciable signs of tension. Good. It looked like Archangel hadn't been detected.

How far was she from her objective? She must be pretty close. He hadn't been able to detect her signature through clairvoyance, so she was within the perimeter beyond which his gift could not take him.

That meant minutes only until those defences went down, unless she and her team were killed or captured in the effort.

'Everything is ready, Scholar,' said a gruff voice from behind.

Karras didn't need to turn. 'No change on the walls yet, Omni. No sign. They haven't tripped any alarms, at least.'

'I'm betting on Archangel and her team.'

Karras nodded. 'This kind of thing was her daily bread in SOD-F. She's better suited to this kind of thing than I suspect you or I will ever be.'

Voss drew up beside him and smiled. 'I'm starting to forget what a good, stand-up fight feels like.'

Aye, thought Karras. *I doubt any of us thought Deathwatch service would be like this. But the Watch and the ordo operate as they must. It's a special kind of war they wage.*

'What's the mood back there?' he asked.

'Positive,' said Voss. 'Eager, even. Prophet is griping as usual, but I think he's secretly happy about the role Archangel gave him.'

'It's where he can do the most good.'

'If it keeps him out of the way of the rest of us, so much the better. Chyron is getting restless, though. The Elysians are giving him a wide berth.'

'It won't be long now.'

'Can you truly not see into that place?'

Karras turned and looked down at his short, stocky brother. 'Whatever is stopping me is strong. The closer we get to it, the less access I'll have to my gift.'

Voss paused. He seemed to be considering whether or not to say something out loud.

'What troubles you, Omni?' asked Karras. 'Speak freely.'

'I was recalling Chiaro, Scholar. I remember looking back at you surrounded by genestealers while the rest of us ran for the exfil point. What I saw you do that day... You obliterated them. Until then, I had thought us more or less the same. But not after that. You're something else entirely. I've wondered since why you need the rest of us at all.'

Karras found himself both saddened and troubled by those words. He did not want to be different. Any barrier between him and the rest of the squad could only be a negative. Cohesion and trust were everything.

'It was a desperate moment, brother. Had I any other choice... I cannot tell you the depth of the risk I take every time I have to depend on my gift to that degree. It is my very soul with which I might ultimately have to pay the cost one day. I'm sure the brothers of your own Librarius feel the same. Often do I wish I did not have access to this power at all. When I need it most is the very time it is most likely to destroy me.'

Voss nodded slowly. 'When I saw you rip those 'stealers apart in mid-air, I admit I envied you a little. I thought I could do so much more if I were gifted like you. But to hear you speak of the price you pay...'

They stood in silence a moment, each with their thoughts.

'Lend me your strength, Omni,' said Karras. 'With you and the others at my side, perhaps I will not need to risk my soul like that again.'

'You don't even have to ask it, Scholar. It's yours. In Dorn's name.'

Fine words, and he meant them, but both Space Marines knew Karras would have to risk his soul again and again regardless.

They were Deathwatch, assigned to Sigma. There would never be an easy op.

'You should get back,' said Karras. 'The sign will come any moment. And when it does, I want Reaper flight in the air in seconds.'

Voss turned and moved off into the shadows of the tunnel at the back of the cave, leaving Karras alone again, looking out over the last changing colours of the dying day.

Soon, thought Karras. *Soon, it'll be time to go in, whether Archangel is successful or not. Live up to your reputation, woman. Open the way.*

TWENTY-FIVE

Progress was slower than Copley would have liked. The halls and walkways were frequently swept by security drones. The unit's ordo-issued camo-suits masked body heat, scent molecules, even the sounds of breathing and heartbeat, but none of that would have mattered without the patience and skill she and her men had honed over long years of special operations training and deployment.

The t'au drones were all but silent until they got within about eight metres. From there, the pulsing hum of their anti-gravitic motors could be heard. Copley and her people held their collective breaths every time one of the damned things drifted past. Twice, they made cover just in the nick of time. Copley knew she was sweating, but the camo-suit masked that, too, locking the moisture away in a micro-weave layer. Half-seconds counted when avoiding the drones. Any flicker of unexpected movement caught by their lenses would bring investigation. And it wasn't just drones. Sometimes, a fire warrior would accompany them, routinely patrolling the corridors with the drones floating along behind. But the patrolling soldiers looked bored and listless. This was no task for a born warrior. T'au soldiers longed to be on the front line, fighting to expand their race's empire.

Being stuck out here for years without conflict or intrusion had made them complacent by default. Try as a commander might – any commander – it made little difference; long periods lacking stimulation or surprise dulled the edge of even the best blades. Copley was more anxious about the drones than any flesh-and-blood foes.

Being spotted meant being fired on, and that would mean losing what razor-thin advantage they still currently held. Trip one alarm, alert a single enemy, and the whole base would go on lockdown. Copley and her team would be cornered and exterminated like rats.

Most would have cracked and slipped up, but tension was like high-octane promethium to special forces operators. Pressure brought out Copley's best. The ordo didn't hand out command to just anyone. With a series of last-second evasions and silent kills, she and her team finally reached the door to the central control chamber with situational advantage still intact.

No time to breathe easy, though.

It was almost that time in which stealth would have to be abandoned.

Almost, but not quite.

The door was a large, solid-looking disc of advanced t'au super-ceramics set deep in a thick, blast-proof wall. A seam ran down the middle where the door would split in two and retract into the frame on either side. There was no point trying to blow it or cut it. Too strong. She'd assumed from the start that success would come down to hacking. There was no other way she was getting in there.

She whispered to her team, the sound picked up by her throat mic and transmitted to their earpieces over the squad's encrypted, short-rage vox-net. 'This is it. Morant, take a look at that panel and tell me what you think.'

'If I can pry off that housing, ma'am, and get access, then the module could–'

Grigolicz cut in. 'If that thing is rigged with anti-tamper alarms, man…'

'What would *you* do?' said Ryce.

Grigolicz pointed to the ceiling.

Above them, the corridor was lined with pipes and cables, all threaded through solid ceramic support struts. Some of those lines carried power and data. Others as thick as a man pushed fresh air in and pulled stale air out. Nothing they could crawl through, but…

'We wait up there,' said Grigolicz. 'When one of the blue bastards goes in or comes out, we drop, kill him and storm the room while the door is still open. Smoke or gas – lady's choice.' He looked at Copley. 'Me? I'm for smoking it and shooting them all, but if you'd rather put them to sleep, ma'am…'

Copley processed her thoughts for all of three seconds. The door access panel's casing might well have alarms attached. Fifty-fifty. Grig's idea had better odds. 'We gas them,' she ordered. 'I might want some of them alive at some point. Any fire caste, though, we kill outright. Clear?'

'Crystal, ma'am,' said Triskel, standing on her left. He patted one of the nerve-gas grenades on his webbing. 'I knew these babies would come in handy.'

'Up!' said Copley. She leapt and grabbed one of the support

struts above her, then hauled herself up and over the thickest bundle of pipes. The others, looking up, saw her disappear completely from view. 'Ryce and Morant will make the kill together. One in front, one behind. No noise. Grig, you and Triskel drop with me and go in hard. Triskel covers the right, Grig, you're on my left. I'm taking centre. The second we're in the room, throw. A good spread. By the look of these outer walls, we're probably talking about a large, split-level chamber. We've seen how the t'au like to configure their control rooms. Security will be the upper control banks. General operations will be the lower.'

'And the door?' asked Triskel.

'Morant, I want you on that before the gas clears. The second you and Ryce are done with the kill, I want the body dragged in and the door locked up tight again. Use the module if you need to. Work fast. Once we're all in, I want absolute control. Let's make it so they'll have to cut the door to get to us.'

As they listened to her, the four men hauled themselves up over the pipes and cables until they were perched there, hidden from the view of any that might pass below. Then they waited, bodyweight spread out as much as possible, looking down through gaps in the cabling, ears attuned for the first sound of footsteps or disengaging locks.

Copley thought of Talon Squad and the rest of her men waiting for the signal she had promised. Time was getting on. Every one of them knew just how much depended on her taking down the anti-air systems here.

The whole operation was so damned tenuous. A single mistake and they'd all be flying to their deaths. And after that? The t'au would know. They'd know that the ordo had located Epsilon. They'd know that Tychonis had been put on the Imperial map again. And they'd start locking the planet up. They might even move Epsilon off-world depending on her value to them, on how much she was giving them.

Just stay switched on, she told herself. *Stay focused.*

There was a click and hiss from below. The ceramic circle split in two. Yellow-white light spilled into the corridor. A shadow appeared, cast on the corridor floor by light from the control centre. A second later, the short, stocky earth caste tech to whom it belonged emerged, moving briskly.

Ryce and Morant didn't need to be told.

They dropped with barely a sound, one in front of the t'au engineer, the other behind.

The alien's eyes went wide for the briefest instant. Its mouth began to open, ready to cry out in alarm.

Too late.

From the xenos' rear, Ryce's arm snaked around to the front. He clamped his hand over the blue-skin's mouth.

At that same moment, Triskel thrust his blade up and under the alien's ribcage, cleaving the heart as Triskel yanked hard, upwards and backwards, on the handle of his blade.

The t'au shuddered in Ryce's grip and went slack. Together, the two operators lowered the body to the floor. Barely three seconds. They hadn't bent even halfway before Copley and the other two dropped and bolted through the open control centre door.

'Gas,' Copley barked.

At her voice, the aliens inside turned from their consoles.

Too late.

Three small cylindrical canisters rolled into the room, each coming to a stop a good four metres away from the others. Even before they stopped rolling, clouds of thick yellowish vapour began to hiss and billow out.

Copley watched along the barrel of her lasgun as shocked t'au began clutching at their throats. One after another, in rapid succession, they started dropping to the floor. Behind her, Triskel and Ryce had already dragged the earth caste tech's body inside.

With the gas thickening, obscuring her view, Copley switched her goggles to infrared and ran to the upper level. There she found the prone forms of several fire warriors. She put a single lethal round through each of their skulls.

From down below, she heard the door hiss shut and the locking bolts engage. 'That's us locked up nice and tight, ma'am,' Morant said, 'unless they built in a bypass code. I'll need time to find it.'

'Get to it,' she said. 'Triskel, Ryce, hog-tie the blue-skins down there and gather them in the middle of the room. Tris, you'll keep them covered in case they wake up.'

'Yes, ma'am.'

'Grig, get up here with me. Morant, you too once you've finished with the door. We'll need the module up here if the control systems are all encrypted. Ryce, you'll stay down there with Tris. Stay by the door. You hear any movement outside it, I want to know about it.'

'Aye, ma'am.'

Orders given, Copley went straight to a central console and started working her way out from there, checking the main function of each. The control system for the installation's defences had to be here. It had to be on one of these panels.

The gas had cleared now, pulled out by the room's extractors. She switched back to standard optics.

It took around three full minutes for her to find the t'au cogitator station she was looking for.

She allowed herself a moment – a brief, bursting moment – of relief. Then she started tapping on the glowing holographic glyphs of the station's runeboard. Menu after menu flashed up. She didn't have time to read them all. She was looking for one particular string of glyphs. Just as she was starting to think she'd never find it, there it was.

'Got you!'

Finally, after all the sneaking around, all the tension of trying to get here undetected, she had it. She tapped her way carefully through a series of prompts. Red glyphs flashed in front of her, asking for confirmation. Did she really want to power down the auto-defence systems?

She jabbed her finger on a small square of projected light.

Immediately, other monitors around her started displaying power-level data as energy was cut off from the weapon emplacements on the walls and rooftops. More typing, and Copley had control of the locks on the facility's main gates and security doors.

A failsafe query shimmered in the air before her.

One more glyph to press.

Her finger stabbed hololithic light.

Outside, set in the facility's thick walls, locking mechanisms disengaged. From another console, Grigolicz called out to her. 'That's done it, ma'am. Lots of activity out there.'

It was inevitable. She'd known that the very moment she powered down the defences and unlocked the gates, the vipers' nest would rouse.

'Well done, gentlemen,' she told her four-man squad. 'This facility is now open to visitors.'

The Deathwatch would be watching from afar. They'd have seen the defences power down. Reaper flight would be inbound within minutes. Copley and her people had to keep control of the room until the birds were on site. Those anti-air batteries had to stay dead. Already, t'au forces would be racing towards the control room. She couldn't let them retake it. She and her men had to dig in hard.

'Don't be too long, Deathwatch,' she muttered as she turned from the console to oversee the defence of the control centre.

Three kilometres away, from the mouth of the high cave, Karras watched by the light of the planet's two bluish-silver moons as the glow of targeting displays and status panels on the t'au defence turrets suddenly started winking off, one after another.

Awareness of the sudden shutdown spread from tower to tower, the fire caste soldiers becoming abruptly active, though not frantic. There was no obvious sign of an assaulting enemy, after all. It must be a technical issue. Then a Fireblade squad leader, broader and more muscular than the rest, burst out of a tower door and began barking and gesturing at the others. The t'au snapped into action, racing to the edge of the walls, raising the blue-skin equivalent of magnoculars to their eyes to scan the canyon.

'She's done it,' Karras rasped on the task force channel. 'Arcturus, lock and load. The turrets are down. We're going in.'

'About bloody time!' Zeed replied.

Barely two minutes later, three heavily modified and unmarked black Stormravens screamed in along the canyon floor, kicking up great clouds of dust as they tore towards the objective, their metal bellies filled with Ordo Xenos stormtroopers and Deathwatch Space Marines.

No more hiding. No more waiting.

Time to kick down some doors.

TWENTY-SIX

Canyon walls, blackened by the new night, whipped past Karras as he leaned out of the starboard-side hatch of Reaper One.

Up ahead, the walls and towers of Alel a Tarag stretched towards a sky now pricked with bright stars. Reaper flight was closing on those walls fast.

Archangel and her team had secured the Stormravens their approach window. Karras hoped she was still alive. Heavily armed response teams would be converging on her position in the control centre by now.

With the Stormravens roaring into visual range of the t'au on the high walls, a dense barrage of pulse rifle and burst cannon fire began blazing out, lighting up the night. Little threat at this range, but things would get nastier in a few seconds. The t'au would be scrambling to get heavier man-portable weapons out on the walls in lieu of their disabled batteries. The Stormravens were too high and too fast to worry about the current barrage, but they'd have to hover in an aerial kill zone just long enough to make their individual drops. They'd be highly vulnerable when stationary. Before that, the t'au had to be taught to keep their heads pulled in.

Fire warriors were streaming from their barracks into the installation's central courtyard, their armour lit in sharp relief by the muzzle flashes of their companions already firing up at their uninvited guests.

A missile from Reaper Three streaked past Karras, so close he almost felt the wash of heat from it. He watched it arc in towards one of the deactivated defence emplacements, this one bristling with t'au seeker missiles. It struck dead centre. Seeker warheads detonated in a rippling series of secondary explosions that tore the entire top of the tower to pieces. Rubble rained down on those below. Fire warriors scrambled out of the way. Fireblade leaders yelled at them to stand firm, to keep firing. A dozen or so were crushed, others had bones shattered. They collapsed to the ground in agony. Their comrades pulled them into cover, calling out for earth caste medical techs.

So much fire was pouring into the air now as more and more infantry filled the open spaces below that it seemed the Stormravens were flying into a blizzard. Pulse rounds hit Reaper One's wing just in front of Karras, smacking into the underside and leaving little black burn marks. But although those inside could feel the impacts, the assault craft shrugged them off, utterly undaunted, and swung around, levelling its nose-mounted twin-linked heavy-bolters at a cluster of fire warriors on the roof of the north cell block.

A familiar deep drumming sounded over the muffled rumble of stealthed jet engines. Explosive bolts poured down at the t'au, punching through armour and ripping into blue-grey flesh beneath. T'au blood sprayed dark patterns on moonlit rockcrete as dozens were gunned down.

In seconds the roof was cleared of all but smoking corpses.

'North landing zone clear. Moving in for the drop,' reported Ventius from the cockpit.

'Watcher, you're up!' barked Karras.

'I should be storming the main block with you,' growled Rauth.

It was the second time he had protested the splitting up of the kill-team for the assault. It was the second time Karras denied him.

'No! You will secure the north block, brother. We can't be sure Epsilon is in the sub-levels. I need you to take this block and hold it. If she is here, it will be on you to get her to one of the Stormravens. Do not fail me.'

'Witchblood,' said Rauth, 'I never fail.'

After unleashing a suppressing torrent of lethal fire at t'au on the nearest wall walk, Reaper One dipped into position, as low as possible. Rauth kicked out a zipline, ordered his fire-team of five stormtroopers to line up ready for the drop, then stepped out into open space.

The stormtroopers clipped themselves to the zipline and dropped after him, each a study in cool efficiency, not speaking, no hesitation, resp-masked faces unreadable.

Having watched the last of them drop from across the hold, Karras turned and looked down from his side hatch at the rooftop below. He watched as Rauth stormed towards the stairway access door, the stormtroopers chasing hard to close ranks on him. At a run, they descended into the section of the prison reserved for human inmates. Karras tested his witchsight, trying to send his astral vision down into the block. He could dimly sense human souls there, but the barrier to his power, whatever it was, resisted his attempts to project his awareness out of his body. Here, this close to its source, he was locked inside himself.

A fresh fusillade of glowing plasma and pulse rounds stabbed through the air in Reaper One's direction. Rounds struck the thick plate of the closed assault ramp at the front of the craft. The Stormraven shuddered.

Ventius' voice was tense. *'Taking heavy fire from the walls, Talon Alpha. Need to move!'*

'Clear the central block rooftop and get me in,' replied Karras. 'Missiles at your discretion.'

'There may be structural damage. Risk of collapsing the only access.'

'Take it. Archangel is in there. If she's still alive, she's going to need support fast. The longer she holds the main control centre, the better our chances. Get me in.'

'M'lord.'

The gunship's nose swung twenty degrees right, giving Karras a view down into the busy courtyard where fire caste officers and sergeants were trying to marshal their troops. Some were directing fire up towards Reaper One. Glowing rounds whipped past Karras as he watched. Other fire cadres were running for vators to take them up to the wall walks, hoping to pour additional fire on the assaulting aircraft from there. Earth caste techs were working frantically at the disabled turrets, trying to bring them back online.

Karras cursed. The t'au engineers might find a way to override Copley's hack. If those anti-air batteries came back online, no one was getting out of here alive. Not by air.

There was a great roar to his left. He watched Reaper Three swing in from about two hundred metres away, angling its nose at the upper levels of the south cell block. Front-mounted heavy-bolters blazed. The muzzle flash lit the whole roof. The t'au forces there were chewed apart, turned to dark smears and shattered plate. Some were hit close to the roof's edge. They tumbled backwards, out into the air, their bodies plummeting to the ground below.

A massacre.

The Stormravens were shadows of death in the night, cutting down xenos like wheat before scythes.

Suddenly, blinding streams of blue light lanced up towards Reaper Three, missing by what must have been centimetres.

Karras tracked the trajectory back to its source and saw two Crisis Battlesuits – XV8s – stalking out of the armoury doors on the south-west side of the base, their massive rail rifles aimed at the sky.

Their strange gait, both machine-like and alien at the same time, immediately brought back memories from the sensorium feeds at Damaroth and the vid-picts he had studied on the *Saint Nevarre*.

Highly mobile and with serious hardware – he had seen how deadly the blue-skin battlesuits could be.

'Reaper Three,' Karras voxed over to the other aircraft, 'make your drop and pull back. You're drawing heavy fire. Two XV8s down below.'

'I see them, Talon Alpha!'

As the pilot swung his craft over the lip of the south block, the battlesuits fired upwards again, this time striking the corner of the building. Reaper Three had shifted out of their line of sight just in time. Where the hyper-accelerated rounds struck the prison block walls they erased the reinforced rockcrete completely.

The XV8s were the biggest threat to the Stormravens. For missiles, there were countermeasures. For railguns, there were none.

Karras put out a call over the vox alerting all task force elements to the threat.

Muzzle flashes from up ahead caught his eye. A fresh storm of rounds started arcing towards him from the roof of the central building. More t'au squads were streaming out to reinforce their comrades.

'Reaper One, why are there still hostiles on that rooftop?' Karras demanded. 'Clear those xenos out and get me down there.'

Reaper One angled left, dipped its nose and surged forward, bolters blazing. *'Spear two,'* voxed Ventius, announcing missile launch. From the wing-mounted pods on either side of the Stormraven, a single lethal dart dropped. Rocket fuel ignited. The missiles leapt forward, streaking through the night.

Everything flared white and yellow as payloads detonated on contact. From his place at the hatch, Karras saw t'au bodies cartwheeling off into the dark, falling to the courtyard, their combat fatigues ablaze. A few were left alive on the rooftop, stunned and deafened. They staggered blindly, disoriented by the explosions.

Karras took aim and added his own fire to that of the nose-mounted bolters. He picked them off with ease. Heads snapped backwards. Rounds detonated within alien skulls, blowing them apart. The pilot gunned the engines and the Stormraven surged forward.

Reaper One tilted in over the roof of the central block and settled in to a dangerous but necessary hover. There she hung, roaring and restless, impatient to be off again and laying slaughter on the foe.

Small-arms fire smacked her sides from atop the nearest wall, but at least here, in the centre of the roof, she was beyond the line of sight of the ground-based forces and the two XV8s.

'In position, Alpha.'

At Karras' feet, a coil of zipline was already fixed to the floor lug. He wouldn't need it, but those following him would. He kicked it out of the side hatch.

On the other side of the Stormraven, one of Karras' Elysian assault team members kicked out another zipline. At the rear hatch, another Arcturus trooper dropped a third.

Now, three ziplines extended down from the hovering gunship. Two operators clipped themselves onto each of those lines. The remaining two would follow them down, and one more operator would precede Karras on his side. The Space Marine would drop last.

Karras moved back from the hatch and gestured to the waiting Elysian. The man nodded and moved into place, clipping himself smoothly to the line.

Karras barked the go order over the fire-team vox-channel. As one, the first three troopers plunged from their respective hatches.

Leaning out again, the Death Spectre watched all three hit rockcrete within milliseconds of each other. He saw them move out from the ziplines, drop to a knee, lasguns to shoulders, and secure the drop zone for those that would follow.

An instant later, two more sets of boots hit the roof. Those troopers quickly moved into covering positions too.

Karras ignored the zipline. He didn't need it at this height. He stepped out from the hatch and dropped like a three-hundred-kilogram bomb.

He hit the roof heavily, right in the centre of the five-man team, ceramite boots fracturing the surface, power armour shock-absorbers soaking up the impact. He began moving at once, bolter raised, muzzle trained on the open stairway access to which he was running.

'On me!'

Behind him, the stormtroopers broke into a run.

They had covered half the distance when a squad of t'au with pulse carbines burst from the doorway at the top of the stairs. Whatever they expected, it wasn't a massive Space Marine in black thundering towards them. That tiny instant of recognition and shock was all they got. With tight, controlled bursts, Karras put bolter rounds into each of them – two shots, centre-mass. The stormtroopers with him didn't even have time to fire. As the bolter rounds exploded inside each alien chest, the t'au were knocked from their feet, some thrown backwards onto rockcrete, others tumbling back down the stair.

Without breaking step, Karras kept on, ready to pour fire down on any xenos still foolish enough to try to ascend. He and the stormtroopers stacked up at the top of the stair in partial cover of the doorway and leaned in, weapons ready, eyes alert for any sign of movement.

Nothing. Just bodies broken and tangled, the walls around them splashed with blue blood.

Karras descended. His unit followed. They were in the main block now. He just had to establish vox-net contact with Copley and find out where the hell Epsilon was and how to get there.

At the bottom of the stairs, he found himself in a corridor lit by orange lumes. The ceiling was low enough that Karras could've reached up and punched a hole in it.

'Archangel, this is Scholar,' he said over the tactical command channel. 'Respond.'

Static.

'Archangel, this is Scholar. Respond.'

Nothing. Assuming she was still alive, something was wrong with comms. Could the t'au be jamming the vox somehow?

'M'lord?' asked one of the troopers.

'We push on,' said Karras, 'and try to pick up a signal as we go deeper.'

Again he cursed the strange barrier here that was stoppering his abilities. What the hell was it? He was certain now that it wasn't just some type of old anti-psyker ward. It seemed somehow familiar, but...

Right now, all he could do was push on and hope to disable it at the source somehow.

The t'au would have noted the rooftop drops. Reaper flight would continue to harry the forces amassed outside, but fire cadres would be pouring into each block, sweeping floor after floor from ground level up, intending to cut the invaders off as they descended from the roofs. Barricades would be thrown up at key exits. Escape routes were likely being cut off even now. The t'au would try to funnel the assaulting elements into killing zones. How far would they go to prevent Arcturus from securing Epsilon? What was her value to them?

He switched vox-channel. 'Talon Squad, this is Talon Alpha. Respond.'

Nothing.

He switched channel again as he and his team pressed on. 'Reaper One, this is Talon Alpha. Respond.'

Again nothing.

No link to the outside at all now.

Despite rotating frequencies and high-level auto-encryption, both standard for ordo special operations, it seemed the t'au had found a way to jam Imperial comms, at least from within the central building.

No access to his talents, and now, no analogue comms.

This keeps getting better and better.

He had to get to Archangel fast. If she still held the facility's command centre, there might be something she could do.

Because without any ability to coordinate the assault, this op was a lost cause.

TWENTY-SEVEN

Solarion squeezed the trigger.

His rifle kicked.

One moment, the Fireblade leader was standing on the wall, yelling and barking like a mad dog, frantically trying to coordinate his squad's fire on the Stormraven overhead. The next moment, he had no mouth to yell with. The round obliterated his lower jaw and then punched through the back of his neck with such force that it tore the skull free. The body dropped to its knees, then pitched forward, landing awkwardly, limbs at angles, hands still gripping his carbine.

The fire warriors on either side of their slain leader roared in grief and rage and redoubled their efforts to shoot down the gunship. Two of the xenos brought forward rail rifles, easily spotted by their long barrels. Pulse carbines and pulse rifles couldn't do much against the Stormravens, but if a rail round struck an engine or a fuel line...

'Brace for missile evasion!' shouted the pilot over the vox.

Solarion grabbed a grip-rail on the inner rim of his hatch. The Stormraven pitched left violently. Had the Ultramarine been a second too late to grab on, he'd have rolled straight out the far side.

The missile screamed by him, missing the Stormraven by a scant three metres. The pilot, angered by the close call, dipped the craft's nose and unleashed the fury of its heavy-bolters. Rounds stitched the courtyard, cutting down a dozen t'au infantry, but the Crisis Battlesuit that had fired the missile was already on the move, leaping to cover on bursts of blue flame from its back-mounted jump jets.

As the Stormraven levelled out, Solarion sighted down his scope, zeroed in on one of the t'au with the rail rifles and squeezed off another perfect shot. The round took the target in the chest, hitting like a meteor.

Without halting to take satisfaction, Solarion aimed at the other rail rifle wielder. He was about to make the kill when Reaper Two lurched high into the air.

'Brace!' shouted the pilot. *'Missile locked onto us!'*

'Damn it!' cursed the Ultramarine.

'Launching countermeasures!'

There was a great blinding burst of flares and irradiated chaff. The missiles swerved away from the Stormraven, giving its occupants a moment of relief.

'Bring us around on that bastard,' raged Solarion. 'Get me an angle! We have to stop those XV8s!'

'They've split up, my lord,' replied the pilot. *'We're taking fire from direct front and far right. We have to keep moving.'*

'Then move! But get me a line on one of them so I can make the damned shot before they take us out!'

* * *

Zeed made ready to drop from Reaper Three onto the roof of the south block with five of Copley's killers. At this point, Chyron was still attached by magna-grapple to the back of the Stormraven, so the Raven Guard and his stormtroopers were forced to drop from side hatches only.

Before Zeed leapt, he turned and looked at Voss, who, with Chyron and his own fire-team, would drop into the courtyard to assault the armoury.

'No rounding up, paper-face!' said Voss with a grin. 'Confirmed kills only.'

Zeed grinned back. 'You're the one who needs to round up. By my count, you've lost the last three.'

They gripped wrists.

'This one's mine,' said Voss. 'But don't go embarrassing yourself. Give me a challenge, at least.'

The Raven Guard chuckled. 'In your dreams, tree stump.'

It was as close as the two friends ever got to telling each other *Don't die out there*. They were Adeptus Astartes. They didn't die easily. But against these odds...

Zeed and his team dropped from the hatches. They hit the rooftop hard and fast, their formation flawless. As Reaper Three swung around, Voss watched his friend and the Elysians make for the stairwell down into the south cell block where the t'au prisoners were held.

Voss pitied the Elysians deploying with the Raven Guard. If they slowed him down for any more than an instant, he'd likely leave them behind. In pursuit of a decent fight, he was likely to go off mission anyway.

Nothing to be done. He had his own team to think of.

He turned his attention to the central courtyard. T'au fire warriors, having witnessed the rooftop drops, were streaming into the main buildings now, aware that the fight had moved inside.

Where Epsilon is sure to be, he thought.

Voss and Chyron weren't part of that search, but if they failed in their objectives, no one would be flying out of here.

Over the vox, the Imperial Fist addressed the massive Lamenter. 'Ready to unleash some rage, Old One?'

'Get me on the ground, brother, and you will see!'

Voss smiled and voxed the pilot. 'Clear some space and get us down. As near to that armoury as you can.'

He, his fire-team and Chyron would be facing the most resistance, drawing the heaviest and most prolonged fire. For those inside the prison blocks and central tower, the fighting would be corridor by corridor, bloody and close, just the way the kill-team had so rigorously trained in the kill-blocks back on Damaroth.

For the Imperial Fist, the Lamenter and those with them, things would be more chaotic. That armoury had to be breached and any vehicles within either crippled or destroyed. That meant a drop under heavy fire on open ground and, once the armoury was dealt with, the distinct possibility of getting pinned down inside. Chyron was supposed to be the solution for that. Voss was counting on him to keep the bulk of the t'au forces at bay until he and his team could rejoin him outside and push the xenos back.

The moment Reaper Three swung out over the edge of the prison block and back into view of the ground forces, wave after wave of bright rounds blazed up at it.

The Stormraven strafed the ground in response, bolters blazing, cutting down entire squads. Then something screamed past the cockpit, too close for comfort.

'Missiles!' warned the pilot.

Voss barked over the vox-link. 'Prophet! You're supposed to be taking out anti-air threats. We almost got hit!'

'I haven't missed a kill yet,' snapped Solarion. *'But there are two XV8s down there and I can only get an angle on one of them. If you can't stand the heat–'*

Voss ignored that and addressed the pilot. 'Put a missile on the cluster nearest the hanger. Light them up, then drop us in right on top of the bodies. Is that clear? I want Chyron free the moment we have that ground.'

'They can still get a lock, m'lord. It's too dangerous while–'

'We're not here to play safe,' growled Voss. 'We're here to get a job done. Now light them up and get us down!'

'Aye, m'lord.'

The craft dipped violently.

'Spear two, spear two!'

Twin trails of fire and smoke lanced from under the Stormraven's wings. The two missiles screamed towards a cluster of t'au warriors defending the armoury from hastily deployed barricades. They struck close together. The ground erupted. Fire blossomed into the air. Body parts rained down. The barricades were blasted apart. The ground beneath was blackened in a great ring.

Reaper Three arrested its drop and swung in, taking multiple hits on the hull from enemies on either side. Engines roaring, the Stormraven settled hastily into position, the pilot pulling back on his yoke and hauling the craft's nose up. It stopped, hovering for just a moment about three metres above the ground. Blinding t'au fire stitched the craft but the armour held. Still, at this volume of fire, and at this range, the risk to the engines and fuel tanks was too much to bear for long.

'Disengaging magna-grapples!'

Chyron dropped from the back of the Stormraven and hit the ground with a shudder. His piston legs hissed as they took the force of the impact. He swung his armoured chassis around, surveying the enemy ranks before him even as they turned their weapons on him.

His assault cannon cycled up with a whine. A deep, booming stutter erupted from it. Tracer rounds stitched the enemy in a broad arc. Armour shattered. Blue blood sprayed. The weapon's overwhelming noise drowned out the screams of dying blue-skins.

The Lamenter stomped forward, swinging and firing in sweeps, slaying fire warriors to left and right, ignoring the rounds that smacked into his thick plate. He was utterly intent on clearing the area for Voss and the Elysians to drop in behind him.

'I have the landing zone, Omni,' he boomed. *'Drop and do some work!'*

Voss didn't need to be told. He'd seen everything from the starboard-side hatch. At a gesture, his stormtroopers stepped out from the hold and into open air, dropping on their ziplines. When they had formed a cordon, weapons facing out, already blazing, Voss dropped right in the centre.

Between Chyron's blizzard of fire and the hail from the heavy-bolters of Reaper Three, the t'au found themselves heavily suppressed. It was enough to allow Voss' team the drop they needed. No fatalities. No wounds. Now they were down, however, t'au rounds began whipping in their direction.

Voss ignored them, even as several smacked into his right pauldron, and led his people at a run towards the armoury. The rolling metal doors were gradually lifting. The t'au were bringing out armour to meet the Imperial assault. He had to get this done now. No mistakes.

'Tell me you've got this, Lamenter! Tell me you can hold!'

'I have it,' roared the Dreadnought. *'Be about your business.'*

Voss sprinted, his kill-team right behind him, running full tilt to keep up. Voss had deployed with a meltagun, the better to deal with enemy armour. As heavy as it was, it didn't slow him. Still, the armoury doors were already at head height when he reached them. He ducked under, barely slowing his pace, and barrelled inside. Before him was a broad hangar, the air within humming noisily with anti-gravitic engines and the powering up of deadly energy weapons.

The t'au were bringing out their big guns to take down the Stormravens. Voss had to make sure they never got that chance.

Fire whipped down at him and his team from gantries and metal stairwells.

'Drop them!' he barked.

Hot-shot las-fire cracked the air.

Alien bodies fell limp, their flesh cratered and burned, but the enemy vehicles were powered up now. They began to turn towards him, eager to bring their weapons to bear.

He raced straight for the nearest.

'Melta charges! Get your backsides in gear!'

The turret of the TX7 Hammerhead at which he was running almost had a bead on him, but Voss threw himself forward onto his back, skidding under it on a trail of sparks, and fired a blast from his meltagun straight up into its smooth metal underbelly.

The massive tank trembled. A gaping hole appeared in its armour, edges glowing white hot. Voss rolled out fast. Underneath a dying tank was not a good place to be. Just as he got clear, there was a dull *crump* from inside, a secondary explosion. The gravitic motors suddenly failed. The Hammerhead hit rockcrete. A second later, pieces of its curved hull exploded outwards, filling the air with hot fragments.

Under fire from the drones attached to the other tanks, Voss saw his Elysians run in at their own targets. They moved fast. One of them, Irych, slapped a melta charge on the radiator of a Devilfish transport and angled away, springing hard.

When the charge blew, the pilot of the craft lost control. The hovering tank swung left and crashed straight into the side of another. More charges detonated. Both vehicles exploded into burning scrap.

'Covering fire,' shouted Voss, pushing himself up and off towards the last target, another Hammerhead, his melta already charged to fire again.

All around him was smoke, flame and the chaos of battle.

He was smiling under his helm.

Right in the middle of the maelstrom.

Nothing else even came close.

TWENTY-EIGHT

The missile screamed so close to Chyron it almost grazed him. He was turning to cut down a t'au squad trying to flank him. A second earlier or later in the turn and the missile would have clipped him, detonated, bitten through his thick shell, possibly knocked him from his feet.

Out in the open, besieged from several sides, that could mean death, and not one he could feel proud of. It was no easy thing for a Dreadnought to right himself. The thought of dying that way filled him with sudden fury.

He roared with rage as he strafed a fire cadre of six, cutting them to pieces, then turned his attention to the source of the missile.

The XV8s were fast. For all their size, they were able to jump like fleas. Space Marines with an assault squad loadout might keep up, but all the Dreadnought could hope to do was soak up the punishment until a good kill angle opened.

Chyron saw moonlight and muzzle fire gleaming momentarily

on his attacker's carapace before it vanished behind the corner of a barracks building.

His hail of bullets was half a second too late. Rounds punched holes in the wall, chewing the corner to pieces, but the XV8 had already repositioned.

And there was still the other to watch for.

Chyron knew he was in trouble. He couldn't see either, had no idea where they were now. They were so damned nimble. And he was the biggest target – the only target – on the ground right now. Both XV8s were working together to get a kill angle on him while the t'au infantry kept him pressed. One would draw him, the other would flank and slay.

Except I know what you're about, you xenos curs. It will be harder than you think!

Where was that bloody Imperial Fist? Why hadn't he exited that armoury yet? The longer Chyron had to hold the courtyard alone, the greater the chance of failure.

'If you're in there much longer, son of Dorn…' raged the Lamenter over the vox.

As if in answer, the stocky Deathwatch operator barrelled out of the armoury door with his squad of Elysians in tow. One was missing, his ruined body cooling in the armoury, cut down by pulse cannon fire from the gun drones of the last Hammerhead tank before Voss had blown it to scrap. The four remaining stormtroopers immediately added their lasgun fire to Chyron's fusillade as they ran. Behind them, explosions rippled through the building. Great sections of the metal roof began to fall inwards. Thick smoke billowed out.

'Feeling the heat, Lamenter?' voxed Voss as he slid to a stop by Chyron's side, slung his meltagun, ripped his bolt pistol from the mag-lock on his left cuisse and started taking down a squad of t'au infantry that were trying to pin them from portable barricades on the south side. 'More hardware in there than we anticipated, but we handled it.'

'It won't matter if we can't take out their damned battlesuits,' Chyron said over the roar of his assault cannon. 'They're working on a suppress and flank.'

'We still have sniper support,' said Voss. He voxed Solarion. 'Prophet! What's the word on those XV8s?'

The Ultramarine sounded hard-pressed. *'I've got other problems right now. They've deployed man-portable missile launchers on the walls. A lot of them. Multiple locks. All three Stormravens are running dangerously low on countermeasures. Scholar needs to get that damned woman out now so we can leave this hellhole.'*

'If we don't secure the exterior,' said Chyron, 'it won't matter!'

'Listen, Prophet, as pressed as you are, we need you to take down one of the XV8s. We can't get both from down here. They're too manoeuvrable. We need air support.'

'Damn it, Omni. I just told you–'

'I thought you were the best,' bit back the Imperial Fist. 'Those XV8s are honour kills. Biggest threat on the field. But if one of them is beyond you...'

Voss knew he had him. It was too easy. Solarion went quiet. Then, *'I am* the best, *you stunted oaf. Just watch for the kill-shot. And mark it well.'*

'Get us up,' Solarion barked at the pilot. 'I need a clean angle on one of the battlesuits.'

'M'lord, the second I take us out of cover, we'll have every launcher on those walls locked right on us.'

'How many more times can we deploy countermeasures?'

'Six. They get a good lock after that and we're going down. I can evade one, maybe two, manually, but more than that...'

Solarion switched to the tactical channel for all air support. 'This is Talon Three. Listen up. I want maximum fire on wall walks, towers and rooftops. Ignore ground targets until further orders. Is that clear?'

'M'lord,' voxed Ventius, Reaper One, *'that leaves Talons Four and Six without close support. They're under heavy fire down there. We–'*

'They're the reason I'm ordering this, damn it. We need to clear the heights so I can take down one of those XV8s. If I can't do that, our ground team won't hold. Don't make me repeat myself. Turn all your attention to the walls, towers and rooftops. Clear them, whatever it takes!'

Orders given, he turned his attention back to the pilot of Reaper Two. 'Graka, you heard me. Get to it. Or Talon will be down two Space Marines and the Death Spectre will take your head!'

TWENTY-NINE

Karras found the door to the command centre. The t'au were trying to cut through it with a powerful laser. Fortunately, the quality of their own construction was working against them. They didn't even have time to turn before Karras and his squad cut them down, bolts and beams ripping into them, turning the corridor outside the door into an azure bloodbath.

'Talon Alpha to Archangel, respond.'

No. The vox was still out.

Stepping over smoking bodies, Karras ripped out the power feed to the cutting laser and batted the machine aside. He removed his helm, raised a hand, spread his fingers and placed his palm on the surface.

The field suppressing his gifts was as powerful as ever, but Copley was just on the other side, maybe a dozen metres away. If he pushed hard enough, if he really tried, there was a chance, slim perhaps, that he might manage to reach her.

Closing his eyes, he called his power forth from deep down inside his mind.

He tried to push his consciousness out beyond the confines of his physical body. He couldn't. The suppression field was too strong.

He focused harder, drawing forth more power from the warp. As it rose up from within, white witchfire began to manifest, licking his armour and flickering around his smooth, chalk-white skull.

The troopers beside him retreated a little and turned to cover the corridor behind.

Karras pushed harder. With effort and unusual slowness, his astral self at last emerged from his body and phased through the door. On the other side, the souls of Copley and her people shone brightly, drawing him forward.

Copley's soul was by far the brightest. So easy to distinguish. Focusing hard, he pressed towards it.

When he was right in front of her, he reached into her light. It was turbulent in there. She was in control, but tense. Her mind was racing, processing visual data from the security feeds all across the base.

'Major!' Immediately, he sensed her attention shift. 'Copley,' he said. 'Open the door. It is Karras.'

He felt her confusion. Had she just heard a voice? Was it her imagination?

She tried to message him over the vox. When that failed, she pulled up a holo-display from one of the feeds outside the control room. She saw the corridor, saw the Death Spectre and his team there.

Karras felt her relief and stopped resisting the suppression field. He snapped back into himself, and the eerie white light around him guttered and vanished. A moment later, the heavy doors to the command centre began to split.

'Inside,' Karras ordered his team. 'You'll cover the corridor from there.'

He strode past them to greet Archangel face to face.

The visual feeds told a story of ordered chaos.

Standing at Copley's side, dwarfing her utterly, Karras watched on banks of t'au monitors as members of Talon Squad and Task Force Arcturus exchanged fire with a dwindling alien force that still greatly outnumbered them. Had it not been for the air support of the Stormravens, the sheer deadly might of Chyron holding the central courtyard and Omni's destruction of the t'au armour, things would've been very different out there.

The situation was still highly fluid. Nothing was certain. The balance could tip either way at any moment.

And still no sign of Epsilon.

Chyron was being hunted by the XV8s. The Stormravens had yet to get Prophet the kill angle he needed. Using the t'au's own barricades against them, Voss and his team were doing their best to support the Dreadnought, keeping the t'au infantry from deploying anything heavy enough to complicate matters. But there was little room to manoeuvre and time was against them.

Copley expressed deep concern.

'They will overcome,' Karras said. 'We must trust to that and focus on finding Epsilon.'

The woman pointed to a holo-monitor on the right. 'That is the entryway to a dedicated vator that goes down to the basement levels. There is no other access. None of the feeds show us what's down there. Whatever it is, t'au command did not want or need the personnel at these stations to see it.'

'I need to get down there now,' said Karras.

He glanced at the other monitors. Watcher and Ghost had taken control of the north and south internment blocks. They had yet to release the inmates, but each level was littered with the bodies of blue-skin guards.

'Without the vox-link,' he said, 'I can't order them to release the prisoners. It would aid us greatly to have the t'au suddenly overwhelmed by desperate escapees.'

'I can't say why vox isn't working in this particular block. I've had Morant going through their systems. There's nothing like that. It must be something in the basement.'

'Whatever is suppressing my gift is there also. I was able to reach you through the door only through proximity and great effort.'

'Both of your brothers are occupying cell block control rooms. I could try the facility's hard-line comms. Send a visual over to the monitors in those rooms. If they're watching, they'll get it.'

'Do that,' Karras said. 'Get them to release every last prisoner in those blocks. We'll flood the t'au in the courtyard with too many targets. Prophet and Chyron will take down the XV8s. But I need to get below, and you need to sabotage this place and get your team outside. Help hold the exfil point. I need your best lock-breaker with me. And your second best as insurance.'

'Morant is your man. I'll send him with you. Carland from your own fire-team would be second choice. It's a distant second, so don't lose Morant.'

'I don't intend to. Keep those vators running, but sabotage

the rest of their systems. Blow this room if you have to, but those vators must stay operational.'

He turned and left her at the displays, descended to the lower level of the command room and strode powerfully towards the door.

Copley watched him, finding herself abruptly and powerfully conflicted. Only now did she realise that she had automatically and completely deferred to him. It was so hard not to. His very presence practically demanded it.

Her pride won out. She called down to him, her voice sharp with anger-edged authority. 'You're forgetting who gives the damned orders around here, Deathwatch!'

Karras stopped and turned to stare up at her from the level below. He removed his helm so he could look her in the eye.

As she held that blood-red gaze, she felt a wave of self-doubt wash over her. *Look at him!* Splashed in the blood of aliens, his armoured bulk carved with skulls, he looked like a mythical battle-god made real, and she felt suddenly and totally inadequate before him.

She quietly cursed. Had pride just made a fool of her?

Karras, after a long second, simply grinned up at her. 'My apologies, major. With your permission…'

Copley swallowed and threw him a nod. 'Get to it, Talon. We're counting on you!'

Karras gave a shallow bow, replaced his helm and strode out the door.

Copley shouted for Morant and Carland to follow him, and the two men raced off after the Space Marine. He was moving fast. They had to sprint to catch up.

Copley then called out for the attention of everyone left in the control centre. 'Listen up, you meatheads! We're going to sab every system and circuit in this place with the exception of the vators. Then we get out of here, rendezvous with the Dreadnought and the fire-team in the central courtyard and hold the exfil point until extraction. Is that clear?'

'Yes, ma'am,' they called back.

'Good. We've got three minutes! Let's do some damage!'

THIRTY

Karras skidded to a halt and thrust up one gauntleted fist.

'Hold!' he barked.

Morant and Carland slid to a stop beside him. Karras ushered them back against the wall.

The next stretch of corridor was the last between him and the vator, but the t'au were present in force. A squad of twenty, entrenched behind portable barricades, guarded the only door. Three heavy weapons had been mounted. Between them, they covered the north corridor down which Karras would have to come and each of the side corridors, east and west.

The firepower he was facing here was formidable. Had it not been for the heavy weapons, he knew he could have walked straight in among them. Without full access to his gift, which might shield him or massively magnify his speed and Space Marine reflexes, he and the Elysians might well be cut to bloody pieces.

'No way around them, m'lord?' asked Carland. He was the younger of the two Elysians by a decade, but his eyes already had the coldness of the seasoned special ops veteran.

Karras pulled a Deathwatch-issue thundershock EMP grenade from a bandolier around his armour and chambered it in the grenade launcher under the barrel of his bolter.

'Why go around when we can go through? I'm going to hit them dead centre and disrupt their hardware. The moment it goes down, give them everything you've got. But stay behind me. Do not try to rush ahead.'

'Understood,' said Morant.

Carland nodded.

'Ready yourselves,' said Karras. 'When this round detonates, there may be interference with our own equipment. Nothing serious at this range, but be prepared.'

With that, he leaned around the corner and fired. Pulse rounds smacked into the wall in front of him. There was a *thunk* followed by a loud zap.

'Now!' shouted Karras.

He burst from the corner and began systematically gunning down every target he laid eyes on. The Elysians followed, one to each side of him, lasguns blazing death.

Alien voices cried out in anguish.

The t'au had looked well prepared, but they were too dependent on their technology. As soon as the thundershock disrupted their optics, they started desperately trying to throw off their battle-helms. Some had been bareheaded before it detonated. These few were still stunned by the noise and light of the detonation, but they quickly rallied and started to return fire, filling the corridor with crackling blue plasma and beams of lethal energy.

They focused fire on Karras, desperate to stop him as he

tore towards them, but his armour could soak up more small-arms fire than this before systems and integrity started to suffer. It was the heavy weapons that posed the real threat. Karras prioritised the killing of their gunners. Each fell with a wet blue crater where his face had been.

Three bolt rounds.

Three grisly kills.

The other fire warriors ducked behind the barricades, safely out of the storm if only for a moment.

Karras was about to order the Elysians to throw frags when suddenly, from the west corridor, he saw a grenade arc smoothly over the barricades and land right in among the foe.

It detonated sharply, slaughtering those in cover.

Of the ten remaining t'au, seven were instantly killed. The other three were injured badly.

Karras had a feeling he already knew who had tossed that frag.

He was right.

Rauth was a blur of black and silver as he came into view, leaping over the barricade to kill the rest of the t'au with his combat knife.

Karras signalled to the Elysians to follow as he walked forward to meet his squad brother, bolter now lowered at his side.

'You're supposed to be holding the north cell block, Watcher!'

Rauth looked up from wiping his knife on the beige combat uniform of his last alien victim, sheathed the blade at his lower back and said, 'The stormtroopers can manage now. I'm going down there with you.' He thrust his chin in the direction of the vator doors. 'You don't know what you're walking into.'

'Neither do you,' replied Karras.

'So we go together,' said Rauth. As was his way, he didn't seem to be giving Karras much choice, despite the matter of rank.

Karras eyed him a moment, then said, 'Great is the worth of he who would walk beside you into that darkness where no man has stepped before.'

'Cervesta's *White Road to Stramos*. Thirty-second millennium.'

Karras grinned. 'I can't seem to get away from you. Perhaps I should feel blessed.'

'No,' said Rauth. 'You should not.'

Karras ordered Morant forward to the door panel. 'How long?' he asked as the Elysian pulled a hacking panel and cables from a pouch on his webbing.

Morant was kneeling, already at work when he answered. 'Solid encryption. Three levels. Estimating full vator control in four to six minutes, m'lord.'

The fresh sound of boots on the corridor floor reached Karras' and Rauth's enhanced ears.

'Scholar, we've got incoming. A lot of them.'

'Carland,' said Karras. 'Get into cover with a fire arc on the north corridor. Rauth, cover the west. I've got the east.'

Carland nodded. 'M'lord's command.'

All three got themselves into position.

'If they cluster,' said Karras, 'use frags.'

The first of the t'au squads to arrive began firing from the cover of the corner around which Karras and his Elysians had only just come. Pulse rounds smacked and fizzed on the outward face of the barricade.

Karras checked his current mag, cocked his bolter and said to Morant, 'Make it three minutes, soldier. They're about to throw a lot of pressure our way.'

With that, he raised himself above the lip of the barricade and took aim.

THIRTY-ONE

Guns blazing, the Stormravens strafed the walls and rooftops mercilessly. T'au bodies were ripped apart by the dozen, splashing the walkways blue. Others were punched over the edge by rounds that struck them centre-mass. They tumbled screaming to the unforgiving ground below.

As the gunships systematically cleared the walls and towers, missiles streaked into the air, leaping up on trails of fire and smoke to try and strike them down. Even so, as the walls and towers were being purged, the lock-on alarms in the cockpit of each Stormraven began to blare less and less frequently. Each time the warning runes lit, the pilots would hit a countermeasures rune, sending out a cloud of flares and irradiated chaff. Guidance systems became confused. Missiles detonated harmlessly in mid-air. Each time they did, however, the pilots threw increasingly anxious glances at their readouts. All too soon, the stock of countermeasures would be gone, and there would be no choice left but to outfly the missiles. At that point, their skills would be measured against their lives.

It was not a competition any pilot won for long.

'It's working,' Solarion told Flight Lieutenant Graka. 'Keep the pressure on them. The heights are almost clear!'

The Stormravens hadn't been able to risk a hover since the moment they had dropped the assault teams. Now, with the t'au threat all but cleared from the walls, it was time for Solarion to take his shot.

Leaning out of the right-side hatch, he ordered the pilot to circle while he looked for a kill angle on one of the XV8s. Down on the ground, in positions of barely adequate cover between the barracks, hangars and prison blocks, he could see Voss and Chyron more or less pinned down, doing their best to hold fast with the support of Copley's soldiers. A couple of bodies in black assault gear lay beside them in growing pools of red. Some of the Arcturus operators had already paid the ultimate price in their duty to the Golden Throne.

One of the XV8s emerged from behind the corner of a barracks building and fired searing blue bursts at Talons Four and Six. Chyron, being the bigger and wielding the most firepower, was the obvious target. He shuddered and staggered backwards as the beams struck his dense armoured chassis. Two glowing craters the size of melons marked his black body now, smoke drifting into the air from each.

The Dreadnought shook it off and returned fire, but the XV8 had used its jets to dash at blistering speed to fresh cover.

The shells from Chyron's assault cannon tore the wall of the barracks to pieces, revealing the plasteel supports beneath the rockcrete, but the XV8s were just too fast for the Lamenter to get a proper bead when cover was so plentiful.

No kill angle on that one. Not from here.

'Where's the other?' Solarion wondered.

Then, as Reaper Two swung around on the western edge of the battle, with the sky's first hints of dawn on the far side, he saw movement between the north block and the central tower. It was fast and large. It had to be the other battlesuit.

He barked orders to the pilot, and the Stormraven swooped in for yet another kill.

Siefer Zeed's lip was pulled back over his teeth as he looked at the monitors in the control room of the south cell block. The rest of Talon was deep in combat, already revelling in his beloved dance of death. And where the hell was he? Stuck in a cell block control room, watching it unfold on a bunch of damned holo-screens.

'Enough!'

'My lord?' asked Corporal Gaman, the most senior of the troopers Copley had assigned to him as support.

'I said it's enough, by Terra!' Zeed swung to face him, his flawless white face creased with cold fury. 'I can't languish here watching it all from a distance.'

Gaman, for all his years as a hardened xenos killer, could only look back into those coal-black eyes for a moment. He broke his gaze away to look at the firefight on the monitors.

'M'lord should be out there,' he said, 'where the fighting is. You were born for that, m'lord. Go take the Emperor's wrath to them. We' – he gestured to the other Elysians in the room – 'will hold the block until the major orders us out.'

Zeed was already on his way to the door when he heard Gaman add one more thing.

'We'll be watching on the monitors, my lord. And if we might ask a favour...'

'Ask it,' said Zeed.

Gaman grinned. 'Make it worth watching!'

Zeed grinned back, punched the command glyph for the control room doors and broke into a run.

His blood was already up at the thought of throwing himself into battle. His secondary heart began to pump. Combat chemicals flooded his system, sharpening his senses.

He moved through the cell block like a freight train, his pauldrons smashing rockcrete from the walls as he rounded tight corners. Soon, all that separated him from the battle outside was a set of metal doors at the end of the final corridor. As he thundered towards them, he felt elation and excitement flowing through him. He flexed his fists eagerly.

He was just metres from the doors when they exploded inwards – a great wash of fire and heat and deadly debris.

The blast knocked him from his feet.

THIRTY-TWO

The corridors were filled with a smoky haze and the sharp smells of ionised air and t'au blood.

'Carland,' moaned Morant.

The sergeant knelt by the motionless body of his fellow operator, cradling his head. No response. Carland was already gone, deep cauterised holes bored through his armour and the flesh and bones of his chest. Smoke still wisped upwards from them.

The fighting had been fierce, the t'au desperate to prevent Karras, Rauth and the Arcturus troopers from getting below. They had thrown a wall of blistering fire at the Imperials behind the barricade. When that hadn't worked, they'd tossed smoke and tried to rush them.

Foolish and desperate.

Karras looked down at Morant holding his dead comrade. He was conditioned to be cold in battle, but he knew what Morant was feeling. Even Space Marines knew grief. The

Death Spectres had faced long odds and come through many, many times, but the price had often been painfully high.

He could see colours of deep sorrow and loss, tinged with flickers of survivor guilt, coruscating around Morant's kneeling form.

He placed a heavy, gauntleted hand on the Elysian's shoulder. 'He fought with honour. His place is assured. Do not grudge him a worthy death just because you must go on without him. This was his time.'

Morant took a deep, ragged breath and sighed. 'He was young.'

'Fruit falls when ripe, but a man may die on any day,' stated Rauth.

Karras recognised it. *The Fourth Book of Thoule* by Duris Trant. Trant had been eaten alive by razormouth squid on Ashika while swimming in a lake. There had never been a fifth book.

Behind Karras, the hacking module Morant had set up chimed. The vator doors gave a mechanical hiss and slid back into their housing.

Karras turned to see the open vator cage waiting for them. At the same moment, he noted the hurried approach of more booted feet closing quickly on their position.

'Take his tags, Morant,' he told the grieving soldier. 'It's time to go!'

Rauth strode into the vator, turned and raised his weapon to cover the others. He, too, had heard the rush of feet on the corridor floor.

Morant grabbed the tags and tugged them from Carland's neck. 'See you when it's my time, Car.'

He stood, bowed his head briefly and made the sign of the aquila.

Just as he was turning to the vator, beams of blinding t'au fire scored the air around him. Rounds smacked into the walls on either side of the vator doors. One found its mark on Morant's left arm, burning away a bite-sized channel of flesh. The Elysian cried out and dropped into a crouch, nerves singing with agony.

From the cover of the vator doors, Rauth leaned out and sent bursts back at the t'au.

'Scholar!' he snapped.

Karras was already moving. He grabbed Morant by the combat webbing on his back and tossed him into the vator. Morant hit the far wall with a moan and dropped to the floor.

The t'au began blasting away in earnest, rounds peppering the walls in their hundreds.

Rauth hit a rune on the panel inside the vator and the doors began hissing shut.

As they did, Karras threw out a hand to stop them. Soaking up several shots on his arm and pauldron, he reached round to the outside of the vator and grabbed Morant's hacking module. Then he ducked back inside and let the doors resume closing.

Through the narrowing gap, glowing pulse rounds and burning beams scored the metal of the vator cage's back wall, but the t'au had missed their chance.

Whatever lay below, whatever the t'au were hiding here, Karras was about to see with his own eyes.

THIRTY-THREE

Zeed shoved a block of rubble from his breastplate with a grunt and pushed himself to his feet. Dust from the destruction of the cell block doors filled the air. The impact had killed the lighting in the corridor. Daylight was dawning outside, but its illumination hadn't reached the canyon floor on which the Tower sat.

Space Marine eyes needed only a tiny amount of light, of course, to see perfectly well. Ahead of him, he made out a hulking armoured form on its back. It was half blocking his route out.

He slung his tactical bolter over his shoulder and slid his fists into the housing of the lightning claws mag-locked to each of his thighs. His weapons of choice. Nothing else compared. No high ever came close to the battle-rush of hand-to-hand combat. He often entered a half-mindless peak state in which his whole body was given over to the ultimate expression of the life-and-death struggle between mortal foes.

He was different from the others. Duty and honour were important, yes, but it was the battle-high that gave his life meaning. He could never get enough.

With the claws locked into place, he sent a thought impulse through his armour's neural connection. A lethal power field activated just millimetres from the metal surface of each claw – a deadly invisible addition that made a mockery of most amour, even that of tanks.

This done, he moved forward to investigate.

He found himself standing over a t'au battlesuit with two perfect holes punched in it, each about the size and shape of an armour-piercing bolter round.

He opened a vox-channel, noting how weak and filled with static it was. Undaunted, he said, 'I'm down here admiring your handiwork, Prophet. Nice of you to open the door for me.'

'I don't know what you're talking about, Raven Guard,' Solarion snapped back. *'Don't bother me while I'm busy!'*

One of the Ultramarine's rounds had struck the XV8's apparent head dead centre. What looked like a head, of course, was actually part of the suit's sensor array and control systems housing. Essentially, knocking it out had removed the suit's advanced sensory feed, fire control systems, even some of its AI-assisted mobility systems, but that wasn't how one killed an XV8. That was how you winged it.

The second shot had been the kill-shot.

The round had lanced straight through the thickest armour plating on the whole suit. If Zeed were to cut that plate off right now, he'd find that the round had obliterated the skull of the pilot inside. The cramped cockpit of the suit was awash with alien blood and bone fragments.

'Hell of a shot anyway, you sour-faced son of a squig,' Zeed muttered to himself, stepping over the outstretched right arm of the dead machine.

Now he was outside. The sky was a pale violet, but the facility was still deep in shadow, lit only in flickers and flares by the battle that raged within its walls.

Zeed wished he had a jump pack. Higher mobility would mean a higher kill count. Alas, he was confined to the ground this time.

Never mind, he told himself. *Still some fun to be had.*

All that gunfire meant it wasn't too late.

Over the vox, he called out, 'Hey, tree stump! What's your count so far?'

'Forty-eight, not counting vehicles,' replied Voss. He paused for a moment, then added, *'Forty-nine. Yours?'*

Zeed had slain twenty-eight t'au soldiers while storming the prison block and taking the control room.

'You're way behind,' laughed Voss. *'Better give it up this time.'*

Zeed was already running towards the sound of the nearest t'au squad. With his armour's sound damping and photo-reactive camouflage cells, the t'au wouldn't know he was among them until it was too late. They would be focusing all their fire towards Voss, Chyron and the Arcturus troopers.

He would claim many xenos lives before the order came to exfiltrate.

Such a pity the t'au were poor prey without their battlesuits. They were smart and strategic, and their technology and tactics were solid at long range. But to Zeed, they didn't provide enough sport at close quarters.

He was thinking this when a massive object struck the dirt right in front of him. A few more metres and he would have been crushed.

He looked up and found himself staring into the scanner

lenses of an armoured figure three full metres taller than himself, all heavy plate and oversized weapons. It was mostly shadow, but red lights on its head and torso winked through the clouds of dust. This close, he could hear the humming of its powerful generator, could feel it vibrating his armour.

Despite Zeed's stealth systems being fully activated, the giant, angular form immediately focused on him, trying to bring its weapons to bear. Its advanced sensory suite had picked him up easily at such close range.

To Zeed, it was as if the universe had just granted him a wish.

Here was the fight he wanted. Here was a proper challenge where he'd expected none.

He dropped into combat stance, arms splayed, lightning claws out to either side, blades angled edge forward at his foe.

'My lucky day,' he said with a laugh. 'And your last. Don't disappoint me, blue-skin.'

Violence exploded. Machine strength and AI-boosted reflexes clashed with flawless combat genetics, centuries of training and a love of battle that bordered on madness.

I am an angel of death, thought Zeed as he slipped aside a lethal diagonal swipe and slashed his claws across the battlesuit's left knee, severing cables and hydraulics. Coolant and lubricant splashed his black cuirass.

And I will never be beaten at close range. Never.

THIRTY-FOUR

Karras and Rauth emerged from the vator cautiously, weapons raised.

It was quiet. *Too* quiet.

'This is wrong, Scholar,' breathed Rauth. 'No resistance? They must know we're here. Those above would have called it in.'

Karras had other things on his mind. The force which had been suppressing his gift had been getting progressively stronger the closer he came to this place. Here, he felt the flow of energy from the immaterium cut off from him utterly.

'Karras!' growled Rauth impatiently.

Karras raised a hand. 'Give me a damned moment, brother.'

Rauth guessed the Death Spectre was working one of his fell magicks, sending some astral projection of his mind along the corridors ahead, perhaps, and kept his silence.

Morant hung back in the vator cage, adjusting the field dressing Rauth had helped him apply to his wounded left arm. His lasgun was slung over one shoulder. His hacking module was back in its pouch on his webbing. He couldn't wield the lasgun anymore, but he had a hot-shot laspistol holstered at his right hip and a combat knife with a mono-molecular blade that could cut through standard t'au infantry armour with ease.

If there was fighting to be done down here, pistol and blade would have to suffice. He was no Space Marine, but he was still in the fight. He would do what he could to support the dark giants in front of him.

Karras had finished processing some troubling thoughts. He'd come to his conclusion.

'They're pulling out. That's why there's no force to meet us. Whatever is down here, they're getting ready to leave with it.'

He turned to Rauth. 'We don't have much time, Watcher. We have to get to Epsilon!'

The corridor stretched out in two directions, north and south, both curving round to the east, cutting off the view ahead at about twenty metres.

'Which way?' demanded the Exorcist.

Without his gift, Karras had no way of knowing. He had a hunch that the corridors would eventually merge, forming a complete circle. If he was right, it didn't matter which direction they chose.

If he was wrong, they'd lose precious, maybe even critical time.

'Left!'

The two Space Marines broke into a jog. Morant followed, running hard to keep up. Karras called back to him. 'Try to stay with us, soldier. We cannot afford to slow for you. If you fall behind, keep running. I believe we will have need of your skills again very soon.'

Morant pushed thoughts of his wound aside, though every step sent fresh waves of pain surging through him. *I will not falter. I will not fail!*

He put on all the speed he could manage. Even so, the two giants were quickly pulling away.

Thick, windowless doors marked with t'au glyphs whipped past them. Karras and Rauth had mastered the t'au script. They read each door as they ran.

Storage, maintenance, and then a series of cells, the purpose of which could only be guessed at.

Suddenly, Karras halted. Rauth ran on a few steps, then stopped and turned. 'What is it, Scholar?'

'I don't know,' murmured Karras. 'Something...'

He reached out with a gauntleted hand, pressing it against the door in front of him.

Nothing. The psychic suppression is too complete. So why did I stop?

Morant caught up to them, a light sweat on his brow.

'I cannot say why, brother,' Karras told Rauth, 'but we have to check this room.'

Rauth shrugged. Karras' power was a dark thing, a thing not to be trusted, but its value could not be denied. He had no idea that the gift in question was currently not a factor.

'Morant,' said Karras.

The trooper moved to the access panel, connected his module and began to work. On the tiny screen, thousands of t'au glyphs scrolled by at an almost unreadable speed. Suddenly the flow stopped. Morant had found what he was looking for. He reached for the keypad on the access panel and tapped in a seven-glyph code.

Seals disengaged within the door housing. Thick bolts slid aside. The door retracted upward into the frame.

Rauth looked at Karras expectantly. Karras nodded him through, then followed, bolter raised.

They found themselves in an observation room. The left and right walls were transparent, made of a tough polymer that was the t'au equivalent of glass.

What Karras saw in the chambers beyond made his breath catch in his chest.

In the room on the right, hanging by their arms from ceramic restraints attached to the ceiling, were five figures of unmistakable size and musculature.

'Space Marines!' snarled Karras.

'Epsilon's kill-team,' added Rauth.

Karras moved closer to the window. He nodded. 'Sabre Squad, but missing three members.'

The Space Marines of Sabre Squad were still wearing the black bodysuits that sat between skin and power armour, but of their armour itself there was no sign.

They were breathing, though each of their faces was masked with some kind of sensory-deprivation helmet. None seemed injured.

'Another over here, my lords,' said Morant. There was no mistaking the heaviness in his tone. 'The xenos bastards have made a real mess of him.'

Rauth crossed the room to stand by Morant. What he saw made him bare his teeth, and a dark anger filled his heart, he who was the least emotional of all Talon Squad.

'Vivisection,' he breathed. 'See those machines connected to the body? They dissected him alive, Scholar.'

Karras joined them at the window, and his heart, too, filled with righteous rage. 'How?' he muttered through gritted teeth. 'What in Terra's holy name brought them to this?'

'The others are alive,' said Rauth. 'But Karras... if Epsilon and the t'au are moving out as you say, we can't spare time for this.'

'My lords!' gasped Morant. 'Surely we–'

Rauth whipped his head around to the trooper. 'Silence! This is a Space Marine matter!'

'No time,' said Karras. 'You're right, Watcher. But we both know we cannot leave them. I will push on ahead with Morant. I charge you with releasing them and catching up to me.'

Rauth was quiet for a brief moment – just long enough to communicate his disapproval. But he knew the truth of what Karras had said. Whatever waited up ahead, neither would rest easy knowing they had left brothers imprisoned here.

'On your order then, Alpha,' said Rauth. 'Now get out of here and let me work.'

As Karras and Morant left, the Exorcist was thumbing plastic explosive charges into a breaching pattern on the thick window between himself and the five Space Marines on the other side. They were already running, their feet pounding the corridor, when they heard the crack of the explosion and the crash of the window breaking into a million pieces.

But Karras couldn't think about that now.

Up ahead, the corridor straightened for fifty metres and ended at a large door. *So,* thought Karras, *the corridors didn't join up after all. Let us hope I made the right choice.*

The door was marked with t'au glyphs:

Main Operations

Extreme Caution Beyond This Point

Karras and Morant jogged to a halt in front of it.

Karras gestured to the door. 'You know what to do, soldier. Crack it. Fast.'

THIRTY-FIVE

Main Operations seemed as deserted as the rest of the basement level. Karras and Morant stepped into a hallway with another large security door at the far end. On either side, smaller doors led into surgeries and observation rooms. There were banks of t'au cogitators and monitors, workstations arranged in rows, but they were all dead. Here and there, a chair lay toppled. Sheaves of crystalline printouts covered in t'au glyphs lay scattered where they had fallen. The place had all the signs of a rushed evacuation.

'When the t'au clear out, they clear out fast. Doesn't mean they won't be back,' offered Morant.

Karras spoke without turning. His eyes were on the far end of the hall. 'Get to work on that door.'

Morant bowed and jogged over to it, steadfastly ignoring the pain of his wounded arm.

Karras began investigating the side rooms. No t'au. No

sign of Epsilon. And yet, he had a strong feeling, a feeling in his gut, that she was here, that he hadn't come too late.

The surgeries and observation rooms had been ransacked. There was nothing left to show what had been happening here. Still, there was a heavy feeling in Karras' gut. Something familiar and foreboding. The faintest hint of a familiar scent hung in the air. For some reason, his mind called up memories of the mines under Chiaro's surface.

Morant stood from his hacking module and disconnected it as the massive door slid upwards into the ceiling. A vast, echoing space gaped beyond.

He called out to Karras, and the Death Spectre strode over to join him.

Together, they looked through the portal at the massive chamber beyond.

It was cool in there. Cool and damp and gloomy. The ceiling was high and hewn from solid rock. There had been a natural cavern here. The original Imperial inhabitants had exploited it to make this space. Thick pillars supported the roof every ten metres or so. Blocky. Human-made. None of the smoothness or roundness so beloved of the t'au.

All along the walls stood monitoring stations and storage units. Lights shone from the fixtures halfway up the pillars, illuminating the floor but leaving the ceiling in shadow.

That floor was a patchwork of metal and transparent polymer. Stretching out in a grid across the whole space were railing-lined walkways. Between these, sunk deep in the floor, were holding tanks of some kind. The ceiling of each tank was floor level. Were one to simply jump the railings, one might walk straight out across them.

Karras walked to the nearest of the tanks and looked down into it.

Empty, but the walls had been raked repeatedly by something sharp.

He moved on along the central walkway, bolter raised and ready. He was deeply uneasy. Angry, too, that something was suppressing his gift when he needed it most. Just what the hell was all this?

Morant fell in behind him, clutching his pistol tightly, eyes wide, alert to any movement.

When they reached the next junction on the walkway, they both looked down into the second holding tank.

'Throne and saints!' whispered Morant.

Karras just glared down at what he saw, his lip twisted in a snarl.

There below him, packed tight, were a dozen twisted forms of chitin and claw.

'Tyranids,' said Morant.

'T'au-genestealer hybrids,' said Karras. They were unmistakable. Where human hybrids still bore a nose, or at least nostrils, these creatures bore the olfactory facial slit of the t'au. But, no, it was more than just that – their lineage was just as clear in their lipless mouths, their flatter facial bone structure, their three-fingered hands...

Karras' mind was on overdrive. What were the t'au doing with a tank full of abominations? What did Epsilon have to do with this?

Now he knew why his mind kept bringing him back to Chiaro, to *Operation Night Harvest*.

This is no coincidence.

One of the hybrids glanced up and saw him. It tossed back its head and loosed a long, throaty howl. The others looked up. When they saw the soldier and the Space Marine staring down at them, they went into a frenzy, clambering over each other to get closer and try to fulfil their genetic imperative – to kill and consume for the proliferation of their foul species.

A few leapt from the backs of others and slashed at the polymer ceiling with curving black claws, leaving white scratches. But they couldn't break through. The t'au weren't sloppy.

'What were they doing with them?' Morant wondered aloud.

For Karras, things started clicking into place. *A Geller field. That's why my power is being suppressed. To create hybrids, they'd need purestrain 'stealers. And the t'au would have to prevent those 'stealers from guiding the hive-mind here. Otherwise the whole planet…*

And if that were true, it was highly likely that Epsilon herself had provided the Geller field generator.

He spun on Morant. 'Get back to the upper levels. Get word to Copley. She has to pull everyone out. Now! Get everyone on the Stormravens and get them out of here!'

'M'lord?'

Karras pointed at the monsters in the tank. Then he ordered Morant to follow him and marched to the next. There, he found what he knew he would – purestrain genestealers. They stood at rest, swaying slightly, armoured backs glistening in the light from the lamps on the pillars.

Karras growled. He had seen enough of them back on Chiaro – the bony, almost fleshless heads; the twisted, razor-lined mouths; the four lethal, black-taloned arms.

'Why?' gasped Morant.

'Epsilon,' said Karras. He was starting to see. 'Epsilon must have brought some project to the t'au here. They wouldn't know to use a Geller field to isolate their specimens otherwise. I'll wager it was she who made this possible.'

'Why would an ordo member work with the t'au on something like this?'

'I'll find that out when I ask her,' said Karras.

'No, Death Spectre,' rumbled a voice like distant thunder. 'You won't.'

A bulky black figure emerged from behind one of the central pillars up ahead. Red visor lenses glowed. Light shimmered on silver and black ceramite. A bolter was raised, aimed straight at Karras.

'Get behind me, now,' Karras muttered to Morant. 'And be ready to run for the door the moment I say go. Don't question me. Get everyone off-site as fast as you can. This place will be a smoking crater very soon.'

'What about you, m'lord?'

Karras didn't answer. The figure in front of him had his full attention. Now another, similarly clad in black power armour, stepped out of cover.

The first spoke again, his voice deep, even for a Space Marine. 'We would have you turn back, Lyandro Karras. We would not see Adeptus Astartes blood spilled. Leave with haste and put as much distance between yourself and this facility as you can.'

'You know my name,' said Karras. It wasn't a question. 'And I know yours, Khor Kabannen of the Iron Hands. And yours, Lucianos of the Scythes of the Emperor. What I do not know is why you betrayed the rest of your kill-team into xenos hands and are helping Epsilon betray the ordo and the Imperium.'

Kabannen shook his helmed head. 'You cannot begin to comprehend what is at stake. This game is too big for you, Death Spectre. Turn around and leave it to those better informed. For your own sake and the sake of your brothers.'

'I have orders,' Karras shot back. 'A duty. We are here to retrieve Epsilon. Join us in getting her back into ordo hands, or face judgement as traitors of the Imperium.'

'He talks of duty,' said Lucianos, his voice higher and sharper than his counterpart's. 'Brother, few know the meaning of duty as we do. Sacrifice. Honour. Things are not as you believe. Do not seek to judge. Go back the way you came.'

The door at the very far end of the chamber slid open and a slender, feminine figure, all in black like her bodyguards, stalked towards them. When she was level with Kabannen, she stopped and looked Karras over.

He found himself staring into the pale golden eyes of a beautiful woman, her skin almost as white as his own, her hair so black it seemed to drink the light.

She smiled.

'So this is Talon Alpha.' She glanced at Kabannen and Lucianos. 'Who else could it be? Death Spectre iconography, Deathwatch-issue wargear. M'lord Omicron would, of course, command Sigma to find me. He would trust no one else.'

'The Ordo Xenos orders you to return with me, inquisitor,' said Karras. 'You are officially operating beyond your remit. You must return and account for your actions, else be branded a traitor subject to excommunicatus.'

Epsilon scowled at that word. 'Do you think I wanted to put myself in t'au hands? Think, Alpha. Would a loyal inquisitor reveal Imperial secrets to the t'au on a whim? I am so close now. I alone have come to the t'au offering a sliver of hope in their fight against the Great Devourer. Their Empire may well live or die on the success of our work together. And for that… for *that,* they will grant me passage to Al Rashaq.'

Karras squinted at her. Al Rashaq? It was the first time he had heard the name. In all his reading, he had not come across it. Was it a place? A thing? Why was it so important to this woman that she would deliberately put herself in enemy hands?

'I know nothing of that,' he boomed. 'It would not matter if

I did. My duty is simple. I have been charged with returning you. Come with me now. Do not let this turn to bloodshed and regret.'

'You are outnumbered, Death Spectre,' laughed Kabannen. 'Two to one. The man with you will be of no consequence.'

'You seem to have miscounted, Iron Hand,' Karras shot back. Beneath his helm, he was grinning. 'Isn't that right, Watcher?'

Photo-reactive camouflage flickered off to reveal Darrion Rauth standing just inside the chamber door with his bolter pointed straight at Lucianos.

'How fine it is to see in the dark,' quoted Rauth, a line from a thirty-fourth-millennium play by Orchaeo. 'But so much better to *be* the dark.'

Karras raised his bolter and pointed it straight at Kabannen. To Morant, he said, 'Go, now! Get everyone away from here. And do not wait for us. That's an order!'

'Emperor watch over you, my lord,' breathed Morant. 'I will see it done!'

He ran.

'Khor!' said Lucianos, ready to gun the man down before he reached the door.

'Let him go, brother,' said Kabannen. 'He matters not. Their game is utterly lost.'

'What makes you so sure?' Karras demanded.

At a sign from Epsilon, the two Deathwatch bodyguards began retreating towards the chamber's far door, weapons still trained on Karras and Rauth.

Epsilon spoke over her shoulder as she walked. 'Return to your master, Talon. Ask him to have faith in me and the patience to let this play out. I must see this through, no matter how it looks from the outside.'

When she was almost at the door, she paused. 'There will come a time, soon, when you will understand all of this. On that day, you will be glad this moment did not descend into bloodshed. Brother should not slay brother, after all. And the prize at the end of this road is great indeed. Far greater than you can imagine. It may change everything for mankind. Everything.'

Karras walked forward, daring the inquisitor's bodyguards to shoot. 'Answer me this!' he called out. 'Is that the same damned lie you fed the rest of your kill-team before you handed them over to be vivisected by the xenos?'

Lucianos took an angry step towards Karras, finger on trigger.

'No, brother!' barked Kabannen.

Reluctantly, Lucianos backed down and retreated to the doorway.

'The death of Sabre Three was unfortunate,' said Kabannen, 'but he woke from cryosleep before he could be properly restrained. He opted to disobey me and fight. Many t'au died before we could restrain him. We almost lost our chance at cooperation. The t'au demanded his life as a marker of the fresh accord between us. In the end, we had no choice. As she has already told you, ultimately, in retrospect, the Ordo Xenos will understand and approve of her actions.'

'Did you see his body?' growled Karras. 'Did you see how they defiled it?'

Neither Kabannen nor Lucianos answered. Weapons still levelled, they backed out the door. And then they were gone.

Karras and Rauth both broke into a run at the same time, determined to chase them down.

At that moment, there came the double crack of two small explosions in close proximity. Glass shattered. Alien screeching filled the air.

Up ahead, between himself and the doorway through which his targets had just vanished, Karras saw a taloned hand grasp for a metal railing. Another reached up. Then another. A large, powerful body hauled itself from the holding pen, jaws dripping with noxious saliva. Its violet eyes locked onto Karras. It loosed a chilling scream into the air.

Rauth's bolter coughed once.

The genestealer's head snapped backwards. It tumbled back into the holding tank. Others spilled up and out, climbing frantically, ravenously.

Karras opened fire, bolts ripping into alien bodies and exploding inside, bursting them apart. Every bolt struck its mark, but the 'stealers were fast and there were many.

'Like old times,' said Karras, half to himself, as the slaughter intensified. It was something Ghost would probably say.

But it wasn't just like old times. Because this time, his true power was cut off from him. *Arquemann*, the great force sword on his back, was still silent. No call for artful slaughter itched at the edge of Karras' mind. With the Geller field interfering, the relic sword could not communicate with its owner, could not channel his power through the psy-resonating crystal matrix in its blade.

The Geller field generator was still close enough to be a problem, but there might be enough time. Epsilon wasn't out of range quite yet. Karras and Rauth could still turn this around.

'Forward, brother!' Karras yelled. 'We break through!'

They ran. A score of slashing talons reached for them, raking their pauldons as they went, but their bolters continued to bark and the tyranids could not stop them.

As they passed through the doorway, Rauth slapped a demolition charge on the wall and kept running.

They emerged into a wide, well-lit loading area. Up ahead, Epsilon, Kabannen, Lucianos and a cadre of fire warriors were boarding some kind of hovering train carriage. Karras saw a t'au with the marking of a supreme commander glance his way, bark orders to the blue-skin soldiers and disappear into the passenger carriage.

Coldwave!

There was only one passenger car. All the others were for freight, each loaded with bulky cargo covered by sheets.

The fire warriors on the platform formed a firing line and began taking shots at Karras and Rauth.

Behind the two Space Marines, determined tyranids began to spill from the doorway. Rauth had been waiting for that. He squeezed the detonator in his left hand. There was a deafening crack and a blast of heat. Tyranid bodies were ripped apart with vicious, pulverising force.

The doorway collapsed, along with much of the wall, bringing large chunks of ceiling down with it.

'Satisfying,' said Rauth as he turned to concentrate on the t'au. 'But we've one less exit.'

Karras dropped to an armoured knee and began picking off fire warriors with his bolter. 'Never mind. We weren't leaving that way anyway!'

The t'au mag-train began to hum noisily, rising a metre higher in the air. It moved off, picking up speed quickly, disappearing into a tunnel leading north-east.

'Damn it!' spat Karras.

He and Rauth downed the last of the fire warriors. The loading terminal fell silent. Smoke wisped from bolter muzzles and the broken bodies of the xenos they had slain.

'What now, Scholar?' demanded Rauth. 'Our mission objective just got away.'

'We've got more immediate problems,' said Karras. 'Start running!'

He broke into a sprint. At the edge of the platform, he leapt down onto the mag-tracks and began racing along them in the same direction Epsilon had gone.

'What do you mean, more immediate problems?' demanded Rauth as he paced Karras, bolter slung over right pauldron, feet pounding the flat metallic track.

Karras felt his power returning to him. At first just an itch, just a tiny trickle, but quickly more, and more, until it was back with all the force it had ever had. He could feel *Arquemann* again, could sense the sword's soul reconnecting with his.

'Run for all you're worth,' Karras gasped as he put on an added burst of speed.

He knew what the retreat of the Geller field meant. The t'au could never afford to risk purestrain genestealers calling out to the tyranid hive-mind. That would draw the hive-fleet down on Tychonis. Everything here would die.

The removal of the Geller field generator from the Tower while there were still tyranid life forms present spoke of Coldwave's intent in plain terms.

I hope the others get away in time, thought Karras.

At that moment, the ground shuddered so violently that he and Rauth were thrown from their feet.

Karras landed hard, the speed of his sprint carrying him forward half a dozen metres on his side.

He pushed himself to his hands and looked back the way they had come.

A bright light appeared. Blinding. Soundless. All-consuming. Pieces of rock riding the forward wave of the blast struck his armour like a hard rain.

With all the haste he could manage, he wrenched open his inner gates and called forth the dangerous power of the immaterium.

Rauth had risen to his knees just to Karras' right. He faced the racing wall of fire and rock as it bore down on them both.

'Ah,' he muttered.

It was said so calmly.

Karras didn't hear it. All he could hear was the cruel laughter of a thousand voices.

The power he desperately needed in order to save them had a terrible price. How high would it be this time?

He was about to find out.

THIRTY-SIX

Morant's vox-bead crackled. Without any explanation, he was suddenly hearing comms chatter from the rest of Arcturus. He had no idea it was down to the removal of the Geller field generator. The moment he realised he had comms again, he voxed Archangel directly.

He was sprinting along the corridor to the vator in which he and the Space Marines had come, but he slowed momentarily so he could be understood. His arm throbbed wickedly. He spoke through gritted teeth as he explained to Copley what had transpired here in the sub-levels.

Copley kept her response short, then addressed Arcturus over the main tactical channel. *'Everyone will converge in the courtyard for extraction. And I mean* now! *Ground team, I want that courtyard secured for dust-off.'*

Each of the separate assault elements confirmed their orders.

As Morant continued his race against time, he came upon

the Space Marines of Sabre Squad ripping apart room after room as they headed towards the vator Rauth had told them about.

When Morant skidded to a halt, they rounded on him, eyeing him suspiciously. The largest by far in both height and frame stormed over to him and blocked his way.

'Who are you?' he thundered.

'Sergeant Morant, my lord, of Task Force Arcturus, Ordo Xenos. I'm with the Space Marine who freed you.'

'Where is he?'

'He has gone deeper into the facility, my lord. I was ordered to evacuate with all haste.'

'I am Androcles of the Sons of Antaeus,' said the giant. 'Deathwatch. Callsign *Sabre Four*. We cannot find our weapons, Morant, nor our armour.'

The Elysian gulped and glanced at the others. All so massive. All so grim. The scars, the tattoos, the broad, impassive faces and hard eyes. One had all-black eyes like the Raven Guard of Talon, but his teeth were like triangular razors. He was almost as terrifying as the tyranids Morant had just witnessed in the holding tanks.

Others, like Androcles, looked more noble, more like Karras, more like the glorious illustrations in Imperial storybooks.

'My lords,' said Morant with a look of regret, 'would that we had time. Talon Alpha believes the t'au are about to destroy this entire base. We must evacuate now, while we still can.'

One of the others spat a curse. 'We cannot leave our wargear!'

Androcles looked down at Morant. He could see that the Elysian was flush with adrenaline and desperately wanted to get away. The threat seemed real.

'Brothers,' said the giant, his tone so deep it shook the air, 'we honour and treasure our weapons, our armour... but that we live to fight for the Emperor is the priority. I believe the t'au *will* destroy this place. There is no time. We go!'

The black-eyed, sharp-toothed one muttered something in a tribal tongue.

'Sergeant Morant,' said Androcles. 'All we know of this place is the cell where we were held. Lead us out of here so we can live to take our revenge on the xenos.'

'M'lords,' said Morant. 'This way!'

A vator ride later, they were on ground level, charging through corridors Karras and Rauth had filled with t'au dead. They passed the corpse of Carland. Morant glanced at it with a twinge of sorrow, but there was no time for anything else. At any moment, the t'au would turn this whole prison into a giant crater.

They had to get away.

Copley and her squad were clambering into the hatches of Reaper Two when Morant bolted from cover with the remnants of Sabre Squad in tow.

Solarion was still aboard. He hadn't left his sniping position since the assault began. He looked over his shoulder and nodded at Copley as she entered the hold, then noticed the five unfamiliar, unarmoured Space Marines behind her.

By their tattoos, he quickly counted three as being from Ultramarine successor Chapters – the Howling Griffons, the Marines Errant… and the massive one with the slightly sleepy look on his face? He was from the Sons of Antaeus.

The Sons were not well honoured on Macragge. Something had gone wrong in their creation process. They were a product of the so-called Cursed Founding.

No matter. Surely all three would show him due respect as progenitor. He could see them noting the proud Ultramarines icon on his right pauldron.

He did not acknowledge them, however. Instead, he returned swiftly to his search for fresh targets, for any t'au determined to interfere with the extraction.

There would be time for introductions later.

As he scanned the buildings and the shadows, he heard Copley shouting orders to her people.

Archangel.

Despite his anger at the initial insult of Sigma putting a woman in charge of Space Marines, the major had proven adequate to her task. Karras and Rauth were still down there, in the bowels of the facility, facing Throne knew what, but such was their duty. Task Force Arcturus had got them in, had given them the shot they needed. Now, time was up.

Reaper Two was almost fully loaded. Reaper Three swung in to land and start picking up more of the Arcturus survivors. Reaper One circled in the air above, continuing to provide deadly fire support to those on the ground as they whittled away at the last of the t'au forces.

Copley had no idea how much time she had left. She trusted Karras' message, relayed through Morant. It made sense. If there were tyranids here, especially 'stealers, and the t'au were being forced to pull out by the task force assault, t'au command – meaning Coldwave – would want to make sure no loose ends were left. A single stealer loosed into the wild would eventually infect the populace. At a certain tipping point, the genestealer infestation would be so widespread that the psychic call to the hive-fleets would bring inescapable doom to this world. And from here, it wasn't so far to the next t'au world, and the next after that.

She knew Karras was right. Coldwave was about to purge this whole area. How long did they have? Seconds? Minutes?

Where are you, Karras? How will you get out? Or do you no longer expect to?

That thought stung her. She had come to respect, even like, the red-eyed albino. He was a lot easier to deal with than most of those he commanded, with the exception, perhaps, of the easy-going Imperial Fist.

Don't die, Death Spectre. I don't know how you'll get away. But don't die.

Reaper Two was ready to take off.

Copley yelled over the vox. The rest of her operators started falling back from their firing positions towards the black belly of Reaper Three.

'Brother Chyron,' she added. 'Move to Reaper Three and prepare for magna-grapple attachment.'

The Dreadnought answered over the whine and roar of his assault cannon. His ammo was almost out, having been spent chewing t'au cover to pieces then chewing apart the bodies which had been sheltering behind it. *'There are xenos yet breathing, woman! The slaughter is not yet done!'*

'Talon Six, comply with your orders *now*!'

'It's time to go, scrapheap,' laughed Zeed over the vox. *'Here, I brought a present for you.'*

Looking out of the rear of Reaper Two, Copley saw the Raven Guard appear from between two barracks and casually toss something at Chyron. It was smooth and metallic. It clanged against the Dreadnought's armoured chassis.

Chyron shuffled backwards and angled his visor down to look at it. 'The head of the last XV8. A curse on you, Raven Guard. That honour was to be mine.'

Zeed was making for Reaper Three, ignoring the t'au fire that still hissed in the air about him as if it were nothing at all. His confidence struck Copley as bordering on madness.

Had he been a normal man... But, of course, he was not. How great it must be, she thought, to have such power, such strength. Even for just a moment, she'd have liked to know what it felt like.

'Stick to what you're good at, Old One,' laughed Zeed. 'You're too slow for some foes. Leave the fast ones to me.'

Chyron growled menacingly.

'Stop your grumbling. Your kill count is high enough. As the lady says, it's time to leave. Get yourself secured to the Stormraven if you don't want to walk all the way back.'

Zeed waited at the rear of the Stormraven. After a moment spent wrestling with his desire to continue killing, Chyron broke away from the last vestiges of t'au resistance and stomped angrily over to the back of the craft. The Raven Guard and two of Copley's people connected him to the grapples. The winches turned, groaning at his weight as they lifted him from his feet.

With Chyron suspended from the rear, Reaper Three was by far the heaviest and slowest of the three gunships. Copley ordered it up while the others were still loading.

Voss and the remains of his support squad – two had been lost in the firefight – were the last to mount up. The rear hatch of Reaper One was still closing behind them when the Stormraven lifted into the air to join the others.

'Are Scholar and Watcher still out of contact?' Voss asked over the vox.

'They're on their own,' said Copley.

With all three Stormravens in the air, the bedraggled remains of the t'au force on the ground moved forward and fired up. Their shots smacked harmlessly off black-armoured hulls and wings as the gunships turned east and engaged their jets. Soon, they were out of range.

A wind blew into the courtyard, stirring the smoke, tugging at the clothing of the dead.

The t'au left alive moved among their fallen, finding friends there. Brothers. Some cried out. Tears ran down blue-grey cheeks.

Aboard Reaper One, Voss was still brooding over the need to leave without Karras and Rauth.

'Listen, there's nothing we can do for them,' said Copley sullenly.

'Why worry, tree stump?' voxed Zeed. *'You said it yourself before – Karras is a hard bastard to kill.'*

Pure bravado. Zeed was as worried as Voss. He just refused to show it.

'Hard to kill, maybe, but he's not invincible,' Solarion muttered back.

The Stormravens put on more speed, accelerating away from Alel a Tarag as fast as their turbine engines would allow. The roar of their passage echoed off the canyon walls, filling it.

The sun was up and glaring in the eastern sky. The sky was blue.

Copley watched the prison walls shrink into the distance on one of the monitors linked to Reaper Two's rear picter. Dark smoke poured up from inside the compound and was dragged south on a light wind.

Suddenly, the monitor crackled with bands of static. She saw a sphere of blinding white light engulf the facility.

'Brace!' she shouted over the vox. 'All hands, brace!'

There was a strange moment of stillness, then a vast, towering cloud rose into the sky in the shape of a great mushroom. On the ground, a raging wall of fire and dirt came racing along the canyon towards them.

One of the Sabre Squad Space Marines was at her side, watching over her shoulder. He was pale, like Karras, but lacked the red eyes.

'Nuclear,' he said matter-of-factly. He reached up and gripped the crash net fixed to the ceiling. 'This is going to hurt, woman.'

Copley called out to the pilot, 'Get us up and out of this bloody canyon. All the speed you can muster. Or the walls will channel the blast straight at us! That goes for all Stormravens!'

Reaper Two started bucking and shuddering. Gravity shifted violently as the pilot swung the craft up over the edge of the canyon and out into open desert, low to the ground. Reapers One and Three were only half a second behind.

But the wall of fire and dust was fast, expanding like a solar flare, hungry to swallow them. It was slowing as it came, spending its power as it expanded, but it still caught up with them easily and swept them into its rage.

The Stormravens were snatched from the air then swatted to the desert floor like bugs. Flying low as they were, they hit the sand at a shallow angle, carving long wakes as they slid to a halt in a ragged, uneven triangle. Those onboard were thrown against their restraints. Unsecured weapons slammed against the walls. Then silence.

Around Copley, all internal lights and monitors flickered and went out. Red backup lighting kicked in.

'Reaper Two down,' reported the pilot over the force-wide channel. *'All systems offline.'*

No one heard him. Comms were dead. He was speaking to himself up there in the cockpit.

'Reaper flight, report!' barked Copley.

Nothing.

'Reapers One and Three, do you copy?'

'The link is dead, ma'am,' said Morant, picking himself up

from the floor. He had a cut on his head. Some of the others had been thrown around, too. They groaned as they got to their feet and then helped their fellows. The Space Marines had remained standing, holding on to the crash net above them. Some of them helped the Elysians up. Solarion and the one with the razor teeth did not, Copley noted.

That Ultramarine was easy to respect as a sniper, but damned impossible to like. The other one she didn't know. He looked like a monster from a bad dream.

Her people were looking at her, awaiting her command.

'Crack that rear hatch manually,' she barked, 'and get an eye on the other Stormravens. Check on the Dreadnought, too. I need a full damage report. I'm going up front to talk with Graka.'

'That was thermonuclear,' said Solarion. 'You crack that hatch and you know what it means for your people. We Space Marines will be fine, but not you.'

Copley glared at him. She didn't need it spelled out like that in front of her men. She knew damned well what it meant. What choice was there?

'We can't lie here in the dirt. How long till t'au fighters start running sweeps, looking for us? We have to get in the air and back to Chatha na Hadik. So we have to go outside. We take that chance, or we die here, three crippled birds waiting to be shot to pieces.' She looked around at her people. Reluctant, but resigned. They knew she was right. 'If we're lucky, and if he's still alive somehow, maybe Talon Alpha can get word to us while we're doing the repairs. We'd all better hope so. Because if he's dead, we have no idea where we stand with Epsilon. *Operation Shadowbreaker* is not over. Do you all hear me? This op is not over until we have the target! Now get out there. We have work to do!'

Triskel held up a hand, his auspex scanner in the other. He was glaring at it, his mouth a tight line. 'Not safe to open the hatch, ma'am. Radiation levels in the red.'

'Since the other options are get caught by the t'au or just wait to die, I'm afraid we don't have a choice, Tris.'

'You need not venture out,' said one of the Space Marines, his voice so unnaturally deep and resonant compared to Triskel's and Copley's. He gestured to his brothers. 'We will be unharmed. It is we who shall effect the repairs.'

Copley bowed with gratitude, but said, 'That'll mitigate it somewhat, my lord, but either way that hatch has to open.' She turned to her men. 'So get to it, lads.'

Her troopers went into action. They tried furiously to crack the hatch, but it was jammed with sand from the outside. It took the prodigious strength of Brother Androcles to open it at last.

The Elysians watched in quiet awe as he did, his raw strength far superior to all of theirs combined. They were the best, hard men who completed hard missions, but to a man, they felt like children next to the Space Marines.

When the hatch was open, daylight flooded the inside of the compartment. Hot, flinty air rushed in, strong with the smell of burning silicates. The Space Marines, unarmoured but utterly undaunted by thoughts of radiation, stepped out into the blazing desert light.

'I'm going up front to speak with Graka,' Copley announced.

As she turned towards the cockpit, Morant put a hand on her arm. 'Ma'am, about the Death Spectre... Much as I want to, I don't think even a Space Marine could have survived that. Not even Talon Alpha.'

Copley didn't look at him. She brushed his hand off, saying nothing. She needed to believe Karras was still alive, that it hadn't all gone to shit like this. Morant's words made her angry, because they meant *Shadowbreaker* was a lost cause, a failed op. She had always been able to pull bad ops back from the abyss before now.

Had she been depending on the Deathwatch too much?

Should she have gone into the lower levels with them?

Morant was right. The chances were high that Karras and Rauth were dead. No way for anyone on foot to escape a thermonuclear blast radius that size. Hell, even at full speed, the Stormravens hadn't managed it.

The knowledge of what had happened down there after Morant was ordered away would lie dead with them forever.

Operation Shadowbreaker had always been a long shot. Too many variables. Too many unknowns.

Karras and Rauth were gone. Swallowed up in the blast.

The rogue inquisitor and the t'au commander had pulled out and blown everything sky high.

Epsilon slipped us. Our one shot, and she slipped right through our hands.

Somehow, though, a tiny voice in Copley's head told her it *wasn't* over.

She shook her head. If things hadn't been so bad, she'd have laughed at herself. Who was she kidding? *Shadowbreaker* was a mess. They'd lost people. The target had got away. And even now, she and her people were being irradiated to potentially lethal levels because they needed to effect emergency repairs or die out here on the open sand.

No one wins all the time.

But the voice in her head was persistent. She was still alive. And if she was alive, she was still in the game. And if she was still in the game, she could still win.

It wasn't over. She still had a job to do.

THIRTY-SEVEN

From blinding light to deepest darkness.

Karras felt himself being pulled down, dragged deep into a black void. Around him, he could hear things moving, breathing, slithering, their claws scratching on stone. He heard a chorus of voices in terrible anguish and another chorus mocking them cruelly. He heard songs sung in forbidden languages and chanting that both repelled and entranced.

His own voice was weak and quiet in his mind, all but drowned out by the cacophony around him. He concentrated on his own thoughts, violently rejecting everything else that sought to smother him.

Was I fast enough? Did I throw up the barrier in time?

The blast had been powerful. Definitely thermonuclear.

He had never been forced to defend against something of that magnitude. Given time to think, he might not have tried, certain he could not. But he had acted on reflex, as much to save Darrion Rauth as to save himself.

Still, the price…

Was his desperate, reckless use of ethereal power about to cost him his soul?

Familiar laughter. Unnatural. Inhuman.

It echoed in the vastness of Karras' inner universe, that bottomless well of the simultaneously infinite and infinitesimal self.

It emanated from a growing presence, rising up from below to meet him as he plunged further from physical reality.

Karras tried to recoil from it, revulsion washing over him.

The laughter grew louder, until it was so loud it seemed to Karras that he himself might be the source.

'You insist on disappointing me, Death Spectre,' said a dozen voices at once, each of different tone and timbre. 'I thought I made myself clear about what the consequences would be.'

Unbidden, the monstrosity's name rang loud in Karras' mind.

Hepaxammon. Prince of Sorrows.

Again, the laughter. 'Names I chose to give you. Among a thousand peoples on a thousand worlds, I am known by many others. You cannot begin to imagine the sphere of my influence. I am older than your petty Imperium, Space Marine. And you have made the mistake of underestimating me. Ah, such consequences you will face!'

In Karras' mind, there flashed a sequence of images, each so vivid they might have been real, as if he were being skipped across the surface of time and space like a flat stone on still waters, forced to witness places and times of the daemon's choosing.

The Death Spectre war fleet departing Occludian orbit en masse.

A titanic battle in space. Several Space Marine fleets including that of his Chapter locked in desperate combat with a vast tendril of the tyranid incursion. Hopelessly outnumbered, unable to fall back.

Ships aflame, shedding sections of hull as they crashed white hot through a thick planetary atmosphere before knifing into the ground like thrown javelins.

And Space Marines, so many Space Marines, staggering from a thousand burning wrecks only to be swarmed upon, their desperate defence easily overwhelmed by a living tsunami of tyranid bioforms.

Space Marine deaths on a scale Karras had never seen.

Brave brothers eaten alive by bio-acid, or speared and sliced apart by talons as long and sharp as the power-scythes of the Death Spectres First Company, the War-Geists.

Massacre. Hopeless, bloody massacre.

The end of the Chapter, its fate the same as that of Chyron's Lamenters.

Hepaxammon's voice whispered to him now, as if only centimetres from his ear, as soft and coaxing as a lover's but dripping with poison and bile.

'You doubt, Death Spectre, but you will see. You cannot imagine the extent of my influence, the depth of my machinations. Men of such rank and power. Names that would shock you. Wheels within wheels. That you are here, now, with the Exorcist, is no matter of happenstance. I warned you. You did not heed me. The extent of your punishment will strike you to the core. The Death Spectres will be commanded to deploy in full force. And none will see Occludus again.'

Karras roared in denial. 'The tongues of daemons drip with lies! Your words are hollow!'

Hepaxammon's presence retreated a little. Karras could

feel it, though all was still blackness and void. Why? Was it pushed back by the strength of his conviction?

'You will learn in time,' it told him. '*Jormungandr.* Remember that name. The end of the Death Spectres. No, not just their end, but their damnation. I will not stop with simply destroying them. In the aftermath, I will cause others to question their decisions. The loss of a thousand worlds will be placed at their feet. The losses of other Chapters, too. Thousands of dead Adeptus Astartes. I will make it so. Your beloved brotherhood will be dishonoured for all time.'

The abomination paused, then added, 'This I do because you disobeyed me. There is no more bargain to be made. Now, I will speak to Darrion Rauth. I cannot sense him, but he is here. I know you sought to save him. Your thoughts have given him away.'

Karras sensed the daemon focusing elsewhere, preparing for something.

The last time he had encountered this horror, he had been saved by Athio Cordatus, mentor and friend. The Chief Librarian had foreseen the daemon's intrusion into Karras' reality. He had placed a psychic safeguard along several of Karras' prime futures.

But there was no such safeguard now.

My khadit, thought Karras, *did you not foresee this too? Am I too far along a shadowed path?*

The daemon's presence suddenly flooded Karras' consciousness. He felt it surge into him like icy water into the lungs of a drowning man. He felt himself overwhelmed, swept up and tossed around as if by an unstoppable tidal wave. Karras desperately scrambled for something to hold on to. He reached for mantras and litanies long committed to memory, but the daemon deflected him from them easily.

'I have waited long for this,' Hepaxammon hissed with obvious satisfaction. 'Darrion Rauth evaded me once. Broke his oath. Betrayed his vow. Through you, Lyandro Karras, he will finally pay. Watch through your own eyes, listen with your own ears, powerless to intervene as I take my due!'

Karras found himself looking out through his own eyes. He could feel his body, feel his armour around him, his pulse, his breathing. He saw his hand flexing and his mind flooded with panic and rage, because it was not he who had flexed it.

He was no longer in control. He was a passenger.

'Enjoy the ride,' said Hepaxammon.

Karras' eyes fixed on movement to his left. There was Rauth, pushing himself to his feet.

The Exorcist was looking back the way they had come. Most of the tunnel down which he and Karras had run had collapsed. Nothing could be seen of the loading area, just a wall of fallen rock.

He turned and looked the other way, and saw that the tunnel ahead of them was still intact. Karras' barrier hadn't just saved them – it had prevented the collapse of the tunnel beyond them.

The Death Spectre's sorcery had stopped the fury of a nuclear blast. He had saved them...

Rauth turned to Karras and regarded him for a moment. He walked towards him, unfastening his helm as he did.

Three metres from Karras, he stopped and said, 'Your helm, Scholar. Take off your helm.' His bolter was aimed straight at Karras' head. 'I need to see your face!'

Rauth knew he shouldn't be alive. For the Death Spectre to save them, the amount of power from the warp must have been dangerously high. And now he sensed that something was deeply wrong. His training on Banish had been comprehensive and very specific. His instincts never lied. His subconscious was powerfully attuned to the presence of evil, and it was itching now, telling him Karras had opened the inner gates too wide. Something fell had forced its way through.

'You heard me, Scholar,' he growled. 'Helm. Now.'

Karras got to his feet, but did not remove his helm.

'First, a question,' he said, and Rauth's lip curled. The voice was nothing like Karras'. Rauth had heard it before. He'd once struck a bargain with it, commanded to do so by those in charge of testing neophytes on his Chapter home world. Strength, speed, power and glory for a thousand years unbroken.

And the price?

Just his immortal soul.

Every Exorcist had to summon a daemon and risk the bargain. It was the first part of the final test. Reneging on the deal and exorcising the monstrosity back into the warp was the latter part.

Most of the aspirants who failed their tests in other Chapters simply died. Those that failed the tests of the Exorcists lost their souls to an eternity of torture and madness in the warp.

And most didn't make it. Eight in ten became possessed with no hope of recovery and had to be destroyed. But not Rauth.

He had tricked Hepaxammon. The daemon had tried to take its due early, to trick the trickster, but Rauth's soul had already been hidden away, out of the daemon's reach. It resided inside an infant, a clone of Rauth himself kept permanently in cryosleep. While the clone slept, the soul was hidden. Hepaxammon would never find it.

And without his soul inhabiting his conscious body, Rauth had become impossible to track. It was only through Karras, damn it, through his herculean effort to save them both, that the beast had found him after a century of searching.

The question came. Rauth had known it would.

'Where is the soul you promised me, cur? Where is my due?'

Rauth's finger squeezed the trigger of his bolter, then stopped just before the biting point.

It was Karras that stood before him. His Alpha.

Though the worst had happened, the very thing Rauth had been assigned to Talon to watch for, now that he had to deal with it, he found himself holding back. The Death Spectre had proven himself a force to be reckoned with, a brother not to be underestimated.

As bad as things looked, Rauth just couldn't fire.

If he gave Karras time, might the Death Spectre find a way? Was he fighting Hepaxammon from within even now?

The daemon laughed, unfastened Karras' helm and dropped it to the ground.

Rauth saw that the chalk-white face of his squad brother was already changing. The red eyes had turned black. The perfect, even white teeth were now wickedly pointed. As he watched, red seams appeared in Karras' cheeks. He opened his mouth and they split apart with a spray of blood. His jaw began to protrude like a wolf's muzzle.

'Where did you hide it, Exorcist?' demanded the daemon.

The air had turned icy cold and there was a foul stench on it, like corpses rotting.

Karras' armour began to mutate, the ceramite and plasteel growing sharp spines and barbs, the pauldrons morphing to form hideous, leering faces where once there had been symbols of honour and pride. The fingers of Karras' gauntlets stretched into long, curving talons, and the air around him began to shimmer and churn as if he were surrounded by a swarm of black flies stirred into frenzy.

The foul stink of brimstone emanated from his body as it hunkered down into a bestial half-crouch.

There was a wet, throaty chuckle. 'You cannot fire on me, Exorcist, and you know it. You would only be slaying your brother.'

'Scholar will understand. It was inevitable, after all.'

'Ah, yes,' breathed the beast. 'How ironic. You were assigned to Talon to safeguard against this very thing. And yet, it is your very presence on Talon Squad that caused this. How does that make you feel, deal-breaker?'

Rauth dropped his bolter to the ground, took a step back, drew his combat knife and settled into a fighting stance. With his left hand, he drew something small and metallic from a pouch on his webbing. This he held in his closed fist. The daemon's eyes flicked to it, but the beast could not see what it was.

'I don't think I'd enjoy just blowing you away,' said Rauth. 'I'll get a lot more satisfaction from carving you up.'

The abomination dropped to all fours, its form so twisted that it barely seemed to be Karras' body at all. 'When I destroy your physical form, Exorcist, your soul will awaken in the place where you have hidden it. I will know. I will sense it. And I will hunt it down and devour it. There will be nothing you can do to stop me.'

Rauth raised his knife and began circling right. 'Weaker the mantis who talks too much,' he told the daemon.

Blood of Armageddon, by Sonolocus. Karras would know the quote. If he still existed in that hijacked body of his, maybe he heard it.

Fight, Scholar, thought Rauth. *Fight your way back up.*

He tightened his grip on the tiny relic in his left hand and felt the weight of all his hopes resting on it.

If you can regain control for just an instant, all may not be lost.

THIRTY-EIGHT

The beast was fast. It had all the speed of a Space Marine's body plus its own raw, reckless power fused together in one.

Rauth found himself on the defensive from the start.

The beast opened by leaping at him, faking with a low swipe of the left hand, those claws so long and black, then slashing diagonally down with the right.

Rauth's reflexes were all that saved him, his subconscious programming moving much faster than conscious thought could manage.

He slid the downward blow aside by inches and slashed out in a backhand strike with his knife. But he had to be careful. He had to make the beast believe he meant business, but he also had to give Karras a chance to regain control. He couldn't afford to carve up the Death Spectre if he was to have any hope of saving him.

And Darrion Rauth wanted to save him.

Since they had met, he had known he would have to kill

Karras one day. Sigma's coven had seen it. The psyker's greatest asset was also his greatest weakness, and one day, they said, it would overwhelm him. Rauth was charged with watching him, waiting for that day, duty bound to step in and end the threat, destroying the very Space Marine who would be leading him.

Fate was cruel.

Rauth had tried not to like Karras. It was usually easy for him to remain cold and closed off to others, but their back and forth in quotes, their mutual love of written works – some extremely rare – had forged in Rauth's mind an unspoken bond. He respected Karras. The Librarian committed everything, all he was, all he had, to every desperate fight he entered. Such a shame he had been born with the psyker gene. Things would have been much easier for him otherwise.

As Rauth and Hepaxammon circled each other, the Exorcist's mind raced for a way to reach the soul trapped inside. If Scholar was still down there, a prisoner in his own hijacked mind, there was a chance, albeit small, that he could be drawn back up.

If he couldn't, Rauth would have to slay him, and Hepaxammon would retreat from the physical realm, but it would drag Karras' immortal soul with it to be tortured in the depths of the warp for all eternity.

It's a fight for Karras' soul, and I cannot afford to lose.

An idea occurred to him – a ridiculous long shot, but better than nothing at all.

'Unending is the vigilance of the Adeptus Astartes.' He said it loud and clear as he circled right, keeping a careful eye for sign of the beast's next lunge.

Karras was powerless to answer, but he saw Rauth speak it, heard the words in his ears. He would have answered, too, but that his voice was no longer his own.

His inner voice, however, remained to him. He finished the quote.

And boundless is their honour, their sacrifice, their service.

Adelus Gayan's *Ode to Strength*. Thirty-third millennium.

Hepaxammon heard his thoughts and laughed. To Rauth, it said, 'Words will avail you nothing, deal-breaker. You cannot save yourself or the Death Spectre. And his pathetic Chapter had such high hopes for him. Such a pity!'

It laughed, jaws wide, then suddenly lunged, grasping for Rauth's wrists and twisting its head sideways to bite at his neck.

Again, Rauth was just fast enough. He slipped his head to the side of the jaws, then smashed it into the daemon's brow, opening a cut that bled into Karras' right eye, blinding it.

Struck so, the daemon loosened its grip. Rauth immediately twisted his knife arm away and brought the butt of the blade hammering into the side of Karras' head.

The daemon staggered, roaring in pain, lifting its clawed hands to its skull.

Looking at its terrible, twisted form – a mockery of Space Marine glory – it was hard to think of this thing as Karras now. Rauth had to remind himself that it was still the body of his battle-brother. That all wasn't lost quite yet.

'Honour is the only currency they seek,' he boomed.

Again, Karras' imprisoned soul heard. Again, he recognised the quote and finished it.

Honour is the price of their service. By that service is our doom held at bay.

The Shadow of the Shepherd, by Annaria Ixia. Thirty-eighth millennium.

The daemon faked at Rauth again, feigning a lateral right slash before spinning with its left talons extended in a wide backhand sweep.

Knife-like claws raked Rauth's breastplate, sending out a shower of short-lived orange sparks and leaving deep gouges in the ceramite. Rauth was almost knocked from his feet, such was the power of the blow. Any closer and his chest would have been cored like an apple.

He steadied himself and dropped into a lower crouch. His grip tightened on his knife and on the little relic in his left hand. So far, he could see no sign that he was any closer to being able to use it. The daemon's grip on Karras' body was too tight. The Death Spectre's soul was too well bound.

Do something, Karras. Find a way to push through. Anything. You only have to surface for an instant, and I will be on him. If you cannot do it soon, I may have no choice.

Rauth knew he was physically outmatched. The daemon's raw, inhuman power married to Karras' superhuman strength and speed, not to mention the addition of power armour now twisted to serve daemonic needs, was an overwhelming combination.

The Exorcist could hold the beast off, but not for long. The daemon would never tire. And it didn't need to hold back as he did.

One more time, Karras. One more time. But you have to try. I don't care what it takes, but you have to do something.

Karras raged helplessly as the beast in control of his body slashed deep into Rauth's breastplate. He saw Rauth stagger backwards and knew that this was a fight the Exorcist was not winning. Why had he abandoned his bolter? Why had he not taken the kill-shot when he'd had the chance?

You know why. He's intent on saving you. And if he keeps it up, he's going to get himself killed.

Hopeless anger blazed inside him. He was desperate to

undo this, to wrestle control back from Hepaxammon before he had to watch his own distorted hands deal the killing blow.

Again Karras thought of Cordatus. Was there truly no chance that the Chief Librarian had foreseen this and set up some kind of pre-emptive defence along the timeline? Or had Karras' prime futures become too complicated, too clouded for there to be any hope of salvation?

He cursed.

I cannot always expect him to appear and rescue me, damn it. If those days are over, so be it. If I am worthy of the Chapter's expectations…

He thought of the day Cordatus had plucked him from the air over the chasm. He thought of his people under attack by red giants, of the burning forest, of…

Aranye. The eldar witch.

She had warned him of horrors ahead. It was she who had first spoken the name Tychonis to him.

She was powerful, and she claimed some interest in his fate.

But she was xenos! She could no more be trusted than the daemon!

Even as he thought this, he knew it wasn't true. Aranye had clearly indicated that the denizens of the warp and those in service to them were common enemies.

She had some stake in Karras' fate, and she had his psychic signature. Much as he hated the fact, his time in the eldar healing machine on Damaroth had marked him, made him easy for her to find.

And if he was so easy to find…

It was worth a shot. There was no other.

With the daemon possessing him, the flow of the warp was both strong and close – more than ever before. Its strange currents boiled and churned all around him, feeding the beast its strength, allowing it to exist in the realm of matter, to keep its hold on him.

Maybe that strength could be its undoing, just as it had been his.

Karras turned all his focus inwards, concentrating hard on tapping into the ethereal tide. He cast himself into it completely, felt himself get swallowed up in it. His mind surged with a fresh sense of power and presence.

Hepaxammon did not sense this, occupied utterly with tormenting the Exorcist, but Karras knew that might change at any moment. He would get only one chance at this.

He felt the current rise to a momentary peak and called out with all his strength.

A single word.

Aranye.

The thought rippled powerfully through the warp.

Hepaxammon felt it. Responding at once, the daemon snatched Karras' consciousness from the flow of power and bound it tighter, cutting off his senses again, casting him back down into inner darkness. Karras plummeted deeper and deeper, descending so far that surely it would be impossible to ever climb back out.

At least he had tried. It had been a desperate move with almost no chance of success. Cordatus couldn't help him. Rauth couldn't help him.

What chance did he have with a xenos witch who couldn't be trusted in the first place? The eldar served only the eldar.

But as his mind continued to descend further and further from physical reality, he heard it – a familiar voice, feminine and musical, yet somehow still repellant, for though it spoke to him in High Gothic, it was no less alien.

'I told you I would be watching,' said Aranye. She sounded impossibly close. 'And I warned you that the path would be narrow.'

Karras felt his essence grasped by a vastly more powerful force. Where Hepaxammon exuded a churning, filth-filled darkness and the stink of rot, Aranye's essence was almost blindingly bright.

Bright, but not warm. It was harsh and cold and alien.

She halted his descent, enveloped him and surged powerfully up towards physical reality.

'Do not speak,' she said. 'The daemon is attuned to you. It will hear you. It has not yet detected me.'

Further and further they rose. Karras could feel his awareness getting closer to the physical realm.

'I will hold him,' Aranye continued. 'I cannot maintain it for long, for I am some distance away, but it may be long enough. When I do, you must take immediate control of your body and signal to the other who hopes to save you – the one with the displaced soul, he who caused this trouble in the first place.'

There was no chance to ask what Aranye meant by that.

'Before I do this, mon-keigh, you will swear an oath to me. You will put yourself in my debt.'

Karras could not question her on this, since to answer aloud would alert the daemon, but he radiated uncertainty and distrust.

Aranye noted it. 'There will come a time soon,' she said, 'in which your mistaken notions of duty will call for you to obstruct me, perhaps even to kill me. I will have your silent oath now that you will remember your debt to me and stand aside when the time comes, that you will raise no hand against me nor my retinue. Swear it now or lose your soul and the soul of the other!'

The last thing Karras wanted was to put himself in debt to a damned xenos, but her words were true. He had no other options.

She sensed his resentful acceptance of the bargain. 'On your life and the honour of your Chapter, then, I accept your solemn oath.'

They had risen close to the edge of physical reality now, ready to push through from mind alone into mind and matter, from the well of the inner self to the conscious world of the senses.

It was time to make the only move available.

'Now!' cried the eldar witch.

She cast Karras' consciousness forward, then threw her full power against the mind of the daemon, smashing her will against it, staggering it, wrenching its control of the body away as it reeled under the psychic impact.

As if from a hammer blow, Karras was struck with immense physical pain. He was back in his body, fully restored to his senses, and the agony of its corruption was almost too much to bear. He dropped to the ground.

Through misshapen jaws, he barely managed to form a single word. 'Watcher!'

He raised his bleeding head and locked eyes with the Exorcist.

And Rauth saw that those eyes were red again, not black. It was the sign he had been waiting for.

Dropping his knife, Rauth rushed forward, grabbed the back of Karras' head with his right hand, as tight as a vice, and pressed the relic in his left hand to the Death Spectre's forehead.

Immediately, he began chanting in an ancient language most thought lost in Terra's ancient past, a sacred tongue of great power if spoken by those trained in its use. Only two Chapters existed in all the Imperium who knew that tongue and what it could do.

The Exorcists were one of them.

In his head, Karras could hear Hepaxammon giving vent to his rage. A hundred foul voices roared in denial as he wrestled with the burning presence of the eldar Farseer.

'I can hold the daemon no longer, Space Marine!' said Aranye, her voice strained with the effort.

Her grasp on Hepaxammon's essence broke, and the daemon threw her off, surging forward to reclaim control of Karras.

But Rauth was already deep into the ancient rites.

The relic pulsed with purifying power against Karras' forehead.

As Hepaxammon pushed forward, scrambling for dominion over Karras' body, the holy power of the relic lanced into him like a spear of light.

The daemon screamed.

Rauth continued his litany, voice rising, his chanting more and more intense. Moment by moment, Karras could sense the daemon's presence withering and his own getting stronger and stronger.

When he felt himself restored, he turned his mind fully against the daemon and joined his own litanies of protection and banishment to Rauth's.

There was a psychic firestorm raging inside him now, all its power turned against the insidious entity. Holy light was tearing the daemon to pieces, burning it to cinders and blasting those cinders back into the warp.

As the final fragments of Hepaxammon's presence were burned away, it railed at Rauth and Karras one last time. 'This is not the end. Jormungandr, Death Spectre. Mark me well and know that you have condemned your brothers.'

The voice sounded as if from a great distance now. 'Jormungandr,' it said again. 'And I will have my due. I will collect. The Exorcist will not evade me forever.'

Then it was gone.

Rauth's litany came to its end. Breathing heavily, he removed the relic, kissed it reverently and returned it to its pouch. Karras, barely able to focus on anything but the agony wracking his every nerve, never saw what it was.

Rauth stepped over to where his bolter lay on the tunnel floor, picked it up and returned to Karras. He pressed the muzzle against the Death Spectre's still-misshapen head and waited.

Karras was on his knees, roaring in pain through gritted teeth. With the daemon gone, his body was restoring itself, but the pain caused by flesh and bone returning to their natural form was excruciating.

Shakily, he held up a hand for Rauth to wait.

On that hand, the talons were retreating, melting back into their original form – human fingers encased in ceramite armour. Spines and barbs receded. Twisted faces melted back into symbols of the Chapter and the Watch.

Before the Exorcist's eyes, the true form of Karras was restored. In a matter of moments, one would have found it hard to believe it had ever looked any different.

'Prove to me now that I should not kill you,' said Rauth. He had faith in the rites he had performed, but there was still a risk that this was a trick of the beast. He had to know. 'Prove to me that the daemon is gone.'

Pain subsiding, Karras struggled to his feet and said, 'How do I prove it, brother? You saved my soul, and perhaps your own, but I have no more proof for you than my word and the form in which I stand before you.'

Rauth eyed him up and down with open suspicion. He wanted to believe. His gut told him no foul presence remained. He felt deep down that the exorcism had been a success, that he would have known this for a trick if such it were.

At last, he lowered his bolter. 'It will have to do for now.'

They looked at each other, silence stretching out between them. There was so much to say. Rauth had saved Karras, but Rauth was also the reason the daemon had come.

'It claims a right to your soul,' said Karras. 'Why?'

Rauth held his gaze a moment, then turned and started walking up the tunnel in the only direction available to them.

Over his shoulder, he said, 'I cannot answer that for you, brother. I am sworn to silence. I am sorry you became embroiled in this, but what's done is done. I cannot untangle you from it now.'

Karras scowled and shook his head, but he started walking. Behind them lay the ruins of the Tower. Ahead, cutting north-east, the tunnel extended into darkness. He caught up with Rauth and they walked together in silence a while.

'We need to find a way out,' said Karras after a few minutes. 'We have to get word to the Stormravens. They may still be within range.'

'Archangel and the others will think us dead. *They* may be dead.'

'Why didn't you shoot?' asked Karras. 'You've been watching for it since the day we met. I wager it was the reason Sigma assigned you to Talon Squad in the first place. And yet, you yourself seem to be the reason–'

'I took a dangerous gamble. I will not do that again.'

Karras let that hang between them a moment, then replied, 'Let us hope there is never again a need. But this Hepaxammon is tenacious. It is not finished with us.'

Rauth glanced at Karras from the corner of his eye. 'I will be better prepared.'

Around a slow bend in the tunnel up ahead, there seemed to be a source of light. Rounding it, Karras saw bright daylight filtering in through a natural gap in the ceiling.

'There's our exit,' he said. 'We need to hurry. And hope the Stormravens are still in vox range.'

Together, they jogged forward and began hauling their bodies up the rocky wall of the tunnel. Soon, they emerged into the baking heat of the day.

They found themselves on a spur of beige rock. All around them, golden dunes stretched out to the horizon. The sun was piercingly bright, the sky a deep azure, flawless in all directions but south. To the south, the remnants of the mushroom cloud were still hanging in the air, a great, broad column of smoke and dust that dominated the skyline.

The two Space Marines climbed to the top of the tallest dune nearby.

'Talon Alpha to Reaper flight,' voxed Karras. 'Reaper flight, do you copy?'

Nothing. Just static.

'Talon Alpha to Reaper flight. Respond.'

Again, nothing.

Karras squinted into the distance and saw smoke on the far horizon due west-north-west of their position. Tentatively, even somewhat anxiously, he sent thin tendrils of psychic energy questing in that direction and picked up familiar signatures. Talon Squad. Unmistakable. The only member who didn't have a psychic signature was standing right beside him.

There were others, too – a mix of Adeptus Astartes and humans. Sabre Squad and Copley's people, plus the pilots of the Stormravens.

'That way,' said Karras, gesturing with a nod. 'They must have gone down on the periphery of the blast.'

He and Rauth set off down the dune face in the direction of the smoke.

'It must have burned out their electronics.'

Karras nodded. That would explain the vox silence. 'We run.'

As they put on some speed, carving a channel across the hot sand, Karras anxiously searched his consciousness for any trace of Aranye. Was she still in there, silently monitoring him? She seemed able to trespass upon his mind with such disturbing ease.

He found no trace of her. The eldar witch was gone. Her words, however, echoed in his mind, bothering him.

Remember your debt to me. Stand aside when I ask it.

He had sworn an oath on his life and on the honour of his Chapter. An oath to a filthy xenos, true, but a xenos that had saved his soul from damnation and disgrace. It was a heavy debt.

She was truly powerful, her gifts well beyond his own. He could never have survived without her intervention.

So now he owed her.

Did he dare break their bargain? She was xenos, and he, Deathwatch.

When the time came, would he dare to keep it?

THIRTY-NINE

Six powerful presences, their warp signatures far denser than those of the tribespeople that formed a seal of souls around them, the exception being Agga's.

Unanticipated, these six. Troubling.

Karras detected them as soon as Chatha na Hadik began to emerge through the grey skirts of pouring rain in which the Stormravens flew.

From the hold of Reaper Two, Karras reached out to Agga's mind. Her relief at his survival was foremost, and she welcomed him back warmly, but there was an unmissable undercurrent of tension and fear.

'Others have come, my lord,' she told him, mind to mind. 'Resh'vah, like you, but *not* like you. Their leader has a turbulent soul. My people fear him greatly. He has ordered my son imprisoned under guard – a hostage to ensure our cooperation. Had there been a psyker among them, it would be I...'

'I will be with you soon,' replied Karras. 'Do not risk your cover. You are unsanctioned. For now, let them believe they have the Speaker, as your people believe it. I will assess things when I arrive.'

Agga withdrew, emanating faith and gratitude, but her fear and tension had abated little.

As the landing platform finished lowering the Stormravens into the hangar, Copley ordered all her people to get their gear in order. The wounded would need to be taken to the medicae facilities immediately. Bones needed resetting, wounds needed stitching, and much more besides.

She caught Karras' gaze and tilted her head across the Stormraven's hold to the Space Marines of Sabre Squad. Oblivious to just how strong their enhanced hearing was, she murmured, 'Will they commit to us, Scholar? Can you convince them to lend their strength to Arcturus until *Shadowbreaker* is over?'

Karras looked over and met Androcles' gaze.

Wounded pride, thought Karras. *Dishonour. Their handler and their Alpha betrayed them into xenos hands for some reason we don't yet fully understand. And rage in abundance.*

They will *join us,* he thought. *Redemption in their own eyes demands it, as it would of me.*

And what of his own honour? Epsilon had slipped his grasp. What of his redemption?

Arcturus could not afford to grant the t'au time to get the inquisitor offworld, but neither could they move until she was located again. For that reason, more than anything else, they had returned to the Kashtu stronghold. The Speaker's haddayin would be watching. Word would come.

It had to.

Karras emerged from Reaper Two's hold to see a Thunderhawk gunship, far larger than a Stormraven, beloved and trusted of all Space Marine Chapters. It sat silent, a great sleeping dragon with scales of black ceramite. Fuel lines snaked from its belly. The rear ramp was down, but all the lights were off.

He didn't recognise it, but it bore the iconography of both the Deathwatch and the Ordo Xenos, and he could see that the armour was stealth-coated and that the engines and exhausts were modified for noise reduction.

Standing just in the shadow of its boxy nose, a few metres from the forward landing gear, was a large figure in distinctive Terminator armour, all black with silver on the left arm and pauldron.

Copley was busy barking orders at her people as they unloaded wargear from Reaper flight. The Space Marines of Talon and Sabre were filtering down ramps. Chyron was being uncoupled from magna-grapples.

Karras stood regarding the figure in shadow.

Neither moved.

He heard Talon come to stand behind him, lining up in silence, all staring at the figure in front.

Sabre formed up on Androcles and watched quietly from a few metres back.

'Who's the shy one hiding under the gunship?' said Zeed as he stepped abreast of Karras.

Karras put a hand out and halted him. 'Stay here,' he told his kill-team.

Zeed shrugged. He and his brothers watched as Karras strode forward to meet the shadowed hulk.

As Karras neared, the other moved out to meet him.

An ancient, nigh-indestructible suit of tactical Dreadnought armour here on Tychonis when things were so precarious should have been a welcome sight, but Karras could read the aura of the wearer, and that aura was as dark as the Deathwatch black in which it was painted.

They stopped, facing each other. As tall as he was, Karras had to look up to meet the eyes of the Space Marine in front of him. The Terminator stood a full head and a half taller than he. At a glance, he registered the iconography of Chapter, kill-team, honour markings.

'You are Jannes Broden, Scimitar Alpha, battle-brother of the Black Templars,' said Karras.

'And you are Lyandro Karras,' said the other.

Karras inclined his head in a slight bow. 'Well met, brother.'

Broden glared down at him, pointedly not returning the greeting.

The Templar's face was of typical cast for a Space Marine. The brow was heavy, the nose strong and aquiline, the jawbone square and broad. There were structural similarities to Voss', naturally, the Black Templars being a successor Chapter of the Imperial Fists, but here was none of Omni's warmth and openness. Broden's face was as hard and cold as frost-rimed rock, made all the more fearsome by the profusion of scars and claw marks, testimony to a life of intense close-range combat.

Couched in the gorget and cowl of that Terminator suit, Broden's face was all the more fearsome. But Karras was unmoved.

'You understand the reason for my presence here,' said Broden.

'I can guess,' said Karras.

The Templar scowled, then cast his glance over the Talon members watching from further back. 'Talon and Arcturus have proven inadequate to their mission. Epsilon evaded you. *Shadowbreaker* is a failure. It is over.'

'It's *not* over. Epsilon remains on Tychonis for now. We need only locate her and–'

'No!' snapped Broden. 'It is I, Karras, who need to locate her. You need only do as you are told from here on.'

He stepped in close, towering over Karras like a Warhound Titan.

Karras cocked an eyebrow, utterly unimpressed. Was this really what passed for *the best of the best* among the Black Templars?

'I have been placed in operational command, charged with salvaging this debacle,' said Broden. 'Archangel's powers will be limited to tactical command of her people, as yours will be to yours. Both of you are now directly under my command.'

Karras cursed. 'Show me,' he demanded.

Broden held out his right hand and opened his fist. There in his palm was a red holo-crystal in a setting of silver. With his thumb, Broden activated it.

Hololithic light began to shimmer a foot above the crystal. The iconography of the Ordo Xenos rezzed into view, followed by the skull symbol of the Deathwatch, then several authentication codes that the sensors set in Karras' power armour verified as current and legitimate.

Reams of data began scrolling before Karras, imprinting on his retina, coding itself into the memory centres of his brain.

Broden spoke the truth.

Sigma was handing *Shadowbreaker* over to the command of the Black Templar. All task force elements were now answerable to him.

The display ended, and the Templar closed his fist over the gem once again and dropped it to his side.

Karras searched his face for a sign of the smugness that had crept into his aura, but that face betrayed nothing.

'I have also imprisoned the rebel leader, this Speaker of the Sands, to be executed if his people do not comply absolutely. He is unsanctioned and will be dealt with post-mission, but, for now, he provides leverage.'

'The Speaker has shown nothing but full support for our mission,' hissed Karras. 'Rebels fought and died to ensure the t'au forces at Alel a Tarag were not reinforced during our assault. Your decision is an open betrayal of their loyalty to the Emperor. It will only cause resentment and alienation. It is not the way to play this!'

'You had your chance, Death Spectre. You and Copley played things your way and got nowhere. Had you done your jobs, I'd not be here at all.'

'Then go back,' growled Karras, his fists clenched at his sides. 'We have it in hand.'

He knew Broden was baiting him, getting him to display emotions he should have well in hand, but the Templar had attacked his honour and his pride – two things guaranteed to push a Space Marine to the edge of his self control.

Karras forced himself to calmness. He held Broden's eye, saw satisfaction glinting there.

'Scimitar Alpha has operational command,' he said coldly. 'Talon Alpha acknowledges. The Will of the Emperor will be served. Does the commander have instructions?'

Broden looked over at the members of Sabre Squad. They stood there, still clad in black bodysuits, watching things unfold in silence.

'The remains of Epsilon's kill-team,' said Broden.

Karras nodded. 'Betrayed by the rogue inquisitor and two of their own. One of those was their Alpha. A third was… killed by the t'au.'

'The Son of Antaeus is the new Alpha by default. Cursed

Founding or not, he's the ranking member, so he will have tactical command of his team. Tell me of the others.'

Karras turned to look at them and ran through what he knew. The four remaining Sabre operators stared back, well aware they were being discussed, able to hear every word.

There was Striggo of the Carcharadons, whose aura, Karras noted, was so dark and stormy with feral violence that he seemed likely to lean towards berserker tendencies.

Next to him stood Pelion of the Marines Errant, somewhat fine-featured for a Space Marine but missing most of his left ear.

Gedeon of the Howling Griffons stood next to Pelion. The two were of equal height, but while Pelion was beardless and short-haired, Gedeon looked wild, his hair and beard the same bright red as Darrion Rauth's. They framed his battle-scarred face like a lion's mane, which was appropriate given the somewhat leonine cast to his features.

Roen of the Revilers was last – eyes black, skin chalk-white, both a genetic inheritance from his Chapter's progenitor, the Raven Guard.

'They look diminished,' said Broden when Karras was done.

Karras snorted. The Templar could not see the fire that flared and danced in their auras. 'Their wargear was never recovered. There wasn't time. If diminished, then in number only. And defeated, not at all. They are eager to redeem themselves and see Epsilon and the traitors brought to account. And they long for t'au blood.'

Broden nodded. 'They will operate under my command with the rest of you.'

'That will be their choice,' said Karras. 'They are not Sigma's assets. They have no obligation to you.'

'If they seek redemption as you say, they have no choice,'

said Broden. He gestured with a tilt of his head to the Thunderhawk behind him. 'There is no power armour for them, but we have weapons and other supplies. They will be equipped as well as we are able. I leave it to you to make sure they understand the new command structure. I will inform Major Copley of the changes myself.'

'Her people fought hard,' said Karras with genuine feeling. 'They exemplified the qualities of ordo special forces. And without their systems intrusion work, the assault would have been a disastrous bloodbath. Archangel is highly capable. I advise you to ask her counsel on all operational matters.'

Broden waved that off with an armoured hand. 'She failed in her command. If it were up to me, she'd face an ordo court martial. But your assessment is noted. I dismiss you now to see to your wargear and to inform Sabre Squad of the new order of things.'

A court martial? thought Karras with suppressed outrage. *This one would cut off his hand to spite his arm.*

'If my team are to work with yours, Broden…' he said.

The Black Templar was already moving off, each step shaking the rockcrete under him, but he paused and half-turned back towards Karras. 'Introductions will wait, Death Spectre. Just make sure your people understand the situation. If anyone steps out of order, I will hold you responsible. And you will not find me very forgiving.'

Karras' jaw rippled and his fists flexed as he watched the giant stomp away from him.

He knew already that he didn't like Scimitar Alpha.

He had met such Adeptus Astartes before – overzealous, arrogant, inclined towards overkill tactics and unrefined force. Not uncommon traits among the ranks of the Imperium's greatest warriors. It was something about the martial path – it led one either to humility or arrogance, and seldom anywhere in the middle.

To this Broden, Talon Squad, Sabre Squad and Arcturus would be little more than pieces on the board. He'd place his Scimitar Squad for maximum glory in whatever lay ahead.

So the real question, when the bullets started flying and the air was filled with deadly plasma, pulse and railgun rounds, was not so much *if* Karras would have to defy him, but *when*.

He and his Talon brothers had come a long way together.

He would not stand by and watch them die for the honour and glory of Jannes Broden.

FORTY

No time. No time!

Azhan Amin had to focus hard to keep his hands from trembling. His heart was in his mouth. Its rapid beating drowned out everything else.

As for his vision, it was hyper-sharp, enhanced by fear and adrenaline.

Of all the haddayin in the spaceport town of Kurdiza, he alone had a cover role that granted access to part of the spaceport's defence grid.

He alone could open the approach window for the Adeptus Astartes.

He sent word of the time, the place, the length of the gap he could create. Four minutes only, and those four fixed with no margin for error. If he messed the timing up, noble Space Marines would die, their craft ripped out of the air by t'au missiles and AI-controlled railgun fire.

Blue clip to white node.

Black clip to black wire.

Almost done. Almost done.

He looked at his wrist chrono. Ten seconds more to finish rigging the charge. Forty seconds to race back to his assigned work route, to checking the air-cooling control circuits on the first and second floors.

As soon as he was there, safely away from the blast, he'd watch the last seconds tick off, then hit the remote detonator in his pocket.

The earth caste would rush into action, desperate to find the problem and reroute power and control through secondary channels. That would take them four minutes, so that was the hard limit on the infiltration window.

By then, the resh'vah will be within the perimeter, and I will slip away in the chaos.

Almost done. Right on schedule.

His fingers released the last clip, its metal teeth cinching on exposed wire.

That was when he heard the shout from behind him.

It was in T'au at first, clipped and harsh, but the speaker soon switched to Tychonite Gothic on noting the full head of black hair and the nut-brown skin of the neck exposed above the collar.

'Worker! Stop what you're doing and explain yourself!'

The voice was gruff, commanding, dense with that peculiar accent only the water caste ever managed to shed.

Azhan had no weapon. It had taken all his guile just to get the small explosive through security.

Twelve years he had spent solidifying his cover here. A perfect service record. Unremarkable, but no black marks either. No haddayin could afford to be noteworthy.

All for this. All for this day, this moment.

He looked again at his chrono. He was several seconds behind now.

He turned and saw the speaker, a squat, square-faced earth caste flanked by a stern-looking fire caste soldier whose blue, three-fingered hand was resting close to the pistol on his right hip.

Azhan waved them closer.

Familiar faces, but they weren't known to him by name. They must have seen him on the monitors and come down from the upper floors where he seldom worked.

They were walking towards him now, flat faces stern.

Eager to get away from the bomb he had just placed, he walked out to meet them.

'No,' snapped the fire warrior. 'Stay where you are. And keep your hands in plain sight!'

The earth caste technician muttered to himself in T'au as they neared, assuming as the blue-skins usually did that a human worker could never understand his race's rich and highly nuanced tongue.

Azhan translated easily in his head: *This stinking five-toes isn't supposed to be here.*

I have to get away now, he thought. *I* have *to!*

Again, a quick glance at his chrono.

His heart sank. The window he'd promised couldn't be changed. It *couldn't.*

Space Marines' lives…

The liberation of his people…

Vengeance on the filthy pogs…

Suddenly weary, his soul heavy with all the years of lies, of suffering their proximity, he committed to the last course of action available.

'I'm glad you're here,' he told the t'au as they closed on him. 'I was looking for a flaw in the air-cooling control line when I found something unexpected. I don't think it's supposed to be there. If the noble earth caste will take a look...'

The t'au technician clacked his tooth-plates in disdain and pushed his way past Azhan, the soldier following suit, peering over the technician's shoulder to where Azhan was gesturing, right at the bomb.

Azhan took another quick look at the chrono on his wrist and started counting backwards in his head.

Truly, he would have liked to live.

But I am haddayin, he told himself resignedly. *I will find my reward by the Emperor's side.*

The stocky technician leaned forward and stared hard, raising a hand to his short, square chin.

'That is no t'au device. It is a gue'la thing!'

Azhan put his hand in his overalls pocket and gripped the detonator. 'Ah, you're right,' he said as his thumb found the trigger. 'I see what it is now. How stupid of me. I should not have troubled you.'

The fire warrior looked round at him, impatience creasing his blue-grey brow. 'Then what is it?' he demanded.

'You stupid, ugly pog,' said Azhan with a final smile. 'It's a bomb.'

He pressed the trigger. Right on time.

The blast killed all three of them instantaneously.

Tower Six, covering the north-north-east approach on the spaceport's perimeter, abruptly went dead.

Defence control consoles in the spaceport's main control centre leapt to life, alarm glyphs rezzing into the air above them. T'au engineers began jabbering at each other. Senior techs began barking at aerospace monitoring personnel. The latter frantically searched their holo-displays for any sign of inbound contacts.

They found nothing.

No scanner returns.

No detections.

Only expected traffic, and most of that was fighter patrols at high altitude, placed on special duty when Commander Coldwave arrived two days ago. The shas'o had immediately ordered both a massive increase in security and a temporary cessation on all non-military activities at the spaceport.

It could be no coincidence that Kurdiza's automated defence perimeter now had a gaping hole in it.

It was almost precisely three and a half minutes after the blast that fire warriors in Tower Six found the charred remains of three bodies in a smoke-filled corridor. Even as they frantically relayed this information back to central defence, claiming deliberate sabotage, it was too late.

Reapers One and Two had already dropped Talon Squad and Sabre Squad by zipline within the spaceport walls, then pulled back out to a safe distance to wait.

With quiet speed, ten shadow-clad figures split into two groups of five and moved off in opposite directions towards their first objectives.

'Good hunting, Talon,' voxed Androcles as he and his squad melted into the darkness.

'Good hunting, Sabre,' Karras voxed back.

Redemption or death.

FORTY-ONE

'You were right, inquisitor,' said Coldwave as he stood looking down at a holo-screen. The woman in black stood by his side, her focus on the same display.

Behind him, glaring over his shoulders, towered her two giant killers.

Coldwave hated when they came close like this. They stank, and the smell was so offensively unnatural. It never seemed to communicate any other emotion than their lust for killing.

Did they never think of anything else?

Despite how they made his fingers itch, he was certainly not about to give them the satisfaction of seeing him in discomfort at their proximity.

His tone was flat, giving nothing away, but Epsilon knew he was irritated at the thought that his gambit in the desert canyon had failed. Talon Squad's survival of a nuclear blast would only add to the tales his fire caste troopers were telling each other out of earshot of their officers.

'I told you they would not be easy to erase,' she said with a slight smile.

Was the woman a complete fool? She actually seemed amused. Coldwave was most definitely not, but he gave the blue-skin equivalent of a shrug and said, 'They come to meet their death, in any case. They will not be allowed to interfere with our departure. I have issued deployment orders. No matter their number, they will find us unyielding.'

One of the giants spoke, his voice so deep and rough that Coldwave sometimes had to strain to make out the words. Both pretended not to know the T'au language, but he was certain they did. They simply refused to use it. The speaker was the one called Kabannen, he of the ugly all-mechanical arms and legs.

Why was his order known as the Iron Hands, Coldwave wondered, when they obviously boasted titanium prostheses that extended well beyond their hands?

Stupid Gue'la!

He smelled, by far, the worst of the two.

'Do not underestimate the Deathwatch,' he told Coldwave. 'You did so before, shas'o, and the Tower of the Forgotten was lost to you along with hundreds of your people. The size of your force does not matter to the Adeptus Astartes of the Deathwatch. We can turn any situation to our advantage. Talon Squad may use your very confidence against you here today.'

He nodded towards the other, called Lucianos. 'But we are here. That bodes well for you. They will not prevail.'

Again, thought Coldwave, *that arrogance, that pride when they speak of this Deathwatch. How can they speak so smugly of a thing they have already betrayed? As if they still belong to it somehow. I don't understand these damnable creatures and their constant twisting of identities and loyalties. They are as changeable as the winds in the storm season.*

He had told his people to watch the inquisitor's bodyguards constantly. He trusted them not at all. They might explode into mayhem and slaughter anytime it suited them. His accord with the woman was all that held them back.

It wouldn't last. He was certain they would try for his life eventually.

But not while the woman still needs us. Not while she still petitions for access to the star systems that interest her so.

When he and the inquisitor finally stood before the High Council of Ethereals on T'au, he would secretly petition the Auns to send an exploratory force to the region. He had to know why the woman was so desperate to gain access. What did she expect to find? Until he had his answers, she could not be allowed the permission she sought.

For now, she still had much to share in the effort to create the ultimate weapon against the Y'he. That was her only value. The moment it was no longer a factor, he would take great personal pleasure in watching the light go from her eyes.

She was more dangerous than a pit of pregnant firefangs.

He walked away from the monitor, thankful that the smell of the Space Marines did not follow him.

Before him curved the great, broad hull of the ship that would take them into orbit, there to dock with the interstellar craft the High Council had sent.

From Tychonis, further east. Rimward. Deeper into t'au space.

It would be several weeks of skipping across the surface of the void, what the gue'la called the warp, before they would arrive at their destination.

The breeding project would continue throughout the trip.

The inquisitor's Geller field generator would continue to isolate their specimens from the tyranid hive-mind.

How perilously critical that generator is, he thought unhappily.

If it ever faltered for long, the purestrain genestealers and even, perhaps, some of the t'au-tyranid hybrids they were transporting would suddenly find themselves able to signal the hive-mind.

Such a signal would, as he understood it, bring the might of the Devourer down on this entire sector of space. Tychonis and the system in which it sat would be consumed and left dead in the wake of that unquenchable hunger.

Again, the importance of what they were doing here struck him.

The Council should never have brushed him and Aun'dzi aside all those years ago, posting them to such an insignificant world as this. Pure politics. Less honourable servants of the Greater Good had schemed and brought influence to bear behind the scenes. Coldwave had been originally marked for a far greater posting. Aun'dzi, too, was to be honoured with a rich and vibrant world on which to share his guidance and wisdom.

It mattered no longer. Their political rivals had thought themselves victorious, but in truth, they had accidentally seeded the ground with an opportunity for redemption and glory beyond all expectation.

Was it Fate that had intersected the inquisitor's path with his? Or was it all down to her machinations? Had she chosen Tychonis well in advance?

No matter. The accord had placed in t'au hands the first real chance to save their entire race from its greatest threat.

And old rivals will know, they will see, and they will bow their heads in shame.

A senior earth caste tech saw him gazing at the ship and hustled over in that particular way unique to the shortest and physically strongest of the t'au.

'Shas'o,' trilled the tech.

Coldwave turned and gave a curt nod. 'How close are we to readiness?'

The tech gestured to the ship's rear, where its massive engines hummed, the exhausts glowing a hot, dull red. Thick cables snaked away from ports in the ship's sides, running to reactors and vast cylindrical tanks. Earth caste techs in non-military exo-suits were loading heavy crates via ramps at the fore and aft.

'Within the decacycle, honoured hunter.'

'Then we are behind,' rasped Coldwave.

The tech began exuding a particular scent, a mix of guilt, resentment and unworthiness, tinged with a little dislike.

'Forgiveness, hunter, but the *special cargo* presented... unique challenges.'

'My orders on that were executed precisely,' said Coldwave. It was anything but a question.

'They were, hunter. I saw to it myself.'

'For the Greater Good,' said Coldwave.

'Always,' said the tech. 'My life for the Greater Good.'

'Very well, I hold you to the decacycle. Do not disappoint me. In doing so, you disappoint the Aun, a stain on your standing you might never remove, builder.'

He strode off, leaving the tech staring at his back, exuding that mix of emotions even more strongly than before.

Two air caste pilots – one male, one female – tall and willowy, frail-looking in their tight-fitting flight suits, moved to either side of him but stayed half a pace back in respect.

'Word has just reached us, hunter,' said the one on the

right. 'The Kashtu and Ishtu rebels have attacked our airbases at Na'sol and Zu'shan. The fighting is heavy. Many dead.'

Coldwave whirled to face them. He met the gaze of one, then the other. 'Should I request air support from those bases, I need it delivered. Did they get fighters into the air?'

Again, it was the one on the right who spoke. 'Our pilots were not able to take off. The assaults were very sudden and carefully coordinated. It is your fire caste brothers fighting to restore control on whom we must depend. If they can clear the runways, even temporarily, we can get Razorsharks and Sunsharks into the air.'

'I don't need bombers,' snapped Coldwave. 'Kurdiza must remain operational after our departure. Prioritise the launch of fighters. I want to know as soon as you have them in the air. I want to know how many and how long it will take them to get here if I should need them. Is that understood?'

The tall, slender t'au touched the fingers of their right hands to their upper abdomens and gave brief bows.

Coldwave left them to follow his instructions. It was time to make his own preparations.

The Space Marines, this Talon Squad the black giants kept talking about, had somehow survived. The bombing of the perimeter air-defence tower and the rebel attacks on the neighbouring airbases could only mean one thing.

They were coming for the woman.

Under other circumstances, Coldwave would have gladly given them her cold corpse.

They were coming, but the line stopped here. This time, he would obliterate them personally and destroy the dark legend that was growing around them among his soldiers. Space Marines bled like everything else. They died. They just took a little more killing than most.

He entered the sub-hangar housing his battlesuit. It gleamed in the light of the lumes, beautiful and noble, a martial masterwork of his people, calling to him, eager for union so that they could relish the surge and flow of battle again, the grace, the power, the freedom.

Here was the doom of his enemies, the vehicle of his glory and honour, his success.

'Patience, mighty one,' he told the silent giant. He ignored the curious looks of the techs still busy arming and priming its advanced combat systems. He was grinning, aware that he was exuding eagerness and confidence and a hunger for violent victory. What of it? He had every right.

He strode forward and placed a proud hand on the smooth, armoured leg of the machine.

'The blood of powerful foes will be shed today. They are on their way, foolish and eager to die. They are coming, and we shall oblige.

'For the Greater Good.'

FORTY-TWO

Less than an hour till sunrise.

The t'au would have plugged the gap in their perimeter by now, rerouting power through other circuits to bring the sabotaged Tower Six back online.

As he led Talon through the darkness, Karras glanced at the sky, saw the spray of bright stars there, the tiny, distant orb of Tychonis' only moon, Goetha. Sigma had to be in-system somewhere, the *Saint Nevarre* cloaked and undetectable to the t'au. Broden and Scimitar couldn't have travelled here otherwise. Thunderhawk gunships couldn't traverse the warp.

There was a t'au craft up there, too. Agga had told him. She had seen it in a scrying. She could not read Epsilon's prime futures, but the chances were high that the ship had come for the inquisitor and her research project.

This assault on the spaceport really would be a last chance.

So far, only Talon and Sabre were on the ground. The

only way to get the rest of the assault force on site was to knock out the t'au air-defence network for the whole facility.

Two options, then. Take it down via the defence control consoles in the command centre of the main spaceport building – heavily defended, and a surefire way to bring every t'au in the region running straight to your location – or knock out power for the whole damned town – a more temporary solution, but a lot more viable given the available assets.

With primary power down, the circuits would switch over to drawing power from stations outside the immediate local area. Those were outside the task force's reach, but the switch from a primary local source to secondary distant sources would take the t'au an estimated eleven minutes.

Eleven minutes in which the Thunderhawk, callsign *Black Eagle*, along with the Stormravens of Reaper flight would do a missile run, knocking out as many of the armed turrets as they could manage before the spaceport power came back online.

The whole town around the spaceport would be seething with ground forces by then. Enemy air elements were being held at bay by the rebels, but that could change anytime.

Situational advantage was so tenuous. The pendulum could swing against them at any given moment. Karras could only deal with what was in front of him, however. He pushed the later stages of the assault from his mind.

Sabre Squad would hit fuel silos and cause a disaster. Fires would spread. The t'au would have to deal with that or see half the town destroyed.

Talon would hit the power station and open the way for the others.

He led Watcher, Prophet, Omni and Ghost through the shadowed streets, fully armed and armoured but stealthed and all but silent.

They passed through the main warehousing area where off-planet imports were stored before distribution. Twice they encountered small t'au patrols, the fire warriors made complacent by the late hour and the years of uneventful duty. Tychonis had been too peaceful for too long. Even with Coldwave on site, bringing extra fire caste forces with him, the average t'au soldier saw little cause for heightened vigilance. Events at the Tower had been kept contained, data shared on a need-to-know basis only, and most t'au simply did not need to know.

Each patrol met a quick, quiet end courtesy of silenced bolt rounds.

Both times, Karras, Rauth and Solarion lined up their targets and fired simultaneously on a vox-whispered three-count.

Heads exploded into dark, wet mist. Bodies hit the dirt, then were dragged off into cover.

With each patrol eliminated, Talon pressed closer and closer to their goal. They could see the tall, curving structure of the main power facility up ahead, towering over the storehouses, machine-works and admin buildings that surrounded it. Red lights, a warning to low aircraft, winked in the night from towers and antenna masts.

'Almost there,' voxed Solarion quietly from his point-man position twenty metres ahead of the others. 'The streets end here. Open ground around the power station, with fire caste gun towers looking out over about thirty metres of killing ground. Searchlights and heavy weapons. Two blue-skins per tower. Hard-wall perimeter, not fencing. Ten metres high, so we either go through the main gate or blast our own. Noisy either way. Suggest we use cables to go over.'

It would be easier for Zeed. He had deployed with a jump pack. Broden had left loadout selection to Talon Alpha's discretion. Karras had opted to let his team deploy with the wargear of their choice. The Raven Guard went with the high-mobility option, knowing that most of the fighting would be outdoors, at least for Talon. The t'au were notorious for trying to stay at mid to long range. He'd rob them of that choice. The jump pack would allow him to stay right on them, no matter how much they moved.

Here, it would get him over the walls with a single thought impulse and a brief flare of jets.

Karras wanted a proper visual before he would commit to an entry method. Up ahead, he could see Solarion waiting, his right pauldron jutting slightly from the cover of the shadows at the end of the street.

'Prophet,' voxed the Death Spectre. 'Go high. We'll follow you up. Once I've got a good visual on things, I'll decide how we'll handle it.'

Solarion grunted an affirmative. The edge of the pauldron melted into the shadows. A few moments later, looking up, Karras saw the Ultramarine on the roof, briefly silhouetted in black against the dark navy of the star-frosted sky.

Karras followed him up, shouldering his bolter and jumping several metres to grab a ledge. From there, he moved to an outer stairwell that led to the roof's north-east corner. Once on the roof, he moved at a crouch to the corner where Solarion lay belly down, looking through the scope of his beloved, personally modified sniper rifle.

On another rooftop to the right, Rauth, Voss and Zeed took up observation positions.

Karras assessed the scene before him.

Through booted feet, he could feel the generators and exchangers vibrating even from here, a constant low hum.

Solarion had been right – it would be easy enough to take

down the t'au in the gun towers, but blowing a hole in the wall or trying to rush the main gate seemed ill advised.

The longer he could keep the t'au guessing, the better.

He dipped into his power, murmuring the Litany of Sight Beyond Sight, and sent his astral presence beyond the walls.

As he had suspected, there was a reasonable fire caste presence within the grounds. A TX7 Hammerhead was sitting just inside the main gates. Its engines were powered down, but its weapons systems were fully activated.

'Armour,' he told the others. 'Just inside and to the left of the main gate. Ion cannon and two gun drones. A squad of ten infantry beside it. Three more squads of five running clockwise patrols, each escorted by two drones.'

'That complicates taking down the targets on the towers,' grated Rauth.

'Can't have bodies falling from the towers,' said Zeed. 'They all have to go down nice and quiet and steady.'

'Wake me when you've a proper challenge,' said Solarion.

'I hate to agree with the Prince of Macragge,' voxed Voss sarcastically, 'but at this range, it should be a breeze.'

The Imperial Fist had opted for an Infernus heavy-bolter – extremely large, noisy and cumbersome. Had anyone else chosen such a weapon, Karras would have vetoed it, but Voss wasn't just anyone. Heavy weapons didn't slow him down as they did others. As much as the Infernus wasn't ideal for the opening phase of the op, Karras knew they would all be glad of its power later, when the fighting started. Once the sneaking around was over and the t'au were properly roused, Voss' affinity for seriously heavy firepower would prove its worth.

For now, Voss lowered it to the rooftop and tugged his silenced bolt pistol from the mag-lock on his right cuisse. He flicked the safety off and chambered a round.

'Ghost, Watcher,' said Karras. 'Circle around and establish good kill angles on the north-east and north-west towers. Omni has the south-east. Prophet, go cover the south-west. I'll take the two towers at the main gate. When you're in position with a good bead on your targets, vox in and wait.'

He felt them move off more than saw them, tracking their souls automatically, with one obvious exception. Then Karras rose from his position, slipped back to the rear edge of the roof, dropped to the sandy ground below and, with the buildings around him as cover, pushed south until he was sure he was parallel with the main gates.

Soon, he was in position, crouching on the corner of a storehouse rooftop with a good view of the main gate and the towers on either side of it.

With the exception of Solarion, who had the farthest to go, the others voxed back that they were ready. Solarion confirmed a few seconds later.

'Scholar,' voxed Rauth. 'We need to do this *before* Sabre blow the fuel silos to the east. The whole town is going to wake up when that happens. It will put these blue-skins on immediate alert.'

'Agreed,' replied Karras. 'Now listen carefully, all of you.'

And he told them exactly how five Deathwatch Space Marines cloaked in shadow were going to overcome thirty-one alien soldiers, six armed drones and a heavily armoured battle-tank.

FORTY-THREE

Space Marine scout armour with a layer of photo-reactive optical camouflage cells under a transparent coating of las- and plasma-ablative polymer.

Light. Easy to move in.

Pity it offered so little real protection.

The feeling didn't even come close to full power armour. Still, Androcles was grateful nonetheless. The Black Templar, Broden, was as cold and contemptuous a Space Marine as he'd ever met, and it was all too apparent that he saw Talon and Sabre as little more than tools with which to shape his own success. Despite all that, how could the Son of Antaeus feel anything *but* gratitude? From being a t'au prisoner just days ago to armed and loosed upon the foe, as it should be.

A shot at redemption. At retribution.

This is the Emperor's will.

He placed the last of his demo charges and moved off to the rendezvous to await the others. The Carcharadon, Striggo, was already there, hunched in the darkness, breathing like an animal through his razor-lined jaws like he always did.

He and Androcles nodded at each other in the dark. The Carcharadon had never been much for words.

Gedeon of the Howling Griffons joined them next in the shadow of the guardhouse where they'd left the corpses of the fire warriors protecting the silos. Four swift, silent blade kills. No alarms raised.

Androcles was proud of his brothers. Their time in captivity had done nothing to blunt their edge. Each had wisely spent their days of imprisonment in deep meditation and visualisation, a powerful tool that kept important neural pathways from degenerating while out of active use.

'Charges placed,' whispered Gedeon. 'It'll be quite a show.'

Gedeon was honourable, dutiful, steadfast. Androcles liked him. But, as newly named Sabre Alpha, Androcles had also had to deal with something he hadn't seen coming.

Gedeon had caused a serious problem back at the rebel capital.

On his introduction to Scimitar Four – Van Velden of the Executioners – old hatred had surged to the surface. The Executioners had wreaked havoc on the Howling Griffons during the Badab War, reducing their numbers drastically in a tragic clash that should never have happened.

An old wound, but one never healed. Though the Executioners had been sentenced to a century-long penitent crusade in recompense, nothing would ever be enough in the eyes of the Howling Griffons.

Gedeon had struck Van Velden full in the face before anyone else could act. It was Lyandro Karras who had torn them off each other, tossing them apart with a psychic snap of his terrible power.

Androcles had caught the look Broden had thrown Karras then – wary of where the real power lay in that room, despite operational rank. Few Space Marines, if any, stood a chance against a battle-hardened Librarian. They were a different animal entirely. The apparent ease with which Karras rendered two Space Marine veterans all but helpless had clearly unsettled the Black Templar.

Rightly so. They seemed as children before his power.

Gedeon had raged at being pulled off the Executioner. For all his honour on the battlefield, he was unable to control himself in the full fire of his inner anger and hate.

Androcles had removed him, talked him down.

Temporarily.

Once the operation was over, if both lived, the fires of retribution would flare in him again.

But later was later. For now, it mattered more that his mind was on the mission.

Pelion and Roen joined the rest, charges placed. All looked at Androcles.

'We don't blow the silos till we're well away,' he said. 'Burning fuel will flood the area. Fires will spread quickly. Buildings will burn. The t'au will respond hard, sending troops in force, doubling or tripling patrols, running drone sweeps. I want us well on our way to the spaceport grounds by then. To the true fight.'

'To Kabannen and Lucianos,' growled Pelion.

'To the back-stabbing whore,' hissed Striggo, eyes flashing.

'I will see traitor blood spilled before this day is through,' Roen insisted.

The Reviler was typically almost as quiet as Striggo, but there was real venom in his words. He spoke for all of them.

Androcles found himself picturing the faces of the three

who had betrayed them, faces he had trusted, respected once. Aye, it was hard not to want blood, but the woman could not be harmed, and he reminded them of this.

They would have to make do with the blood of the brothers who had turned against them. The ordo would deal with the woman. Traitors to the Inquisition did not die quickly.

'My mind is as yours,' growled Androcles through gritted teeth, 'but revenge is not why we are here. We are Deathwatch, and we have a job to do. If we are to have a chance at justice, the Emperor will give it to us when the time is right. Now, move out.'

As one, they slipped away from the silos, heading southwest through narrow streets, silently slaying t'au foot patrols where they found them and hiding the bodies as best they could.

Soon they reached the edge of the effective range of their detonators. With consummate stealth, the cells in their armour bending what little light there was around them, blending them into the dark pre-dawn, they climbed to the roof of a storehouse and looked back the way they had come.

'As one,' said Androcles, holding forward the detonator in his left hand. The others raised their own.

The Son of Antaeus grinned.

'It's morning. Let's wake the blue-skins up to the worst day of their lives!'

FORTY-FOUR

One word. A dozen deaths.

'Now!'

Karras had already opened his inner gates to a trickle of power from the immaterium. He channelled it into speeding his perceptions and reflexes, slowing down the flow of time as he experienced it.

With the main gate boasting two gun towers, he had twice the number of t'au lookouts to kill than anyone else. Only this way, utilising his gift, could he execute his part of the plan.

With his bolter's crosshairs on one fire warrior then another, he squeezed the trigger twice.

Two soft coughs from his weapon's muzzle.

Two heads twitched – one, then another – as rounds struck dead centre in each skull. No explosions. Solid rounds for this, not mass-reactive. Solid rounds were cleaner, quieter, but rarely seen outside Deathwatch ops like this.

With his synapses still psychically supercharged, time flowed like mud rather than water. He zeroed in on his targets in the second tower. His first two kills hadn't yet dropped to their knees before his bolter coughed again.

Once. Twice.

Two more heads struck dead centre.

Job done, he lessened his draw on the warp. Time snapped back into standard flow. Four bodies dropped in rapid succession, disappearing from view behind waist-high walls.

One after another, his squad brothers voxed in their success.

Karras sent out questing strands of psychic awareness. The t'au stationed below the watchtowers were oblivious to the kills above them. All around the power station perimeter, the xenos on lookout had dropped silently in pairs.

None had fallen from their nests. Flawless, but now it got harder.

Each Space Marine knew what to do.

Karras gave the word.

Zeed wasn't about to argue – Karras had been clear.

Use of the Raven Guard's jump pack was a risk. Even ordo-modified, it would probably tip off the t'au on the ground. So he'd ordered Zeed to go by zipline like everyone else. It was the quietest option available. Zeed had to concede that.

Once everyone was in position above the circling patrols and the squad inside the gate, they would unleash death in synchronicity. No heroics. No reckless mistakes. Not Zeed's style at all, but he saw the need well enough.

The main power station structure was typical of t'au construction, all smooth curves and sloping sides, but there was a walkway, an encircling balcony halfway up that led to several emergency exits, presumably for the earth caste techs inside to use if there was an accident. Talon Squad would cross to it before dropping on the foe.

Zeed fixed the zipline harpoon attachment from his webbing to the muzzle of his silenced bolt pistol. From his perch overlooking the power station, he took aim at a point on the wall some two and a half metres above the balcony, enough to clear the railing there.

Around the power station, the others voxed their readiness. Karras counted them down.

Five plasteel harpoons bit into the outer surface of the building, ziplines spooling out behind them then going taut. An anchoring round was then fired into the rooftop at each Space Marine's feet, fixing the lines in place.

Zeed checked that his armour's stealth systems were fully engaged, masking the bright Deathwatch silver of pauldron and left arm. All good.

'Ready, Scholar.'

The rest of the team confirmed.

Karras gave the word. From five positions around the station, dark shapes quietly crossed the air above the heads of the t'au patrolling within the outer walls and landed with practised agility on the walkway.

Zeed unclipped himself from the line and walked south around the building to meet with Karras above the main entrance facing the gate. He found him there, looking down on the Hammerhead tank and the squad standing not far from it.

'Scholar.'

'Ghost.'

The tank's turret hatch was open. The gunner was standing half out of it, drawing lungfuls of smoke from a small cylinder of compressed leaves not unlike the tabac popular among Imperial Guardsmen. The habit was a lot less common among the t'au. This one would pay the price for it. His addiction presented Karras with a perfect means by which to quickly deal with the armoured threat.

Voss, Solarion and Rauth called in, confirming their readiness to drop on the patrolling squads and their drones.

'You ready?' asked Karras.

Zeed nodded and rolled his armoured shoulders. At a single thought impulse, a rune on his retinal display switched from red to green. His lightning claws gleamed with the power field now activated around them.

'On your mark, Scholar.'

Karras slung his bolter and drew his combat knife. 'Do it!'

They leapt over the railing together, propelling themselves out over their targets in a wide arc.

Heavy in full armour, they dropped fast.

Zeed struck the ground right among his marks. Before they could gasp, three were down, carved apart with ease. The others barely had time to raise weapons. Zeed was a tornado of slaughter among them, a dark blur of long razors and ceramite shell, apparently unhindered by the jump pack at all.

Blue gore splashed armour and dirt. Bodies collapsed like toppled dolls.

Karras hit the tank's turret just behind the gunner and thrust his knife straight into the alien's skull. He tugged it free, then hauled the body out of the hatch and tossed it. It bounced off the sloping sides of the tank before it hit the dirt.

He pulled a frag grenade from his webbing and pulled the pin, then dropped it into the hatch and leaned back.

A sharp crack. An outpouring of thick smoke.

A side hatch was thrown open and one bloodstained, wounded t'au crawled out groaning, followed a second later by another. They lay on the ground, desperately trying to staunch the bloodflow from grievous shrapnel wounds.

Atop the tank, Karras raised his bolter to his shoulder and put two silenced rounds in them, one in each skull.

'Report!' he voxed to the others.

'Talon Two, targets eliminated,' replied Rauth.

The others called in their kills.

Karras turned towards the main entrance and saw an access panel on the wall just right of it. Unbidden, his mind threw up a memory – Morant hacking the vator back at Alel a Tarag while he, Rauth and Carland held off the retaliating t'au.

Sorrow hit him like a chill gust of wind.

Copley's people had been irradiated in the aftermath of Coldwave's nuclear blast. They'd had to go outside the Stormravens to restore systems. Soon, they'd be dropping with Scimitar Squad for the main assault, but each of the Arcturus troopers was already beginning to suffer the first signs.

This would be their last mission.

Let it bring them some honour, at least.

He shook himself clear of such thoughts. It was not the time.

'Ghost. One of those bodies is a Fireblade. He'll have an access card on him. Get it!'

Zeed found the t'au officer quickly, easy to distinguish by his white cloak, black braid and the honour markings on his armour. The access card was around his neck, a disc of flexible polymer with t'au glyphs on it. Zeed ripped it free and tossed it to Karras, who was already over by the access panel.

'Watcher, Prophet, Omni, back up on the walkway, ready to breach those emergency exits. Novas. Flash and clear when I give the go.'

Confirmation came back from all three, then the word that each was in position, charges placed, ready to breach.

Karras gestured over to Zeed, who got into place. They'd crack the front door and go in together.

'Same for us,' said Karras. 'One nova each. Flash and clear. Pistol first, understood?'

Zeed mag-locked his claws to his cuisses and drew his bolt pistol.

Karras swiped the card. T'au glyphs flashed on the access panel's screen.

The door began to crack open. Halfway open now.

He gave the order.

From the walkway above, the *crump* of breaching charges could be heard.

He and Zeed tossed their nova grenades.

Inside the building, twin flashes of blinding light exploded, each with a concussive bang. As soon as the flashes were over, Karras and Zeed were in, weapons coughing, ending the lives of every t'au they laid eyes on. Squat, stocky bodies in earth caste uniforms went down, skulls and ribcages punched apart.

From the upper level, voices sounded over the vox.

'Clear.'

'Clear.'

'All clear, Scholar.'

Karras gestured to Zeed and together they moved further into the building.

'Good work, Talon,' voxed the Death Spectre. 'Let's shut this place down so the real work can start. Keep it tight and check your corners. There may be more of them. None gets out alive. Omni, you're on demolitions. Get it done.'

'With pleasure, Alpha,' the Imperial Fist voxed back.

Six minutes later, primary power for the whole of Kurdiza went down. The missile and railgun towers encircling the spaceport went dead, targeting AIs offline, holo-displays suddenly blank.

Karras ascended to the walkway outside and switched the vox over to the operational command channel. 'Talon Alpha to Scimitar Alpha. All dark as ordered. Bring the light.'

'Don't get cocky, Talon,' snapped Broden through a crackle of static. *'Just get your kill-team to the next objective on time.'*

'Confirmed, Scimitar. Try not to get killed before we arrive. Talon, out.'

Karras smiled to himself, imagining Broden's expression. The Black Templar was probably cursing him to the deepest pits of the warp right about now.

Good.

The Death Spectre swung his plated legs over the railing of the walkway and dropped to the ground, fracturing rock-crete when he hit. He walked around to the front to reunite with the rest of the squad.

'They'll be coming,' said Solarion. 'TX4s, first. Piranhas.'

Voss nodded. 'Fastest response on the ground. If we go by the rooftops, we'll be spotted from the air as the sun comes up. Any fighters on site will be taking to the air as we speak.'

'We'll stay low,' said Karras, leading them out through the station's main gate. 'Stick to the streets where our stealth systems still give us some edge. They'll be bringing out armour and infantry in force, setting up at least one defensive perimeter around the spaceport landing fields. We need to move fast, but I want us undetected for as long as possible. Keep to the shadows and follow me.'

FORTY-FIVE

In the spaceport's air control centre, located at the top of the tower overlooking all three of the broad circular landing fields, members of the fire and earth castes alike were in a frenzy. The soldiers were relaying information to Commander Coldwave and taking orders. The techs were desperately trying to switch facility systems over to secondary power sources as quickly as possible. Local backup generators couldn't power the defences. They were too low-yield.

The most immediate solution was to draw from the cold fusion station at Ki'tekh, three hundred kilometres to the west-south-west. It would take around eleven minutes. Fast, but not nearly fast enough.

Damage reports were flooding in. A massive fire was spreading out of control near the north-east wall. The geothermal power station just west of there was a ruin, no chance of repair. Dozens lay dead inside and around it.

At the seven-minute mark, word of air strikes came in.

By the time the spaceport's main systems *did* come back online, *Black Eagle* and the three Stormravens of Reaper flight had laid waste to ninety per cent of the perimeter anti-air systems.

The last minutes of darkness before dawn were bright with flame.

In the hangar where he waited impatiently to depart, Coldwave took a calming breath, centred himself and studied the view on the holo-monitor.

Earth caste and fire warriors bustled around him like agitated bees, racing to finish take-off preparations or ready their gear for combat.

The visual feed showed him a horizon ablaze.

He opened a comm-channel to the Fireblades on site and his senior support staff and said, 'Initiate *Bastion* protocols. Ready yourselves for battle. By the glory of the Greater Good and the will of the Aun, we will show them what it means to put one's hand in the daggerhead's jaws.'

The inquisitor was overseeing the loading of her personal cargo while her two bodyguards loaded and primed their ugly, brutish weapons. The Space Marines glanced up when he stopped in front of them. The inquisitor did not look his way. She continued her work, but he knew she had registered him in her peripheral vision.

'Soon, I will go to meet your Deathwatch in battle,' he told the Space Marines. 'They will not survive it.'

He was defiant.

The one called Lucianos grinned.

Kabannen kept loading rounds into a bolt pistol magazine as he said, 'Better for all were you to stay on the ship with m'lady, shas'o. Who will speak your words to the Ethereal Council if you lie dead on these landing fields?'

'But I will not die,' said Coldwave. 'Instead, I will show you why the t'au need fear no one. Our destiny cannot be denied.'

Kabannen shrugged. 'Grand words, blue-skin. But should the killing of Talon Squad prove beyond you, let me put your mind at ease. They may get through you, but they will not get through us. M'lady will get off-world and deliver the data and proposals to your Ethereal High Council. Again I say, better you stay back from the fight and live to accompany her.'

'My survival is not in doubt,' snapped Coldwave. He whirled to face Epsilon, his joy at the thought of the coming battle robbed somewhat by his anger at the insolence and arrogance of her murderous guards.

'Inquisitor,' he barked. 'Caution your Space Marines. All three of you yet draw breath only through my good graces and the good graces of the Aun. Know that even our patience and tolerance have their limits. Your protectors tread perilously close to them.'

Epsilon threw Kabannen a mildly chastising glance, then turned her attention to Coldwave. 'I will watch the battle with great interest, honoured hunter. I have no doubt you will be victorious this day. We shall soon be bound for T'au, and the salvation of both your people and mine will be assured. Fight well, and may the winds favour you.'

This last struck him, for it was an ancient thing said among plains hunters before the t'au had yet become a unified race. Staying downwind of prey was critical. Winds that changed suddenly could ruin a hunt.

She knows far more about us than I thought. Truly, we must kill her as soon as is prudent. Until then, ever more caution. We have climbed into our cots with a serpent most poisonous.

Her words stayed with him as he stormed away, but they

passed from his mind entirely as he started climbing the metal stairs that led to his battlesuit's cockpit.

I am ready, hunter, his battlesuit seemed to sing to him as he climbed inside. *I have waited for this.*

His techs plugged in his neural connectors and pilot-support systems, then sealed him in. Holo-displays and neuro-optical projections flickered to life all around him. He gave himself over to fusing his mind with the advanced AI support systems and felt an overwhelming sense of power, almost indescribable, flood his mind and body.

He felt uplifted, transformed.

Many battlesuit pilots became hopelessly addicted to that feeling. For some, disconnecting, living outside them, caused an acute form of depression. Coldwave had known it once in his first days of piloting an XV8. He had hated the feeling of inadequacy, of weakness, whenever separated from the machine.

Had he not soon overcome it, he would never have risen to shas'o.

It had not affected him since, but still, there was no feeling quite like engaging a foe in a battlesuit. Nothing even close. It had been so long. He almost felt grateful to the intruders.

Today would be a great day. Within the next hour, he would feel more alive than in all the years since he and his people had defeated the Tall Ones and rescued this pitiful world.

He tested the link's neural response times. Glyph readouts told of speeds even better than expected.

The earth caste had been working hard. His kills today would honour their efforts.

'Kabannen,' said the inquisitor.

The Iron Hands veteran looked over at her. 'M'lady?'

'I have told you before. I will not repeat myself again – cease your antagonising of the shas'o. Our accord is tenuous enough. Press him like that again and he will likely try to kill you. Both of you.'

'He will find that beyond him, I assure you,' grunted Kabannen.

'You underestimate him, Space Marine,' replied Epsilon angrily. 'Perhaps today he will show you the error of that. In any case, his patronage is critical. You know what we fight for. You know what we seek and what it could mean.'

Kabannen stopped what he was doing and turned his head to face her. 'I am Adeptus Astartes, lady. A sworn xenos killer. I have allied myself to your cause, turned brother Space Marines over to a xenos race I detest, and do not murder them though my honour and oaths demand it. All of this I have done because I understand the possibilities, the promise. You confided in us because you knew, you *knew*, that only Lucianos and I would understand, that we alone had the vision to go to the necessary extremes.'

She held his gaze, accustomed to feeling dominant, in control.

But not this time. This time, she faltered. She had seen something unexpected in the Iron Hand's usually unreadable face.

Commitment. Absolute and fierce.

She realised then that he was every bit as invested as she. He had already paid a high personal price to come this far. Lucianos, too.

'I am a Space Marine, m'lady,' Khor Kabannen rumbled as he resumed loading and oiling his weapons. 'And I must find Al Rashaq for the sake of *all* Space Marines.'

Especially those I have betrayed for it.

FORTY-SIX

Black Eagle cut across the sky above Kurdiza, upper and lower holds filled with hardened warriors, every last one eager to get groundside and into the fight.

Broden, in the front hold, cast an eye over his kill-team, all in full plate, armed to the teeth, Deathwatch iconography gleaming in the light of the red lumes that signalled an imminent drop.

The Thunderhawk's dorsal-mounted turbo-laser destructor had already made rubble and slag of the spaceport's deadly perimeter defence towers. Not alone, of course. The time taken for that would have seen power restored too soon. *Black Eagle* would have been cut from the sky. The Stormravens had done their part, sharing the work.

Though the t'au had power again, it was too late to matter. The spaceport's static defences were out of the equation, a critical element of the operation achieved.

Not quite freedom of the skies, though.

The moment the xenos recognised that they were under attack, air caste fighter pilots had been ordered out onto runways. Several AX3 Razorsharks were now in the air, racing to engage. But engage what? The Deathwatch gunships were far from standard. Stealth fields, radar absorbing plate, heat signature dampers, electronic countermeasures – all blessings of the Machine Cult of Mars. There was nothing on t'au scanners to lock onto. The air caste would need a visual in order to engage.

'Time until sunrise?' Broden voxed his pilot, Tarval.

'Sixteen minutes, m'lord. The sky is lightening already.'

We'll be on the ground in three, thought the Black Templar. *We just needed darkness to get us in.*

'Any sign of those fighters?'

'Auspex returns show three running defensive sweep patterns over the airfields, m'lord. Correction, one of them just broke away, heading east.'

East.

Reaper Three was flying in to the LZ on that vector, the Dreadnought, Chyron, in its grapples and Spear Team Three in its hold, a third of Major Copley's special forces operators. Broden needed the Lamenter on the ground, wreaking havoc. He couldn't afford for Reaper Three to be knocked out of the sky.

Reaper Three's pilot, Dargen, would have noted the Razorshark breaking off towards him. Mostly likely, the t'au were tracking him visually from the ground, following the passage of his glowing jets across the sky. The Razorshark wouldn't get a lock. It would need to get close and target the Stormraven manually.

Still, its speed and the power of its weaponry presented a problem.

Broden opened a link to Reaper flight. 'Scimitar Alpha to all Stormravens. Reapers One and Two are to support Reaper Three. Take down that shark and escort to the drop zone. Once the Dreadnought and Spear Team Three are on the ground, provide close support. Confirm orders.'

The Reaper pilots confirmed.

Broden addressed Tarval again. 'Time to drop site?'

'One minute forty seconds, m'lord,' reported the Thunderhawk pilot.

'Be ready. We're about to take a lot of heat from the ground. I want all weapons systems brought to bear.'

'Always ready, m'lord. They made me that way.'

Broden grunted. At first, he'd been offended that a Thunderhawk, especially the one assigned to carry him, was to be piloted by a non-Adeptus Astartes. Outside the Deathwatch, it was unheard of. To the Ordo Xenos, however, Space Marine assets were too important to leave in a cockpit when they were most needed on the ground. The ordo instead recruited decorated veterans from the Imperial Navy, luring them in with the promise of unparalleled aircraft, technological resources, honour and glory. With a price, of course. Those that accepted were modified. They became... What? Man-machines, Broden supposed. Like servitors in some ways, but not quite. They became the living brains of their aircraft, fused with them permanently, the airframe becoming their body, responding to their thoughts the way his power armour responded to his.

He still wasn't sure he approved, but he had seen the results. He could not doubt their effectiveness.

'Scimitar,' he barked at the battle-brothers in front of him. 'Final weapon checks and litanies. Make your obeisance. Bless your weapons. And bring honour to our name this day!'

'For honour and the Emperor,' bellowed the kill-team in unison.

Valo, as always, bowed his head and added a brief oath to the Omnissiah. Not something Broden liked, but the rest of Scimitar didn't see the God-Emperor quite as he did. They did not consider him truly divine in the religious sense. Blind, they were, and the teachings of their Chapter woefully incomplete, but forgiving their ignorance was the only way to make things work. He had come to terms with that on his first deployment as Alpha.

As they were offering obeisance to their wargear, he opened a channel to the upper hold.

'Spear Teams One and Two,' he voxed, addressing Copley's own squad and the squad assigned to her second, Captain Vyggs. 'Ninety seconds till drop. Have your people ready, Archangel. I will personally punish any slips. The Deathwatch demands excellence of those who deploy in support of it. Your people may be sickened, weakened, but they have a duty to fulfil. Be glad of this chance. Today will be your last shot at glory in the God-Emperor's name. A last chance to elevate your souls for all eternity to come. Do not squander it.'

In the upper hold, Copley could barely contain her anger at his words. Yes, her people were dying, but they knew it well enough. They did not need it spelled out for them by one who was immune to the very thing that was killing them.

Back at Chatha na Hadik, her stormtroopers had taken powerful meds to counteract the worst of the symptoms during this final operation, but if any of them lived through this, it would not be for very long. Days at most.

Truly, Coldwave had killed them the moment he had opted to destroy Alel a Tarag.

It will be a cruel, slow death, she thought. *But the Templar bastard is right about one thing. That the death is slow gives us this one shot.* Shadowbreaker *can still succeed. Arcturus can go out on a high note. My people are ready, and if the Emperor is watching over us, he will let us die in battle as true warriors deserve.*

The thought of a slow, withering death, of vomiting greater and greater amounts of blood while sores erupted on the skin, while organs failed and liquefied…

Such thoughts chilled her blood.

A pulse round to the skull would be welcome.

For all she hated the xenos, all the years she had dedicated herself to the war against them, it would be better to die at the hands of a worthy enemy, a smart enemy, an enemy she could respect. And she had always held a grudging respect for the t'au. Anything less would have been self-delusion.

Defeating the blue-skins today at Kurdiza would do little to hurt their expansion. They were relentless, vigorous, filled with the fires of ambition and entitlement. They would continue to encroach on Imperial space, bringing into the fold other races with promises of unity and prosperity for all.

It hardly mattered if those promises were a glamour only. They worked.

And one day, the Imperium, *her* beloved Imperium, would find itself in crisis, having underestimated the allure of the T'au'va.

Human worlds would fall like dominoes.

But I'll be dead by then. I have today to make a difference. Only today.

'Archangel to Scimitar Alpha,' she voxed, making sure her voice was loud enough in the hold for her people to hear. 'Arcturus stands ready. Do your part, and we will do ours. Archangel out.'

She closed the link.

Vyggs was looking at her with that expression again. He no longer tried to hide it now that he knew they would soon die. She hardened hers.

Don't say it, man. Please don't. I know well enough. But let it pass unsaid, for both our sakes.

He had loved her for years. He had never spoken of it, but she knew, as all women know when a man's gaze lingers overlong and warm on them, even when they can't see his face behind an omnishield helm and resp-mask.

She had appreciated his affection somewhat, deep down. What person, man or woman, hated to be valued and adored?

But she had resented it, too.

Vyggs saw her as she had never allowed herself to. He saw a woman, and desired her. She had spent her whole life building herself into something else, a warrior and leader every bit the equal of her men. As a woman, it was not enough to be equal. She'd had to work far harder than any male officer. The Militarum had denied her her due so many times, throwing her over for promotion, choosing men with half her record or less.

The Inquisition had not been so blind. The Ordo Xenos had seen her worth. It had vindicated her.

Ordo service has been the best years of my life. I will not fail the ordo now. Shadowbreaker will succeed. On my life, on the lives of my men, Shadowbreaker will succeed.

She checked the power cabling and connectors on her hotshot lasgun, then ran a final check on the rest of her kit. Silenced bolt pistol, grenades, knife.

She checked the stealth systems and photo-reactive camouflage of her combat bodysuit and carapace armour, her helm optics, comms and filters.

All green.

Gravity shifted. The Thunderhawk was swinging around on the drop zone.

Noise erupted. Explosions. The rattle and smack of pulse cannon fire. The deep growl of the aircraft's twin-linked heavy-bolters. The hiss and zap of its lascannons. Then, the angry buzz and shuddering boom of the turbo-laser destructor.

'All brace,' voxed the pilot. *'Drop zone is hot.'*

'Wake up, Spear teams,' she shouted above the noise.

Her people snapped to attention. She tried to ignore that a few were stifling wet coughs.

'Time to do what we do best,' she told them. 'Now remind me one more time where you ugly, tough-looking sons-of-grox were all born and raised!'

Every right fist in the upper hold was suddenly thrust into the air. As one, they roared, voices drowning out all else.

'Elysia!'

'Elysia!' Copley yelled back, her face split with a broad grin.

There was a judder as the Thunderhawk's landing stanchions hit solid ground.

The doors to the lower hold jerked open. Muted daylight was already flooding the space.

Scimitar was charging out into battle.

Copley heard the roar of a heavy flamer, the thump of a Deathwatch frag cannon.

She was still grinning when she ran down the ramp to the lower hold, then led her people out at speed into the maelstrom that awaited.

Up ahead of her, she immediately saw her objective, the atrium of the Kurdiza spaceport main building. Behind it, the air control tower thrust upwards into the early morning air, lights shining bright in the control centre windows.

T'au were everywhere, pouring onto the rooftops and walkways of the two large terminal buildings on either side and from the roof and balconies of the atrium itself. On the ground, they fired from behind man-portable barricades of energy-absorbing alloys and ceramics.

From all these places, they rained pulse, plasma and ion fire towards the Thunderhawk and the Imperial forces which spilled out onto the rockcrete. From *Black Eagle*'s front ramp to the main entrance of the atrium lay seventy metres of open ground – ground that should have been impossible to cross. But the Thunderhawk's heavy-bolters were chewing apart the t'au cover, forcing their heads down, tearing apart the bodies of any foolish enough to dare return fire.

Even so, during the mad, breathless sprint towards the broad windows and glass doors of the atrium entrance, two members of Vyggs' team, Keel and Arlen, were evaporated, turned to ash and burning scraps of cloth by a t'au heavy weapon that managed to get off a blinding, stone-scorching blast.

Black Eagle's hurricane bolters turned the offending position to rubble and dust. The screams of t'au wounded were drowned out by continued drumming as the bolters then strafed the walkways left and right.

Dozens of fire warriors were ripped to pieces. Weapons and bodies tumbled to the ground below.

Copley registered all of this peripherally, but her focus was ahead of her.

Ten metres.

The t'au saw her getting closer to cover. They intensified their fire.

Black Eagle punished them lethally for that, forcing them back down.

Faster!

Eight metres.

The hurricane bolters couldn't cover every angle. The t'au were determined that Spear Teams One and Two would not make the cover of the atrium.

Faster, damn it!

Six metres.

Pulse rounds sang through the air so close she felt their deadly heat through her combat suit.

Four metres.

Two metres.

One.

Copley fired at the glass, weakening it.

Then she charged straight through it, head tucked. The window exploded inwards. She skidded to a halt, lasgun raised.

The atrium was wide and filled with light. There were slate-black holo-displays everywhere – on walls, on pillars, hanging from the metal beams of the high ceiling – but they were dead now. No timetables or safety information flickered and danced over them today. There were strange plants, too, blue in colour, some reaching as high as the second-floor galleries.

It would have been easy to imagine this place on a normal day, filled with a multitude of beings from all the races the t'au had embraced, a mix of military, commercial, political...

Today, it was a battleground.

T'au defenders burst from cover or leaned from pillars to open fire. The Elysians dived for cover of their own. Several tossed frags.

There was a sharp staccato of explosions. Unbroken windows shook.

T'au infantry staggered from cover, uniforms stained blue, flesh punctured by deadly shrapnel. They were gunned down immediately.

Others still were concussed and stumbled into view. Lasgun fire ended their lives.

Those still fighting were soon suppressed and flanked, the last of these shot in the back as he tried to flee through the far exit.

'Spear One to Scimitar Alpha,' voxed Copley as her people secured the stairs on either side of the hall and proceeded to clear the second floor. 'We've taken the reception building. Proceeding to objective.'

Broden's answer was terse, his focus given over to battle flow. *'Be quick about it, woman. I want Epsilon found!'*

Copley's eyes narrowed. She cut the link.

Arrogant piece of…

Clearly, not all Adeptus Astartes were equal.

'Second floor cleared, ma'am,' voxed Vyggs.

Copley ran up the right stairway. Vyggs and his team were stacked at the end of the second-floor hallway by a row of broad doors that opened onto covered walkways outside.

The doors to the left and right would take them to the east and west terminal buildings – east for atmospheric traffic, west for traffic going offworld.

The central walkway was the one they wanted – it would take them to the main control tower.

Vyggs thrust his chin at its ornately carved doors. 'No way we can just walk straight in, I suppose.'

Copley knew he was grinning under his mask. She shook her head. 'You know better.'

The t'au would have rigged it to blow the minute they knew the spaceport was under attack. They'd know someone was coming for the control room.

'Rooftop access?' she asked.

'Stairs far left and right through those exits over there.'

Addressing everyone, she said, 'We're going up. There will be t'au still on the roof, so clear them out. We'll run lines from the roof to the control tower and go in through the windows. They can blow the walkways if they want. It won't make a difference. But be ready. Get to cover the moment you're through the glass and secure the room for those coming in behind you. Clear?'

Spear Team One took the left access. Spear Team Two took the right.

Two minutes later, they crashed through several windows on the second floor of the air control tower and cleared that floor.

In the main hall, they found two vators. Vyggs didn't have to ask. The t'au would have rigged them, too.

There was only one stairwell leading up. Spear Team Two took the lead.

'Stack up on that door,' Vyggs told his team.

Copley's team covered them from the rear.

'Smoke the stairwell on entry and go in on infrared,' ordered Vyggs. 'Gaman. Ludo. You're my first-footers. On three, two, one.'

Doors were kicked. Smoke was popped. Sergeant Gaman and Private Ludo raced in.

Lasgun fire lit the smoke like a strobe. There was a scream. Bodies dropped from the landings above, t'au and ISF both.

The Elysians surged inside and began their ascent.

FORTY-SEVEN

'Ghost. Go high.'

The Raven Guard didn't need to be told twice. At a mental command, his jump jets flared, launching him up and over, onto the rooftop of the tallest hab.

The rest of Talon went into cover and, shadow to shadow, pushed up the street, closer to the t'au blockade at the intersection ahead.

There were blockades at every intersection now as Talon pushed closer to the spaceport and the rendezvous with the rest of the task force.

Fire caste patrols and drones were sweeping the streets and rooftops, looking for those that had blown the power station and the north-east silos. Karras and his kill-team brothers evaded those they could and killed those they could not.

The blue-skin response to the Imperial incursion had been swift and comprehensive, typical of t'au organisation and efficiency.

The spaceport town had never needed much in the way of a garrison. Two hundred infantry. A dozen Devilfish transports. Half that again in Hammerhead tanks. Two Skyray anti-air units. The defence towers had been designed to make the garrison all but redundant. The t'au hadn't imagined they might be brought down so easily from the inside.

Karras peered out from the cover of a recessed doorway. Behind the barricades ahead brooded the sleek form of another TX7 Hammerhead. Deadly enough on its own, this one was accompanied by twelve fire warriors and their Fireblade officer, plus two of those damned drones the blue-skins were always depending on.

Sharp as his eyes and autosenses were at this range, Karras needed to be sure neither of those fliers was a shield drone.

'Scholar,' breathed Zeed over the vox. 'I've got a good vertical flank. Say the word.'

'Drone types?' said Karras.

There was a pause. 'Shield drones,' said Zeed. 'Both of them.'

That complicated things. Karras might destroy them with psychic force, but only if he had a solid line of sight on each, and the way they were positioned within the barricades, that would mean putting himself out in the open.

His armour could soak up enough of the standard t'au small-arms fire to give him a window on *one* of the drones, but the Hammerhead's powerful railgun would be on him, stealth systems engaged or not, before he could crush the other. He couldn't kill it and shield himself at the same time.

He called up the pict feed from the Raven Guard's helm and considered the enemies' relative positions.

'Ghost,' he voxed. 'You'll drop right down on the left drone. The second you do, those troopers on the east edge of the barricade are going to turn their weapons on you. Don't give them time. The instant your drone is down, you jump back to cover.'

'I can handle them, Scholar. I'll stick to them until they're meat.'

'You won't. You'll jump as ordered. Clear?'

Zeed snorted. 'Your game, your rules. Got it.'

'Watcher, flank left. The minute both drones are down and Ghost is out of there, hit the front of that Hammerhead with a thundershock grenade.'

'EMP won't knock out a Hammerhead, Karras. You know that.'

'It *will* knock out the gun drones in its nose. You'll take them out, then turn your bolter on the infantry. Frag them if they cluster.'

'Understood.'

'Prophet, you'll flank right, find cover, and put crosshairs on the Fireblade. When the shield drones go down, take his head off. After that, kill at will. The t'au on the west side will be firing up at Ghost. Drop them.'

'Moving off now,' said Solarion.

'Scholar,' said Voss, hefting his Infernus heavy-bolter a little higher than usual, as if to say, *Put me to work!*

Karras nodded to him. 'You're with me, Omni. We're going right down the middle. I'll take out the right-side shield drone first, but I'll be dangerously exposed after that while I deal with the Hammerhead's railgun. You'll suppress the infantry out in front. Bolt or flame or both, just keep them off me.'

'As good as done, Scholar.'

'Get yourselves into position. The chrono is ticking and I could do without an earful from Broden.'

Black shapes separated from each other.

Two minutes later, the intersection erupted in violence.

Three minutes later, it was silent, awash with blood and black smoke. Not a single t'au drew breath.

Five minutes later, a patrol came across the scene of the carnage and called it in.

Talon Squad was already half a kilometre away, moving at speed, pushing south to the landing fields and the battle that was already raging there.

Reaper Three swung west for the spaceport landing grounds. Chyron, hanging under its tail, held there by magna-grapples, turned his optics to the fires and smoke below.

To the left and right, Reapers One and Two paced his craft, just a little to the rear in delta formation, watching the skies and their scopes. There were still two Razorshark fighters out there within striking distance.

From this position, his view largely obscured by black hull, Chyron hadn't seen much of the fight with the first. He had heard the vox chatter, had known one of the t'au jets was on an intercept course. At the last moment, as the Razorshark was just opening fire, the other Stormravens had swept in on its flanks and torn it to pieces.

Chyron had seen a flash, and then the burning wreckage had appeared in his vision as it spiralled groundward. It smashed into a large storage facility, igniting whatever was kept there.

Settling into formation, the three Stormravens pressed on towards the spaceport.

Broden's plan had tested Chyron's patience already. He had had to remain hooked up to the assault craft while it took down its share of the town's perimeter defences during the initial assault window.

Three of those towers lay in ruins thanks to Flight Lieutenant Dargen and his gunship. As the Stormraven had screamed away, fire caste soldiers had flooded onto rooftops with man-portable missile systems to try to close the new gaps in the perimeter. Stealthed and with full electronic countermeasures active, Reaper Three was impossible to lock onto. Not invisible, however. At this altitude, just a few hundred metres up, the glow from her turbofan engines was visible from the ground. That was how t'au infantry had guided the Razorshark in, and ultimately doomed it.

As the three Stormravens cut the distance to the spaceport in half, then half again, bright pulse and plasma fire arced up into the night.

Chyron growled. As he swung to and fro in the clutches of the magna-grapples, he felt helpless and frustrated. Xenos were firing on him and he could not retaliate.

'Get me groundside,' he snarled, but only to himself. There was no point taking it out on Dargen. He couldn't fly any faster.

Besides, Chyron felt a strange kinship with the Stormraven pilots. Not much of one, but it struck him that each was as permanently a part of his machine as he was himself. In essence, they were all loyal Imperial souls locked in mechanical bodies, living for duty, living *through* their duty.

Maybe they were as he was – maybe duty was all they had left.

Had they lost everything else, just as he had?

Several streams of pulse fire just missed him. A few of the rounds smacked into the tail of the craft, glowing there momentarily until their deadly energy dissipated, leaving a small black crater.

Reaper Three dropped a little altitude and angled slightly north. The others did likewise.

'Be ready, Talon Six,' voxed the pilot. *'You too, Spear Team Three,'* he added for the Elysians in the hold.

'Drop site in view, and it looks damned hot down there!'

FORTY-EIGHT

Broden and his kill-team, under cover of the Thunderhawk's armoured wings and hull, added their fire to the assault craft's own, helping to buy Spear Teams One and Two the opening they needed to get into the atrium and begin their push to the air control centre.

Now they were inside and Scimitar needed to be about its own objectives.

Kurdiza had three large, oval landing fields. Fields One and Three were given over to commercial traffic, surrounded by vast warehouses, refuelling stations and cargo loading bays. Field Two was military, and likewise surrounded, but with barracks and a large armoury. One and Three boasted three large hangars apiece. Field Two had only one, but it was double the size of any other.

Somewhere in all this, Coldwave and Epsilon were readying for departure, trusting in the fire caste to eliminate the Imperial threat before take-off.

Broden didn't know where Epsilon intended to go from here. Further from the reach of the ordo, he imagined, in order to continue her fell business with the t'au.

It didn't matter.

He wasn't going to let her get offworld. He would do what Talon and Arcturus had been unable to, those unworthy dogs. He was a breed apart, scion of the Black Templars, and he would prove it today for the honour of the God-Emperor and the primarch, Rogal Dorn.

To the west lay the main transit station serving the spaceport – a t'au thing, some kind of fusion-driven, high-speed mag-rail node that probably served commercial distribution interests most of the time. But it *could* be used for bringing t'au reinforcements right into the heart of the battle, and he couldn't allow that.

Just west, about three hundred metres, lay the closest of the commercial hangars attached to Field One. The search would start there.

'Scimitar to *Black Eagle*,' he voxed. 'We're clear. Take to the air. Keep us covered as you rise. Once you're up, I want that transit station obliterated. I need it unusable. Bring it down. Is that understood?'

Still firing furiously, the Thunderhawk cycled up its turbines. '*Black Eagle* copies, m'lord. Good hunting.'

'Good hunting,' grunted Broden.

With Adeptus Astartes battle-sign, he signalled his kill-team – including the Crimson Fist Techmarine, Valo, and his two slaved servitors – to make speed for the first of the hangars.

Black Eagle was nosing into the air. Scimitar broke from the cover of her shadow and pounded across open rockcrete, Broden the slowest in Terminator armour but moving with all the alacrity that the almost indestructible suit could manage.

Fire warriors pressed forward, eager to exploit the advantage of having their targets on open ground. They sent a withering hail of fire at Scimitar, only to have their rounds shrugged off, Adeptus Astartes power armour more than equal to the task.

That eagerness to exploit what the t'au thought was a great opportunity was, in fact, their undoing. From the cockpit of *Black Eagle*, Tarval saw them and turned his gunship's bolters on them, shredding the t'au in a wash of mass-reactive shells.

The landing field became wet with xenos blood. Smoking bodies twitched.

Then she was up, swinging her boxy nose east, dipping to bring her massive dorsal weapon to bear on the transit station. The turbo-laser destructor's coils began to glow and an angry buzz filled the air.

Black Eagle loosed a bright blast that struck the station building dead on, turning it to dust and burning ruins. Then she flared her jets and hauled herself higher into the air.

'Target eliminated, Scimitar. Reaper Three reports arrival in one minute. Black Eagle *will stay on station to provide air support for Reaper Three during the drop. With your permission, m'lord.'*

Broden was running full tilt, not stopping to fire at the few t'au left alive as they took shots at him from the handful of barricades that remained intact. 'Permission granted,' he replied. Then, over the command channel, 'Reaper Three, your drop zone is Landing Field Three. Talon Six, you will give fire support to Spear Team Three, who are tasked with searching each of the hangars east of the main terminal building. Be swift, but operate with caution. And stay in contact. Reaper flight will offer close support from the air. All confirm!'

Responses were loud and clear.

'There are still two Razorsharks up here,' voxed Ventius of Reaper One. *'Orders regarding them, m'lord?'*

'Don't let them draw you away from the battle here,' Broden said. 'The t'au have yet to show us their teeth. The Razorsharks must have been ordered to hold back for a reason. They may be awaiting more air support, or perhaps some opening we cannot foresee. Watch your auspexes. Keep me apprised. We must be ready.'

Power armour allowing far faster running than Terminator armour, his Scimitar brothers had already reached the outer walls of Hangar One West. They slammed their backs against it. A moment later, Broden joined them.

Several thick metal doors led inside. The main entrance was the massive rolled shutter through which aircraft could enter or exit. This was closed and far too heavy to breach.

No windows to look through, either. Just plasteel-reinforced rockcrete and the metal side-doors, all sealed.

A simple breach and clear. Broden was used to going in hard. In Terminator armour, impervious to most fire, he would also be going in first.

'Stack up on south, west and north,' he said. 'Two to a door. Caenan, you're with me, but you'll stay well back until I give the word. Once I'm in, the rest of you will monitor my pict feed, mark your targets and breach on my order.'

'Affirmative, Alpha,' grated Valo, voice modulated by the permanent augmetics that covered his nose and mouth. The others replied in kind.

'On your say then, brother,' said Caenan of the Doom Eagles. Bolt pistol in his right hand, chainsword gently purring in his left, he looked more than ready. The Apothecary's ferocity in close quarters was something to behold.

Broden stepped out, faced the door, then, having activated

the energy field around his power fist, threw a blistering left that exploded it inwards in a shower of hot metal shards.

He surged inside.

Immediately, from positions of cover all over the interior of the hangar, from both ground level and upper gantries, a deadly rain of fire began scoring the air in bright white and blue. Plasma rounds struck his breastplate. Pulse rounds scored his greaves and cuisses.

The barrage was intense, like being caught in a rainstorm. Broden grinned beneath his fearsome ceramite muzzle. Tactical Dreadnought armour was made for far harsher storms than this.

Far from being pushed back, he boldly stepped forward into the blizzard of xenos rounds, mocking the efforts of the blue-skins to stop him.

Marking t'au positions pointedly for the brothers following his pict feed, he lifted the nose of his assault cannon and pressed the trigger. The clustered barrels began spinning. A muzzle flare licked out, two metres long.

The weapon's unique, deadly whine filled the air.

Rounds began chewing cover apart, cutting the bodies behind it to pieces. Screams were drowned out. Fire warriors died by the dozen, unable to draw back without exposing themselves.

'Breach,' said Broden almost casually.

Two other doors exploded inwards.

Sundstrom's frag cannon coughed. Van Velden's heavy flamer roared. The silenced Stalker bolters and bolt pistols of the others made barely any sound at all.

All too soon, the hangar fell silent. Smoke and dust swam in the air. Blood dripped from gantries above.

'Clear,' said Broden. 'Not even a ship in this one. We press on. The chrono is against us.'

As they were turning to leave, Sammet of the Night Watch, ever the most observant, spotted something on a plasteel support pillar, halfway up towards the ceiling. It was small and dark with the tiniest of blinking lights.

He looked at the other pillars holding up the hangar roof. On each he found a similar small device.

He realised the blinking was accelerating. Rapidly.

He almost managed a shouted warning before the t'au charges detonated, ripping through the hangar, filling the space with bright fire, shearing straight through rockcrete and plasteel.

Broden and his kill-team barely had time to look up as blazing heat and light engulfed them and the whole structure collapsed upon their heads.

FORTY-NINE

Kurdiza was built by men.

Its first incarnation was so far back in the colonised history of the planet that records of those days no longer existed. There was a single, simple reason for its location here on the lower edge of the mid-northern latitudes, south-west of the Ghadda mountain range – it was here that the first ever human craft had landed. No one alive on Tychonis today knew this, of course.

Large sections of the spaceport and the surrounding town had been rebuilt many times. Sometimes, an accident – usually a lifter crash or a plasma generator explosion – was the cause. At one time, it had been the assaults of the dreaded dark eldar in the days before the t'au had driven them off.

In the years since, t'au efficiency being what it was, only minor changes had ever been made. The blue-skins were content to adapt human structures to their needs. Ugly and boxy as they were, they served their function.

The air control tower was no different. Much as it contained significant t'au technology and personnel, it was still a typically human place, its layout more or less the same as such towers on countless Imperial worlds.

From the second-floor admin rooms into which they had crashed via zipline from the roof of the spaceport atrium, Copley had led Spear Teams One and Two up flight after flight of metal stairs, gunning down defenders as they went, ascending at last to the highest level.

Now, with Spear Team Two stacked against the doorway, ready to breach into the main corridor of the uppermost floor, Copley and Spear Team One hung back, keeping to the landing just below, giving Team Two room to work.

Copley knew the t'au would have rigged the door on the other side. There would be fire warriors lying in wait, highly alert, senses sharp with adrenaline.

All the ordo's cards were on the table now. Coldwave and his forces knew about the Thunderhawk, about Scimitar, about the survival of the force that had attacked Alel a Tarag.

If the blue-skins didn't quite recognise the precise level of threat they faced, Epsilon and her traitorous bodyguards certainly did. They knew better than to take an ordo task force and three Deathwatch kill-teams for granted, even with an entire hostile world against them. The inquisitor would make sure Coldwave understood what he was up against.

'Door's rigged, ma'am,' Vyggs said.

'Counter charges, captain. You know the drill.'

'Copy that.'

Vyggs had Willix, his best with explosives, set up small charges on lock and hinges, then pulled everyone back to a safe distance.

'They'll be in the halls,' Copley told everyone. 'Probably

barricades at corridor junctions and corners. The control room entrance will be well defended. Expect overlapping fields of fire. They may have gun drones, possibly shield drones. You all know how we deal with that. Questions?'

She knew there would be none. They knew their jobs, knew the protocols.

'All set,' she told Vyggs. 'Give the word.'

'Breach in three,' Vyggs said, 'two, one.'

The charges cracked loud in the stairwell, blowing the door inwards. The t'au charges on the other side immediately detonated, filling the air with the bright, hot flash of a lethal plasma reaction. Pulse and plasma fire immediately began pouring through the blasted doorway, but Vyggs had his people in cover well back from the opening. He signalled two of them, Dewer and Yann.

They moved up into the hard cover of the doorframe. Yann tugged a grenade from his webbing. Dewer was carrying a grenade launcher and adjusted the round selector on its fat magazine instead. He threw Yann a wink and a nod.

Yann pulled the pin, counted to three and tossed his grenade.

A two-count later, the bright flash and snap of a powerful electromagnetic pulse reached them from down the hall.

All enemy fire suddenly stopped.

Dewer leaned out and fired a round from his launcher. It exploded right among the t'au, hot shrapnel ripping through xenos flesh where it was least armoured. Cries of agony rang out.

'First fire-team,' barked Vyggs. 'Smoke. Optics on infrared. Secure the corridor.'

Dewer hit his weapon's round selector and fired again, filling the corridor with heavy smoke. Four storm troopers surged past him, weapons raised and ready.

The sharp crack of lasgun fire sounded, then died off abruptly.

'Barricade cleared, captain,' reported Sergeant Vanoff. 'We're in the cover of the walls. They have another nest covering this position from right down the hall. Permission to take it, sir?'

'Hold in cover,' said Vyggs. He led the rest of Spear Team Two into the corridor. Copley and her team held back, still covering the rear, alert for any sign of t'au flankers on the stairwell below.

Vyggs voxed her after he had assessed things from the first barricade. *'Two gun drones, but the EMP took them out. Grere, destroy those things before they come back online. Four blue-skin infantry killed. One injured.'* There was a pause, then the bark of a single pistol shot. *'Five killed. Team Two moving to clear other nest now. Team One clear to move up.'*

'Morrow, Caulsen,' said Copley, turning to two of her men. Each nodded their helmed heads.

'Hold here. Razor sharp. You understand me?'

'Razor sharp, ma'am,' replied Morrow, the older of the two. He slapped the other man's shoulder. 'You and me get the dog's job this time, tough stuff.'

Caulsen groaned resignedly.

Copley ordered the rest of her people up and through the breach.

Vyggs and his team had used the same tactics on the second barricade. So long as shield drones were in grenade range, they could be knocked down briefly with EMP. Outside that range, they were a nightmare, allowing t'au sharpshooters to punish attackers at long range with almost total impunity.

Thank Terra for close, tight corridors, thought Copley.

Vyggs confirmed clearance of the second barricade. Copley moved up to join him. With a thin, flexible vid-picter, its tiny lens peeking around the next corner, they surveyed the corridor between them and the final barrier to the tower's air control centre. On the device's display, they could see another t'au nest bristling with weapons, shimmering with projected energy shields.

Copley felt an unpleasant tingle on the back of her neck.

'The main room is right there, ma'am,' said Vyggs. 'The corridor goes from here right towards it, but at the door, it splits off left and right, and they'll have squads covering the entrance from both directions. We can take it, but we won't be clear until we take down both those squads, and that'll have to be done at once.'

Copley was silent, trying to work out what had the hairs on her neck standing up.

'Ma'am?' said Vyggs.

Copley shook her head. Something was definitely wrong. 'The t'au don't sit still if they can help it,' she muttered, mostly to herself. Suddenly, she grabbed his arm. 'They're going to blow the walls! Everyone! Against the back wall, right now!'

Just a second too late.

There was a ripple of explosions.

Some of her people cried out in pain. They staggered and stumbled into the walls, concussed by proximity to the twin blasts.

'Engage! Engage!' shouted Copley.

In the smoke and dust, two fire warrior breacher teams spilled into the halls right on top of the Elysians.

Pulse blasters fired at close range, their rounds biting through armour into human flesh and bone. Arcturus was hit hard. For the first few moments, confusion reigned. Then hard training took over. Well-trained minds switched into reflex and conditioned response.

Those unhurt brought their fury to bear on the t'au.

Intense. Messy. Desperate.

When it ended, six Elysians – Drake, Becker, Ryce, Gaman, Yann and Ludo – were dead. One more lay mortally injured, his life leaving him. Copley knelt beside the wounded man and removed his helm.

Vyggs had stepped across to cover her back just as a fire warrior unloaded his pulse blaster at her from three metres away. Even as Vyggs' torso was being hollowed out by the t'au bastard's white-hot rounds, he managed to fire his lasgun on full auto right at his killer's head, the beams punching straight into the expressionless, backswept alien helm.

The captain had saved Copley's life. The price was his own.

Copley removed her helm and looked down into his eyes, but the light was already gone from them. They were dull and flat. Gone was that unwelcome intensity with which they had always shone when he looked at her.

This one time only, she wished it was still there.

Around her, the rest of her operators covered the corridor and the breaches in the walls that the t'au had made. They didn't turn to stare at their commander. Duty was foremost in their minds. Sorrow would have to settle for second place. They had a job to do. Right now, that meant covering the major while she made her farewell.

She didn't have time to make much of one. The t'au would hit them again, confident their numbers had been reduced. She pulled Vyggs' tags off and pushed them into a pocket.

I know you loved me. Thank you for not saying it. I couldn't have returned it. I think you knew. It's just not in me to give. But I'll be seeing you soon. We all will. Hang back a while and meet us at the gates, and we'll all go to the Emperor's side together.

Imagine that. Arcturus all together, marching into the Emperor's light.

Gently, she lowered his head to the floor.

'Get tags from the others,' she commanded, her voice taking on an icy hardness.

'Already done, ma'am,' said Morant, standing at her side. He put a hand on her shoulder.

She shrugged it off and straightened to face him, eyeball to helm lens. 'None of that,' she growled. 'You hear me?'

Morant, tough as he was, as grizzled as any of them, looked at the floor, abashed.

'Vyggs and the others got warriors' deaths,' she said. 'Well earned. And we'll be joining them soon enough. Before that, we've got a bloody job to do. I need the rest of you to take up the slack. Because now more than ever, how good you are is going to make all the difference.'

Morant stepped back a wide pace and threw up his sharpest salute. 'Ma'am.'

Over the vox, Copley called in Caulsen and Morrow. 'Leave the stairs. I need you here now. Move.'

Seconds later, they joined the rest.

She looked at what she had left. Eight men. And her. It would be enough because it had to be.

She thought of Spear Team Three. They were out there under Broden's command, searching the hangars for sign of Epsilon. She hoped they were faring better than this.

The t'au had made two breaches in their surprise attack. Beside Vyggs' body lay the snake-picter she had been looking at when the t'au teams attacked. She swept it up and walked to the nearest hole in the wall. There, she poked the lens around the fire-blackened corner and studied the screen.

Satisfied, she handed the device off to Morant, who was standing beside her. He was the most senior man left alive, the last of her sergeants apart from Grigolicz, but Grig was out there leading Team Three.

She told the others, 'From now on, you're all Team One. Morrow, sling your lasgun for now and pick up that grenade launcher.'

Morrow crouched by the body of Drake, a man he'd fought alongside for almost two decades. There had been close calls before, but they'd always made it through.

Archangel had always got them through.

'It couldn't last forever,' muttered Morrow to the ruined body of his friend as he tugged the grenade launcher free of the dead man's grip. 'But I'll keep making them pay while I can.'

He stood with the weapon and nodded to Copley.

'The rest of you,' she continued, 'strip the bodies of everything we can use. That goes for the blue-skins, too. They'll have grenades. Be quick about it, because in four minutes, I want us inside that main control room.'

She jabbed a thumb at the hole in the wall. 'The blue-skins just gave us two new avenues of attack, and we're going to make them regret it.'

FIFTY

'What word, brother?'

Four Space Marines looked at Androcles expectantly. It was Pelion who had asked, but it was to all of them that Androcles said, 'Nothing. No response. I cannot raise Scimitar on the vox.'

'So the t'au are jamming us now,' observed Roen. He let the other possibility sit in the air unspoken.

Striggo spat a curse and turned away.

Gedeon frowned at the Carcharadon, then said to Androcles, 'Broden knew he was putting his head in the lion's mouth, going straight for the landing fields.'

'The Black Templar is a contemptible bastard, but not a fool,' said Roen. 'The Stormravens could have picked us up and flown us in fast to support him, but he wanted us on foot. Why? So that we would be outside the t'au noose when they closed it. Broden was keeping us back for a reason.'

Androcles voxed Captain Tarval aboard the Thunderhawk. The moment he heard Tarval's voice, his heart sank. The t'au weren't jamming after all. Broden and his kill-team were probably down.

'I cannot raise Scimitar Alpha on the vox,' the Son of Antaeus told him. 'Can you?'

The pilot tried, then reported that he could not.

'Do you have a visual?'

'Swinging back around. Hold on.'

While Androcles waited, Gedeon told the others, 'If Scimitar is out of the game, it's all on us and Talon now. And Archangel's people. We need to get to the landing fields fast.'

'I don't like it,' muttered Roen. 'Coldwave knows our objective is Epsilon. All around the spaceport, the t'au armour is waiting. The blockades are for show. He knows all our elements will have to converge on the landing fields to get to her. He'll lock the place up tight as soon as he thinks everyone has entered his trap.'

'In our favour,' said Pelion, 'he has no real idea what constitutes *everyone*.'

'So far as *we* know,' said Roen.

Tarval addressed Androcles over the link. 'Black Eagle *to Scimitar Alpha. The hangar is a ruin. Smoke, dust and rubble. No sign of Scimitar. No movement. The t'au have surrounded the site. Infantry and armour.'*

'So they *are* down,' said Androcles heavily. 'What of the Elysians?'

'Spear Teams One and Two are engaged with t'au defenders inside the spaceport building. Spear Team Three has just hit the ground with Talon Six. They're moving to search the hangars around Landing Field Three.'

'What of Talon?' asked Androcles.

'Talon reports that they are en route to the landing fields. Still outside the perimeter. There are several t'au armour and infantry

blockades between them and the objective, but they are pressing ahead as fast as they can.'

'What were your last orders?'

'Scimitar Alpha ordered us to circle the spaceport, keep t'au air support off their backs and provide close support when called on. Reaper Three is providing air cover to Spear Team Three. Reapers One and Two are on standby, watching for air threat, ready to provide close support as needed.'

'Apprise me of any changes, *Black Eagle*.'

'Of course, m'lord.'

Androcles dropped the link. 'It's grim,' he told the others. 'Coldwave couldn't have known about *Black Eagle* and Scimitar, or even how many survived the fall of the Tower, but he prepared ground forces here for a full assault. I don't think we've seen the true extent of what we're up against. Not yet.'

'With Broden down,' said Roen, 'he'll expect all other elements to race to the spaceport to try and fill the gap. He'll know we can't let Epsilon get airborne.'

'What choice do we have?' said Gedeon. 'He knows where we have to go as well as we do.'

'Androcles,' said Gedeon. 'How do you want to proceed?'

The giant considered it only briefly. 'We can't let Spear Team Three run the search alone, and we can't expect Talon to hold off Coldwave's forces single-handedly once they're on site. T'au air support is almost definitely on its way, perhaps additional infantry and armour, though it will be slower to arrive. We have to make the best of the situation we have now, before it gets worse. I can't see any way to avoid Coldwave's noose and still get to Epsilon. Our forces are stretched too thin. So we go, and trust to our strength as Space Marines.'

'The xenos will fall before us,' said Gedeon with feeling, 'no matter their number.'

'As will Kabannen and Lucianos,' said Roen.

'I will eat their primary hearts!' rumbled Striggo.

The others looked at him with a mix of amusement and mild disapproval. There was a good chance the Carcharadon actually meant it.

'What about their secondary hearts?' asked Gedeon with a grin.

'Those I will crush with my boot,' said Striggo.

Gedeon and Roen laughed.

Androcles grinned, but he said, 'No, brothers. I seek retribution just as you do, but the objective is Epsilon. Stay focused. If the Emperor is smiling, the one will give us the other.'

'Then may his smile be blinding,' said Pelion.

'Maintain stealth,' said Androcles. 'We'll move faster if we can avoid engagements. Is that clear, Striggo? No killing until I say. It will only slow us down.'

The Carcharadon's black eyes flashed, but he nodded. 'My killing I will save for later.'

The increasing presence of drone patrols as they neared the landing fields made moving roof to roof a bad idea, and infantry walked the streets, so they moved through shadowed alleyways and evacuated buildings as the sky lightened above them.

They passed barricades where Hammerheads and Devilfish sat shining in the rays of the new day, engines humming, the air beneath them shimmering and shifting.

They went carefully past these places, well aware that the blue-skins' advanced optics and scanning systems might pick up on the tiny thermal, infrared or ultraviolet traces they left in passing. Even air displacement and sound might give them away.

Their modified scout armour was a blessing here. Without

the power pack of full Adeptus Astartes power armour, there were no tell-tale traces of ionised air that the t'au drones might have registered.

Shadow to shadow, cover to cover, they made impressive time, and soon they were stacked up behind a hangar on the northern edge of Landing Field Three. They could hear gunfire to the south-east.

'Sabre Alpha to Reaper Three,' voxed Androcles as he and his team circled around in that direction. 'We have sounds of battle to our south-east. Status report on Spear Team Three.'

Flight Lieutenant Dargen responded. *'Spear Three found a mid-sized trans-atmospheric in Hangar Four East. They are assaulting with Talon Six. I'm on station providing close support, but the fighting is inside. I can't help them directly.'*

'Four East,' repeated Androcles. He pulled up the memory of the spaceport layout as he had studied it back at Chatha na Hadik.

'Four hundred metres south-east of us,' said Roen.

'Reaper Three, be advised,' said Androcles. 'Sabre Squad is moving in to support. We'll be breaching through the north wall.'

'Acknowledged, Sabre Alpha. Will keep any blue-skins off your back. Spear Three is on channel eight-gamma-two. Talon Six, likewise. Good hunting.'

Androcles moved Sabre at a run. Soon they were stacked up against the wall of the hangar. Like all the hangars around the landing fields, it was vast, large enough to house a heavy lifter or even an atmosphere-capable interstellar barge. It was two hundred metres on a side. Within it, brought to their enhanced hearing despite the thickness of the walls, Sabre Squad could discern the rattle and crack of a fierce firefight.

For the first time that day, Androcles wished he was wearing an Adeptus Astartes battle-helm. He could have patched into a visual feed from Talon Squad's Dreadnought and got an idea of what he was leading his kill-team into.

Instead, he'd have to trust in rapid assessment and Space Marine reflexes. They'd never let him down before.

'Sabre to Spear Three,' he voxed. 'My team is stacked and ready to breach the north wall. Request heavy suppressing fire on your targets, Spear Three. We will breach and smoke them, take them up close. Watch your fire when we do.'

'This is Sergeant Grigolicz, Spear Three Leader. Confirmed, Sabre. Glad of the assist. We have a large Imperial craft dead centre of the hangar. I'd guess you're going to recognise it. T'au infantry in heavy cover behind cargo crates and atop the fuselage.'

He broke off to return fire at the blue-skins, then continued. *'There's an XV8 with two shield drones slaved to it. We're having trouble with that one. So far unable to knock the shields out. Talon Six can't slay the XV8 until we do. Your assistance there…'*

Androcles looked at his brothers. Pelion and Gedeon had finished planting charges on the outer wall. They moved to a safe distance and nodded to Androcles. The others stood with them, rounds chambered, safeties off.

'Suppress now, sergeant,' said Androcles. 'Sabre breaching in three, two, one.'

Chyron's storm bolter chugged from under his massive power fist, spewing mass-reactive shells at the t'au positions.

Helmed xenos heads ducked back behind plasteel crates and containers. Those on the back and wings of the black spacecraft dropped to their bellies.

Around him, the men of Spear Three rose from their own cover and unleashed a furious volley of lasgun beams and grenade rounds.

The hangar shook with the noise.

Only the damned XV8 battlesuit dared to stand in the full fury of the human attackers' wrath, flanked on either side by each of its troublesome shield drones and partially protected in front by a reinforced ceramic barricade.

Hot-shot lasrounds smacked harmlessly into the invisible barrier around it. Everywhere they hit, the wall of energy rippled with incandescent colour.

The battlesuit pilot was fixated on Chyron, the biggest and most dangerous target in his sights.

For his part, Chyron wanted the XV8 just as dead, but he had already been frustrated in that, his twin-linked lascannon beams smashing against the energy barrier without effect.

The XV8's pulse cannon barrels whined as they spun. A torrent of bright blue rounds stitched the air in Chyron's direction. A dozen smacked hard into the Dreadnought's armour, staggering him, forcing him back behind a dull red container the surface of which glowed hot wherever it was hit.

'I'll take the wretch's head,' Chyron roared.

There was a *crump* of explosives. The hangar walls shook.

Smoke began to billow up in great, thick clouds around the t'au.

Chyron emerged from cover and saw muzzle flashes and the bright flash of energy rounds lighting up the smoke from within. The fighting inside the dense veil was intense. Chyron saw a chance to press forward. On the vox, he ordered Spear Team Three to move up.

The Dreadnought stormed forward on piston legs, shaking the ground. Sergeant Grigolicz and the six troopers still left to him – Loran and Rush having been gunned down mere moments ago – pushed up in Chyron's wake, cover to cover, unable to fire into the cloud lest they hit Sabre Squad.

Extractors in the hangar's ceiling were starting to thin the smoke. Figures began to form, just shadows, but it was easy to distinguish friend from foe.

The Elysians began firing again, gunning down t'au infantry while they were focused on the Space Marines attacking them at close range.

The xenos on top of the ship were less pressured. They spotted Chyron and Spear Team Three pushing further in and sent a deadly rain of fire down upon them. Rounds rattled on Chyron's massive shoulders like rain, biting into the ceramite surface but going no deeper.

Corporal Skye went down screaming right next to Chyron. Plasma had struck him between plates of carapace armour and buried deep into his chest, incinerating the flesh and bone.

Chyron sent a storm bolter burst at Skye's killer, but the fire warrior dropped down again in the cover of the spacecraft's broad back.

A Space Marine emerged from the last of the smoke then, storming along the spine of the ship, his Stalker-pattern bolter spitting death at the t'au infantry lying belly down there. Within four seconds, Gedeon had cleared the top of the spacecraft.

The smoke was all but gone.

Striggo, bolter slung on his back, a short power sword in each hand, had found the shield drones in the melee and cut them down.

The XV8 whirled on him, too close and too fast to dodge.

He suddenly found himself on his back, swords cast aside, each hand gripping a barrel of the XV8's pulse cannon as the pilot tried to force the weapon down towards the Carcharadon's snarling face.

Striggo's muscles rippled under his tight-fitting stealth suit. Veins stood out like power cables on his thick forearms.

For all his formidable strength, however, he was not winning the fight. The pulse cannon barrels were almost at his face.

Had he still a man's face, Chyron would have smiled. The ugly, bestial-looking Space Marine had just given him a gift.

He fired.

Searing lascannon beams as thick as a man's arm lanced out and ripped into the XV8, centre-mass, blasting it backwards with a great smoking crater in its armoured torso.

It hit the floor of the hangar and skidded, lifeless, its pilot and power systems dead.

Striggo rolled and grabbed his swords. Rising, he nodded in Chyron's direction and scrambled to cover as a volley of ion and plasma rounds chased him.

Sabre Squad fired back while the remains of Spear Team Three flanked right.

With the XV8 down and their numbers depleted, the t'au in the hangar were broken. The sounds of battle died off as the last of them were slain.

Two had tried to surrender. Striggo grinned hideously as he separated their heads from their bodies.

Androcles scowled. He approved of the execution, but not the way his squad brother revelled in it. There was no glory in killing a broken foe. As Alpha, he knew he would have to bring Striggo into line sooner or later. But not today.

Sabre Squad, Chyron and Spear Team Three converged at the lowered rear ramp of the ship.

'*Song of Scaldara*,' breathed Gedeon.

She was typical of an Inquisition stealth-infiltration craft, her lines sleeker, less blocky, than a corvette or cruiser. Far from elegant, but there was something of a great, dark bird of prey about her, a brooding thing, a silent watcher that missed little.

'I'd not thought we'd ever see her again,' said Pelion, staring up at the smooth black hull.

'Now that I'm in front of her,' said Gedeon, 'I feel nothing. I remember only the foul betrayal of her mistress.'

'Just a ship,' rumbled Chyron, 'and not the one we seek.'

'So Epsilon will travel on a t'au ship,' said Roen. 'That makes sense. The t'au executed our Navigator. They'll use their own people to get wherever they're going.'

Mindful that Scimitar had been buried under a hangar such as this, Androcles had everyone search for explosives, but none were found.

Over the vox, Dargen of Reaper Three addressed him. *'Sabre Alpha, you have t'au forces converging on your position from the west. Reaper Three moving to engage, but they have a Sky Shark. In daylight, their missile AIs can get a visual lock. High risk. Advise you move things along down there.'*

Chyron was already stomping towards the hangar's main entrance. His power fist had ripped the heavy plasteel shutter apart at the beginning of the attack, gaining him and Spear Team Three initial entry. Through the ruin of the shutter, he spotted a broad line of enemy forces approaching. His battle lust suddenly reignited. Inside his armoured chassis, what remained of his original organic body flooded with adrenaline and excitement.

'Androcles, Grigolicz,' he boomed. 'Go scour the other hangars. I will keep these curs busy.'

'Pelion,' said Androcles, 'search the ship then catch up to us.'

From outside there came the familiar drumming of heavy-bolters.

Reaper Three screamed from the sky, raking the t'au forces, ripping into a dozen infantry and blowing one of the Sky Shark's impulse jets.

The anti-air tank rocked sideways with the explosion of its left engine. Its right side scraped rockcrete, throwing up a shower of sparks. As it did, it managed to turn its turret and lock onto Reaper Three. There was a roar and a flash of fire. A seeker missile slid from its pylon and lunged into the air after the Stormraven.

The rest of the t'au column, spread in a broad battle line, continued to advance.

From just inside the hangar, Chyron lined his twin-linked lascannons up on the Devilfish armoured transport in the centre. He aimed roughly at where the craft's reactor would be and loosed a shot.

Beams buried deep into the curving, tan-coloured hull.

The machine froze, then the reactor detonated, blasting the armour apart from within, hurling shrapnel into the closest infantry and cutting down seven of them.

Chyron chuckled to himself. 'A good kill to start things off,' he boomed to the others.

There was no one there.

They were already moving north to the next hangar at a run.

'Bah! I never needed an audience anyway,' he said happily, and broke from cover to throw himself in among the foe.

As he thundered forward, his next lascannon blast struck one of the Sky Shark's remaining five seeker missiles and started a stutter of explosions that ripped the tank and surrounding infantry apart.

'Reaper Three,' he voxed. 'Sky Shark destroyed. You are free to re-engage with impunity.'

No answer.

He noticed a column of thick black smoke five hundred metres south, tilting with the wind as it rose.

He stitched the advancing t'au line with storm bolter fire now that they were in range, then stole a quick look south that confirmed his suspicions.

Reaper Three was down, scattered over Landing Field Three in a thousand twisted pieces. The Sky Shark's missile had knocked the Stormraven from the sky.

The Lamenter remembered his momentary feeling of kinship with the pilot, unified with his craft, the machine becoming the body. And now Dargen was dead, killed by puny t'au.

At least he had died in battle. Chyron envied him that.

His spirit would have peace.

T'au rounds rattled off his chassis, drawing him back. The xenos were closing, trying to deploy heavier, closer-range weapons that might stand a chance of bringing the Dreadnought down.

They wanted to get closer? Good!

He would crush them, pulp their bodies with his power fist. That would be much more satisfying.

With a terrifying roar amplified by the vox-grilles on his glacis, he surged towards them, giving himself over completely to the savagery within.

When he was done, the rockcrete around him was awash with blue blood.

'More,' he growled. 'Not enough. Bring me more!'

He remembered the report of t'au converging on the ruin of the hangar which had been brought down on top of Scimitar.

Infantry. Armour. He barely stopped to think.

On piston legs he cursed for not being faster, he struck out across open ground, making straight for the far side of the landing fields and the larger fight he hoped to find there.

FIFTY-ONE

Copley grabbed the earth caste supervisor's body by its collar and wrenched it backwards off the console.

It hit the floor with a thud.

Behind her, half of her remaining people were dragging xenos corpses out of the way. The other half were either welding the outer doors shut or hunched over the t'au consoles, pouring over holo-menus for any subsystems they could put to use.

Copley let her gaze run over the displays and glyph boards in front of her. *We've got everything here. Holo-vid feeds from practically everywhere. Long-range aerospace scanners. Even orbital satellite links.*

She just had to get control of it.

From the tower windows, she had an unparalleled view. Fires still blazed in the north-east where Sabre Squad had hit the fuel silos. Black smoke still rose into the sky from the ruins of every defence tower the Imperial gunships had hit in the opening stages of the assault.

She couldn't see *Black Eagle* or Reaper flight, but if she could hack the holo-feeds, she'd have a much better picture of things.

'Archangel to Scimitar Alpha,' she voxed. 'Spear One has the control tower. I say again, Spear One has the control tower.'

She awaited Broden's gruff response.

Nothing.

It was Morant who called her attention to a holo-feed from the periphery of the landing field to the west.

'Flattened,' he said grimly. 'They brought the whole hangar down. Scimitar must've been in there. See the t'au surrounding the rubble?'

Copley squinted at the display. Morant was right. The t'au had deployed infantry, Devilfish transports and a Hammerhead tank in a broad semi-circle around the ruins.

'Archangel to Scimitar,' she voxed, desperation edging her voice. 'Respond.'

Silence.

'There's something else,' said Morant. He thrust his chin at another display.

'Chyron,' breathed Copley. 'What's he doing?'

The hulking Lamenter was pounding in the direction of the ruined hangar and the t'au surrounding it.

'He's going to engage them alone,' said Morant. He couldn't keep the incredulity from his voice. The Dreadnought was fearsome, true, but didn't he see how badly outnumbered he was? If the t'au saw him coming, and they surely *would*, the Hammerhead's powerful ion cannon would cut him open like a can of beans, no matter how thick that chassis armour was.

'Reaper Three,' voxed Copley. 'Assist Talon Six. Run a flyby on Landing Field One and strafe those damned t'au.'

Static. No response.

'Reaper Three. Dargen.'

Morant put a hand on her arm. 'Ma'am...'

Copley followed his gaze to the top-left holo-display.

At the edge of the holo-picter's field of view, she saw smoking metal strewn across the rockcrete.

A lot of it.

The familiar shapes of several of the larger pieces left no doubt.

'We're down a Stormraven,' said Morant.

'All Imperial air units,' voxed Copley, 'Archangel has the control tower. I want a sitrep. Now!'

Graka, Reaper Two, was the first to respond. *'Engaging ground forces, Archangel. Just north of your position.'*

She looked north and saw a black shape there, fast-moving, silhouetted against the sky.

'They're tightening the perimeter, major, pulling back from the junction barricades and pushing for the landing fields. I'm doing what I can to whittle them down.'

'Understood, Graka. Stay on them till further orders,' said Copley. 'Reaper One, status.'

Ventius sounded tense. *'Strafing ground targets north-east of the landing fields. Can confirm Reaper Two's report. T'au ground forces converging en masse around the spaceport. They've abandoned their blockades. Coldwave is tightening the noose.'*

Morant glanced anxiously at her. She didn't meet his gaze. Instead, she studied the other holo-displays.

Where the hell is Epsilon? No sign of her or Coldwave yet.

'*Black Eagle*, are you reading me?'

'Black Eagle *copies. Go ahead, Archangel.*'

'What's your status?'

'Engaging the Razorsharks, ma'am, but they keep dancing just out of range. Best I can do is keep them off our ground teams.'

Copley stepped back from Morant's console and took in all the displays above it at once.

Why did she feel so exposed right now? Something was definitely wrong. Those hairs on her neck, again…

A voice called out from the other side of the control room. It was Triskel.

'Major, I've got air contacts leaving Zu'shan and Na'tol. ETA eight and eleven minutes respectively.'

'Read their glyphs.'

'All fighters, ma'am. No bombers. No transports.'

Copley's shoulders sank. She felt a deep aching in her muscles and joints. Tiredness was creeping up on her. Post-adrenaline crash. Or were the meds she'd taken wearing off already? The harsh, wet cough that repeatedly reminded her of their degenerating condition was getting worse among her men.

Behind her, Vanoff had finished welding shut the doors. Before that, he had set trip-lines and frag mines out in the hallway. No one was getting in anytime soon. Certainly not in the eight minutes it would take the first of the damned air caste jets to arrive.

When they did, *Black Eagle* and the Stormravens would be badly outnumbered. Easy prey. Once they were down, she and her team would be sitting ducks up here in the tower.

'This shitstorm is about to get a lot messier,' groaned Morant.

She could hardly argue with him, but the others didn't need to hear it. 'Arcturus has handled messy before,' she said for everyone's ears. 'We'll handle it again.' She pressed a finger to the transmit stud of her vox pickup. 'Talon, where are you?'

Karras' voice came back, deep and somehow reassuring. At least the Death Spectre was still in play. He was something different, powerful in ways she didn't understand. For some reason, he made her feel like almost anything might be possible, even here, with *Shadowbreaker* barely holding together at all.

'Talon on site now, Archangel. We remain undetected. Spaceport north side. I can see Reaper Two above us. Still no word from Broden?'

'Nothing,' replied Copley. 'I'm taking back operational command, Scholar. Any objections?'

'None,' said Karras. *'Let's get this done. Orders?'*

'Talon Six is making for the hangar where Scimitar went down. Heavy t'au presence... He's on his own, Scholar. Not responding to hails.'

Karras was briefly silent. *'Chyron can handle himself, Archangel. Suggest we focus on finding Epsilon.'*

Eight minutes. Just eight minutes.

'Agreed, Talon. Be quick. We're about to lose air control. Fighters inbound. Eight minutes out.'

'Talon hears, Archangel. We move.'

'Black Eagle,' voxed Copley. 'Coordinate with Talon Squad. Keep the t'au from slowing them down.'

'Understood, Archangel. Black Eagle *moving in to support.'*

'Reaper Two, I want you running close support for Sabre Squad. They're sweeping the hangars around Landing Field Three. And watch out for Sky Sharks. We've already lost one gunship to anti-air. Can't lose another.'

That left only Reaper One. Ventius. It was all she could do for the Dreadnought, give him the last of their air support and hope it would be enough. Maybe the Dreadnought's fight would draw additional t'au forces away from the kill-teams.

Maybe not.

Reaper One confirmed orders.

A moment later, a bulky black shape with Deathwatch and Ordo Xenos markings screamed past the tower so close it shook it – Ventius on his way to aid Chyron.

Copley covered her mouth and coughed. When she looked into her hand, she saw red flecks there.

She wiped her palm on her thigh.

No, she told herself. *Not until this is over.*

FIFTY-TWO

As he bore down on the t'au around the destroyed hangar, Chyron laughed at himself. He knew the odds were not in his favour. His chances of survival were poor. It excited him. Maybe he would finally die in battle.

He'd have preferred tyranids, selling his life dear against the foe he hated most of all. But xenos were xenos. Honour was honour. And death in service to his oath and the Emperor would see him reunited with his brothers at last.

Before that, he would revel in carnage.

Archangel tried to direct him elsewhere, to support Sabre Squad and Spear Team Three. He was having none of it. They would manage. They had a Stormraven on station overhead. He had made his choice.

Full credit to the woman, though – she hadn't used armour lock on him for failure to obey. Sigma would have.

Closer now.

Up ahead, he saw fire warriors in sand-coloured armour

moving methodically over the great mound of plasteel and rockcrete that had crushed Scimitar Squad. They probed the rubble, searching for signs of the bodies underneath.

Hard to believe Broden had been taken out of the game so early and so easily, but the Black Templar had seemed the type to make hasty mistakes. All bluster, no brains.

Like knows like, Chyron thought, and laughed aloud.

The sound boomed from his vox-grilles, harsh and clear, carrying to his targets. Those closest heard him. They spun and saw his black bulk powering towards them like a runaway train, little over a hundred metres off.

Fireblade officers began gesturing and shouting. Those among the rubble stopped what they were doing and ducked into cover to take up firing positions. The others, out in the open, dropped to a knee and levelled their guns at him.

The two Devilfish transports swung around to face him, their gun drones and pulse cannons zeroing in. The Hammerhead turned its turret in his direction. Its railgun was the only weapon they had which was capable of one-shotting him.

You're first, thought Chyron.

He sighted his twin-linked lascannon on the t'au tank. The ion cannon was powering up, the muzzle aglow.

Pulse and plasma fire filled the air like a sudden squall, pouring at him, smacking into his glacis, scoring the thick ceramite of his huge, boxy shoulders.

He was about to fire when something dark plummeted from the sky above like a diving falcon. There was a sound somewhere between a low bark and a rattle.

The t'au Hammerhead shook, armour-piercing bolt rounds rippling over its turret, biting deep, shredding armour.

Reaper One screamed back up into the air, out of range, and swiftly banked for another run.

In her wake, the railgun's powercell detonated, a flash of blue light that turned the tank into blazing scrap. Grav-engines died. It dropped, hitting the rockcrete hard.

Kill denied, thought Chyron, part rage, part admiration. It had been a graceful kill, pleasing to watch.

His lascannons swung left, locked onto one of the Devilfishes and cut right to its machine heart.

Reaper One screamed in and strafed the ground again, this time smacking a dozen t'au from their feet, spreading them across the landing field in wet blue smears.

Grisly and merciless.

Chyron cored the other Devilfish, then charged forward again, ignoring the rounds biting fist-sized craters in his armour. He pushed into storm bolter range. Raising his power fist, under which the storm bolter was mounted, he raked blistering fire across the infantry, cutting down seven in the first sweep.

He laughed, lost in the rush, his mind unclouded. In battle came the only reprieve from his sorrows. It was all that made continued existence worthwhile.

As he killed, he prayed for more. More enemies. More armour. More risk. Greater odds. More!

Don't let it stop. Don't let me win. Make this the day, damn you. Give me a foe to equal my solemn wish!

From further along the edge of the landing field, hangar shutters began rolling upwards. Fire warriors spilled out, followed by the flowing shapes of more t'au armour.

The infantry taking cover in the rubble on his left began peppering him with shots.

Above him, Reaper One banked left and angled in again.

'Yes!' Chyron roared into the air. 'All of it. Unleash everything you have at me. We will all die together in a mighty clash of metal and flesh! To me, xenos filth. To me! The last Lamenter is ready!'

Talon Squad stacked up against the wall of the only dedicated military hangar at the spaceport. Far bigger than any other, it sat on the northernmost edge of Landing Field One.

T'au forces on site were unaware of their presence. The kill-team was still operating under full stealth. As Karras looked at his brothers, all he saw of their physical forms was a shifting and bending of light, as if each were made of slightly smoky glass that distorted what lay beyond.

Karras pressed his left hand to the wall and muttered the Litany of Sight Beyond Sight, pushing his astral awareness through plasteel-reinforced rockcrete and into the echoing space beyond.

Under a plasteel-beamed ceiling some eighty metres high, a great black form lay sleek and silent and still. No Epsilon. No sign of the two Space Marines who had betrayed Androcles and his brothers.

All around it, however, were fire warriors in hard cover, guns at the ready. Soulless things, they barely registered in the warp at all. Karras could not read their mood, for they had no aura, but he could see how anxious they looked, how tense, primed for a fight.

He read the name on the side of the ship, knowing already what it would say.

Song of Scaldara.

In every detail, she matched the picts Sigma had provided.

In her hold, he detected the spirit signatures of human crew, but no tyranid or hybrid specimens. No active Geller field. He would have felt it pushing him back into his physical body.

Satisfied, he pulled his hand from the hangar wall.

'Epsilon's ship,' he told the others. 'She's not with it. There are crew inside, but no Navigator. No astropath.'

'So we ignore it,' said Solarion sharply. 'We have four minutes till these skies are buzzing with Razorsharks. None of us will be flying out of here once that happens.' He turned his head to the side and muttered, 'I knew *Shadowbreaker* would be a bloody debacle.'

Zeed was priming some remark when there was a sudden, ear-splitting ripple of charges detonating.

The kill-team operators all reacted at once, whipping their heads around towards the landing field that was the source of the noise. There they saw black smoke rising in a ring some six hundred metres across. A series of small charges had blown, creating a long circular channel in the surface.

As they watched, the rockcrete within this ring sank a full metre and split straight down the middle. Each half began to pull apart, creating a growing gulf between the two, turning the circle into a vast, gaping hole.

The ground began to shake.

'Copley,' voxed Karras. 'Eyes on Landing Field One. Are you seeing this?'

Copley didn't need the monitors. From the north-facing window of the control tower, she could see it happening with her own eyes.

No wonder we couldn't find them in the hangars. They were underground all along.

The great, broad back of a t'au ship had started to emerge now. The platform on which it sat rose slowly to ground level. Even from here, she could see that its engines were already well into their warming-up procedure.

T'au infantry surrounded it, along with clusters of crates,

loaders and everything else the t'au needed to prep a ship for travel. She couldn't see the far side of the field, blocked from view by the bulk of the ship, but it was a safe bet to assume there were just as many fire warriors there, too.

'Triskel,' she muttered. 'Those fighters...'

'Three and a half minutes out,' replied the corporal.

We're screwed.

Talon Six and Reaper One were still fighting armour and infantry on the western landing field. Heavily outnumbered, with Chyron more or less pinned down now, pressed into cover by missile and railgun fire behind the remains of the ruined hangar's south wall.

Sabre Squad and Spear Team Three were fighting a tide of foes spilling out of the last two unsearched hangars on the eastern field. They were facing heavy pressure there. With the emergence of the t'au ship, all the xenos that had previously been lying in wait must have been ordered to engage aggressively. Coldwave had decided this was the moment. A storm of bright fire blazed in all directions, las against plasma, bolter against pulse rounds.

And north, right where the ship had appeared, were Talon Squad and *Black Eagle*.

Already, the XV8s had turned their attention to the Thunderhawk. So, too, had several t'au infantry wielding man-portable launchers. Copley saw t'au missiles leap into the sky. *Black Eagle* launched countermeasures. Explosions blossomed in the air above the t'au spacecraft. *Black Eagle* roared out of range, then began to swing around, her turbo-laser glowing as it charged up.

'Reapers One and Two, move to the north field immediately and target the engines of that ship. It must not get into the air, is that clear? This is where we stop them. For Emperor and honour. This is where it ends.'

'Archangel,' voxed Reaper One. *'If I leave the Dreadnought now–'*

'Epsilon is priority one, Ventius. We have to stop that ship taking off. You have your orders.'

Chyron's voice broke in over the link. *'The woman is right,'* he rumbled. *'This fight is mine, flyboy. Stop the rogue inquisitor. She must not escape.'*

There was a pause. *'Reaper One confirms. Breaking off to engage t'au ship.'*

'Reaper Two confirms.'

'Black Eagle,' voxed Copley. 'Cripple that ship! Hit the engines!'

From the tower, she saw *Black Eagle* swoop in, ignoring the hail of rounds that surged up to meet her. Her bolters were blazing, ripping into any exposed t'au they could get an angle on, but, just as she was ready to fire on the t'au ship's port engine, something leapt into the sky.

Something imposingly large, but so fast it was a blur.

It landed on the back of the t'au ship, levelled a large, long-barrelled weapon at *Black Eagle*, and fired.

Searing light scored the air, biting into the Thunderhawk's armoured belly. She shook hard. Half a second later, her turbo-laser fired.

A second beam of light slashed down at the t'au ship, thick and powerful and utterly deadly, but it smashed harmlessly into an invisible wall of force. Colours rippled outwards from the point of impact, revealing the overlapping twin hemispheres of the energy shields that had stopped the shot.

Shield drones!

Black Eagle pulled up and away, a long scar on her underside glowing angry red.

The giant figure on the back of the t'au ship turned, tracking her. A dozen missiles burst from two shoulder-mounted pods and screamed after the Imperial craft.

Chaff and flares burst into the air in *Black Eagle*'s wake. Eleven of the nimble little missiles burst into fire, but the twelfth, furthest behind, speared through the countermeasure cloud and tagged the Thunderhawk's port-side turbine.

Black Eagle staggered and leaned hard to the right, bleeding a trail of thick black smoke into the sky.

'Blood of saints!' cursed Copley. 'To think they kept that in reserve until now…'

Over the vox, she called out, 'All task force units, be advised. The ship is being defended by an XV104. Do you understand? There's a Riptide out there. Bet your souls that Coldwave is the pilot.'

A Riptide! And just three minutes until the air was buzzing with t'au interceptors.

All eyes in the control room were on her. She could feel them. Not the eyes of men giving up. Arcturus had crawled through the fire of impossible odds before. She could feel her men willing her to fight on, to stay on top of this despite how sick, how tired, they all felt.

While we're still breathing, we can still win. It's not over.

'Talon,' she voxed. 'You have to take out that Riptide. Fast! *Black Eagle* can kill those engines, but not while that damned battlesuit is in play.'

Karras' voice betrayed neither confidence nor doubt. *'Moving to engage Riptide, Archangel. Reaper flight, buy us some room to move. Keep the rest off our backs if you can.'*

'Reaper One copies, Talon,' voxed Ventius. *'Moving to assist.'*

'Reaper Two likewise, Talon,' said Graka.

'Black Eagle *coming around again,'* voxed Tarval. *'Get me a clear shot and I'll deliver, Talon.'*

'Major,' said Triskel. 'The first of the Razorshark reinforcements just passed the twenty-kilometre line.'

Damn it.

Now that time was against them, now that they were down to minutes only, Coldwave had finally put his cards on the table, and they were all aces. All the pieces were in play. In a few minutes, the t'au would have total air superiority and that ship would be hauling its odious cargo skyward, leaving the Imperial assault force either dead or cut off with no hope of achieving the primary mission objective.

We'll die on a fail, thought Copley, and the thought burned in her, scorched her uncompromising, unrelenting warrior soul like a splash of acid.

'Listen up, all of you,' she snapped. 'Leave your stations. Come here.'

Eight of them left. They stood facing her, upright and ready despite the biological breakdown that was silently advancing inside each of them.

Warriors all. But for the sporadic fits of coughing, no one would ever have known they were dying.

My lads, she thought. *My lions.*

Hard to express how proud she felt.

This one had been a mess from the start. The Ultramarine had said it often enough, though the other Adeptus Astartes had paid him no mind. How could Sigma have underestimated Epsilon and Coldwave so badly?

That didn't matter now.

She held the gaze of each of her men. They knew her only too well. They knew what was coming. She already saw the assent in their eyes.

She grinned at them, knowing they needed no explanation. Drawing her bolt pistol from its holster, she said, 'Let's go then. Gear up, all of you.'

They grinned back at her, eyes bright at the thought of

taking the fight back out there and maybe dying like fighters should. Maybe even making some kind of difference, however small.

Copley raised her pistol and shot out the control room windows.

Fifteen seconds later, all nine were ziplining down to the rockcrete below. The moment they hit it, they were off at a run.

Copley coughed a little as her feet pounded the rockcrete. She ignored the blood on the back of her hand where she'd raised it to her mouth.

She'd have time. She didn't need much.

Up ahead, the noise of the t'au ship's engines was gaining volume. All around it, an intense firefight flashed and blazed. She saw fire warriors being punched from their feet by powerful rounds, their wounds exploding a second later, blue gore spuming into the air.

She saw others screaming, clutching wet blue stumps where a second before there had been an arm or leg. A black shadow slipped and spun among them, taking limbs and lives in a deadly dance.

She saw walls of bright yellow fire gush forth from another black shape, pouring out in great sweeping arcs, reminding her of a child's tale she'd heard, a story of a monster that breathed such flame.

Where the fire touched, charred black figures flailed and toppled.

Welcome, woman, the battle called out to her as the distance halved. *This is right where you belong.*

FIFTY-THREE

Coldwave watched the beam from his ion accelerator cut into the Imperial gunship's belly as it roared down at him.

He marvelled that the craft had no energy shield, just dense armour plating. Idiot gue'la. Everything they built was so clumsy, so inelegant.

He had been hoping to punch through to the gunship's reactor, but he wasn't familiar with this craft. His targeting was best guess. Apparently, the guess was off.

The gunship's dorsal laser unloaded its own deadly beam, targeting the port-side engine of the ship on which his Riptide stood. It was what he would have done, why he had placed his shield drones there.

Everything hung on getting offworld. If he failed, all his sacrifices, all the stains he could never wash off, all the deaths, the horrors, the doubts, the guilt, the shame... all if it would mean nothing.

But he wouldn't lose.

Couldn't.

Soon, he and the precious specimens would be far away from here. He just had to protect the ship until the engines were fully powered up and his air support arrived. He couldn't risk leaving any foes to strike it out of the sky while it tried to climb. The ship was heavy and slow in atmosphere.

The Razorsharks were almost on site.

The gue'la were too late. They had scoured the hangars as expected, wasting their time while the trap continued to close around them. He had known they would, had planned it so.

Still, their resilience surprised him. They ought to be dead already. He'd arrayed more than enough armour and infantry against them. Their survival made no sense. The inquisitor's foul-smelling bodyguards had not been making idle boasts after all. They had warned him not to underestimate this Deathwatch to which they belonged. How he hated them, hated that they had been right.

If not for the hidden underground hangar…

Silently, he gave thanks to the earth caste engineers who had conceived of it, had built it on the chance that war with the Y'he would one day come to Tychonis. It had been planned as a way to get the ruling Aun safely offworld in the event of a ground war. The need for it had come sooner than expected, and under different circumstances.

The human gunship's powerful dorsal laser struck and was nullified. Waves of coruscating light pulsed across a bubble of protective force. Coldwave turned and, with a thought, locked his smart missile system onto the gunship's fiery tail. So inefficient, the damned gue'la. The craft's three turbines were putting out prodigious heat.

His Riptide trembled as a salvo of missiles leapt from its launchers.

He watched them tear through the sky. High on the rush of battle – it had been *so* long – he felt almost as if they were an extension of his own body, that he was reaching out an impossibly long arm to strike the gunship down, to swat it like a fly.

His lip curled in anger as he watched the gunship defy that strike, causing his missiles to detonate short of target with a cloud of chaff and bright, hot flares.

One, just one, got through. He saw it bite.

As the gunship roared off, lilting to one side, wounded, Coldwave's armour rattled, its shield absorbing a torrent of fire from the ground. Surprised, he spun and saw his forces around the spaceship engaged by bulky black-armoured forms rezzing out of some kind of stealth field.

Cries rang out. Bodies dropped. His infantry were being cut down mercilessly.

Space Marines!

He turned to bring his own armament to bear but was again struck but a fusillade of explosive shells.

His shield prevented any damage, but the impact shook him and sent red warning glyphs scrolling across his retinas.

With a savage scowl on his blue-grey face, he engaged his jump jets and leapt from the back of the ship, landing on the rockcrete below with the cushioned smoothness and grace of cutting-edge t'au technology.

To his immediate left, he saw a Space Marine with long, shining claws eviscerate three fire warriors in a sweeping blur.

As fast as thought, he dashed towards it and swept the barrel of his ion accelerator in a whistling lateral arc that would break the Space Marine in half.

He hit nothing. The Space Marine wasn't there.

On jump jets of its own, it had leapt onto the back of the t'au ship.

Coldwave had been baited. The gunfire had brought him down to join the fight, leaving his drones open to close-range attacks.

His jets flared. He boosted back up into the air.

In the second that it took, the clawed Space Marine had already shredded one drone. Sparking wreckage was strewn across the port-side wing of the craft.

As Coldwave locked eyes on him, the Space Marine bridged the gap to the other drone and thrust the claws of his right hand straight through it.

There was a snap and a burst of blue sparks. The drone fell. Its lights flickered out.

Both of the shield drones were down. The ship's engines were open to attack.

Coldwave yelled his anger and denial and sent a missile roaring from his racks.

The Space Marine was incredibly fast. The missile should have killed him, but he turned from destroying the drone just in time, thrusting up the claws of his left arm like a shield.

The missile struck and exploded, blowing him straight off the wing, hammering him heavily onto the rockcrete below.

Racing to finish the job, Coldwave thundered forward across the back of the ship and looked down. No sign of the Space Marine. He had vanished.

Warning glyphs flashed.

Another stream of rounds struck his battlesuit's energy barrier and detonated fiercely. This time, the fire had come from the air.

The gue'la gunship roared overhead. No, not the same one. This was smaller and faster, less heavily armed and armoured.

His Riptide was out of missiles.

As the ship arced away from him, Coldwave locked on with his ion accelerator. The weapon kicked hard, shaking the whole suit.

The lance of deadly light missed the nimble Imperial craft by a finger's width, blistering the stealth-coated starboard wing. The craft banked hard to the right, racing out of lethal range. Cursing, Coldwave turned his attention to a small force of humans and partially armoured Space Marines running towards the battle from the south-east.

He snarled, targeted them, and loosed another blinding blast from his ion accelerator, atomising one of the humans and scoring a long black gouge in the rockcrete. The others dived or dropped to a knee. Some returned fire, but they were still too far out. He had no time to erase more of them. His shield was struck again, hard, this time from below and to the side.

He saw a short, bulky Space Marine with an oversized weapon unleashing a furious barrage of rounds up at him.

Coldwave flared his jets and leapt from the back of the ship once again. On his HUD, he saw that his Razorsharks were now just two minutes out. It was almost time for him to get inside. He opened a link and ordered the ship's rear ramp to be lowered.

Very soon now, he would leave this damned world behind. How he hated Tychonis.

His posting here had been a grievous insult from the start. Only the presence of Aun'dzi had ever made it worthwhile. They both deserved better. He would make sure the Aun was called to T'au, was recognised, was given his due. He would not leave his beloved leader to languish here.

Ahead lay honour and a brighter future for both.

Ahead lay priceless redemption and vindication.

Ahead lay the salvation of their race, their glorious destiny.

Shas'O T'kan Jai'kal would not be denied.

FIFTY-FOUR

Androcles dived left, hitting hard.

It saved his life.

The Riptide's shot scythed across the ground and wiped one of the Elysian stormtroopers, Hamlin, entirely from existence. Not even his boots remained.

Spear Team Three had already lost Nichs, Vint and Norlund in the fighting at the eastern landing field. And now Hamlin. Only two men remained – Sergeant Grigolicz and Corporal Lunde.

The Arcturus people were remarkable, as worthy as any human warriors Androcles and the rest of Sabre Squad had known, but they were sick from exposure to radiation and severely outgunned.

For all his efforts, Androcles hadn't been able to keep them alive.

Just up ahead lay the blackened wreckage of Reaper Three. Though scant and inadequate, the wreckage offered the only cover available. Androcles pushed himself to his feet and ordered everyone into sheltered positions behind it. From there he swiftly surveyed the battle up ahead.

The fighting was intense. Talon Squad were a storm of murder on the t'au, but the blue-skins were many, and in the presence of Coldwave – who else could be piloting that Riptide? – they fought with a ferocity he'd not seen in their kind. They were desperate to effect the escape of the spaceship and their shas'o.

And the ordo traitor. She is aboard.

No sooner had he thought the word *traitor* than, as if invoked, Kabannen and Lucianos appeared, jumping down from a hatch in the ship's starboard side to add their fury to the fight.

Androcles' eyes locked hard on Kabannen. His blood boiled. He had to hold himself back, suppressing a powerful urge to rush from cover with a battle-cry.

He had to get closer first. The traitors were in full power armour. He and his brothers were not. A reckless charge was not the right play here.

Someone should have told Striggo and Gedeon.

The Carcharadon and the Howling Griffon exploded out from behind the wreckage and burst into a full sprint, Gedeon with bolter raised, Striggo with short power swords shimmering.

Kabannen and Lucianos did not see them at first, intent on spotting Talon Squad in the melee.

Space Marines at full sprint cover ground fast.

Striggo was already leaping into the air, swords raised, when Lucianos' senses pricked. He spun around at the last instant and found himself about to be sliced apart.

Fast as he was, his reflexes every bit the equal of the Carcharadon's, there was no way he could avoid the blades at this range. Striggo's eyes flashed with the certainty of the kill.

There was a bright flash, a hiss and sizzle, twin bursts of white sparks.

Striggo stared in disbelief.

Lucianos had thrown up his left arm. It had stopped the blades dead. That arm should have been lying on the ground, and the blades buried deep in the traitor's torso, but it was not so.

Briefly, the two Space Marines stood frozen in the moment, their minds catching up with their reflexes.

Then Lucianos kicked Striggo hard in the chest. The blow knocked him back three paces.

Striggo glared at him, confusion giving way to understanding when his eyes settled on the storm shield. The small, plate-like deflection-field generator was attached to Lucianos' left pauldron where it met his breastplate.

'You fight me shielded, like a coward.'

The deflection field would falter if Striggo's blows could overload it, but he knew now that a single, clean kill-stroke, the beautiful vengeance he had envisioned, would not be possible.

Lucianos ignored the barb. 'You live, brother. I had thought–'

'I am not so easily ended, traitor.'

Lucianos looked genuinely pained at that.

Striggo began circling him, hunkered over in a predatory half-crouch, blades ready to lash out again without warning.

'I never sought your death, Striggo,' said Lucianos, 'nor death for any of you. It burned me to watch the blue-skins take you away. It sickened me. But what could I do? Epsilon gave orders. You sided with Androcles and disobeyed them. It is *you* who broke your oaths to the Watch and the ordo. Androcles never understood the importance of what she does here. I warned you not to listen to him, to view things so simplistically. Now we go where you cannot follow, though I would have it otherwise. It is not too late. Join us. Once you understand the–'

Striggo snarled and lunged, a savage lateral swipe. Lucianos slipped it. Striggo followed through, putting his momentum into a whistling backhand slash that, with another inch, might have taken Lucianos' head.

There was a triple burst of bolter fire from the left.

Striggo barely managed to raise his blades in time. The bolts exploded on the flat of his swords. The impact sent Striggo skidding six metres on his side, his left arm peppered with tiny shards of shrapnel.

Kabannen stepped over the freshly slain body of Gedeon and marched straight towards Striggo. The Howling Griffon's skull was a hollowed-out mess. Kabannen's boots tracked dark red blood on the ground as he closed in.

'The others,' boomed the Iron Hand. 'Who else survived the fall of the prison? And how?'

A stutter of rounds struck his right pauldron, exploding there. They should have bitten deep gouges in the ceramite, destroying the white icon of the Iron Hands Chapter that graced it, but they did not.

Light flickered at the points of impact, Kabannen's own storm shield nullifying the attack.

The Iron Hand turned and saw Androcles striding towards him, scout-armoured only, just like Gedeon and Striggo, but undaunted. Hardly a fair fight, but Kabannen cared little for fairness right now. Outcome was all that mattered.

Androcles' Stalker bolter was zeroed on his former Alpha's head.

'Betrayer,' hissed the massive Space Marine. 'Oath-breaker.'

Kabannen smirked. 'Neither, oaf. Your interpretations are in need of considerable adjustment.'

Pelion and Roen were sprinting off to the left and right, trying to flank the two traitors.

Lucianos saw them, saw Striggo push himself up. Shaking his head in resignation, he levelled his bolter at Striggo and began moving left to cut off Pelion's flanking.

Kabannen faced Androcles. 'You survived.'

'I survived,' said Androcles. 'You won't.'

Kabannen shook his head. 'Look around you. You fight a hopeless battle. Turn around now, don't interfere, and I will let you walk away.'

'What worth, the words of a traitor?'

Kabannen looked left and right emphatically. 'No traitors here, brother. Just two Adeptus Astartes who see the wider view. I tried to tell you. You had every chan–'

Androcles fired again, his rounds aimed straight at Kabannen's forehead. The Iron Hand whipped up his left hand, palm out, and again, the bolter rounds exploded without effect, their force nullified by the storm shield.

'Don't be a fool. You cannot win. Withdraw. Return to Talasa Prime. Or to Damaroth.'

'Honour demands that we fight, Kabannen. Or have you forgotten honour? And we both know I can beat you. You have seen it for yourself. The stories about my Chapter are true. Some call ours the Cursed Founding, but it is no curse. The Sons of Antaeus have never been defeated on solid ground. You will not best me here, despite your wargear.'

'You are flesh,' grunted Kabannen. 'And flesh is weak.'

He slung his bolter, flexed his augmetic arms – each a power ful titanium prosthetic – and drew his long black combat knife.

'You question my honour. That, I will not forgive. Let us do this up close and personal.'

Androcles lowered his bolter reverently to the ground. He drew his combat knife from the sheath at his lower back.

Kabannen grinned, supremely confident.

They closed on each other, circling slowly.

'What are you doing?' demanded Roen over the vox-link. 'He is in full plate! You cannot think–'

'It will not avail him, Roen. You will see. Deal with Lucianos quickly and lend aid to Talon. The Riptide must be slain. Time is against us. Hurry, brothers. Hurry.'

His peripheral vision shrank as Kabannen moved into lunging range. The fury of battle all around the ship became a muted, distant thing, still there in his awareness but a background only. The universe contracted until all it encapsulated was the space in which they fought.

Each dropped into stance, blade arm forward, free hand placed for the quick parry.

Androcles was a giant of a Space Marine. Even unarmoured, he stood as tall and almost as broad as Kabannen did in full plate. His strength was prodigious, his training and experience comprehensive.

He trusted to that now.

Kabannen snorted. 'Let's be at it. I have a flight to catch.'

Their blades flashed towards each other.

Sparks flew.

For one of them, the last fight of his life had begun.

FIFTY-FIVE

'Scholar!' voxed Rauth. 'The ramp!'

Karras turned, saw the ship opening its rear hatch like the jaws of some ocean leviathan.

Abruptly, the fire cadres all around them turned the pressure right up, becoming bolder, more ferocious.

Talon Squad found themselves pressed back into cover behind rows of crates, unmanned loaders and other t'au machinery.

The air all around was filled with fire, ionised particles sharp in Voss' nostrils as he said, 'Hemmed in here. Lots of targets in close proximity. Wouldn't now be a perfect time to fry them all, Scholar? As you did the 'stealers back on Chiaro?'

Karras and Rauth glanced at each other.

The Geller field generator was obviously on the ship, activated, isolating its contents from the warp. Standing forty metres from the hull, Karras could feel its effects, the field pressing against his soul, its resonance stemming the flow of power from the immaterium to his mind. The effect was much more localised than at Alel a Tarag, and far denser as a result. Epsilon, he guessed, must have configured it to the ship's shape and size in readiness for their voyage.

Her specimens were definitely on board.

Even if he *could* have summoned a storm of witchfire as the Imperial Fist had suggested, he would not have taken the chance. No horror he'd ever known had compared to the battle for his soul. A battle he'd not won alone, he reminded himself sourly, and not won by much, either.

He might be First Codicier of the Death Spectres, his gift considered powerful beyond all but that of Athio Cordatus, but he was no longer willing to put his soul on the line. Never again would he be so reckless, so dependent on the warp, throwing open his inner gates completely to the full flow.

Rauth had been all too clear – if Karras' purity was threatened again, the Exorcist would execute him, and rightly so.

'My gift is diminished, brothers,' he said. 'The Geller field generator is on that ship. Epsilon hides within, hoping to run out the chrono. Let's crush that hope.'

'The Riptide will have us the moment we try for the ramp, Scholar,' said Solarion.

'Then you will distract it,' said Karras. 'I must get inside.'

'Big ship,' said Voss. 'Lot of t'au in there.'

Karras reached up and touched the grip of *Arquemann* where the force sword protruded over his right pauldron. He couldn't feel the weapon's war-like spirit, the link between them severed in the presence of the suppressing field, but the flawless blade would make short work of any t'au at close range regardless.

'I hope so,' said Karras. 'My sword has yet to be bloodied.'

'I'll handle the Riptide, Scholar,' said Zeed. 'The rest of you can enjoy the show.'

Voss grunted. 'Milk-skinned idiot. It already clipped your wings. You're only alive because you rolled under the hull.'

'Jets at seventy per cent efficiency, you over-muscled ape,' replied Zeed. 'More than enough.'

Solarion pointed to a tall stack of supply crates on the edge of the battle. 'High ground. I'll be there.' He did a quick check of the rounds in his rifle's magazine and slapped it back into place.

'I'm going after the Riptide with paper-face,' said Voss. 'Two will cause it a lot more trouble than one.'

Zeed shrugged. 'Do your worst, cannonball. The kill will still be mine.'

'Watcher,' said Karras.

The Exorcist threw him a dark look.

'Fine. You're with me. Just stay out of blade range once we're inside,' said Karras. 'That Riptide will have advanced optics and sensor arrays, but let's throw smoke anyway. I'm counting on the three of you to keep him off us. Don't go getting killed.'

Voss leaned out from cover and said, 'T'au infantry moving up, trying to flank.'

Squads were converging on them from three directions.

'Let's get on with this,' said Solarion.

'Optics to multi-spectrum now,' said Karras.

Talon Squad blink-clicked their helm lenses to enhanced-vision mode.

Karras nodded to Rauth and the two fired smoke grenades from their under-barrel launchers. Voss and Solarion tossed grenades by hand. Great clouds of dense grey billowed up, cloaking everything.

To the Adeptus Astartes, the world around them was still

perfectly clear, defined now by heat, radiation and air displacement instead of visible light.

'Go,' said Karras.

Zeed's jets flared white hot. One moment, he was there, right among them, the next, only a churning vortex of smoke remained.

Voss sidestepped straight out of cover. He sighted on a broad line of approaching fire warriors, pressed the trigger of his Infernus and began cutting them down with heavy-bolter rounds.

Solarion set off at a run for the high ground he had marked.

Karras and Rauth sprinted for the ramp, now fully lowered. T'au were spilling out of it by the score, ignoring the smoke, their own helm optics cycled to thermal to negate it.

The Space Marines ran headlong towards them, their silenced bolters coughing death at close range, gunning down the clustered enemy in swathes. Soon, the two Deathwatch brothers were leaping over crumpled bodies and bounding up the ramp into the gaping vastness of the rear hold.

Up ahead, earth caste t'au were securing tanks and crates to lugs set in the floor.

Karras mag-locked his bolter to his thigh and slid *Arquemann* from his back. He and Rauth strode forward, hulking black avatars of death that made the t'au look like children. Their footfalls shook the plating on the floor.

The earth caste technicians turned too late. *Arquemann* flashed in the light as Karras cut them down, their blood splashing the walls and deck.

He and Rauth pressed on down a broad central corridor. There were doors off to the left and right, most too small for a Space Marine to squeeze through. Ahead, a set of stairs ran upwards to the next deck.

The two Adeptus Astartes surged up them, emerging into another large hold filled with rows of cryogenic pods. A dozen larger pods stood to the sides, secured to the walls, arranged vertically. All were sealed and covered.

Hybrids on the floor, thought Karras. *Purestrains at the sides.*

Among the pods, earth caste workers moved back and forth, fastidiously checking readouts on the top of each. Beyond them, a tall, slender shape in black stood tending to a waist-high machine, a thing of strange, ugly geometry and unnatural energy. It was a distinctly Imperial construction, out of place in a t'au ship surrounded by t'au constructions and t'au workers. Just looking at it caused Karras' skin to prick. He felt a stabbing pain somewhere in his head, just behind his eyes.

It's the Geller field generator from her ship.

The woman turned, sensing eyes on her. Black hair shimmered like silk around a pale, narrow face.

'Whatever you do, Deathwatch,' she told them, placing a hand on the surface of the machine, 'do not damage this. You understand what would happen.'

Karras marched towards her, sheathing *Arquemann* on his back. Earth caste techs scurried out of his way, faces tight with fear. Rauth stayed back, bolter raised, glaring at them through red lenses, daring them to make a move.

'We are leaving,' Karras told Epsilon.

She smiled, but there was no warmth in it. She was beautiful by the standards mortal men assigned to such things. He couldn't read her aura within the Geller field, but he hardly needed to. There was a cold, ruthless cast to her features.

She is most definitely a creature of the Inquisition, thought Karras. *She reminds me of Sigma. Any means necessary, and honour be damned.*

He removed his helm.

The woman was unintimidated by the murderous scowl on his colourless features. 'Come with me, Deathwatch,' she said simply. 'Come with me deep into t'au space, to a place left long abandoned, and I will show you the need for all of this. If you judge me wrong then, you may take my life. But I tell you now, once you see it, once you understand, any price will seem a paltry sum, and all I have done will be justified in your eyes.'

'Al Rashaq?' said Karras.

She nodded. 'Al Rashaq. A warp anomaly unlike any other, lost in the past, believed to be no more than a legend. It is real. And, through it, the mistakes of the past could be erased. The Emperor could be spared His eternal suffering upon the Golden Throne. Mankind could rule over all. Our endless war, ended at last.'

'You dance close to heresy, woman,' spat Rauth.

'I am of the Inquisition,' she bit back. '*I* decide what constitutes heresy.'

Karras shook his head. 'You are mad. And I have orders. I must take you back. You have crossed too many lines.'

'I cannot go back. Not now. I have the t'au exactly where I want them. Here on Tychonis, I have advanced *Blackseed* further than anyone at Facility fifty-two could have imagined. Omicron would order you to assist me if he could only–'

'Omicron?'

She laughed. 'You do not even know who you work for. Did you think Sigma sat at the apex?'

'I care not where he sits,' said Karras. He rounded on the woman, gripping her by the upper arm. 'Enough words,' he growled, thrusting his fearsome face at hers. 'You are coming with us. Your business here is over.'

Epsilon's eyes blazed with anger. In a blur, her hand flashed towards his face. She was incredibly fast, neurally augmented, a lethal weapon in her own right.

But she was no Space Marine.

Karras caught her wrist four inches from his cheek. He turned his red eyes to her hand, saw the ring there, the spike that had emerged from it, the black poison on its point.

'It takes a rare poison to kill a Space Marine,' he growled, low and threatening. 'But you'd have access to just such a thing. Wouldn't you?'

He considered breaking her arm. He squeezed it instead, until she hissed in pain through clenched teeth.

'Watcher,' barked Karras. 'Execute them all.'

Rauth quickly and methodically slaughtered the t'au techs, dropping each one with a single shot to the head while Karras marched between them, pulling Epsilon along with him.

As she was dragged helplessly forward, the woman reached her free hand between the folds of her dress. From a holster on her inner thigh, she pulled a small, high-yield plasma pistol and quickly jammed the muzzle to Karras' skull. As tall as she was, she had to stretch to manage it.

There was a sound like a muffled cough.

Her hand suddenly stung, sharp and incredibly painful.

Rauth had shot the weapon from her grasp. She was lucky. By choice, he had left her fingers intact.

He kept his Stalker bolter's muzzle trained on her. 'Next time, woman,' he warned, 'I'll take an arm.'

Karras swung her around, red eyes blazing. Holding his rage in check, he made a decision. 'Sleep a while,' he said, and struck her on the jaw with just enough force to knock her out. He slung her limp form over his left shoulder, turned and walked past Rauth.

'Easier this way,' he told the Exorcist.

Rauth's eyes were on the Geller field generator. 'Scholar.'

Karras paused beside him. 'Speak.'

'I'm not leaving that intact and in t'au hands.'

Karras turned and looked from the machine to Rauth and back again. 'It is the only thing suppressing the tyranid call. To destroy it would damn every living being on this planet, Watcher. The rebel tribes have supported us from the start. I would not damn them by–'

Rauth's bolter barked. Exploding rounds struck the generator, biting great holes in the metal, turning it to smoking scrap. Waves of psychic light briefly danced and flickered around its shattered form, then vanished.

'In Terra's holy name!' spat Karras.

Rauth met his gaze, unflinching.

'You've just doomed an entire world!'

'I've doomed nothing,' said Rauth coolly. 'Give me every piece of explosive ordnance you've got.'

There was a second of tense silence, then Karras hit the release on his webbing and handed it to Rauth.

Rauth took it, stepped around him and strode back into the hold. 'Get her away and leave these monstrosities to me. They won't have time to call the hive-mind.'

Karras shifted Epsilon on his shoulder and continued down the ramp to the lower hold.

The Geller field was down. He felt the warp all around him again, its tides crashing against his inner gates, unable to flow through while he kept them firmly closed. *Arquemann*'s soul was there, a presence again, hungry for lives, its aura bleeding into and blending with his own.

He sensed his battle-brothers outside, their signatures flaring and flowing with the rush of battle.

And something else, something that dominated all, a new ethereal presence of imposing power and weight. He couldn't pinpoint it, couldn't identify its nature or its location. It seemed to be everywhere at once, and yet somehow nowhere.

It was vast and potent, and it defied all his attempts to probe it with his mind.

He knew one thing without a doubt – it was far more powerful than he.

And he had a feeling, seated deep in his gut like a lead weight, that Talon Squad had finally seized Epsilon only to have her taken away.

FIFTY-SIX

Zeed jumped, jets flaring, launching him into the air at an angle just as the t'au grenade went off. It would have taken a leg, maybe both. It hadn't done that, but it had forced him out of cover and up into plain sight.

A hail of fire from the ground leapt up towards him. He cut his jets and dropped hard, straight at the enemy squad engaging him, their fire sizzling and cracking as it smacked into his ceramite greaves.

He landed right on top of one of them, crushing the alien soldier's bones to powder, an instant kill. His claws flashed as he cut the others down before boosting away again, slipping under the fuselage of the t'au ship in time to evade another barrage.

Coming up on the other side, he found himself confronted with the towering form of the Riptide.

The Riptide's AI-assisted sensory suite tagged the Raven Guard immediately. Coldwave whirled the battlesuit around to face him, sweeping the barrel of his ion accelerator in a lateral arc almost too fast to see.

Zeed boosted straight up, his only chance to evade, and crashed hard into the underside of the spacecraft's wing. His jump pack took damage. His jets cut off, unresponsive. He hit the ground. Red runes blazed on his retinas. Adrenaline surged. His primary and secondary hearts raced.

He pushed himself up onto hands and knees, shook off the impact and looked up at the Riptide.

The wide muzzle of the battlesuit's primary weapon began to glow, charged particles gathering there as it prepared to fire.

Not like this, he silently raged. *Not on your knees, Space Marine.*

As he straightened on his knees to face his killer, he tugged a thundershock EMP grenade free and tossed it, a last blow before he was erased from the world.

It detonated just as Coldwave was about to fire.

The glow vanished. The weapon had shorted out.

The thundershock had detonated dead centre, right over the Riptide's cockpit, not with enough force to shut the battlesuit down but with enough to penetrate the shield and interfere with several subsystems.

A halo of light flickered intermittently around it, the battlesuit's shield phasing in and out as the AI-enhanced defence control systems struggled to cope with electromagnetic disruption.

Movement control systems were unaffected. The Riptide stepped forward, Coldwave filled with fresh rage and murderous intent.

As the battlesuit's three-toed foot hit rockcrete, there was a flash of burning light. Twin lances of lascannon fire hammered into the shield generator on the Riptide's left arm. The disc-shaped generator exploded. Hot fragments hit the ground. The Riptide staggered and sank to a metal knee.

Zeed turned towards the source of the blast. To the south, he saw Chyron. The Lamenter was storming towards the battle, and he was not alone. Beside him strode the unmistakable figure of a Space Marine in Terminator armour flanked by five others.

Scimitar Squad lived.

'Their shas'o finally shows himself,' boomed Jannes Broden over the vox. 'And seals his death by that mistake!'

It was what the Black Templar had been waiting for.

Certain that Coldwave wouldn't come out until the last moment, Broden had ordered his kill-team to stay buried, to let the t'au think them dead. Let false confidence ensnare them until that moment, that critical moment, when the fire caste commander could hide no longer, when the ship had to emerge on the landing field.

At that moment only, the full fury of the Deathwatch would erupt and rain righteous slaughter down on the contemptible t'au.

Broden had used the others to keep the blue-skins occupied, to misdirect them. Talon, Sabre and the Spear teams would whittle away at the t'au forces until Scimitar was ready to take the prize.

Now, with the Riptide's shield crippled and a fresh wave of foes closing in, Coldwave was forced to confront the possibility that he might not survive this. At a thought, he commanded his Riptide's pilot-support system to pump neuro-accelerators into his body.

They hit his system hard. Within two seconds, he felt wired. Hyper-aware.

How long until his Razorshark reinforcements arrived?

One minute.

He saw the clawed Space Marine roll under the ship and out of sight. He couldn't follow. Too little clearance under there for the Riptide. He would catch that one on the other side.

Fire struck his left arm again from the south.

His jump jets flared. He was a blur as he leapt away from the danger, arcing north to the other side of the ship, there to be shielded from the lascannon and assault cannon fire by its armoured bulk.

As he leapt, he ordered several fire cadres to eliminate those arriving from the south. Scimitar and Chyron were in the open. The fire warriors dashed to appropriate cover positions and began blazing away.

Chyron and Broden, largest of the targets, soaked up a tremendous amount of fire. They staggered, runes flaring red, cooling and shielding systems struggling to cope, but they didn't stop. They pushed forward. Broden's storm shield negated much of the heat and kinetic energy he had taken, but it was close to shorting out. Chyron's thick plate weathered the worst for him, but that, too, was nearing its limits. It was gouged and pitted so deep that, in places, the titanium frame beneath was beginning to show through.

Sundstrom of the Executioners was hit hard and dropped to a knee, blackened flesh showing through a hole in his cuirass, right over his upper abdomen. He grunted in pain and swung his frag cannon's muzzle around on a cluster of blue-skins on his eleven o'clock.

The weapon chugged, shunting a heavy grenade round in a high arc. It struck behind the fire cadre's cover and detonated, cutting down half a dozen of them. Their wounds were grievous. Blue blood pumped out. Three died within seconds. The others cried out, but their fellows had no time to aid them. The pressure from Scimitar was too great.

'Forward, Deathwatch!' shouted Broden. 'The Emperor's eyes are upon us. Death to the xenos in His holy name!'

On the starboard side of the ship, Zeed slammed himself into cover beside Voss.

'Damned Riptide almost had me,' he growled. 'If old junk-box hadn't fired on him…'

'Looks like the raven has been grounded,' said Voss, noting the significant damage to Zeed's jump pack.

'I'll still never be as slow and clumsy as you, you grox. Besides, I'm rerouting power. My jets will be back to forty per cent in a few seconds. Once they are, I'm taking another shot at that bastard.'

'You've got tunnel vision. My kill count is at least triple yours now.'

The Raven Guard laughed. 'If I take down the Riptide, you lose, whatever your count is.'

He mag-locked his lightning claws to his cuisses, pulled his bolt pistol and started one-shotting t'au infantry that were trying to flank from the right.

'Where are they all coming from?' said Voss. 'They're like ants.'

'So crush them like ants,' rumbled a familiar voice over the vox.

'About time you showed up, scrapheap,' laughed Zeed. 'I see you picked up some strays on your travels. Try to force the Riptide into cover so I can close for a kill.'

'I give the orders, Raven Guard,' snapped Broden.

'You went offline, Templar,' said Voss in reply. 'Archangel is back in command.'

'No longer,' said Broden. 'Does the woman yet live?'

'On your five, Scimitar,' replied Copley on the vox. 'Three hundred metres from you and closing.'

'Why did you leave the control tower? You were ordered–'

'Assumed you were dead, Scimitar. Made a tactical decision. No time to lay it out for you. Look west. Nine o'clock high.'

Voss and Zeed turned and glanced up. Six sleek shapes were screaming in towards the battle.

The Razorsharks from Na'tol.

As the Space Marines were looking at them, two more shapes swung in to join the formation – the two Razorsharks that had been in a holding pattern out of range since early in the assault. Now they had the reinforcements they had been waiting for.

Behind Voss and Zeed, the hum of the t'au spaceship's engines intensified, vibrating the rockcrete underfoot.

'Chyron!' said Voss urgently. 'Start hitting the port-side engine. Your lascannons might be all we have that can take it out.'

'Do it,' ordered Broden.

The Razorsharks were dropping speed and altitude. They'd already marked Chyron and Scimitar Squad. They were out in the open. So, too, were Copley and Spear Team One. Easy targets, all.

Chyron's lascannons blazed. The beams hit the engine housing dead centre, but the armour was thick. It glowed white hot, but the engine continued to power up unhindered. The weapon recharged. Chyron fired again.

'Keep hitting it,' Broden told him.

The Razorsharks were seconds away from raining death down upon them. There was nowhere to go. No cover within reach.

'Moving to engage air targets,' said a voice over the main vox-channel.

Out of the east, three black shapes materialised, engines at full power, guns already blazing. They cut straight into the path of the Razorsharks.

A hurricane of fire was exchanged.

The lead Razorshark was shredded. Its carcass spun, shedding metal and advanced ceramics, striking a storage building on the eastern edge of the landing field and exploding on contact.

Reapers One and Two took the full force of seeker missiles slamming into their cockpits. In the instant before the missiles hit, knowing with certainty that this was the end, Ventius and Graka angled their craft for a mid-air collision.

Reaper Two fell just short, almost grazing the Razorshark on the trailing edge of the formation.

Reaper One turned starboard side up at the last moment. Its wing sheared right through the same Razorshark that had killed it.

Three ruined aircraft plunged to the ground.

Black Eagle, largest and toughest of all, was hit hard by burst cannon fire, but the additional armour on the Thunderhawk's hull saved it.

Or so it seemed.

As the Thunderhawk flew on between two of the t'au jets, their tail-mounted ion cannons locked onto it. They hammered the gunship with streams of glowing rounds.

Black Eagle's armour would have endured, but the dorsal engine was struck dead on. It erupted in flame and black smoke. She was down to one turbine now, and it was struggling. Several cooling lines had been ruptured in the first fusillade. Engine temperature went straight into the red. The last turbine began stuttering and coughing, then spewing out thick black smoke.

The pilot, Tarval, knew his aircraft didn't have long. He wrestled with her controls and managed to turn her north. On a trail of smoke, raining debris as she came, the Thunderhawk gunship streaked towards the much larger t'au ship on the ground.

'Let's make a difference,' he said to his ship. 'One last time.'

Black Eagle smashed straight into the t'au ship's port-side engine mount.

There was a stutter of explosions. Fire and smoked rolled outwards in an angry sphere. The t'au ship was shunted hard, swinging around anti-clockwise on gravitic impellers. The lowered rear ramp threw up fountains of sparks where it scraped a black curve in the rockcrete.

Copley had witnessed the bravery of the ordo pilots. They had saved those on the ground from the Razorshark attack run. She was wordless, powerfully moved by their brave sacrifice.

There were no more Imperial gunships now. No more air support. They had given their last. They had died with honour, exemplars of warrior spirit.

Now, with the remaining Razorsharks banking for another run, she and her Elysians were as good as dead.

It wasn't much, but maybe the smoke from the wreckage of the downed aircraft might offer a slightly better chance. If they could make it...

'Sprint!' she yelled.

The t'au jets were so damnably fast. Rounds began stitching the ground, most towards the Space Marines just up ahead but enough towards her and her men that death looked imminent. The Elysians were still far short of the wreckage when the worst came.

Chyron and Broden were hit hard, rounds drumming on them like rain. Again, dense armour and shimmering storm shield resisted, absorbing and negating the deadly force. Chyron's torso and shoulders shed hot shards of armour at an alarming rate as the fire from the jets staggered him. Another barrage like that would be his end.

Two of the Razorsharks fired seeker missiles, four in total, their guidance systems spearing in with a solid visual lock on the Lamenter.

As the missiles closed fast, Broden cut in front of the Dreadnought, placing himself directly in their path.

A hail of rounds from his assault cannon cut two of the missiles from the air. They bloomed into bright fire just thirty metres away.

The remaining missiles got through.

Broden braced.

His Terminator armour was struck dead on, each missile smashing into his massive breastplate.

As powerful as the tactical Dreadnought armour was, the Black Templar would certainly have been killed outright were it not for the power of his storm shield. The barrier took the full impact of both missiles and turned it aside. Then it overloaded and died.

Broden had been lucky. A third missile would have slain him.

Copley's people had thrown themselves to the ground.

Rounds ripped into the rockcrete all around them. Then the strike fighters, screaming so low on the strafing run that their passage almost pulled Copley into the air, angled up and climbed away.

Broden had steadied himself by then. He turned and fired furiously at the rearmost of the t'au jets. It was moving too fast. His rounds fell short.

'Get to that t'au ship,' he ordered all members of Scimitar and Spear Team Three. 'Now! Before they turn!'

Copley's body ached all over. It didn't want to move. The sickness had almost done its work on her.

Fight! she told herself. *Get up and run!*

She screamed through a clenched jaw as she pushed to her knees, then from knees to feet. She hefted her hot-shot lasgun and turned to the others.

'Up, all of you! We're almost there.'

Only Triskel rose. The others, all seven, lay unmoving.

Copley stared, her eyes roving from one inert body to another. She noted the blackened edges of limbs blasted away, the deep, charred craters cut into smoking torsos.

No.

Triskel stepped in front of her.

She looked up, eyes wet.

'No,' she said, barely a whisper.

'Warrior deaths, ma'am,' said the corporal, hardening his expression against the emotions that were warring inside him. 'Well-earned peace. They'll be waiting for us when we're done here.'

He had dark rings around his eyes. His skin was yellowing. He didn't have much time either.

They turned and looked at the t'au ship. *Black Eagle*'s great metal carcass burned fiercely beside it, the Thunderhawk's prow speared straight into the side. The port-side engine of the xenos ship was dead.

The other engine could still be heard, its tone rising.

T'au infantry were blasting away at bulky black forms in hard cover.

Talon Squad!

Coldwave's Riptide was once again standing boldly on the

back of his ship, looking for a clear shot at the members of Karras's kill-team.

'Tarval has bought us a few more minutes,' said Copley. She coughed. Her breathing was becoming ragged.

Triskel nodded. 'He has that.'

'The mission objective is still aboard that ship, corporal. What say we join the rest of the task force and…'

And what? Even if they secured Epsilon, there was no way to exfiltrate her now. *Black Eagle*, gone. Reaper flight, gone. The t'au had total air control. Epsilon was surely beyond reach now.

Still…

Copley looked at Triskel and gave a weak, tired smile. 'You know, corporal, I think I'd just like to see what the bitch looks like in person.'

Chyron and Scimitar Squad were back on the move, storming towards the ship again, eager to get to cover before the remaining t'au jets banked for another attack.

Copley and Triskel starting running.

They were almost at the ruin of the Thunderhawk, with t'au pulse and plasma fire arcing out to meet them, when Coldwave's Riptide strode to the edge of the spaceship's starboard wing, locked sights on Chyron and unleashed the t'au commander's boundless fury.

FIFTY-SEVEN

Space Marine senses are unlike those of mortal men.

To an Adeptus Astartes, the world is sharper, more vivid, more vibrant in every way. A normal man would be overloaded and overwhelmed.

Even while all his conscious focus fixed on the deadly knife fight with Khor Kabannen, Androcles' back brain was registering and processing the storm of battle all around him.

He heard the screaming approach of the Razorsharks. He registered the bright explosions as they clashed with the Imperial gunships in the air.

He and Kabannen were almost caught in the blast when the dying Thunderhawk rammed herself into the t'au ship.

They parted from their duel momentarily, stepping back from the heat of the flames and the hail of hot metal debris. The impact and explosion shunted the t'au ship almost a full quarter-turn anti-clockwise.

Androcles noted the cessation of heat and light from the engine. *One down. That will stall them, but not for long.*

He tracked the movement of the massive Riptide battlesuit as it thundered across the top of the ship. For a moment, he thought the lethal machine would turn its ion weapon towards them and eliminate him and Kabannen both. But Coldwave seemed content to let them fight it out.

The shas'o had other foes in his sights.

So the knife battle resumed – a hate-fuelled blur of stabbing, slashing, parrying and slipping.

Androcles already had two deep gashes on his free arm and one high on the shoulder of his knife arm. His Larraman's Organ, implanted over a century ago when he had still been a mere aspirant, was already stemming the flow. Healing cells gathered at each wound, forming thick scar tissue.

It was no easy thing to kill an Adeptus Astartes with a blade.

Kabannen had not gone unscathed. Androcles had managed to clinch with him momentarily, long enough to get purchase on the Iron Hand's storm shield and, finally, rip it from its mount.

The price of that was the wound on Androcles' shoulder, the result of a whip-like slash from Kabannen as he pulled back out of range, but it was worth it to remove the energy barrier that was protecting the dishonourable cur.

Eyes locked, they circled each other again.

'You fight well, brother,' said Kabannen, 'but you are outmatched. You know it now.'

Androcles snorted. 'So you wish it, but I am as fresh as when we started, oath-breaker. You overestimate your advantages. I'd be dead already if it were within your abilities. And you're running out of time.'

'Your assault on Kurdiza has failed, fool. You've lost the air. Your forces are dwindling. I have all the time in the world.'

As this was said, Androcles caught a flicker of something in Kabannen's eye.

Instinct moved him faster than thought. He spun, but it was too late.

Lucianos was there behind him, his face mere inches away. He dipped, cinched his arms around Androcles' waist and hoisted the Son of Antaeus up into the air.

Androcles grunted as the traitor's grip forced all the air from his lungs. He glared down at Lucianos and was surprised by the sadness he saw in the traitor's eyes.

Then Kabannen's knife punched deep into his back, right between two vertebrae, severing the nerves.

Suddenly paralysed, knowing that this was his end, Androcles could only watch. He saw Lucianos' eyes become wet with tears, saw his lips move.

'Forgive me, brother.'

Kabannen ripped the knife free, then thrust again, this time up under the fused ribcage and into Androcles' secondary heart.

There was no pain. Androcles registered his murder as if he were a spectator only, disconnected from all feeling, reduced to watching it play out, helpless to act.

Tears spilled over Lucianos' cheeks as Kabannen's knife struck home a third time, cleaving Androcles' primary heart, ending the life of a Space Marine who had been hero and champion to his Chapter brothers, chosen by the Deathwatch, a paragon of honour and integrity.

He deserved a far better death, but Fate and the universe care little for what a man deserves.

Kabannen tugged his blade free and stepped back, flicking the blood from it.

'Drop him,' he told Lucianos.

Lucianos laid the limp body down gently on the ground and straightened, staring at it, guilt and sorrow writ clear on his face.

'I wonder if he was right,' said Kabannen.

Lucianos looked up, eyes narrowing. 'What?'

'I was trying to kill him from the start. It should have been a simple thing. But it wasn't.' He thrust his chin at the cooling body. 'I did not beat him while his feet touched dry land. Had you not lifted him up, brother… But we'll never really know.'

Lucianos turned away, scowling. 'Sometimes, brother, I think I hate you.'

Kabannen sheathed his knife and gestured for them to make for the t'au ship.

Something whined in the air like a mosquito.

Lucianos' skull exploded.

His headless body dropped to its knees, then pitched forward, dark blood pumping from the open neck.

Kabannen whirled, but could see no attacker. *Talon Three. The Ultramarine!* Solarion's prowess with a sniper rifle was said to be unmatched. Where was he? Kabannen had to get to cover.

Before he could move, his senses twitched. On impulse, he threw his mechanical left hand up in front of his face.

There was a buzz and a crack.

The hand shattered into a thousand metal pieces. Shrapnel bit into Kabannen's cheeks and forehead.

He shook off the pain and steadied himself. *Damned sniper coward!*

When he looked up, he saw brother Striggo barrelling towards him like a bull rhinox.

He leapt for his bolter where it lay on the rockcrete, swept it up and levelled it at the Carcharadon.

Two hundred and thirty metres away, the Ultramarine's rifle coughed again. Kabannen's bolter was smashed from his hand. It hit the rockcrete and skidded out of reach.

Striggo was almost on him now. Kabannen saw the razor-lined grin on that ugly, pasty, barely human face.

He met those all-black eyes and saw death in them.

Striggo was his death. He tried to reject the thought, but it insisted on him, refusing to be denied.

Ironic.

It had always been Striggo whom Kabannen had enjoyed the most.

To me, then, Carcharadon. But it will not be easy.

Kabannen drew his knife one more time.

For Manus and Medusa!

FIFTY-EIGHT

Zeed felt searing pain in his left thigh.

He looked down at his cuisse. The ceramite and adamantium had been scored away. The edges were smooth, like melted wax hardened. The coating of stealth cells and ablative resin had bubbled away.

Coldwave had been about to fire on Chyron. With Scimitar and the Dreadnought still on open ground, Zeed had acted in desperation, leaping out to fire his bolt pistol with his left hand while his right hurled a krak grenade.

Had the grenade struck, it would have dealt a solid blow to the battlesuit. Instead, with boosted reflexes, Coldwave had managed to bat the grenade away with his Riptide's ruined shield arm. It exploded harmlessly some forty metres away.

Zeed's gambit had worked, however. The shas'o turned his attention to the closer threat and fired, punished the Raven Guard for his interference.

Zeed, with his jump pack restored to forty per cent efficiency, had barely managed to evade the shot.

The loss of its shield should have made the Riptide a much easier kill. Instead it seemed only to have jolted the pilot awake.

Chyron fired on it and missed. Broden's assault cannon chewed armour from its left shoulder, but the massive machine boosted laterally and the Terminator-suited Templar lost line of sight.

Zeed was back in cover beside Voss now, cursing under his breath. 'Omni, we have to lock him down.'

'If he didn't have so many damned infantry…'

'Prophet, can't you get a bead on him? Shoot out his jets?'

There was a grunt over the vox. 'If he keeps–'

A spear of light scored one of the cargo containers north-east of the ship, cutting it almost in two. It collapsed. The containers stacked atop it slid and tumbled.

'Prophet!' shouted Voss.

'Damn!' hissed Solarion. 'That one was for me. Relocating.'

Zeed saw the Riptide appear on the starboard wing of the t'au ship, gaining line of sight on him and Voss.

'Omni! Watch yourself!' he called out, and boosted forward, surging into the cover of the ship's curving fuselage.

Voss turned and immediately began blazing away at the battlesuit. A dozen bolter rounds hit, biting fist-sized chunks from frontal armour. The Riptide weathered the storm and raised its ion accelerator to return fire.

Voss lunged, barely in time. The cover behind him collapsed into glowing slag.

He felt the heat of the blast through his armour before temperature control systems compensated and shunted the excess away from his flesh.

He was in plain sight now. Nowhere to hide, nothing to shield him. The next shot would bring a quick death.

Defiantly, he planted his feet wide and swung the muzzle of his Infernus around. 'Let's have you then, xenos bastard! I die with Dorn's eyes upon me!'

From his cockpit, Coldwave looked down at the bulky Space Marine and grinned. Here was a bold one, and his boldness would cost him his life. There was great pleasure to be had in obliterating one of the gue'la Imperium's foul-smelling death-bringers. He would remember this moment, relive it in his mind.

Voss saw the ion accelerator glow and thumbed his own trigger. He would die fighting back, as a Space Marine was meant to die.

He had honoured the primarch and the Chapter.

Few Deathwatch ever made it home.

Glowing particles clustered at the muzzle of the Riptide's weapon. Bolter rounds rattled on the battlesuit's front armour again, doing damage but not nearly enough.

The ion glow reached its peak.

A black shape shot into the air. There was a glint of sun-light on shimmering blades.

The glow of the ion accelerator winked out. The weapon's barrel fell away, cut through at an angle.

Zeed's boots and the severed barrel struck the top of the t'au ship as one.

Voss' features broke into a broad grin. 'Audacious ass. I'll never hear the end of it.'

Alarm glyphs flashed red on Coldwave's retinas. The shas'o snarled with rage and kicked out savagely at the jump-packed Space Marine.

Such speed and ferocity.

The Raven Guard took the full force of the kick, dead centre.

From the ground, Voss saw the battlesuit's leg flash out, connecting hard with his brother. He saw Zeed launched from the back of the t'au ship, straight out into the air, fragments of power armour breaking off, falling away as he arced towards the ground.

He hit hard, skidding a dozen metres, sparks flying from jump pack and heels where they raked the rockcrete of the landing field.

The Riptide turned back to Voss. He and Coldwave regarded each other for a moment.

The battlesuit crouched. No weapons left, no shield, but still with full mobility and massive physical power. Still deadly.

It leapt from the back of the t'au ship and struck the ground just in front of Voss.

Before he could fire again, the Riptide kicked him straight in the chest, just as it had the Raven Guard.

Voss tore through the air and smashed into a stack of metal containers twenty metres behind him, making a deep dent before he tumbled to the rockcrete.

Emergency runes and armour alarms screamed for his attention. He tried to push himself to his knees. Power armour functionality was down sixty per cent. Servos whined and grated at shoulder and elbow. He scoured the ground for his heavy-bolter. It lay four metres away, the ammo feed ripped apart and the flamer nozzle hopelessly crushed.

He looked up.

Coldwave's battlesuit had jumped again, back to the spine of the t'au ship where it was now striding towards the stern.

From above Voss, there was the sound of a single suppressed round.

The Riptide's angular head exploded. It staggered, lost balance, dropped to a knee.

Voss grinned a bloody smile. 'Hell of a shot, Prophet.'

Lascannon beams blazed, smacking into the battlesuit's left shoulder, shearing off the whole arm.

The Riptide braced itself on the shorn stump of its ion accelerator. It looked certain to tumble from the top of the ship.

Instead, it righted itself and rose to full height.

'Saints' blood!' hissed Solarion. 'What does it take to kill this damned thing?'

The whine of the t'au ship's remaining engine rose to a deafening roar. The craft began to rise.

The Riptide leapt to the ground and turned.

'He's going inside,' growled the Ultramarine.

'Damn it,' voxed Zeed, coughing. 'I think the bastard broke half my bones!'

Voss watched helplessly as the t'au ship lifted higher into the air.

A fusillade of fire raked its underside and wings. Scimitar and Chyron were unleashing a withering storm, everything they had, but to no effect. The hull was crafted from advanced t'au ceramics designed for atmospheric re-entry. It soaked up everything they threw at it.

Voss saw a formation of Razorsharks racing in from the east, the sun behind them. With the t'au ship in the air and the vast majority of blue-skin ground forces dead, dying or falling back, the xenos jets had little need to consider collateral damage or friendly fire. They would devastate anything and everything left on the ground.

'Death Spectre,' raged Solarion, 'where the hell are you? What are you doing in there?'

The t'au ship climbed higher, its rear ramp still extended.

Coldwave's Riptide flexed at the knees, flared its jets and launched itself upward, landing perfectly, gracefully, on the edge of the ramp.

Far below, Voss swore.

Over the vox, he heard Zeed. 'We're not finished, xenos! We're not done!'

Metre by metre, the t'au ship ascended while they watched in despair.

The Razorsharks were about to begin their attack run.

Scimitar turned their weapons towards the jets. Chyron's lascannons punched one from the sky. It plunged like a burning rock. But the others came on, pulse cannons cycling up to rain death down from above.

Ignoring the pain searing his nerves, Voss straightened, leaned back against the container behind him and watched the window closing on *Operation Shadowbreaker*.

All hope rested with Karras and Rauth now.

With no word or sign from either, it did not look good.

FIFTY-NINE

Karras was halfway across the lower hold, Epsilon still unconscious over his right shoulder, when the t'au ship started to rise.

Out of the back of the craft, he saw the horizon drop away. Cursing, he ran forward, determined to jump while the ship was still low.

'Watcher,' he voxed. 'We need to get off this thing. Now!'

'I hear you,' said the Exorcist.

The ramp was just ahead. The sun was a quarter of the way up the sky, pouring its liquid light through the rear hatchway, almost blinding as it warmed his face.

He put on a burst of speed and stepped out onto the ramp.

As his foot made contact, a massive form materialised right in front of him, leaping up from out of nowhere to land deftly on the edge.

Karras halted, staring at the silhouetted shape of the Riptide just four metres from him, headless, weapon and shield ruined, white sparks pouring from damage to joints and torso.

Coldwave saw him in that same moment.

The battlesuit's arm blurred in the air as it raised the ruin of its ion accelerator to smash down on him.

No time to throw Epsilon aside before they were both turned to paste.

Karras did the only thing he could.

He called forth a surge of power from the warp and hurled it, like a wall of white fire, straight at the Riptide's cockpit.

Coldwave never knew what hit him.

One instant, he was primed to deliver a killing blow, and if the woman had to die too, so be it. He'd find a way to continue without her. The next, he was blasted backwards, smashed from the ship's ramp.

The sky reeled. The ground raced up to meet him. He fired his jump jets, desperate to right himself.

Big mistake.

They drove him straight into the ground, smashing him against it.

The impact jarred the cockpit far beyond the limits of the shock-dampers. Neural connectors ripped free, causing a surge of pain. He cried out. Blue blood ran over his face and neck from a wide gash on his head. He lost all thought impulse control. AI support systems went down. So many warning glyphs were flashing he couldn't process them all.

He stretched an arm back behind his head and scrambled for the interface cables, but he couldn't grasp them.

The holo-vision array was still working, still showing him the world beyond his cockpit. He saw the t'au ship, saw its underside above him. It was still ascending slowly on one engine.

But there was something else now. Something new. He squinted at it, unable to comprehend what he was seeing.

Right above the ship, another shape, far larger and sleeker, was phasing into existence, melting into reality like liquid filling an invisible glass.

Its finished form was eerily familiar. It was a ship, and Coldwave had seen its like only once before. At the battle of Cor'lyth, where he had stood against the Y'he as a mere Fireblade officer, such a craft had been spotted observing the conflict from afar.

His commander had ordered t'au jets to intercept. The strange ship had vanished before they even got close.

Now they were here at Kurdiza, just when things had reached critical mass.

The Val'Sha had come.

SIXTY

Karras stumbled backwards and fell to an armoured knee.

Epsilon slid from his shoulder and landed in a heap. He didn't notice. His eyes were shut tight. He was breathing hard, desperate to regain his equilibrium. All his attention was turned inwards, on slamming shut his inner gates before a thousand dark entities poured forth, drawn by his violent use of the power of the warp.

Hepaxammon would have sensed it. The daemon would be racing towards him, driving others before it, eager to exploit any opening it could find.

Karras would not risk possession again, but there had been no time, no choice. Coldwave's Riptide would have smeared him and Epsilon all over the deck.

With a powerful mantra on his lips, he managed to seal himself off from the flow of the Empyrean. His mind settled. He sighed with relief, opened his eyes and looked up.

The sky above had grown dark.

His relief bled away the instant he saw the unmistakable form of an eldar ship materialising above him – long and sleek, its prow pointed like the blade of a spear.

He watched hull-mounted weapons swivel around. There was a sharp crack, like a thunderclap. Lances of light scored the air in a dozen directions.

Razorshark jets dropped from the sky in ruin. They crashed hard, smashing into the ground in balls of black smoke and bright flame.

As Karras watched them burn, a voice sounded in his head, familiar but unwelcome.

'Fate draws us together again, Death Spectre. It is time to honour your oath.'

Zeed pushed himself up. He felt fire racing along his nerves. A dozen broken bones were already healing thanks to his Adeptus Astartes implants, but that didn't stop it hurting like all hell. Red runes on his heads-up display told him what he already knew – his power armour was in a poor state.

He'd seen the Riptide blasted from the t'au ship's ramp, had seen it fall to the ground and hit hard. It wasn't getting up. And now he saw an eldar warship materialise in the sky overhead. He watched it shoot the t'au interceptors out of the air. He scowled. If the eldar were here to fight, it wouldn't go well for the remains of the task force.

'Omni,' he voxed through teeth clenched in pain. 'Are you still standing? Are you seeing this?'

'Looks like another player wants to enter the game,' said Voss.

Broden cut in on the command frequency. *'Talon Alpha, report!'*

Nothing.

'Karras. Answer me.'

Karras wasn't answering.

Zeed scanned the wreckage-strewn landing field, looking for any sign of the others. He saw Scimitar Squad standing with Chyron some three hundred metres to the south, weapons lowered, just staring up at the t'au and eldar ships.

Someone broke into a fit of coughing behind him.

Zeed turned and saw Major Copley and one of her men, Triskel, walking slowly towards him, both in obvious pain. He nodded. 'You look like hell.'

'So do you,' Copley replied. 'Your armour's a mess.'

Zeed shrugged. 'I've seen it worse.'

When they stopped at Zeed's side, Triskel pointed to the ships. 'What does this mean?'

Copley and Zeed exchanged a look.

'Whatever it is,' said Copley, 'it's not good.'

Zeed was about to lead Copley and Triskel off to join the others when six tall forms rezzed into view about seven metres away. They formed a semi-circle around the humans and levelled their strange, fluted weapons.

'Stay where you are, mon-keigh,' said the tallest, his voice harsh. 'This will not take long.'

SIXTY-ONE

The t'au ship began to descend.

Whether by force or by choice, Karras didn't know, but it moved in a steady, controlled manner as the eldar craft hung motionlessly above it, guns tracking it all the way.

Beside Karras, Epsilon groaned and rose to her feet, still groggy from being knocked out. She squinted up at the underside of the eldar ship.

'You are Deathwatch,' she told Karras. 'In the name of the Ordo Xenos, I order you to protect me.'

Karras glared at her. 'Woman, were it not for my orders to bring you back alive, I would execute you right now for the Adeptus Astartes deaths you have caused. If we survive this, I will petition Sigma to have you burned after your interrogation.'

She snorted at that. 'Fool of a Space Marine. I am a core member of the *Blackseed* project. Why do you think so many lives were risked to recover me? My worth to the ordo is beyond your comprehension.'

She made to walk away from him, towards the edge of the ramp. Karras shot out a hand and grabbed her neck from behind, halting her, almost lifting her from her feet.

She froze. No struggle. Such would be futile. No threat needed to be spoken. Karras could crush her vertebrae with a simple squeeze, and she knew it.

A voice rough as gravel sounded from behind them both. 'Though Janothe's heart soared on wings of vindication, he could not strike the final blow.'

'He felt his son's eyes upon him,' replied Karras, 'and feared above all things the dimming of his light in those eyes.'

'Cordocai's *Vindictum*,' said Rauth.

The ramp of the t'au ship struck rockcrete. It had returned to the ground.

'I don't plan on killing her,' said Karras. With a grin, he added, 'You can keep me raised on that pedestal, my son.'

Over Epsilon's shoulders, Karras could see eldar warriors everywhere, encircling Striggo and the members of Talon and Scimitar. The gore-spattered Carcharadon was all that remained of Sabre Squad.

Karras saw Copley and one of her men, Triskel, with Zeed, surrounded like all the rest.

There must have been a hundred eldar.

He searched for Chyron, certain the Lamenter would launch himself into gleeful slaughter despite the odds. When his eyes settled on the hulking form of the Dreadnought, however, Karras saw that he was powered down. The eldar had neutralised him somehow. He stood utterly quiescent.

Karras shifted his grip to Epsilon's upper arm and forced her off the ramp. Rauth walked abreast of them on the inquisitor's far side, bolter in hand.

'To your left, Death Spectre,' said Aranye's voice in Karras' head. 'Bring the woman with you.'

Karras turned to see a tall, slender figure in shimmering white robes. Her hair shone like pale gold around her almond-shaped face, falling and cascading like a waterfall from her fine-boned shoulders.

As tall as she was – easily as tall as he, even in power armour – she looked fragile, delicate. The contrast of her physical form with the overwhelming psychic power she radiated could not have been greater.

Karras, Rauth and Epsilon passed the wreckage of the Riptide as they moved towards Aranye. Karras glanced at it. The damned thing had almost been too much for Talon, especially given his new reluctance to rely on the power of the warp.

The Deathwatch would need new weapons to combat such suits. The t'au were constantly evolving their technology. If they were to pull too far ahead...

'Your companion is a curious specimen,' said Aranye, glancing at Rauth, knocking Karras from his train of thought. Though within verbal speaking distance, she continued to talk mind-to-mind, her lips unmoving.

'I wonder where he deposited his soul,' she continued. 'I wonder yet more why there was any need, though I can hazard a guess.'

'I am not interested in your guesses,' said Karras aloud.

Rauth glared at him. 'You are speaking with the Xenos witch? Mind to mind? Have a care, Scholar.'

Karras threw him a sideways look. 'Don't worry about it.'

'Only you and the woman may approach from there,' said Aranye.

'You do not command me, xenos,' replied Karras, his expression darkening.

'You think it a choice, mon-keigh?' pulsed Aranye, mild amusement tugging at the corners of her mouth.

She looked at Rauth, mouthed something and made a fist over her heart.

The Exorcist dropped to the rockcrete like a felled tree.

Karras halted, pulling Epsilon to a stop with a yank of her arm. 'What is this?' he demanded.

'He is unharmed,' said Aranye. She gestured at the other survivors of the assault on Kurdiza, all surrounded by her troops. Again, she spoke sorcerous words and made a fist. Shimmering white witchfire danced briefly from her eyes.

With the exception of Karras, every last surviving member of the Imperial forces dropped to the ground.

Karras glared at the farseer. The extent of her power unsettled him deeply. Could even Athio Cordatus stand against such as she?

'This way,' Aranye told Karras, 'they can no longer endanger themselves. My interest is in you, Death Spectre.' She gestured at Epsilon. 'And in her.'

Karras and Epsilon stopped three metres away. For a moment, the farseer and the Librarian stared at each other. Aranye's face was expressionless. Karras could not keep the dislike and distrust from showing clearly on his own.

'I cannot give her to you,' he said flatly.

The farseer cocked a thin eyebrow. 'You must. You made an oath to me. I saved your immortal soul, the soul of your Chapter's long-awaited Cadash. What is the life of this woman against *that*?'

Karras shook his head. 'I swore not to obstruct you. I did

not swear to dishonour myself and my Chapter to do it. You ask too much.'

'The woman is a danger to your people, Lyandro Karras. To all peoples. She imagines herself a saviour on a desperate mission to change the fate of your race. In truth, she is on course to bring about a cataclysm beyond your imagination. She has already set the t'au down a dark and dangerous path. It will cost much to undo that. Next, she will damn your people and mine. I *must* take her. I must gain her knowledge so that I may prevent any other from following such a path.'

Karras shook his head. 'Even if I believed you, I have oaths that far supersede the one I made to you. Do not think me ungrateful, Aranye. But I am a Space Marine. I serve the Imperium.'

He released Epsilon and slung *Arquemann* from his back. 'Withdraw your forces in peace,' he told the eldar witch. 'I would not have bloodshed between us, but I will fight if you force my hand.'

A gunshot sounded.

Karras heard a grunt. The smell of ionised air and burned flesh reached his nose.

Aranye's brows lowered. Her eyes narrowed. The light of day seemed to suddenly dim.

Epsilon collapsed, folding over on herself.

Karras spun.

On the ruin of his battlesuit stood Coldwave, his sidearm raised, its muzzle glowing. The shas'o was covered in blue blood. His tooth-plates were bared in a rictus of hate, but he didn't move. He just stood there, staring at the crumpled body of the woman he had just shot.

Aranye made a gesture with her right hand. Coldwave was hoisted three metres into the air.

He hung there a moment, then, as Karras watched, was pulled apart by an invisible force. The t'au commander didn't even cry out. His blood splashed the Riptide's carapace. The pieces of his body fell, hitting it, rolling off.

Karras turned to the fallen form of Epsilon, rage writ large on his features. *We had her, damn it. We had her!*

On impulse, he reached down and grabbed her by the hair. He twisted her head round roughly so that he could look down into her eyes.

The light was still there, but it was faint and dimming fast.

On impulse, he placed his right palm on her forehead and gripped it tight.

'Death Spectre! You–'

'Be silent,' he barked at Aranye. 'I have never done this before, but it is the only option left to me now.'

He marshalled his power carefully, no great surge, but he was conscious, too, of how little time he had. Her soul was departing. He knew he had to follow.

He dived.

A roaring sound filled his head.

He opened his mind's eye to a scene he knew well. Black waters raged all around him. They formed a circular tunnel that defied gravity, defied sense, defied logic and physical laws. This was a place that did not exist in the realm of matter and energy. It was the Black River, and it existed to pull disembodied souls towards the eternal Afterlands.

Almost immediately, Karras sensed a monstrous presence trying to break through the walls of the tunnel, desperate to force its way through, to get to him.

Such anger.

Such hate.

There would be little time. The daemon had broken through before, back on Chiaro. It would break through again.

Ahead, Karras saw a sphere of light, colours flowing and mixing within it. It was proceeding down the tunnel, pulled along by the ethereal waters.

'Go after her,' echoed Aranye's voice. 'I will hold back the abomination. Hurry, before she passes beyond reach!'

Karras impelled himself forward at speed, his psychic essence riding the currents, adding his will to that momentum, the combination giving him great speed.

Behind him, he felt two formidable powers clash, one of darkness and pain, the other of wilful light and a cold, acidic nobility.

He caught up to the essence of the inquisitor and reached out to grasp it, halting its headlong rush towards the next world.

The inquisitor's soul protested, snatched from what she fully believed was a promise of infinite peace and unlimited knowledge, of unity with the Emperor, of reward for a lifetime spent serving His Imperium, even if few understood the true depths of her service. She struggled to break free of Karras' grasp.

But Karras held on. There was only one way to salvage *Shadowbreaker*. He was not sure what it would do to him, but he had to take that gamble. It was the only shot he had.

He merged the woman's soul into his essence, swallowing it like a phage cell swallows an invading foreign body.

The effect was immediate, like being struck with a thunder hammer. He lost his grip on himself and plunged further down the tunnel, ripped along by the powerful current. The waters got stronger, more turbulent, as he neared the light at the tunnel's end.

'No!' raged Karras. 'No!'

He threw his will against the currents and managed to halt his progress, but the waters were churning furiously around him, unceasing in their attempt to carry him onward.

Struggling to keep himself steady, he began the mantra Athio Cordatus had taught him – the mantra that had saved him from the Black River more than once already. He prayed that it would be enough. He had never come this close to the tunnel's end.

Cordatus had warned him long ago. Those that did seldom, if ever, returned.

He gave all conscious thought over to the words, and slowly, ever so slowly, the black waters began to lose their hold. They started to fade as the mantra lent him strength, empowering him to return at last to the material realm.

He landed back in his body with a jolt. Opening his eyes, he found himself on hands and knees, the taste of blood on his tongue. His pulse was pounding. His head ached and his eyes itched.

He pushed himself up and found Aranye staring hard into his eyes. She hadn't moved, wasn't even breathing hard.

'The daemon,' said Karras.

'Gone,' said Aranye.

He looked down at the inquisitor. She lay on her back, staring up at the sky. Wisps of smoke still rose from the crater Coldwave's shot had burned in her body. Her eyes were lifeless.

She was gone.

Karras searched within himself. *No,* he thought. *She is not gone. I have her, right here inside me, trapped inside my mind – all that she was beyond her physical form.* Shadowbreaker *is not lost. I have her.*

Aranye took a single step towards him. 'There are three ways we may do this, Death Spectre. You will not like any of them.'

SIXTY-TWO

The first option was no option at all.

Karras knew he couldn't match Aranye's power. Were he to attack her now, the others would be murdered by her troops. Even if he *could* hold his ground against her eldritch might, he could not hold against her entire force. Her ship alone had armament enough to raze Kurdiza to the ground.

The second option was to allow her deep into his mind. Karras had trapped Epsilon's soul within himself. He had full access to her knowledge, her memories, her patterns of thought. What the farseer sought could be learned by letting her dive.

He might have conceded to that if he could have trusted her, but she was xenos. And she was powerful. No matter what inner walls he might erect, if he let her in by choice, she would have unprecedented access to all he knew – the ways of the Death Spectres, the existence of the Shariax, everything.

The eldar were the most capricious of all races. He would

never risk the secrets of his beloved Chapter falling into their hands.

Better he die and she learn nothing.

The last option, and the only real option worth considering, was little better, but that little was at least something.

'You will come with me,' said Aranye. She pointed upwards. 'The woman's soul can be encoded into a gem aboard my ship. You will retain her knowledge, but she will no longer reside within you, and I will be able to glean what I need from her without directly accessing your mind. It ought to satisfy your need for secrecy. Be warned, the process is neither quick nor easy, but once it is done, I shall deliver you to an Imperial world, there to do as you wish.'

Her face was expressionless, unreadable. 'What will you do, Space Marine?'

She seemed to care little, or not at all, which option he chose. Aranye would have what she sought regardless. If he chose to fight, Karras had no doubt she would find a way to entrap his soul as he had Epsilon's. She would get what she wanted.

She could not lose.

He, however, could lose everything.

He cast his gaze over the inert forms of his Talon brothers, of Scimitar, of Striggo and the Elysians. Armed eldar were all around them, weapons held ready, awaiting her command.

His eyes settled on Copley. She lay where she had fallen, arms and legs splayed, her head at an awkward angle on Triskel's right shin. Both looked deathly unwell. Perhaps it would be better for them not to awake. All that lay before them was a slow, grisly end.

Something occurred to him then. 'Though it will stain my soul and my honour both, I will go with you,' said Karras, 'and allow the woman's soul to be transferred as you say. But you will sweeten the deal. Two of my comrades are dying. They will not last long. If it is within your power to save them…'

Something changed in Aranye's expression, but hers was the face of the alien. Whatever the change signified, Karras couldn't read it.

'It is within my power. They will have to come with us, and will be dropped with you when we are done, but I will have them healed. Is this acceptable to you?'

'And no harm will come to the others?'

'No harm will be done to them here. I came for information. Your cooperation in this will buy them their lives.'

Karras breathed deep and turned his eyes skyward.

The eldar ship hung above Kurdiza, a dark shadow against the bright blue of mid-morning, silent, unmoving, imposing. The grounded t'au ship looked like a toy by comparison.

The inquisitor's ship, *Song of Scaldara*, was still in a hangar, fully crewed but for a Navigator and an astropath. With stealth systems engaged, she would get everyone back to Chatha na Hadik without the t'au running her down.

Broden had said the *Saint Nevarre* was holding somewhere in-system, cloaked, hopefully hidden from t'au and eldar both. Sigma would slip in and extract his assets from the rebel hold in the north. At least, so Karras had to assume.

Such things were out of his hands.

He returned his gaze to Aranye.

If there were any other way… any way at all…

But there was not.

'Let us be away from here, then,' he said, his tone sharp, edged with anger and frustration. 'I would be done with all this quickly.'

SIXTY-THREE

Agga did not watch the Imperial forces depart, but she felt them. She stayed in the lower levels of the drowned city, as befit her servant role, carefully suppressing her psychic signature, anxious that someone or something aboard that larger ship would yet recognise her for what she was and send someone to end her life, as they had done for her son.

The Imperium, she knew, did not tolerate unsanctioned psykers. Even among allies.

One of the other Space Marines, he with the daemon's skull carved on his pauldron, had come looking for the man he believed was the Speaker of the Sands. Agga had not lived this long without solid intuition. She knew in her bones that this Space Marine had been ordered to kill him. Forseeing this, she had sent her son away into the rainforest with his bodyguards.

When the Space Marine asked to be taken to the Speaker, he was told that the Speaker had gone to lead the fighting in the capital and had been killed there.

The giant's face said he knew it was a lie, as if he could smell it somehow, but he gave no words to such thought. There was no time. The Inquisition ship was ready to depart. He had turned and thundered off to board it with his brothers.

When the Imperial ships were gone, she'd call her son back. She'd continue to work through him – the male face needed to lead the Kashtu and maintain their unity with the Ishtu.

Karras and Copley had, apparently, not told a soul of the Speaker's true identity.

Silently, she thanked them.

As Agga thought again of the armoured giant without a soul who had been sent to execute her boy, she shivered. There was something profoundly wrong about him. How could any man exist on this side of reality without a soul?

And then she reminded herself that these Space Marines were not really men. The stories and legends presented them as such – giant men of greatness and power and of holy lineage – but they were not really men at all.

They were something else, born for a lifetime of constant bloodshed and death, revelling in slaughter. She hoped she would never meet another. Fight as they did for the sake of mankind, they were dark and terrible and unknowable for all that.

She hadn't seen that in a vision, but then she'd never had a vision of her death. Old as she was, she knew even her strange gifts would not keep her alive indefinitely. In all likelihood, it would happen soon. Even two decades earlier, her longevity had already been surprising to her. It occurred to her that perhaps those gifted as she was were spared visions of their own deaths. She couldn't know for sure. There were no others like her on Tychonis to ask.

Lyandro Karras, the Death Spectre, might have known, though he claimed to be no seer. But he was long gone, and he had not departed on the same ship as the others. She'd felt the alien craft arrive, even this far from the battle, so powerful had the presence aboard it been. She had even felt her mind being abruptly scrutinised from afar by that inscrutable being.

Such a cold and remote intelligence. It had examined her soul as some tech-priest might examine some curious but ultimately irrelevant device.

And then it had left.

With the Death Spectre.

Agga had known that the others would be coming back. She'd seen that, seen the coming of the larger ship that would take them offworld and leave the Kashtu and Ishtu survivors to grieve for their dead.

And to take control of Tychonis, to make it ours again now that Coldwave is dead and his troops and machines much reduced. They gave us that, at least – a fighting chance at last. And we'll take it.

She rose from the cushion she'd been sitting on and slowly got to her feet. Old age was such a pain. So much still to do, and this aged body was so slow and weak. It frustrated her.

Her stomach growled and broke her chain of thought. She was hungry.

As she shuffled along a torch-lined corridor towards the kitchens, she thought of the future of her world. Once again, it was down to the old tribes of Tychonis and the t'au. The fight was more balanced now. Fairer. But it could still go either way.

She reached the kitchens. One of the tribeswomen gave her a bowl of broth and a large slice of buttered bread on a tray. Agga took it with her back into the corridor outside. There she sat on a bench, her back resting against the wall, the scent of the spiced broth tugging at her nose.

As she was about to bite into the bread, a piercing psychic screech lanced straight into her mind.

The tray clattered to the floor. The soup spilled out over cool stone. Agga dropped to her knees, gasping in psychic pain.

That sound. Powerful. Inhuman.

It had come from the far south.

Suddenly, her mind was snatched out of her body and thrown violently into the tides of the prime futures.

There, she had a vision like no other she'd ever seen.

She tried to stop it, to turn from its horrors, but she could not. The vision would not be denied.

At last, it ended – a gut-wrenching, heart-breaking and unimaginably bitter end – and her surroundings became solid again.

She felt her mind resettle in her body, felt her old bones and muscles and skin weighing her down.

Her cheeks were wet with tears.

'So,' she muttered to herself, 'we witch-sighted *can* foresee our deaths after all.'

SIXTY-FOUR

Four months Standard Imperial after the battle at Kurdiza, the astropathic relay on the agri world of Rilaea Secundus found itself visited by three unlikely guests.

The guards at the tower gates dared not prohibit their entry, for the leader of the trio was a terrifying figure known to them from legend and storybook, a titan of a man in sculpted armour of silver and black. His blood-red gaze dared them to get in his way. None took up the challenge.

His companions, a man and a woman, had a look of hardened soldiers about them – a certain way of moving and a cold, predatory look in their eyes. The tattoos on their arms marked them as Astra Militarum special forces, though they would not speak of regiment or rank.

Only the Space Marine spoke. He demanded that the relay send an extraction request on his behalf. The codes were of the Inquisition. Ordo Xenos.

Nine days later, a strange black ship appeared in the skies

of Rilaea Secundus. It showed on no auspex scanners. It made no effort to announce itself to the Planetary Defence Force or Navy Aerospace Control.

As quickly and mysteriously as the three individuals had arrived, they were gone, and the black ship with them, leaving the populace to their wild stories and speculation.

No Space Marine was ever seen there again.

SIXTY-FIVE

The torches flickered and danced.

The same two hooded figures sat facing each other across the same broad wooden table, and yet, so much had changed.

'He has been truthful?' asked Omicron.

'There may be details he is withholding, but my analysts assure me that the answers he has given are true,' said Sigma. 'Or rather, that he believes them to be true.'

'The eldar warned us not to pursue *Blackseed.* Clearly, they were not content to leave it at that. For now, at least, it seems the possibility of locating Al Rashaq has diverted their attention.'

'A matter of time, I'm sure,' said Sigma. 'They will turn their eyes to Facility fifty-two soon enough. Al Rashaq will not occupy their attention forever.'

'To think that it exists after all... the warp anomaly described by Acanti. The Adeptus Mechanicus searched for so long. In the end, they decried it as a hoax. Yet the t'au found it.'

'And lost it again in their battles with the Y'he.'

'Had Epsilon not stumbled across the trail, it would have stayed that way.' Omicron was silent a moment, then added, 'She was not wrong to pursue this. She made grave errors in judgement, but her motivation was sound. If Al Rashaq is as legend claims, it could offer an opportunity to utilise *Blackseed* much earlier than expected.'

'The Death Spectre took pains to impress on me the import this farseer places on locating it. He believes we should send a force to secure it before the xenos do. If the eldar believe it of such worth, the Imperium must not let it fall into their hands.'

Omicron pressed his fingers together as he considered that. 'He wishes to go into battle against them? Even after their fortuitous intervention at Kurdiza and the saving of Copley and the other?'

'They are xenos. He is conditioned to detest them. He claims he had no other choice but to put himself in their charge temporarily in order to fulfil his mission objective. The ordo would have been left utterly in the dark had he not found a way to return with the information he gleaned from Epsilon's soul.'

Omicron's avatar nodded its hooded head. 'He is right in that. I'm sure it does not sit well with him.'

'He clearly bears a powerful hatred towards them,' said Sigma. 'The farseer's manipulations cost him much. Honour and pride are ever the weakness of the Space Marines.'

'As well as their strength.'

'He wishes to be deployed as part of, if not in command of, an intercepting force. It would have to depart almost immediately. The eldar have had a significant head start.'

'How have the rest of Talon reacted to his return?'

'There was apprehension at first. The Ultramarine demanded his dismissal, then called for purity tests. For the most part, they trust him. He has told them much of what transpired. I ordered him to exclude certain details, naturally. But his actions saved their lives and *Operation Shadowbreaker* both. They recognise that.'

'Twice now he has pulled operational success from a seemingly impossible situation,' said Omicron.

'At great personal cost each time,' said Sigma. 'Much as I harboured doubts, the predictions were accurate. He seems strangely blessed... or cursed. I cannot quite decide which. Shall I reinstate him as Talon Alpha?'

'See it done,' said Omicron with a nod. 'Let us see how long his destiny serves our interests. There is much the covens still cannot tell us, but still... Fate has chosen this Death Spectre for something very particular. Have the Exorcist continue to watch him. Should Lyandro Karras drift out of alignment with our aims, issue the execution order.'

'What of *Blackseed*?'

'Epsilon's work on Tychonis is exciting in its potential. It's clear that she was very close to a breakthrough. As such, I have issued orders for the capture of more t'au. We will continue her work. However, the progeny of *White Phoenix* is showing all the potential we have been looking for. We will soon be ready for field tests.'

'To be conducted against Hive-Fleet Jormungandr, my lord? Surely a smaller tendril, a splinter of Gorgon perhaps...'

'My coven has scried the hybrid's prime futures extensively. Jormungandr features in all of the most promising. I think it no mere coincidence that the Death Spectres also feature so prominently, but the nature of this link remains unclear. We must watch and wait. All truth is revealed in time.'

'With Facility fifty-two's location now revealed to the eldar–'

'Operations will be moved. I am handling the matter personally. Your focus must be on locating and securing Al Rashaq. Consider the forces you will need. Ordo assets only. I do not want word of this reaching our opposition. Submit your requests to me as soon as possible.'

Sigma bowed.

Silence hung in the air for a moment.

Omicron raised his hand. 'You are about to ask after your sister, my friend. I'm pleased to say that, at last, I have some news on that front, though I ask that you do not take it for more than it is. Remain objective.'

Sigma's avatar leaned forward eagerly.

So malleable, thought Omicron. *Attachment truly is weakness.*

'The work at Facility fifty-two,' he said, 'has recently resulted in two new avenues to a potential cure. I have ordered that both avenues be fully explored. Work is underway. There is some cause to be optimistic.'

'A cure,' muttered Sigma to himself.

'A *potential* cure, my friend,' insisted Omicron. 'The work is difficult and time-consuming. I will tell you more when I have it.'

Sigma wasn't hearing him. Already, he was envisioning a reunion with his beloved sister, the only soul who had ever cared for him in their childhood years. She had been asleep in cryo-stasis for decades, frozen in her youth in order to slow the progression of her mysterious disease.

Omicron watched his underling. Sigma's avatar was hooded as always, but the set of shoulders, the shifting of the hands, these things told him much.

He had not lied to Sigma outright. There *were* new avenues of research which might yield a cure. But even were such a cure discovered, any application of it would have to be held off. There was far greater work to be done, and he needed Sigma's undistracted commitment to it. While that commitment was secured on hope, his sister would remain in stasis, ever youthful while her brother passed decade after decade in service to Omicron's ambitions.

As for the Death Spectre, everything had happened just as Omicron had been told. Even the interfering eldar did not know they were simply another piece on the game board, that they too were being manipulated into position.

Soon, *Blackseed* would be complete. Omicron alone would wield the power to save the Imperium from the tyranid menace. Lauded as a hero, he would quickly ascend to the primacy of the Ordo Xenos, then from there to that of the Inquisition itself. He would take his seat on the Adeptus Terra, and from there, with the aid of his strange benefactor, he would be but one step from his ultimate ambition.

Absolute rule.

He'd had visions of blinding clarity.

He'd heard the whispers in the dark.

As absolute ruler of mankind, he would save his species from the horror and destruction that was closing in on all sides.

And if Al Rashaq were real – if it was indeed the only stable gateway through time that mankind had ever discovered – even better, for the seed of his ascendency could be planted in the past and bring his dreams and ambitions to life all the sooner.

Messiah. Chosen. The new Emperor of Mankind.

It was his destiny. His *duty*.

He alone could do this thing. No other had the fortitude or the knowledge.

That he was deep in the grip of a terrible madness did not occur to him even once.

He dismissed Sigma, ending the meeting in the psychic mindscape. The room dissolved. Minds returned to bodies of bone and flesh aboard ships many stars apart.

As Omicron left the shadowy, candle-lit chamber and its psychic choir, now silent, sleeping, he thought back to the day he had first heard the voice of the great herald, Hepaxammon.

'You are the one,' the herald had said, its tones filled with light and warmth and divine glory. 'You are the saviour to be, and the God-Emperor Himself, beloved of all, has sent me to show you the way.'

EPILOGUE

Across all the worlds of mankind, there are perhaps a dozen species, mostly of the insectoid type, which are said to be capable of surviving a full nuclear apocalypse.

Their names are spoken with a curious mix of disdain and respect, for they are always hideous, crawling, chittering things, but at the same time, men recognise and respect their incredible resilience.

Their genes do not become corrupted. They do not erupt in tumours. Through sheer toughness, they weather what most other species cannot.

They are true survivors.

Tychonis had one such creature. The Kashtu people of the north called it *shukri'sha,* or rattleback. The Ishtu of the south called it *mhur k'han,* the deathless man. Sixty centimetres long, with ten legs and an almost unbreakable shell, this simple creature was always given great respect. To slay one was to bring ill fortune to one's family for generations, for it was said that the God-Emperor took joy in all things that were strong and single-minded, and so he had created the resh'vah.

But it was not a rattleback which crawled unseen from the irradiated ruins of Alel a Tarag, the Tower of the Forgotten, some seven nights after its thermonuclear destruction at the hands of Commander Coldwave.

It was not a so-called deathless man, and it was not a mere sixty centimetres long.

This survivor pushed itself from the rubble with four long arms each ending in diamond-hard black talons. Its tongue flicked out and tasted the air. It stretched to its full height, over two metres tall.

Casting its bony head about, it searched its surroundings through pale violet eyes. Then, with a screech that cut through the night air, it loped off down the moonlit canyon in search of prey.

Just seven years later, the infection rate among the combined t'au and human population of Tychonis was seventy-six per cent.

A great psychic beacon pulsed from the planet.

The hive-mind heard.

The hive-mind responded.

Two years later, Tychonis lay utterly still.

Silent.

Lifeless.

Four years later, the entire subsector lay dead, scoured of all organic matter.

All it had taken was the survival and escape of a single purestrain genestealer from the prison in the desert.

ABOUT THE AUTHOR

Originally hailing from the rain-swept land of the Picts, **Steve Parker** currently resides in Tokyo, Japan, where he runs a specialist coaching business for men and writes genre fiction. His published works include the novels *Rebel Winter, Gunheads, Rynn's World* and *Deathwatch*, the novella *Survivor*, and several short stories featuring the Deathwatch kill-team Talon Squad, the Crimson Fists and various Astra Militarum regiments.

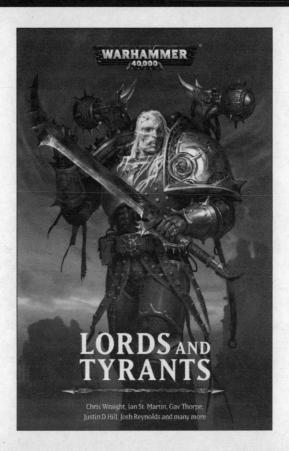

An extract from
'The Reaping Time'
by Robbie MacNiven
Taken from the anthology *Lords and Tyrants*

The figure at the heart of the coral chamber woke with a start. He bit back a cry, fists clenched and shaking around his force staff.

It had been no dream. His kind were incapable of something so human, so innocent. No, this was the third time he had seen the exact same scene – the exact same slaughter – play out since the ship had broken in-system. It was a warning. It could be nothing else.

The figure shifted his cross-legged stance fractionally, the incisor-charms hanging from the leather bands around his wrists rattling. Without his etched blue battleplate and psychic hood, the true horror of his ancient form was revealed. The simple black shift did little to hide the ivory whiteness of his flesh, or the ugly grey denticle-scabs that blotched his elbow joints and neck. It was an affliction, the result of his unique and degraded genetic inheritance. Even more startling were the figure's eyes. They were utterly black, without iris or sclera, as pitiless and unfathomable as the void that was his home.

The figure drew in a long, slow breath. Should he inform Company Master Akia? Not doing so would be a dereliction of duty. But telling him ran complex risks. They could not afford the dangers of a self-fulfilling prophecy. Nothing could be allowed to interfere with the Tithe.

After a while the vox bead in his ear clicked. The figure known to his brethren as Te Kahurangi – the Pale Nomad – listened for a moment, then uncrossed his legs and stood.

The time for contemplation was over. The reaping time had arrived.

The sub-guild quota hall was in an uproar. Every guildmaster and guildmistress present was speaking at once. It took Thornvyl slamming his augmetic left fist – the result of a mining accident almost a century before – against the flank of the hall's lexmechanic podium to bring some semblance of order.

'Panic achieves nothing,' he snapped. 'There may be another explanation.'

'Another explanation for an Adeptus Astartes ship arriving unannounced in our system?' Elinara of the Freehold Prospector Guild demanded. 'A more probable explanation than the Imperium finally coming to investigate the disappearance of the *Praetorian*?'

The arched vault of the quota hall descended once more into wild chatter. The guildmasters, leaders of the mining colony of Zartak, had come together for an emergency session after the augur masts had detected an unidentified vessel breaking in-system. When the logisticators had identified it as a Space Marine warship, the meeting had descended into chaos.

'They are the Emperor's servants,' Thornvyl, Guildmaster of Chronotech Inc., snapped. 'As are we. And we shall greet them as such.'

'Are you insane?' demanded Maron of Broken Hill Industrials.

'Unless you wish to call out the Guard, the local defence force and the mine-militia?' Thornvyl responded. 'Tell me, which course of action sounds more insane?'

The other guildmasters quietened, realising the truth of Thornvyl's words. He pressed on.

'There has been a misunderstanding. We will resolve it, quickly and quietly. Trust me, Guild Brethren, these god-warriors will be gone by tomorrow.'

It was raining hard when the Space Marines arrived. The down-pour made the surrounding jungle canopy hiss, and seethed off the rockcrete surface of sink shaft 1's primary landing plate, sited just beyond the edge of the great burrow-mine habitat.

A behemoth descended from the near-black skies, water cascading from its broad flanks, the white oceanic preda-tor emblazoned on its grey hull glistening. The assembled guildmasters huddled closer together as the mighty gunship screamed overhead, shivering in their drenched finery. The flier's afterburning turbofans whipped at the embroidered hems of their robes and sent one matriarch's shawl twist-ing away through the rain. The engine's painful howl finally dropped to an idling snarl as the transport settled itself atop the plate. The dark muzzles of its many weapons systems gleamed in the rain.

For a moment, nothing stirred. The guilders looked on, fretting. Eventually there was a thump, loud enough to make them jump. The gunship's prow hatch began to lower, vent-ing gouts of hydraulic steam. Through it, their armoured footfalls ringing rhythmically off the plasteel plates, came seven primeval giants.

Each one towered head and shoulders above the tallest

guilder, and all were clad in grey battleplate of different shades. Their eye lenses were black, glittering in the harsh light of the landing zone's jury-rigged lumen strips. Around their wrists and gorgets were bands hung with vicious fangs, claws and incisors, while many parts of their armour were inscribed with flowing line-markings that formed stylised maws or darting fins. They carried weapons in their gauntlets, mighty boltguns and chainaxes, their rotors thankfully inactive.

The seven stepped out onto the landing plate two abreast, forming a line in front of the guildmasters. With a crash of ceramite they came to a halt, the rain pattering from their armour.

For a moment they remained still and silent. Then one, his armour a whiter shade and embossed with numerous brass molecular bonding studs, took one step forward. The guilders cringed.

'Who rules this world in the Void Father's name?' the white-plated giant demanded, his voice crackling up through the arched grille of his helm's vocaliser as though from some great depth. The words were delivered in High Gothic, stilted and unnaturally formal. The guilders didn't respond. The giant said nothing more. Eventually, unable to stand it any more, Fargo Tork of BorerCorp Mining summoned up the few words of High Gothic he recalled from his scholam days.

'We rule as a collective council, sire. We have no one leader, bar Him on Earth.'

For a moment the giant did not respond. The guilders detected a series of low clicking noises. Some recognised it as the sound of an internal vox conversation, held in private over the Space Marines' helm comms. Eventually, the giant spoke again.

'Well met. I am Master Akia, of the Third Battle Company. We are the Carcharodons Astra, and we have come for you.'